Joanne Rock credits her decision to write romance after a book she picked up during a flight delay engrossed her so thoroughly that she didn't mind at all when her flight was delayed two more times. Giving her readers the chance to escape into another world has motivated her to write over eighty books for a variety of Mills & Boon series.

Yahrah St. John is the author of thirty-one books and one deliciously sinful anthology. When she's not at home crafting one of her spicy romances with compelling heroes and feisty heroines with a dash of family drama, she is gourmet cooking or travelling the globe seeking out her next adventure. St. John is a member of Romance Writers of America. Visit www.yahrahstjohn.com for more information.

THE RIVAL

JOANNE ROCK

RED CARPET REDEMPTION

YAHRAH ST. JOHN

MILLS & BOON

First Published in Great Britain 2019
by Mills & Boon, an imprint of HarperCollinsPublishers,
1 London Bridge Street, London, SE1 9GF

The Rival © 2019 Joanne Rock
Red Carpet Redemption © 2019 Yahrah Yisrael

ISBN: 978-0-263-27201-7

1219

Printed and bound in Spain
by CPI, Barcelona

THE RIVAL

JOANNE ROCK

To the new bride Susan Newkirk Heath,
who shares my romantic streak.

One

As she worked in the tack room at Mesa Falls Ranch, Regina Flores caught sight of her reflection in a shiny halter plate bearing one of the horse's names. Even six months after her makeover, it still surprised her sometimes to see another woman's face staring back at her.

Bypassing the fancy dress tack, Regina chose an everyday bridle and rushed back to the stable to finish saddling a second mount. She'd wheedled her way onto the ranch staff as a trail guide the week before and still hadn't found an opportunity to get close to Devon Salazar, whose company was overseeing the social media marketing and launch event for the ranch's rebranding as a private corporate retreat. Getting close to Devon was the only reason she'd taken the job. And she never could have accomplished that if she'd borne any resemblance to her old self—Georgiana Fuentes.

Tightening the saddle girth on the second horse, Regina finished tacking up quickly before unhooking the crossties. She brought both horses through the paddock area before mounting her own and leading the second. She'd heard Devon had a meeting coming up at the main lodge and there was a chance she could talk him into riding there with her. But only if she hurried.

She nudged the bay mustang faster until the main buildings were out of sight. The ranch owners had given Devon a two-bedroom cabin right on the Bitter-root River, a more remote property with beautiful views and a multilevel deck to take in the sights. She'd made careful notes about all the ranch's buildings in order to land the trail guide job. Regina had sacrificed everything to be here now—for this chance to learn the truth about the Salazar heirs.

How much did Devon Salazar know about the book his dead father had penned under a pseudonym eight years ago? A tell-all that had caused life as she'd known it to implode? She'd overheard him deny all knowledge of it to his brother in a conversation last week, but she'd also learned the siblings didn't trust each other, so she didn't put much stock in what he'd told Marcus.

Her private investigator had only recently discovered the identity of the author—two months *after* Alonzo Salazar's death—so she'd had to transfer her need for revenge from the father to the sons. Because she didn't believe for a second that they hadn't benefited from their father's decision to unmask her family's secrets for financial gain.

A light snow began to fall as she guided the horses off the trail to a shortcut that would bring her to Devon's cabin faster.

She should be thankful she bore no resemblance to the woman she used to be. If she'd still looked anything like sweet, innocent Georgiana Fuentes, Devon might have recognized her as one of the thinly disguised real-life characters in his dad's supposed work of "fiction." Or, more accurately, from the endless images of her in the press after a Hollywood gossip columnist had linked the novel's characters to their real-life counterparts.

But stress had stolen thirty pounds from her frame. Relentless workouts in an effort to excise her anger had sculpted a much different body from the soft curves of her teenage self. Even worse, being hounded by the tabloids for her story had caused a car accident three years ago that required enough facial reconstruction to alter her features. Finally, to complete the transformation, six months ago, she'd hacked off her long blond waves to just above her shoulders and dyed the remaining hair a deep chocolate brown. Regina had effectively scrubbed away every last remnant of the woman she used to be.

Devon would never guess she'd once been the spoiled heiress of a powerful A-list actor who'd disowned her and her mother when he learned that Georgiana wasn't his biological daughter, thanks to the tell-all book. She'd done therapy for her anger issues with her family long ago. But she'd then realized she couldn't really start building a new life until she understood why her old one had been taken from her.

And whether or not Devon and Marcus Salazar had profited from the book that had cost her everything.

Leaning back in the saddle, she slowed the lead horse just before Devon's cabin came into view. She needed to brace herself mentally for seeing the man who had almost assuredly built his business empire thanks to her misfortune. He was her enemy.

So it threw her that he was absurdly handsome. His green eyes had sparked an unwelcome heat inside her the only time she'd spoken to him two days ago, when she'd invited him on a trail ride.

Being around him rattled her, but she had to hide it. Had to stay focused. Because she would do whatever was necessary to uncover the truth.

"You're leaving?" Standing in the living area of his two-bedroom cabin on the Mesa Falls Ranch property, Devon Salazar glared at his half brother, Marcus, knowing he shouldn't be surprised by the news.

When had they ever seen eye to eye on anything?

They'd only come to the ranch to honor a deathbed promise to their father before his passing. Because even though they ran a company together, they did so from offices on opposite coasts—Devon in New York and Marcus in Los Angeles. Devon had assumed their father wanted them to spend time in the same place so they would work out their differences and settle the future of Salazar Media. Little did he know Alonzo Salazar had only called them there to drop a bombshell on them, which they discovered in the paperwork he'd left with the ranch owners before his death.

"I know the timing is unfortunate," Marcus conceded, prowling around the living area in a dark blue suit, his sunglasses still perched on his head from when he'd shown up at Devon's cabin twenty minutes ago. His only nod to the fast-dropping Montana temperatures was the wool scarf slung around his neck. "But Lily and I have left you a thorough plan for the launch event. All you need to do is execute it."

Barely hanging onto his patience, Devon stared out at the densely forested mountainside just beyond his luxury cabin's tiered deck.

"All I need to do is execute?" he repeated, glaring

at the sea of ponderosa pines just beyond the big windows. He hadn't been brought up to speed on the client yet, and most of the ranch owners—it was jointly held by six friends—were still aggravated with Devon for showing up more than a week late at the ranch and delaying the work on the relaunch. "While you and Lily gallivant around Europe for a few weeks?"

Marcus had fallen in love with the COO of Salazar Media, Lily Carrington. While Devon had delayed his trip to Montana to hire a private investigator to look more deeply into their father's mysterious past, Marcus had been at the ranch wooing the woman Devon had sent in his absence. Losing both of them during the launch event for a new, prestigious client was a hard hit.

"We did the setup. Now it's your turn," Marcus explained, his usual antagonism noticeably absent. Maybe romance agreed with him. "Besides, I'm hoping this trip turns into an elopement," he confided, the announcement a total surprise.

Knowing what a difficult—and long—engagement Lily had to her previous fiancé, Devon could see the wisdom of that move. Some of his anger leaked away. He and his half brother might not get along, but Devon wanted Lily to be happy. Hell, he didn't begrudge Marcus being happy, either.

"You haven't asked her yet?"

Marcus shook his head. "No. I was thinking of surprising her in Paris. Pulling out all the stops."

"That's a good idea, actually." Funny to think their shared business—and a shared father—had never brought them together, but if Marcus married Lily, they might finally have an effective tie. "I only want what's best for her, you know."

"I know." His sibling's dark eyes met his for a moment before he glanced away. "And so do I. She hasn't taken a vacation in years. She deserves for someone to put her first."

Devon didn't need to be reminded of the particulars. Lily had been raised to feel like an intruder in her grandparents' wealthy world and she'd worked tirelessly to feel deserving of all they'd done for her. Their backgrounds weren't all that different, since Devon's single mother had moved back in with her old-money family after Alonzo Salazar had abandoned her shortly after Devon's birth.

"Agreed." He would find a way to make the launch event work on his own. He would bring in more staff, for starters. "But you realize the bigger issue right now is not the launch, but trying to contain the fallout from whatever new scandal Dad's book could cause."

Hammering out an agreement for the future of Salazar Media—and who would take the helm of the business—would have to wait.

"But for now, no one knows about that. If the secret comes out somehow, we'll deal with it when it happens," Marcus assured him, checking his watch. "In the meantime, I've got to pick up Lily so we can head to the airstrip. We're flying out this afternoon."

Devon resisted the urge to argue. The ramifications of the secret leaking out were bigger than they knew. But Marcus had been the one to nail down the ranch as a client, and he'd kept the situation under control with the owners until Devon had arrived, so he'd done his part. Now Devon would have to find a way to keep any revelations about their father's book from ruining everything they'd both worked so hard for.

"Good luck," he told him simply, extending a hand. Marcus stared down at it for a beat too long, but he squeezed Devon's palm in the end. "Thank you. And you'd better get moving if you want to make that meeting with Weston Rivera. It's almost noon."

Devon swore as he shoved his phone in his pocket and headed toward the coatrack to retrieve a fitted black parka. "I won't bother you unless all hell breaks loose."

"I can give you a ride over there—"

"No need." The main lodge was in the opposite direction from Marcus's cabin. "You added the ranch to our client list. I'll make the rest of it work."

His brother gave a clipped nod before stepping out into the December chill, a burst of cold air lingering in his wake when he closed the door.

Devon shut his laptop and hunted down a hat and a pair of gloves, already mulling over how he was going to juggle orchestrating the kickoff party with digging deeper into their father's secrets. He hadn't wanted to share with Marcus his own reasons for needing to keep the Salazar dirty laundry out of the headlines for at least two more weeks. Devon's socialite mother was set to wed an international banker on Christmas Eve in a highly publicized ceremony. She had found happiness at last, and Devon refused to let a scandal about his father overshadow her well-deserved spotlight.

Maybe Devon's paranoia about his father's secrets leaking now were misplaced, considering Alonzo had kept his double life as an author on lockdown for eight years. But Devon's gut told him that his dad's death was going to bring everything to light.

The papers Alonzo had left for his sons here at the ranch revealed all the details. Under the pseudonym A. J. Sorensen, Alonzo had released an international bestselling novel about Hollywood power brokers and scandals. The book had caused an uproar a year after its release, when a Beverly Hills gossip columnist cracked the code on the identities of the people who inspired the characters.

Real people had been hurt by the book. A Hollywood marriage had been torn apart. A daughter disowned.

Devon pulled a gray knit cap over his ears and tugged open the cabin door just as a light snow began to fall. He spotted a woman on horseback heading toward him. She had a dark Stetson pulled low on her forehead, and it was difficult to see her features through the swirl of snowflakes, but Devon recognized her as the trail guide employed by Mesa Falls Ranch. She'd approached him two days ago about taking a tour of the property to familiarize him with the ranch, an idea he might have jumped on another time, but he'd been reeling from the news about his father's secrets.

Regina Flores had made an impression, though.

With her silver-gray eyes and dark hair, she'd captured his attention right away. She had a thoughtful, brooding air about her; she seemed to be a woman of deep, mysterious thoughts. Until she smiled. She had a mischievous, quick grin that made him think wholly inappropriate things. Today she wore a black duster that flared over her horse's saddle and a purple scarf tied around her neck. She held the reins to a second mount, a sturdy chestnut quarter horse.

"Hello, Mr. Salazar." She flashed a smile his way, two deep dimples framing her lips as she drew to a stop in front of the cabin.

He wasn't a man easily distracted by physical attraction, but something about this woman's ease in her own skin called to him in spite of his looming worries. It made him very aware of how long it had been since he'd shared his bed. He'd been so focused on growing the company he hadn't made time for anything but the most fleeting encounters over the past two years.

"Good morning." He stepped down the deck steps to ground level as the snowfall began picking up speed. "And call me Devon."

Her mustang whinnied a greeting, shaking its mane. Devon stopped near the horse's head to stroke the muzzle, noting the flurries melting on its nose. Safer to look the animal in the eye than its appealing rider.

"I heard from Mr. Rivera that the two of you have a meeting, so I thought I'd offer you a lift." She jutted her chin in the direction of the chestnut mare behind her. "Nutmeg is saddled and ready to go if you are."

"You came all the way out here on the off chance I'd need a ride?" His gaze skimmed up her denim-clad thigh, over her feminine curves, to study her expression. Was there a chance Regina Flores felt the same pull he did when they were near one another?

The idea revved him up.

"I didn't have any trail rides scheduled for today and both these animals were due for some exercise, so my offer isn't quite as generous as you make it sound." Her smile was self-deprecating this time. "I had to get Nutmeg out either way."

She might well be telling the truth.

But the alternative—that she harbored a personal interest in him—was far more intriguing. Especially during a tense week, with his business hanging in the balance. He could see the potential benefit of a distraction.

"To tell you the truth, I'd be grateful for the company," he said at last, reaching up to take Nutmeg's reins from Regina.

He briefly caught her hand in his, leather on leather, before sliding the horse's lead free.

Regina's quicksilver eyes tracked him, her smile fleeing as awareness flickered between them. At least, he'd like to think that she'd felt it, too.

"Do you need a hand up?" she asked even as he slung a leg over Nutmeg's back.

"I'll be fine." He urged the chestnut forward two steps so he was beside Regina.

Close enough to touch.

"Suit yourself." Her gaze darted around, as if unsure where to land. "Just keep in mind some of our horses are more spirited than others. It's a good idea to get acquainted with their quirks first."

"In that case, anything I need to know about Nutmeg?" He was far more interested in getting to know the trail guide than the gentle mare.

"She's a follower." Regina shifted in the saddle and her horse eased back a step from his. "She'll be more comfortable letting me take the lead."

"Fair enough." He opened his hand with the reins still balanced on his palm, giving the horse her lead. "But since I'm most definitely not a follower, next time feel free to give me something feistier." He allowed his words to sink in before leaning fractionally closer. "I like a challenge."

Her swift intake of breath, a soft and sexy gasp, was the most pleasant sound he'd heard in days.

And just like that, he had something to look forward to during an otherwise hellish week. Regina Flores was a welcome feminine distraction when all the rest of his world was falling apart.

Pull it together.

Regina cursed herself for finding anything remotely attractive about a man she knew to be her enemy.

Tall and leanly muscled, Devon carried himself with athletic grace in dark jeans and a fitted black parka. A gray ski cap covered his light brown hair, the knit fabric framing thick eyebrows and pale green eyes. With sculpted features, he was handsome in a way that should have been boringly traditional. Except there was something undeniably compelling about the way his eyes followed her. He didn't seem like the kind of man who paid attention to every random woman in his field of vision. She'd had time to observe him unnoticed, and he was normally all business. Yet, around her, she felt the heated spark of masculine interest.

She put the bay in motion. The hoofbeats were softened by the layer of snow sticking on the trail back to the main lodge at Mesa Falls Ranch. The wind picked up, swirling flakes that tickled her cheeks. She appreciated the icy kiss on her skin, needing something to cool her frustration.

Her keen awareness.

She'd worked too hard to get close to him to lose focus now. Her whole point in bringing Devon a mount had been to talk to him. Earn his confidence. Instead, the moment he'd gotten close to her, she'd felt the most bizarrely unexpected reaction to him.

Blatant physical attraction.

It would have been unsettling enough if it had been one-sided. But Devon's comment about liking a challenge hadn't only been about the horses.

Breathing out slowly, she told herself to let go of the moment and focus on salvaging this time with Devon. His younger brother and business partner, Marcus, was leaving the ranch today with the COO of Salazar Media, Lily Carrington. The pair had fallen in love and spent so much time together during their stay at Mesa Falls Ranch that Regina had had no opportunity to get near Marcus.

Devon was her last chance to find out how much the Salazar family knew about their father's book. She'd risked her cover to eavesdrop on a conversation between the brothers the week before, enough to learn that Marcus and Devon didn't trust each other at all even though they were business partners. And that fact alone called into question everything that had transpired between them.

They'd spoken like they didn't know about their father's book. But could one—or both—of them have been lying?

One thing was certain: she wasn't going to learn any more if she didn't try to get to know Devon better.

Slowing her horse's step, she waited until he was close to her again. She noticed he allowed her to keep the lead, however.

"You ride very well," she observed lightly, daring a glance toward him as they followed the Bitterroot River toward the lodge. "Did you grow up around horses?"

He stared out through the snow-covered field where a few deer picked their way back into a thicket.

"Not really. I went to school with a guy who lived on a Kentucky Thoroughbred farm and I spent a couple of summers with his family." He pointed toward the woods where the deer had disappeared. "Look. The fawn wants to come back and play."

Sure enough, the smallest of the deer hopped out into the field again, running in a circle before it darted back into the trees in a flash of white tail. She felt herself smiling along with Devon until she remembered she had to keep up her guard.

"Now that I know what a strong rider you are, I'm all

the more determined to take you out on one of the trails while you're here." She figured a little flattery couldn't hurt her cause. "You must want to see the full spread of the ranch while you're preparing for the launch party?"

"I do." He turned those pale green eyes her way, his expression serious. "As long as you're my guide."

Her heart pounded harder.

Only because she was circling the enemy, damn it.

She ground her teeth together. *Focus.*

"Deal." She forced a smile as they rounded the last bend before the main lodge came into view. "Name a time. I actually need to put in more trail ride hours myself, familiarize myself with the place, before Mesa Falls Ranch opens to the corporate retreats at the end of the month."

"How's tomorrow morning?" His breath huffed a cloud in the cold air as he spoke. "I can clear my calendar and spend the day taking in the sights."

"Excellent." She'd have Devon all to herself. Surely she'd find out something about his father and what kind of relationship Devon had with the man who'd used Regina's family secrets to make a fortune. "Should I meet you at your cabin?"

"I'll come to the stables." He nudged Nutmeg in the flank, turning her toward the lodge. "You can help me choose the right mount."

"Of course." She wondered if his knowledge of horses was better than hers. She'd had to exaggerate her skills a bit to land the trail guide job. "We can have the kitchen pack us a meal if you think we'll stay out through the lunch hour."

"Absolutely." Devon nodded. "I had a lot on my plate when you first mentioned the idea of a trail ride, but I'll be ready to give you my full attention tomorrow." Slowing his horse to a halt, he let his gaze linger on Regina. "In fact, I look forward to it."

She stared back at him for a moment too long, trying to read the undercurrent between them. Trying to ignore the pull of attraction.

"Sounds good," she said finally, needing to stay polite. Professional. Friendly.

No matter that her feelings for him veered between suspicion and simmering awareness.

Dismounting, he turned to stride into the lodge for his meeting, leaving Regina to bring Nutmeg back to the stables. She watched him walk away, his dark boots leaving an imprint as he charged through the coating of powdery snow.

Tomorrow, he'd promised her his undivided attention. That had potential for her investigation into what the Salazar heirs knew about their father's activities. But he'd also made it clear he was interested in her, and that complicated things considerably. For some reason she was okay deceiving him about her identity, but not okay using the attraction between them as some sort of bargaining chip.

She'd have to find a way to get the answers she needed without succumbing to the draw of the man.

And even after spending only ten minutes with Devon Salazar, she knew that wasn't going to be easy. But failure wasn't an option. One way or another, Regina would find out where the profits from Alonzo Salazar's book were going. If it turned out Devon Salazar had benefited financially from the wreckage of her world?

She would use everything in her power to make sure he paid.

Two

Regina stayed up late and awoke early, wanting to ensure she was well prepared for the outing with Devon. She had studied everything she might possibly need to know for the trail ride—weather conditions, interesting sights along the way, a refresher on the native plants and animals. She'd also spent some time rehearsing a few basic details of her cover story since she couldn't reveal anything personal for fear of giving away her past as Georgiana.

Now she was huddled inside the barn, checking the map on her phone so she didn't get lost during the ride, when Devon arrived.

"Morning." The deep masculine voice warmed her insides even before she turned to see him standing under the arch of the doorway.

Snow stirred behind him in a misty white cloud as he pulled on a pair of leather gloves. From his jeans and boots to his dark sheepskin jacket, he looked ready for the outing and not at all like her idea of a Manhattan executive. Straightening, she tucked her phone in the pocket of her jacket.

"Good morning, Devon." She forced a smile in spite of the weird mixture of nervousness and tamped-down attraction. "Are you ready to ride?"

"I've been eagerly anticipating this." His green eyes lingered on her as he stepped deeper into the barn. "And I hope you don't mind, but I took the liberty of making a few adjustments to the lunch you ordered from the kitchen."

He held up a sleekly packaged parcel that she hadn't noticed he was carrying.

"Perfect." She'd been planning to stop by the kitchen on their way out. She opened one of the saddlebags. "You can slide it in here."

He was by her side in a few steps, the heat and warmth of him blocking the cold air blowing in through the open doors.

He smelled like pine trees and soap. A fact she wished she hadn't noticed. He stepped back from the Appaloosa.

"I see you saddled a different mount for me today." He patted the mare's flank while she closed the flap on the saddlebag.

"I know you hoped for something more spirited. Your brother was partial to Evangeline," she told him smoothly, pretending not to know anything about their enmity. "I thought maybe you'd enjoy her, too."

Leading his horse out of the barn, he gave a humorless laugh. "Marcus and I have rarely agreed on anything, but I won't hold that against Evangeline."

A few moments later, they were mounted and trotting away from the barns at a good clip. Regina tipped her face up into the falling snow, enjoying the fresh air and the beauty of Big Sky Country despite the rider beside her. She found it difficult to relax around him, given her overwhelming need to learn more about his connection to his father and the book that had destroyed her life. But at least his remark about Marcus had given her a toehold into that conversation.

Her cheeks tingled with the chill of the icy snow as she began her most basic introduction to Mesa Falls Ranch, outlining the size and rough parameters of the place, skimming over the ownership, since she assumed Devon knew all about the unique group who managed the property.

"Have you met all of the owners?" Devon asked as they began the steep trek out of Bitterroot Valley.

"I haven't." She hadn't really understood the point of the shared ranch venture. Most ranches were either family owned or held by a major corporation. Yet Mesa Falls was owned equally by six friends who had never made the bottom line a primary concern. "I've only met Weston Rivera, who spends the most time on site over-seeing things." She pointed to a break in the trees ahead. "We'll be able to see his house from just up there."

"I've been to his home. I got to meet a few of the owners at a welcome party they threw at Rivera's place last week." Devon appeared more relaxed than he had the day before, even though his mount was definitely more energetic.

For her part, Regina felt on edge, wanting to remain alert to any clues he might give her about his family, his business and his sources of income.

Swaying with the mustang's movements, she debated the best way to broach those topics.

"I remember hearing about that. Your brother went, too, I think." She knew a lot about Marcus's movements even though she hadn't spoken to him directly. Last week, she'd still been feeling her way around the ranch after landing the job. She'd spied on Marcus more than once.

"He did." Devon's answer was clipped.

"The two of you have a business together, and yet you mentioned you don't see eye to eye on many things." She glanced his way to gauge his expression. "Doesn't that make working together difficult?"

"Absolutely," he said without hesitation. "Thankfully, we have offices on opposite coasts, and that helps."

She wanted to ask a follow-up question but didn't want to sound like she was interrogating him. So she waited.

"Do you have siblings, Regina?" he asked as they cleared a rise. The terrain leveled off slightly as the horses picked their way along the narrow trail under the shelter of the pines.

"No." That wasn't strictly true since she had two half siblings, her father's kids she'd never been allowed to meet. Her birth father's wife was highly protective of her family, resenting Regina's late appearance in their lives. "I've always envied people with bigger families."

Families that didn't disown their children.

Birds squawked in the trees overhead, their movements causing more snow to rain down on them as they disturbed the branches.

"Marcus and I didn't spend any time together growing up," Devon explained as they left the trees behind and arrived on a plateau above the river. "Our mothers viewed one another as rivals, so Marcus and I did, too."

"Yet you started a very successful business together."

He looked sharply at her. "You've done your homework."

Her cheeks heated; yes, she had dug through everything she could find about Salazar Media. Especially since Devon's father had been a part owner. "You and Marcus are the first guests since I've been a trail guide. I figured it doesn't hurt to know who I'm talking to."

"I'm flattered," he admitted. "I'm usually the one doing all the studying about new clients. I can't remember the last time anyone tried to impress me."

His gaze collided with hers and she felt the prickle of awareness all over her skin, even with the cold wind blowing off the mountains. Her mouth dried up as she debated how to respond. Thankfully, he had questions about their direction and the next two hours passed uneventfully enough.

She kept up a running patter about the sights, the history of the Bitterroot River, and the best spots for fly-fishing according to the locals she'd asked. They were far from the main ranch house when she spotted a creek side lean-to that one of the ranch hands had told her about. Built by one of the owners for a winter retreat, the lean-to was open on one side, with a picnic table tucked under the shelter.

"Are you ready for lunch?" she asked, shifting in the saddle to see Devon better. "There's a good spot to make a fire by the water if you want one."

She could see the fire ring between the lean-to and the creek, the spot sheltered from the wind.

"Sounds good." He followed her down the snowy hill to the open hut with its bark and branch roof.

She settled the horses close to the water while Devon unpacked the food. She found a few promising sticks to build a fire, kicked away the excess snow, then got to work starting a blaze. By the time she turned around, Devon had flannel blankets on both benches, a clean linen over the table and two glasses of wine poured into stemless glasses. A centerpiece of bread, meats and cheeses was surrounded by fruit, nuts and even a small jar of honey.

With the fire snapping behind her, the flames giving the winter picnic a burnished glow, things had taken a turn for the romantic.

"Wow." She darted her gaze to his, not sure what to say. "That definitely looks better than the turkey sandwiches I asked the staff chef to make us."

He waved her closer. "I hope you don't mind. But I like to combine work with pleasure whenever I can, and Montana is too beautiful not to savor."

Her heartbeat jumped nervously as she neared him to slide onto one of the bench seats. She needed to be wary of this man's idea of pleasure. She had too much at stake to lose focus now.

"Of course," she tried to say in a normal tone, but her voice cracked like a twelve-year-old boy's. She cleared her throat and tried again. "It's a treat for me, too."

"I'm glad." He took the seat opposite her and waited while she removed her gloves and filled a plate for herself. "So how long have you worked here?"

She took a sip of her wine to steel herself for the inevitable questions and hoped she could change the topic fast.

"I just started last week. I'm having a hard time deciding on a career path since I finished college, so I've been testing out different jobs, trying to figure out what I want to do and where I'd like to live." It was close enough to the truth.

She didn't mention that she couldn't properly get

her life underway until she had the answers she needed about A. J. Sorensen's book and where all the profits from it had gone.

"Really?" Devon stretched his long legs under the table, one knee bumping hers. "Where did you attend college?"

"Online." That wasn't true. She'd taken most of her classes on the UCLA campus—right up until her accident. "It was easier that way, since I enjoy moving around."

"And where's home?" he asked, dipping a corner of the fresh bread into the honey.

"My mother lives in Tahoe." That was true. "I guess home is there." Technically, Regina had only ever visited for a couple of days at a time.

Her mother had left Hollywood as soon as she could after the scandal broke, but Regina had remained in Los Angeles with her grandmother to finish high school. At the time, she couldn't imagine living without her friends, but one by one her friends had all fallen away after the scandal. Even Terri, her best friend, had eventually disappeared from her life when Terri's parents realized how dangerous it was for two teenage girls trying to flee tabloid reporters on their own.

Regina understood—especially after the late-night car wreck while trying to shake the paparazzi had almost killed her during her undergraduate years. But understanding why her friends had vanished didn't make those years any less painful. She nibbled a square of smoked gouda and hoped she could change the subject soon.

"Well, I'm glad our paths crossed," Devon said, lifting his glass. "Here's to finding new friends in unexpected places."

She felt her chest constrict, hating the lies but knowing she had no choice if she wanted to discover the truth about his father's finances.

"To new friends." Raising her glass, she clinked it gently against his.

Their eyes met as they drank. She glanced away fast, but not before she felt an undeniable spark between them. The thought he'd put into the meal, the curiosity he'd shown about her personally, the way he looked at her—all of it added up to frank male interest that would have been flattering if it hadn't been so dangerous to her mission.

"What about you?" She reached for another topic of conversation to steer things away from herself. Away from the slow simmer of awareness in her veins. "Where's home for you?"

"New York. I bought a place on Central Park West when I heard about a potential vacancy and jumped on it before the apartment went on the market." Crunching into an apple slice, he pointed to a low-flying hawk circling nearby. "My family is in Connecticut. Except, of course, for Marcus out in Los Angeles."

She tracked the bird while she thought about how to steer the conversation to find out more about his father. The hawk flew for long moments without flapping its wings, angling through the air in a graceful, soaring flight.

"Do you travel to a lot of different places for work?" She needed to be subtler than she'd been earlier. She might have admitted she'd read up on his family, but she didn't want him to know how much.

"I was in India last week, meeting with an international client, but that's rare." He removed a sheaf of paperwork from his jacket and laid it on the table. She recognized a map of Mesa Falls Ranch with a few of the buildings marked on it. "Montana is new for me, too, and I appreciate the tour today." He spun the map around so she could see it better, then pointed to a few pen markings. "I want to make sure we hit these places."

She recognized two of the owners' homes as well as a peak with renowned views of the valley. But her eye was drawn to the papers that had been behind the map—the ones now partially covered by his forearm. The top sheet appeared to be contact information for someone—part of a phone number and an email address that looked like it ended "…tigations.com."

Mitigations? Litigations? Investigations?

"Of course." Her brain worked double time to come up with other words even as she forced herself to make eye contact with him. "No problem."

Crazy though it might seem, she couldn't shake the feeling the information was related to his father's estate. Or the book. Or something that might shed light on her quest. But how to steal a peek at it?

"Excellent." He started to slide the map back into his stack, then paused. "Did you need this for reference?"

Her gaze flicked back to the sheaf on the table, where she caught the word "April." Or was it a name?

"Sure." She reached for the map, trying not to stare at the place where his elbow hid whatever came after "April."

"That would be great."

He hesitated before passing it to her. "Are you okay?"

She forced her attention back to his green eyes. "Of course. Why?"

Tucking the map into her jacket pocket, she watched him fold his documents and return them to his coat.

"You just seem a little distracted." He studied her,

and for a moment she feared he could see right through her. But then he clinked his glass to hers again. "Drink up, Regina. We should probably pack our things so we have time to see the rest of the ranch."

Nodding, she finished her meal and wondered how to see those papers before they disappeared for good. One way or another, she needed a plan to separate Devon from his jacket as soon as possible.

Something seemed off about the lovely Mesa Falls Ranch trail guide.

Devon couldn't quite put his finger on what it was, though. After they returned their mounts to the stables shortly before sunset, Regina had invited him to brush down the horses with her, one of many little things that struck him as odd. He didn't mind taking care of an animal he'd ridden all day—that was far from the point. Mesa Falls Ranch was positioning itself as a high-end corporate retreat, secondary to its main ranching mission. They had plenty of ranch hands to oversee the stables. If anything, they had too much help in the weeks before the launch party. So certainly, Regina didn't need his help.

As much as he'd like to think the sexy trail guide was unwilling to part with his company, he didn't think attraction factored into her request. There'd been plenty of opportunities to act on the awareness between them today—during lunch especially. But Regina had seemed distracted, her thoughts elsewhere.

He ran the brush over Evangeline's flank, working in tandem with Regina in the quiet barn. The riding arena close to the lodge was more of a showplace than part of the working ranch—here, inexperienced riders could receive pointers about horsemanship, or try their hand at simple rodeo events in a well-monitored setting. Only a handful of horses were housed here tonight. The sweet smell of hay circulated in the cool air from a high, open window.

Evangeline whinnied as he moved the brush down her back, and he caught sight of Regina working silently at the crossties, next to him. Her dark hair caught the overhead lights, revealing a healthy shine. She'd shrugged off her jacket when they'd started working and now he did the same, draping it over the hook near hers. Even with the window open, the big animals warmed the space.

Regina caught him staring then, and for a moment the temperature spiked hotter. Her eyes darted over him before she shifted her attention back to her work. What was it about her silvery gaze that made him so damned curious about her? Maybe the odd signals he'd gotten today came down to attraction after all.

Perhaps she was simply shy. Or maybe she felt an abundance of caution since she was employed by the ranch and didn't wish to risk a new job by fraternizing with a client. While he considered his next move, his phone rang. He'd had it turned off during their ride, so he checked the screen now just in case it was important.

The caller ID showed his mother's photo.

"Regina, I just need five minutes, but I really should grab this."

"Of course." She waved him along, her smile transforming her face from pretty to breathtaking. "Take as long as you need."

Nodding his thanks, he set down the brush and hit the button to connect the call.

"Mom?" He moved toward the barn doors, sliding one open to step outside.

"Hello, Devon." Her voice was lowered, and he could hear what sounded like a dinner party in the background—indistinct music, soft chatter and laughter. "I just saw your note about extending your stay in Montana for the launch party. I wanted to be sure you'll be here for the wedding."

"Of course I will." He thought he'd made that clear in the text he'd sent earlier, but he knew his mother was nervous about her upcoming nuptials. "Mom, I wouldn't miss it for the world. You know that."

"Okay." Her small laugh sounded relieved more than anything. "I thought so, but I wanted to be sure. There's so much booked for the week before that the sooner you can be here the better."

Devon breathed in the deep stillness of the Montana mountains, wishing he could trade places with his mother for a few days so she could enjoy the peace of this kind of setting. Then again, she wouldn't want to travel anywhere that his father had frequented. She'd never forgiven him for not sticking around after Devon was born, and although Devon understood why, he wished—for her sake—she'd been able to put Alonzo firmly in her past a long time ago.

"I'll be at the rehearsal dinner." He glanced behind him at the barn door, which he'd left open a few inches. "Is there anything else going on that I should know about?"

He tried his damnedest to be an attentive son. His mother had never held it against him that he was a Salazar, the way Granddad did, even though Devon had worked hard to make sure he didn't overtly share any of his dad's qualities.

"Most of Bradley's family will be in town, so Granddad wants to roll out the red carpet," his mother explained. Bradley Stewart's family was a force to be reckoned with in banking, a well-connected clan Devon's grandfather would leverage at first opportunity. "There will be a welcome party, a few media interviews, that sort of thing. You're always so good with the press, Devon. I'd love it if you could be here."

He closed his eyes, resenting his grandfather for making this wedding about business. And he hated knowing that news of Alonzo Salazar's salacious book could steal the spotlight from what should be the happiest day of his mother's life.

"The launch party is only two days before the wedding." He couldn't leave before then. Still, guilt gnawed at him that he couldn't be there for her when she'd given up so much for him. "But I'll get a flight as soon as it ends."

"Of course. I understand." The music in the background of the call grew louder. "I'd better go now, darling. Good luck, and I'll see you soon."

He disconnected the call, not happy to disappoint her, but knowing that it was more important for her to have him here—though she'd never understand why.

Devon needed to speak to all the owners of Mesa Falls Ranch to see what they knew about his father's past—about the book, about the proceeds, about their relationship with him. But he needed to keep a lid on scandal at all costs. Keep his family's private business just that—private.

And yet, as he peered through the opening of the barn door, Devon spotted Regina Flores hunched over his discarded jacket, his personal papers spilled over her lap while she helped herself to the confidential contents.

Anger flared—fast and hot.

Shoving open the door the rest of the way, he charged

toward her. Her guilty scramble to stash the papers would have been damning even if he hadn't already seen her reading them.

He stopped a foot away from her, quietly seething. "May I ask what in the hell you think you're doing?"

Three

Regina froze.

She'd thought she'd been keeping an ear out for Devon's return, but she'd gotten engrossed in reading the files she had only meant to photograph. Had he seen her with the papers? Or had he only noticed her rifling through his jacket?

Her heart pounded harder as she relinquished her hold on his coat, letting it fall back on the chair as she straightened.

"I'm so embarrassed." She only had so many ways to play this without alienating him. For that matter, if she didn't find a way to smooth this over, he could have her fired from her job and then she'd *really* have no options left to track down the profits from the book that had ruined her family.

"With good reason." Devon glared at her, his shoulders tight and his jaw clenched. He stalked closer, his dark brows furrowed.

Behind her, Evangeline tossed her head and exhaled on a long, shuddering snort. Regina moved away from the mare, not wanting the animals to feel the nervous energy pinging through her. Stepping from the straw-covered grooming area onto the cement walkway down the center of the barn, she kept her gaze trained on Devon.

"I only wanted to touch your jacket." She knew her cheeks were bright red, and in this case that was surely to her advantage. "I'm sure it's obvious to you that I'm…" She forced herself to pause, wishing there was another way out of this mess. She took a deep breath. "Attracted to you."

It wasn't a lie. She let him see the truth of it in her expression. Her pulse galloped faster while his green eyes narrowed.

"And what did you think you might find out by snooping around in my personal papers?"

Did he know that for certain? Or was he guessing?

"Call me crazy." Shrugging, she folded her arms around herself to ward off the chill of his doubt. "But I just wanted to breathe in the scent of you." That part was—sadly—true, as well. The first thing she'd done when she picked up his coat was to bury her nose in the lining. "And the papers fell out."

Her face must be on fire by now. She swore she could feel where every single capillary pulsed with heat just below the skin.

She was worried about his reaction, yes. And she'd stretched the truth. But maybe the biggest reason for her blush was that she was baring a secret she hadn't wanted to admit—even to herself.

"I find that difficult to believe when you seemed careful to keep me at arm's length today." He spoke softly, studying her carefully as he stood just inches away. "Our picnic certainly offered an opportunity for that."

"Fraternizing with a guest will surely be frowned upon by my new employer." Her breath came fast. Out of the corner of her eye, she could see a stray hair flutter in her exhale. "I didn't think acting on the attraction would be wise." She saw some subtle shift in his expression. His pupils widened, maybe. Or his nostrils flared. "I still don't," she rushed to add.

"Nevertheless." He shifted closer, his right hand grazing her jaw to lift her chin. "I'd like to test the truth of that claim."

The green of his eyes was just the slimmest of rings around the dark centers as he peered down at her. Her thoughts scrambled.

"That I don't think we should act on it?" Her breathless voice sounded nothing like her.

"That you're attracted to me." His thumb skimmed along her lower lip and pleasure trembled through her even though she tried to hold herself very still.

Electrified, she sucked in a breath. And then his lips were brushing hers. Once. Twice. Just feather-soft touches that made her knees weak, right before he kissed her.

For real.

Desire streaked through her and stole her reservations. Her arms fell to her sides for only a moment before she wrapped them around him, drawing him closer. The woodsy bergamot scent of his skin filled her senses while his hands slid around her back, pressing her closer. His fingers flexed against the hem of her sweater, stirring an awareness of how much more pleasure awaited her. The hard wall of his chest called to her palms to explore all the intriguing ridges and planes of muscle...

He broke away suddenly. For a moment, she was utterly disoriented, blinking back at him in the glow of the barn light overhead. Her breath came hard, and she noticed his did, too. His hands lingered on her back, while hers still clutched the shoulders of his gray flannel shirt. With an effort, she unclenched her fingers, letting go of him.

"The chemistry is real enough." He didn't seem in any hurry to release her, his fingers skimming around to her waist. Stroking up her arms. "But is your story?"

His icy words jerked her back to reality.

He let go of her then, pacing away from her. For a moment she didn't even remember what he was talking about. She'd been that caught up in the kiss.

Panic lodged in her throat.

"What do you mean?" She stalled for time, not sure how to fix this.

How could she have let him catch her snooping? And why hadn't she used the time when they'd been kissing to work out a plan B? Absurdly, her lips still tingled from that damned kiss, and it was all she could do not to brush her fingers over her mouth to still the quivery feeling.

"I mean I'm not convinced about your motives." He turned to study her, and she wondered how he could flip the switch from passion to interrogation so fast. "You could be using the attraction as a smoke screen. A very hot, very effective smoke screen, from whatever it is you're up to."

Her throat dried up.

She was on the verge of blurting the truth—that she didn't trust him, either, and she wanted to know what his father had done with all the profits from her misery. But then, Devon took a step closer to her again, his head tilting to one side as if he was considering a new idea.

"Maybe the best solution is for me to keep you close so I can have my eyes on you all the time." His wolfish smile shouldn't have been a turn-on, but she'd be lying if she denied a flare of heat inside her.

"I don't understand," she told him flatly, folding her arms across her chest to quiet all the ridiculous reactions of her body.

"We'll act on the attraction, Regina," he announced, like it was already decided. "Explore this chemistry for as long as we have together." He lowered his voice, the silky tone stroking over her senses like a caress. "Starting now."

Checkmate.

He'd effectively cornered her, and he wondered if she'd give up the game. No more pretense.

Because while there was attraction at work here—without question—he felt like she'd been searching his jacket with a purpose. His every instinct screamed at him that she was looking for something specific. Was she with the press? Had someone in the media gotten wind of his father's secret identity?

Or had she been tasked by her employer to find out more about him before the launch party? Devon suspected the Mesa Falls Ranch owners would have preferred to work with Marcus on the launch since Devon had arrived late and had asked a private investigator to look into his father's doings before he'd arrived. Weston Rivera hadn't been pleased to be contacted by the PI.

Devon had hoped that was water under the bridge

after the welcome reception the owners had thrown last week. But now he wasn't so sure.

"You're suggesting we…date?" When she raised one eyebrow and pursed her lips, there was something familiar about her features.

For a moment, he could almost swear he'd seen her before. But that made no sense. He shoved aside the thought to lock things down with her.

"Date. And wherever that might lead." He wandered closer to her again, taking pleasure in the way her gaze dipped to his lips for a moment.

"I have to admit, now I'm the one confused about your motives." She turned to release her horse from the crossties so she could lead the bay back to a stall.

It forced Devon to back up a step. The scent of hay and horses stirred while the mustang swished her tail, settling into the space before dipping her muzzle into the feed bucket.

"I thought I made myself very clear. I'm attracted to you. The feeling is reciprocated." He shrugged as he moved toward Evangeline so he could put her in for the night, too. "What's confusing about that?"

"You don't seem to trust me." She eyed him warily, opening another stall door and showing him where to lead Evangeline. "That kiss felt like some kind of test. You walked away from it easily enough. And now you toss around the idea of dating like it's a dare."

"In a way, it is." He led Evangeline to the stall, then passed the bridle to Regina. "Do you dare?"

She slanted a sideways glance at him while she waited for Evangeline to get comfortable. Then she pulled off the bridle and latched the stall door.

"That's beside the point. I can't risk my job by dating one of the patrons." She brushed past him with two bridles in hand.

He followed her into the tack room, where the scent of leather cleaner and polish hung heavily in the air. The walls were lined with saddles, blankets and all kinds of riding accessories. There were a few highly decorative pieces, but most were well-used plain leather.

"I'm not a guest of the ranch, though," he reminded her as he watched her wipe down the bridles. "I'm a freelance contractor providing a service. That's something very different. No one will object to you seeing me for the next ten days until the launch party."

He needed to keep her close to him to find out what she was doing. If she was trying to dig up information about his family, he'd find out soon enough. He watched as she hung the clean bridles on an iron peg over her head. She arched up on her toes, fitting the pieces over the hook.

"How do I know that?" She lifted her hands in exasperation.

"I'll inform Rivera personally." He rested his hands on her shoulders, feeling the tension threaded through her muscles under the fabric of her soft chambray shirt. "That way, he'll know I'm the one who initiated this relationship. So tell me, what would you like to do tomorrow to celebrate our first date?"

He caught a hint of her fragrance, something green and fresh like spring. Jasmine, maybe. He could feel some of the knots sliding away as he worked over the muscles. Not all. She was far from relaxed. Because she was nervous? Or was it more of that attraction at work? The kiss had rocked him, too, even if he'd managed to hide his reaction better than she had.

"You're serious about going through with this?" Those silver eyes were so wary.

"I want you," he told her simply. "I'm sure you could tell how much when I kissed you."

He saw a shiver pass over her and it filled him with satisfaction. No matter what other dynamic was at work between them, he couldn't wait to touch her again. Taste her thoroughly.

She gave a quick, fast nod.

"Okay."

It wasn't the most enthusiastic of receptions, but the shiver—and the kiss—had been enough.

"Okay." He confirmed it, gesturing her to lead the way out of the tack room.

She sidled past him, careful not to touch.

He retrieved her discarded jacket and helped her on with it. "Would you prefer I make the plans?"

He took his time easing the heavy duster over her shoulders, then lifted her hair out from under the collar. It brushed in a silky waterfall along the top of her back.

"Maybe that would be best." She turned to face him while he shrugged into his own jacket. "The picnic was nice today," she admitted, a smile animating her features for the briefest moment.

"I'm glad you had fun." He looked forward to getting to know Regina Flores much, much better. "I'll find a way to top it tomorrow."

She tugged her gloves from her pockets and pulled them on, flexing her fingers into the leather. He wondered what she was thinking. Feeling.

There were mysteries in her eyes he couldn't wait to unravel.

"I'll pick you up at six?" He pulled open the barn

door so he could walk her back to her cabin or wherever it was she stayed on the ranch.

Snowflakes still fell in slow whorls. She glanced up at the sky and then back at him as she stepped outside.

He couldn't miss the steely gleam in her eyes when she nodded.

"I'll be ready." Bracing her shoulders, she headed into the wind.

Devon followed and escorted her toward the main lodge. He'd have time to do his homework on Regina tonight, even if that meant asking his private investigator to do some digging on her. And when it was time for his date with the mysterious trail guide?

He'd be ready, too.

She was dating the enemy.

An hour after she'd made the deal with Devon, Regina couldn't decide if she was grateful for her quick thinking that had made her tell him she was attracted to him. Because she sure had put herself between a rock and a...very hard place. Memories of that kiss still scorched her insides if she let her thoughts linger on it too long.

Back in the comfort of her own quarters that night, she tried to focus on what she'd learned from her gamble instead of the dicey situation she'd put herself in. With a pillow propped behind her back as she worked in bed, she recorded everything she remembered from her quick glance through Devon's papers, entering the information on her laptop.

The women's bunkhouse accommodations were snug but comfortable, especially since half of the beds were still vacant. But then, the guest ranch portion of Mesa Falls was all new, with the service positions still being filled. She'd chosen a top bunk in the corner, and between the location and the curtains she could draw closed across the open side of the bed, her work on the laptop was private enough.

One of the other women she roomed with had come in briefly to shower before heading out for the night, and another had gone to sleep early. In the common room where there were a few couches and a television, a couple of older ladies who worked in the kitchens were reading. Someone had flipped on Christmas country tunes in that room, the occasional twang of a fiddle or a steel guitar filtering back to the bunk area. Regina didn't think anyone would disturb her for the rest of the evening with her curtain closed. She had her phone charging next to a bottle of water in a canvas cupholder that dangled from the top rail against the wall.

Regina searched online for the name she recalled from Devon's papers: April Stephens. She was a private investigator. She hadn't recalled the contact information other than that the woman was based in Denver. Regina found her easily and read her bio on a website for an agency specializing in forensic accounting and tracking down hidden assets.

Why did Devon have her card? And whose assets did he need to trace? Delving further into the website, she found links to articles about tracking missing persons. Apparently the two investigative specialties often went hand in hand since tracing missing money often led to missing people.

For the first time, Regina felt a twinge of guilt about invading Devon's privacy. She'd been so convinced he was profiting from the story about her family, but what if he wasn't? What if she was being as careless sifting through his personal business as his father had been with her family's secrets?

The scent of popcorn from the common room pulled her out of her thoughts, making her remember she hadn't eaten since the picnic she'd shared with Devon. Her stomach rumbled.

The other papers she'd glimpsed in Devon's coat were return plane tickets and a printed schedule for an East Coast wedding. A quick scan online confirmed the woman getting married was Devon's mother, Katherine "Kate" Radcliffe. Regina had read about Kate briefly in her earlier investigation into the Salazar family, but since the woman had never been a Salazar and didn't stay with Alonzo for long, Regina hadn't devoted much time to learning about the Radcliffes.

She dug deeper now, clicking through article after article online to discover all she could about Philip Radcliffe, the aging patriarch who oversaw a global pharmaceutical company. It was possible his wealth had helped Devon fund Salazar Media, and not Alonzo Salazar's ill-gotten gains. But an interview with the billionaire in a business publication suggested otherwise. In it, Philip talked about the need for "the Radcliffe fortune to remain in Radcliffe hands" for future generations.

That sounded like a deliberate slight to his grandson with a different last name, and the author of the article had speculated as much.

Fingers hovering over her keyboard, Regina found herself empathizing—at least a small amount—with Devon. She recalled how it felt to be dismissed based on lack of birthright.

While she mulled over the new twists, the sound of footsteps in the bunkhouse made her click off her screen right before a shadow loomed on the drawn curtain around her bed.

"Hon, you still awake?" It was a woman's voice, warm and kind.

Regina pushed aside the lined cotton fabric to see Millie, one of the new line cooks, holding a bowl of popcorn. Millie seemed close to retirement age, but she had an energetic vibe and fully embraced ranch life. Her long blond braid rested on the shoulder of a red thermal shirt that read Santa, I Tried.

"Just doing some research before bed," Regina replied, pointing to the closed laptop.

"We made a second batch of popcorn, so I thought I'd see if you wanted a bowl." Millie winked as she extended a red plastic dish decorated with green horseshoes and Christmas trees, with a paper napkin underneath. "It's got extra butter."

Touched by the gesture, Regina smiled, her mouth watering. "That's so kind of you to think of me. Thank you."

"It's no trouble." Millie was already backing away, her voice quiet as she passed another bunk where one of the room attendants was sacked out cold.

Millie disappeared into the common room, leaving Regina with the popcorn and a surprise dose of holiday spirit she hadn't been expecting. It was strange that she felt sort of at home at Mesa Falls Ranch, given that she'd only come here to learn more about the Salazar heirs. But it had been a long time since she'd been able to work with horses; the man she'd thought was her father had confiscated her beloved Arabian when the book scandal broke. She'd missed that equine companionship almost as much as she'd missed her father figure. More, perhaps, since the horse hadn't discarded her the way her dad had.

Mesa Falls Ranch gave her the gift of horses. And, it seemed, the gift of friendly faces in the form of people like Millie. As Regina munched the popcorn, she reminded herself not to get too attached. Because she was only in Montana for one reason.

To find out where Alonzo Salazar's profits went on the book that stole Regina's life out from under her. And to do that, she was going to get closer to Alonzo's oldest son than she'd ever imagined.

Starting tomorrow, on whatever date Devon dreamed up for them.

She wished she could concentrate on how that would benefit her cause. Yet long after she'd finished the popcorn and tried to fall asleep, Regina's thoughts returned again and again to the spark of awareness she'd felt when Devon had kissed her. And the knowledge that she was getting in too deep with a man who compelled her like no other.

Four

April Stephens tipped her face into the wind off the Bitterroot Mountains, breathing in the freedom of Big Sky Country just before sunset on her first day in Montana.

Gripping the smooth trunk of a sapling close to the campsite she'd just finished securing, April took in the beauty of Gem Lake, a frozen patch of opalescent blue in the gully between sharp gray peaks. Her work as a private investigator for Devon Salazar may have paid for her plane ticket, but that didn't mean her new client owned all of her time. As soon as she'd settled her things in her room at the Great Lodge at Mesa Falls Ranch, April had stuffed her camping gear into a backpack and requested a ranch utility vehicle to take her to one of the trailheads for Trapper's Peak.

She had no need to summit, and there wouldn't have been enough time if she'd wanted to. She just needed this moment in the outdoors with space and air around her, so different from the crammed suffocation of her mother's house, full of things from years of hoarding, every precarious pile providing tangible evidence that April could never save her.

Her trip there this morning, before her flight to Montana, had been a typical exercise in futility. She'd wanted to bring her mom some basic groceries, encourage her to get in the shower and alert her that April was going out of town. Instead, Mom had spent the whole time fretting over where to put a recent purchase of fabric remains from a local shop going out of business. By the time April had left for the airport, her mother—once a beloved schoolteacher and warm-hearted homemaker—had been in tears trying to cram bolts of fabric around the refrigerator in a way that would still allow the fridge to open.

Shoving aside the memory, April breathed deep, savoring the clean air before turning back to her camp and the small fire she'd started. She took a seat in front of the blaze to enjoy the warmth for another hour until she crawled inside her small tent for the night. She needed to be ready to break camp at dawn and get back to the lodge. For now, however, the cold wind tore through her clothes, whipping them against her in a way that felt like Mother Nature shaking out the cobwebs. Snow swirled in white eddies, the damp iciness scrubbing away the detritus of the messy life she kept hidden from everyone.

Was it any wonder she enjoyed tracking down secrets? She spent so much time concealing her own it was a weird sort of therapy to rip away the subterfuge from other people's. Sometimes it felt cruel. But it was cathartic, too.

Like with her work for Devon Salazar, who now wanted answers about Regina Flores on top of his original request. Tomorrow, she would meet with him about his more difficult project—tracking the proceeds from his father's book. But tonight, before his date with the mysterious Regina, she'd had to message him a warning that the woman's identity was an obvious fake.

That facet of the job had been easy—she'd been able to do the search on the flight. Without further information, she couldn't pinpoint the woman's real name. But as for the lady she claimed to be?

Regina Flores simply didn't exist.

The bunkhouse bustled with activity late the next afternoon while Regina dressed for her date. The second-shift workers had already left, and several of the women who held first-shift jobs were also getting ready to go out to local pubs, enjoying the start of the weekend.

Christmas pop music played over someone's speaker while women traded news about the workday. Most of the chatter was about the influx of reservations for the launch party week. Apparently, the lodge was already booked to capacity for the four days leading up to the event, and even now they were near 80 percent.

After pulling a heavy fisherman's sweater over her T-shirt, Regina double-checked an earlier text she'd received from Devon asking her to dress warmly since their date would have them outdoors for an hour. She was curious what he had in mind since the sun went down early this time of year. It was dark outside already.

She grabbed a pair of mittens and her jacket and was heading for the door when a snippet of conversation from the common room caught her ear.

"…I think his name is Devon. And he's smoking

hot," a feminine voice spoke in a breathless rush, bringing Regina to an abrupt halt. "He came into the lodge today to make a reservation and I was so tongue-tied I don't even remember what he said to me."

Regina couldn't help but listen. But the response of the woman's friend was lost to Regina's ears when someone flipped on a hair dryer nearby. Of course, she shouldn't be eavesdropping anyhow, but it seemed reassuring to know she wasn't the only one who found the marketing executive from New York to be ridiculously appealing. Clearly, he affected total strangers that way, too.

Charging into the common room, she gave a wave to the three younger women decorating a small Christmas tree someone had put up in a corner. There were popcorn strands all around it. Regina guessed that was what Millie and her friends had been working on the night before. Now the younger group—all from guest services, she thought—were hanging pine cones and small, glittery stars on the tree.

"Have a good night," one of them called to her as she left for her date.

She hadn't even pulled the door closed behind her when she spotted the sleigh.

The huge wooden contraption rested across the walkway in front of the bunkhouse. It was outlined in white lights and decorated with pine branches and a few red bows. A driver in a parka and Stetson held the reins to matching Friesian horses stamping and snorting in the chilly evening.

Devon stood beside the sleigh in a dark overcoat, jeans and boots, with a bouquet of white poinsettias in one hand.

Behind her, Regina felt her fellow bunkmates jostle

for position to see. One woman let out a dreamy sigh while another squealed. Reactions Regina could completely understand.

But she knew this romantic display wasn't so much for her as a way for Devon to keep close to her. He was as suspicious of her as she was of him, and she couldn't allow herself to forget it.

"Are you ready for a sleigh ride?" he asked, striding toward her.

She met him halfway, bearing in mind the charade was temporary and strictly for the convenience of keeping an eye on her, so there was no reason to feel flattered he'd gone to this much trouble for their evening together.

"Very ready." As her boots crunched in the snow, her gaze fixed on her companion for the evening.

His green eyes held hers, his shadowed jaw calling to her fingertips to test the feel of his skin there.

"For you." His breath huffed in the air between them as he handed her the poinsettia bouquet tied with a red bow. The scent of his aftershave, something woodsy with a hint of spice, made her want to lean closer.

"Thank you." She clutched the cloth bow and inhaled the bouquet made fragrant by the balsam greenery around it. "They're beautiful."

"Good." He nodded his satisfaction, his breath puffing in the space between them. "I hope it's one of many things you enjoy about the evening." His hand landed on her back as he guided her toward the sleigh. "I've heard this tour is fun at night even though you aren't able to see the sights, as well."

Stepping up into the vehicle, she said hello to the driver before taking a seat on the bench padded with blankets in back. She'd worn a short wool jacket over her sweater, but there was a stack of extra quilts neatly folded in an open shelf under the front seat.

Regina set the flowers on one side of her while Devon settled into the spot on her other side. She could see her bunkmates still crowded in the front door, peering out at them. Their relationship had gone public in a hurry. No doubt it all looked wildly romantic to an outsider. Who would ever guess at the strange way she'd fallen into this evening with Devon?

"Did you speak to Mr. Rivera about…us?" She didn't want to give her boss any reason to fire her.

"I did." He nodded as he leaned back in the seat, draping one arm across the back of the bench behind her before giving the driver the cue they were ready. "And it's a nonissue as far as the ranch is concerned. He said they welcome a lot of couples who take temporary jobs together to experience ranch life."

The sleigh ride began while Regina digested the news, realizing there would be no getting out of the date for that reason. For better or worse, she was committed to this fake relationship if she wanted to learn more about Devon. But she planned to proceed with caution since she had the feeling Devon Salazar was a man who wouldn't take kindly to being deceived.

"I appreciate you checking with him," she told him sincerely, figuring if she spoke the truth as often as possible, it would go a long way to putting them both more at ease.

She glanced out over the moonlit snow as the horses trotted away from the ranch buildings on the trail connecting grazing pastures. The lane was well packed here because trucks and ranch utility vehicles used it frequently. The sleigh moved faster, the runners making a gentle swishing sound.

The evening was clear and starlit, but now and then she felt the kiss of snow against her cheeks from drifts blowing along either side of the trail.

"I'm glad I could put your mind at ease," Devon assured her, tipping his head back to stare up at the tree branches when they entered a heavily forested area next to a pasture. "Now that there's no reason to fear repercussions for you at work, we can relax and get to know each other better."

He turned toward her, his presence suddenly very near. Close enough for her to feel the warmth of his chest near hers, the brush of his arm against the back of her shoulders. His leg grazed hers. Her throat dried up at the physical proximity, at the appeal of hard male muscle just underneath a layer of clothes.

She hid a shiver that was more pleasure than worry.

Frowning, he leaned forward to retrieve one of the linens folded beneath the vacant seat in front of them.

"Are you cold?" he asked, already unfurling the red plaid wool and laying it over their laps. "There are plenty of blankets if you want another."

His fingers tugged the fabric around her, tucking it behind her hip, igniting a slow burn of awareness in her belly. And lower.

"I'm fine," she protested, mostly because his hands were a major distraction.

Her breath came faster as they emerged from the trees back out onto an open field, where it was brighter.

"Are you sure?" He studied her in the moonlight. "Just say the word if you want to turn back at any time." His concern sounded genuine.

"I'm warm enough." She fought the urge to lick her dry lips—and battled an even stronger urge to taste her way along his shadowed jaw. She dragged her gaze from him to gesture toward the scenery. "And this is really pretty."

The Montana countryside unfolded in shades of gray and white around them as they skirted the western bank of the Bitterroot River. In the river valley, the waterway was a frozen layer of ice under snow, the area around it devoid of trees.

A few deer lifted their heads as the sleigh neared, keeping watch over Regina and Devon while other members of the herd nosed through the snow for a drink.

"We lucked out with the moon almost full." Devon shifted on the bench seat beside her as the sleigh took a hard turn away from the water. "I'd heard that the sleigh rides are worth it even when it's fully dark because of the sensory experience, but we're getting to see quite a bit, too."

"Sensory experience?" She wasn't quite sure what he meant. She pulled back to look at him.

"You know how your senses are heightened when your eyes are closed? You're more attuned to what you hear or feel? I heard this trip in the dark is fun like that—you can really enjoy the experience of the sleigh ride." A wolfish smile flashed as he lowered his voice. "Sort of like closing your eyes when you kiss so you can appreciate everything else that's going on."

Her belly flipped, feeling almost airborne for a moment.

Her brain refused to think of a single response that didn't sound like flirting. Because suddenly, all she could think about was pressing her lips to his.

Maybe it was unwise to kiss a woman who was hiding something from him.

Everything about Regina Flores—from her fake

name to the way she'd rifled through his jacket the night before—had warned Devon she was trouble. At the very least, she was being dishonest with him.

Yet something about her called to him anyway.

Because he wasn't thinking about kissing the woman who was doing her best to deceive him. No, he was mesmerized by the one who could handle a horse in icy trail conditions and build her own fire. Captivated by the woman who knew about Montana wildlife and whose breath caught when he got close to her.

Like now.

"Should we try it?" he asked her now, skimming away a few dark strands of her hair where they blew across her cheek.

Her ivory-colored knit hat framed her face but didn't constrain her hair.

"Try what?" Her voice was a barely-there whisper of sound that was almost lost in the swish of the runners through the snow, the clop of hooves and the jangle of sleigh bells.

Regina's gray eyes were wide.

"The full sensory experience," he clarified, unable to move his fingers away from her face now that he'd felt the smooth softness of her skin. "The kiss."

Her nod was almost imperceptible. But she let her eyes drift closed, the dark lashes fanning a sultry shadow on her cheek.

Hunger for her surged. He wrapped his arm around her shoulders to draw her close and tipped her chin up to taste her the way he'd wanted to since the first time he'd seen her.

Her lips parted. He breathed in the minty trace of toothpaste and a fruity hint of lip balm before he kissed her. Gently, at first. Her mouth molded to his, lips pillow soft as she sighed into him.

Her fingers traced over his jaw, back and forth, before her hand fell to the shoulder of his jacket where she gripped the fabric tight. She edged closer, the warm press of her curves against him a welcome weight that took the kiss from experimental to simmering.

Awareness flared hotter, and he angled her shoulders to deepen the kiss. The small, needy sound she made at the back of her throat was like a torch to dry timber, desire for her cranking into a slow burn. Devon knew that a sleigh in the middle of a snow-covered Montana river valley was no place to take things farther. Yet that didn't do a damned thing to impede the roll of red-hot thoughts through his mind, the need for her scorching away everything else.

Especially when she fitted so perfectly against him under the cocoon of the wool blanket. Hip to hip. Thigh to thigh. And before he allowed his thoughts to drift any more astray, he forced himself to break the kiss. Slowly he leaned back, inserting an inch or two of space between them where before there'd been none.

The cold December air rushed in, filling the gap. Reminding him how much he needed things to cool down.

"I see what you mean now about the dark heightening the senses," Regina told him as she opened her eyes, her gaze seeking his. "I'm in complete, one-hundred-percent agreement that it's a very real phenomenon."

Devon breathed in the snow-dusted air as the sleigh bounced over frozen ruts in the ranch trail, the big black draft horses never slowing. Long, spikey shadows of pine trees fell over them. He waited for his heart rate to even out after the head rush of kissing Regina.

"I honestly didn't expect to prove the point so thoroughly." He'd planned to woo her into letting her guard down. Letting him see a glimpse of what she was really about. He hadn't expected to be seduced by a kiss. "It was my intention to take you out and get to know you better."

Hell, it had been his plan to confront her about her real motives. Her real identity. Running a social media company had taught him that people in her age demographic rarely if ever left no trace online. Yet that was the case with Regina Flores. The text message from his private investigator had confirmed his hunch—Regina was a fake.

"You asked all the questions at our picnic," she hedged, her fingers threading through the fringed edge of the blanket. "It's me who doesn't know much about you."

"I'm an open book," he protested, not surprised that she wanted to sidestep talking about herself. Maybe he'd do better to share something superficial about his world, in the hope that it would prompt her to share something, too. Like why had she taken the job at Mesa Falls Ranch. And why she was interested in him. "What do you want to know? And would you like some hot cocoa?"

He reached under the seat and retrieved two thermal carafes, passing one to her. He used the time to think through topics he needed to avoid if it turned out Regina was a member of the media looking for a scoop about his father's book.

And, hell, if the conversation got too dicey, he could always kiss her again. The chemistry between them was hot enough to burn away everything else.

"Thank you." She twisted the lid of her thermos to

reveal the spout, and steam wafted out the top. "One thing I'm curious about is your job. Why did you start a media company?"

He seized on the topic to keep his thoughts from straying down the carnal path again. At least for the time being. Once they returned to civilization—maybe to the privacy of his cabin—he would be more than happy to revisit the temptation of Regina's lips.

"My brother, Marcus, has a gift for social media and a lot of ambition." Devon remembered seeing the kinds of things his brother posted in the early days of social media—innovative, creative content that people copied. "We've never had much in common, but I've always respected his intelligence. I had a strong feeling he would be successful, and I wanted to test my own ideas for growing a small business from the ground up."

Regina studied him for a long moment over the stainless steel rim of her drink. "Is it expensive to start a business like that? You must have been young."

"We both were. But there wasn't a lot of overhead at first—just the cost of manpower." He decided to mention his dad, if only to watch her reaction. "Our father invested in us, which helped."

Her head tilted a fraction at the mention of Alonzo. Was it polite curiosity? Or had she been waiting for a chance to discuss the author of the novel that had caused such scandal? He couldn't be sure.

"Nice to have a parent's support." She sipped her cocoa before continuing. "Is your dad an entrepreneur, too?"

"He was an English teacher, actually." He noticed how she peered down as he spoke, making it harder to gauge her reactions. "He died early this year."

"I'm so sorry." Regina's hand covered his, her tone undeniably sympathetic.

"Thank you." He missed his dad even though they'd never been close. If anything, that made it harder since he'd never have the chance to build a relationship with him now. "He taught at a boarding school on the West Coast. The same school the owners of Mesa Falls Ranch attended, in fact. My father remained in contact with them after graduation, visiting Montana whenever he had the chance."

He wondered about that. What had tied his father to the wealthy and powerful men who ran Mesa Falls Ranch? A small part of him resented the fact that his dad made time to see them, yet had rarely made the effort to spend time with Devon.

"No wonder the owners chose your firm to handle their social media as they open the ranch to private guests." She twisted the top closed on her drink and tucked the carafe into an open slot alongside the bench seat. "I'm sure it would make your father proud to know you and your brother are maintaining relationships that must have been important to him."

She sounded almost wistful as she said it, which made him wonder about her family.

"You said your mother lived in Tahoe," he said, recalling their conversation during the snowy picnic. "What about your dad?"

"We…aren't close," she admitted. "He was married to someone else when he had an affair with my mom, so I think I'm a reminder of his bad choices. Especially for my stepmother."

Before he could respond, she pointed into the field on their right. There, seemingly in the middle of nowhere, someone had decorated a pine tree with red and white lights. The blowing snow dulled some of them on the windward side, but the rest shone brightly.

"Are we close to one of the owners' homes?" he asked, trying to orient himself.

All six owners of the Mesa Falls Ranch had houses around the property. They'd seen a few of them on their horseback ride the day before.

She peered around the field, looking from the shadowed mountains to the river and back again. "Maybe Desmond Pierce's, although I don't think he's in Montana this week. And I don't see lights for a house anywhere nearby." She turned her gaze back toward him. "Although I've heard all the owners will be on hand for the launch event. How are the preparations going for that?"

Devon noted that she'd once again dodged the subject of her own life.

But now that she had nowhere to hide from his questions, he prepared to confront her with the bombshell that his investigator had shared with him.

"The preparations are running like clockwork. My biggest concern right now is you."

"Me?" She tilted her head, her expression questioning, but he didn't miss the hint of wariness in her eyes.

He met her gaze, the soft glow from the white lights on the sleigh helping him to see her even in the dark. "I can't figure out why you're hiding behind a fake identity."

Five

Panic bubbled up in her throat.

Not that she feared for her physical safety out here in the Montana wilderness, tucked into the back of the huge horse-drawn sleigh. Devon Salazar wasn't the kind of man to intimidate a woman; his demeanor was calm, his body language relaxed as he sat on the bench beside her. Plus, the sleigh driver from the ranch was right there, sitting high on his perch above the horses, a neutral party under his earmuffs and cowboy hat. He was far enough away from them not to hear their conversation, but close enough to remind Regina she wasn't alone with Devon.

So while she was safe, she was also well and truly cornered. There was zero doubt in Devon's eyes as he watched her every reaction to his accusation. And who knew how much she'd already given away in her shock? Her best option now was to tell him the truth.

Or at least enough truth to ease his suspicions.

"I have an excellent reason for hiding behind a fake identity." She retrieved the carafe of hot chocolate again, if only to soothe her dry throat—and to give her time to think her way through this. "I'm surprised you haven't guessed."

She twisted open the top and sipped the cocoa while the sleigh looped around an open field and turned back toward the ranch. A thin veil of snow kissed her cheeks as a cross breeze caught the flakes stirred by the runners. She welcomed the cooling touch against the knot of confusing emotions she had about this man. Resentment, anxiety and, yes, more than a little desire. She wished she didn't feel quite so much of the latter for a man whose father had been her worst enemy.

"I have ideas, certainly," he acknowledged as calmly as if they were discussing holiday decorations instead of her most closely guarded secrets. "And since you rifled through the papers in my jacket last night, you must know that I'm working with a private investigator, so I'll uncover the whole story for myself eventually." His level gaze revealed nothing. "But considering the draw between you and me, I'd prefer to hear the truth from you first."

Her stomach tightened. She could deny the sexual chemistry all she wanted, but at least he sensed it as much as she did. Why did she have to feel this way about the man she was spying on? Her relationships before now had been predicated on mutual interests. They'd been simple, sensible connections. They hadn't lasted long, but then again, they never stirred this level of heat and confusion.

Steeling herself for the conversation, she lowered her

drink and closed the top again. "I couldn't risk having you shut me out if you knew my real name," she admitted. "But I needed to meet you in person."

"Why?" he pressed. "What do you want from me?"

So many things now that she'd met him. She wanted his touch. His kiss. His eyes on her because he wanted her, not out of suspicion. But she was foolish to think about that when there was something so much more complex between them. Something painful.

"I want answers about your father, Devon. About the book he wrote that destroyed my life."

For a moment the only sound was the rhythmic clomp of the horses' hooves, the soft rattle of their dress tack against their bodies and the swish of the runners through powdery snow.

In the quiet, Devon looked at her with the same stunned expression that she suspected she'd worn just moments before.

"*Your* life?" He leaned forward, his knee brushing hers, the warmth of his body stirring her in spite of everything. "Who are you really?"

She wondered how he would react. Would he have her fired? Or would he leave Mesa Falls Ranch altogether and find someone else to oversee the launch event for his powerful client?

Those questions didn't begin to address the other fears and insecurities that came with revealing her identity. How many times had she been rejected because of her surname? Or turned into an object of scandal, ridicule or curiosity?

"I was born Georgiana. My original birth certificate had my name as Georgiana Cameron." She notched her chin higher, defensive of the girl she'd once been. "But in some ways, that name is far more deceptive than the one I'm using now."

Recognition flicked in his eyes. Something else flitted through his expression, too. Something dangerously close to pity.

"You're the daughter in that book?" He shook his head, eyes wide. "She was little more than a child—"

"I was sixteen when your father's book was released—almost seventeen by the time it was exposed that my parents were the key figures the novel was based on. And your father used a fake identity, too, I might add, for far more nefarious purposes than me. I need the anonymity to protect myself from the tabloids' relentless interest in me. But your dad? He used a pen name to hide behind. Plain and simple." She didn't have a prayer of disguising the bitterness in her voice. "I was twenty-one when I hired someone to investigate the pseudonym A. J. Sorensen, and it took two years to learn it was Alonzo Salazar."

"At which point, you learned he'd died." Devon put the pieces together quickly, but then, he was a sharp man to have taken his company from a start-up founded by two brothers to a globally recognized firm. "But why do you say your birth name is more deceptive than the one you're using now?"

The question tore at an old wound, one that had never healed. The anger it raised was never far from the surface, even in this beautiful, still Montana night.

"Because while I was born Georgiana Cameron, it was based on a lie." That was her mother's fault more than his father's. But there was plenty of blame to go around. "Have you read the book?"

A gust of wind whirled off the mountains and lifted

the edge of the blanket, causing the fringe to dance across her lap.

"No." Devon smoothed the wool back into place as he shook his head. "I read a few reviews of it to get up to speed once I discovered Dad's…connection. So I know the gist, but not all the particulars."

"Lucky you," she said tightly, her fingers fisting in her gloves. "In a nutshell, the book depicts a sordid love triangle between a powerful Hollywood producer, an LA singer and a Brazilian soccer star, where the singer passes off her lover's child as her husband's." How many breathless reviews had she read that said the world it painted was so vivid and real, capturing the seedy side of fame? Tension knotted her shoulders. "But a few details were so particular—like the singer being twice divorced and signing an ironclad prenup that gave her nothing if she cheated—that eventually a gossip columnist connected it to my parents. They were Hollywood actors and my mother's lover was an Argentinian polo player, but everything else lined up."

Her parents had met while her mother was in South America for her honeymoon, of all things, which was a tidbit of truth Regina wished she'd never learned. She'd loved the man she'd believed to be her father.

"It seems like a flimsy parallel—" Devon began, his expression thoughtful as the sleigh bumped from a field onto a path near the tree line.

His easy dismissal of that time in her life stirred a fresh wave of hurt.

"It became a national pastime to find other connections over the next six months. One of the tabloids offered a game with a huge cash prize for whoever found the most real-life similarities." It hadn't mattered for her by then, since her father believed the scandalmongers instantly. Her gut knotted. "But the most telling proof was the way my father—the man I'd believed to be my dad up until then—began divorce proceedings as soon as the story broke. I came home from dance practice one day to find a locksmith at work on the security system to ensure my mother and I weren't allowed back on his property."

She shouldn't feel tears burn at the back of her eyes about that anymore. But she rarely spoke about that day, and, yes, it still hurt.

Beside her, she heard Devon shift closer, his voice gentler. Kind.

"I'm sorry you had to endure that." He placed a steadying hand between her shoulders. "And sorry that you weren't ever able to confront my dad about his actions. Hell, I wish *I* could ask him why he wrote that damned book, and I've only known about it for a few days. I can't imagine how deeply it's hurt you to have no answers."

His empathy touched her, even though she told herself she shouldn't let it. Because she couldn't afford to lose focus on her mission in Montana—to find out where the proceeds from the book had gone. And taking comfort from Devon's kindness would only make her feel worse later if she discovered his business was built on the income from her heartache.

"Thank you for your sympathy." She gave a clipped nod to acknowledge words that didn't heal the hurt of having her past ripped away. "And to your original point about Georgiana Cameron, my mother's husband won a court order to change my birth certificate so that it no longer bore his name."

There'd been a time when she'd had grand visions for what she would say to the man who'd raised her when she saw him in court—for the impassioned plea she would make about how a family wasn't bound by blood ties but by love. In her girlish dreams, she'd thought that could change his mind and make him accept her again. But he'd sent his attorney to argue for him, robbing her of the chance to gain closure by speaking directly to him.

"So Flores is your birth father's last name?" Devon asked.

"No. It's Fuentes. When I came up with a name for myself, I used your father's trick of changing names just a little. In his book, my mother, Tabitha, was called Tempest. The man I believed to be my father, Davis, was called David." She shrugged, not owing him any more explanation than she'd already given. Yet now that she'd started talking about the past—about all the reasons she felt angry—she found it hard to stop. "Even as Georgiana Fuentes, the tabloids hounded me. It was so bad that I got into a car accident trying to elude a photographer. The surprise blessing of reconstructive surgery on my face was that at least I didn't bear as much resemblance to the woman I was before."

The surgeries had been painful. Recovery had been slow. But she'd used the time to formulate her plan for revenge. One that she couldn't abandon just because she was attracted to Alonzo Salazar's older son.

"Georgiana." He covered her hand with his where it rested on the blanket.

Even through her gloves she could feel the warmth of his palm. The sound of her name on his lips was oddly soothing. She hadn't heard it in so long. She'd isolated herself in so many ways, unhappy with the shreds of family she had left after the wreckage caused by that damned book.

"Please." Her throat burned with emotions as the sleigh hurtled faster toward the ranch. "Don't call me that."

She couldn't afford to let her feelings toward him soften. Part of her wanted to call an end to this conversation, but they were still too far from the ranch for her to get out and walk. She would have to sit tight, see how the conversation—and the attraction—played out.

"Regina, then," he corrected himself, the gentleness in his voice and his touch unnerving her. "I wish I could take back what he did. Or even help you to understand it, because I don't understand myself."

She willed herself to pull away from him but couldn't quite do it. Her emotions were ragged, and she feared one false move would dissolve all her boundaries and send her hurtling into his arms to seek what warmth she could in his embrace, to forget herself in the seductive power of his kiss.

She wanted the heat of their attraction to burn away everything else, if only for a few hours. And that was a dangerous desire when she should be focused on her end goal finding out where the proceeds of that book had gone.

A goal she wasn't ready to admit to him. Because what if he thwarted her efforts to unravel the truth?

"So find the answers now," she challenged. "You said you hired a private investigator." She knew his budget would be far bigger than the measly amount she'd been able to pay someone to track the mystery author in the first place. "Why not ask the PI to find out your father's reasons for writing it?"

Devon studied the myriad emotions on Regina's face, visible even in the dim Christmas lights strewn around the outside of the sleigh. Her confession had rocked him, though he'd gone into the evening knowing that she wasn't who she claimed to be. Yet he hadn't expected anything like this—a revelation that she was a woman who'd been personally devastated by his father's book.

Even after all the ways she'd come clean tonight, Devon couldn't help the lingering sense that she'd held some piece back from him. Some part of the bigger picture he wasn't seeing yet.

Soon enough, he would. He just needed to bring himself up to speed on her and her family. Learn all he could about the Camerons, the Fuenteses, and about how his father's life had intersected with theirs. It seemed that the biggest mystery remained; Devon hadn't known his father at all.

For now, his need to stay close to Regina was stronger than ever. And not just because the air between them sizzled every time they looked at one another. But because he had to know what she was really up to in Montana this week. He didn't believe for a second that she'd come all this way, taking a job as a trail guide, just to learn more about his father's motives. Was she hoping to sue his family? Or look into his father's past for skeletons as some sort of payback scheme? She could certainly cause a scandal for him if she hoped to get even with the Salazars. There was more at play here, and Devon intended to uncover it.

More important, he planned to keep a lid on it until after his mother's wedding.

"Good idea about the investigator," he told her, still holding her hand. Still wanting her in spite of everything. "I'll ask her to explore my father's past and see what she can come up with. I wasn't aware he had ties to the show business community, so I'm not sure where he would have unearthed information about your parents' private lives."

For that matter if Regina was considering a lawsuit against his father's estate, it might be beneficial to have the investigator's findings ready to shore up a defense. But Devon hoped it wouldn't come to that.

Regina slid her hand out of his and hugged herself. He mourned the loss of her touch.

"When I came to work here, I thought you might have those answers for me." Her restless gaze roamed the lights of the guest ranch buildings in the distance, momentarily visible from a high hill. "Knowing the author's reasons for exploiting my family might help me finally gain some closure, so I can put the past to rest for good."

Her words sparked a feeling of defensiveness for his dad, but not strongly enough to outweigh the empathy he felt for what she'd been through. Besides, whatever wrongs had been committed didn't detract from the simple fact that Devon wanted her with a hunger unlike anything he'd ever experienced.

"I wish I had answers, but all I have right now are more questions." He shifted closer to her, resting his fingertips lightly on her cheek to encourage her to meet his gaze. A thrill shot through him to touch her this way; her skin was cool and soft. "And right now the most important of those questions is this. Will you have dinner with me?" he asked, looking deep into her gray eyes.

Her gaze lowered to his mouth and lingered.

"Dinner?" she asked after a long pause, pulling in a breath that huffed lightly along his palm.

Desire for her sharpened. Tightened. Crowded his chest.

"At my cabin," he clarified, wanting her to be very

aware they would be alone. "I ordered catering for our return, but I don't want to be presumptuous. We can go out if you prefer."

Her tongue darted along her bottom lip.

"You still want this to be a date?" she asked, her voice wary. "Even now that you know who I am?"

"Knowing your identity doesn't change the attraction." If anything, the outing had only reinforced it. The memory of that kiss had never been far from his mind.

He stroked a light touch along her jaw, feathered a caress over her lush mouth.

Her eyelids fluttered but didn't close. "But my name…complicates things."

The sleigh skidded to the left down a hill and her body collided against his. He caught her, held her steady just long enough to feel the rapid-fire beat of her heart, the soft swell of her breasts. He wanted to feel her naked against him just this way.

He burned for her, his skin on fire. He breathed in the slightest hint of her jasmine fragrance, different from the cedar and balsam all around them.

"I think the rewards will make the complications well worth it." It took a superhuman effort not to pull her closer. To slide his hands away. "But it's your call to make."

"You want me to decide." She worried her lower lip with her teeth in a movement as erotic as any touch.

He steeled himself, wondering how any woman could have this kind of power over him. Particularly a woman he shouldn't trust.

"I already know that I don't want tonight to end. But are you ready for more, Regina?" He kept his hands at his sides.

He knew his touch could sway her answer. That

wasn't egotistical. It was a simple fact that they combusted when they touched each other.

And he refused to tip the scales unfairly. He needed her to be sure. To want this as much as he did.

The sleigh slowed down, and Devon knew they must be approaching the remote lodge where he was staying. The scent of wood smoke from a chimney fire teased his nose, reminding him he'd left a blaze burning in the river stone fireplace while the catering company set up service for the meal.

Fragrant cooking spices drifted on the breeze as the sleigh came to a stop. The driver remained in his seat, though he did turn around expectantly.

And still, Regina hadn't replied.

"Should we return to the ranch?" Devon didn't want to part company, but if that was her preference, he would wait.

Find a way to tempt her into another evening with him tomorrow.

"I don't run from complications, either," she finally said, certainty evident in every word as she peeled away the blanket and tossed it on the seat in front of them. Sitting forward, she gave him her hand. "And I signed up for a date tonight."

Six

Stepping over the threshold into the cabin perched above the Bitterroot River, Regina breathed in the savory scent of roasting spices along with the sweeter hints of nutmeg and clove. Devon took her coat from her before excusing himself to speak to the catering team.

In short order, the three staff members exited through a back entrance, leaving Devon and her very much alone. Warming trays filled the kitchen island, while the dining area table had been set with festive red candles and decorated with scattered pine cones on green boughs. The table was tucked into a nook of bay windows, but the sky remained too dark to see beyond the glass into the densely forested woods.

In the living area, a wood fire burned in the stone fireplace, casting an inviting glow over a deep leather sofa and a narrow holiday tree bare of all decoration except for white lights. The wide plank floors were covered with twill weavings in muted cream, gold and brown, in patterns she'd seen often in this part of Montana. Moose antlers hung over the fireplace.

Sliding off her boots, Regina left them by the front door and padded deeper into the lodge, pausing near the holiday tree. She tested the soft needles of the balsam pine, surprised to discover it was fresh.

A thrill shot through her as Devon's footsteps sounded behind her. She'd thought long and hard about his invitation here before setting foot inside. And now that she had made up her mind to be with him, she wasn't sure she could wait to kiss him again until after dinner.

"Regina." His voice was just over her shoulder.

His nearness made her heart gallop faster, the warmth of him close enough to make her nerve endings tingle with awareness. She was done questioning it. Done asking herself why she had to be so attracted to this man of all people.

The need for him was so strong she couldn't think past it.

She wasn't sure how to express any of that as she turned toward him. But when she met his gaze, she realized that she didn't need to try to articulate it. The sizzling connection sparked to life on its own, a magnetic draw so strong she couldn't say who moved first—him or her.

Their lips met. Fused. Arms wrapping around each other. Hers around his neck. His around her waist. The full-on impact of his body against hers was hot enough to take her breath away, stirring all her senses. She wanted time to appreciate every nuance of those sensations, and at the same time, she wanted more. Faster. Now.

His hands skimmed up her sweater, pressing her tighter. Her fingers raked through his wavy hair. The ripple of muscle under his shirt was enough to make her stomach tighten with breathless anticipation. Her pulse pounded harder in every tiny vein, making her whole body feel like a drumroll, a vibrating precursor to the big finish she craved.

When he broke the kiss, she made a sound of wordless protest, but then his lips fastened on her neck. She closed her eyes again to give herself to the feel of his tongue stroking along the exquisitely sensitive place behind her ear. Then the tender hollow at the base of her throat. Every sensual glide across her skin deepened the need to get closer. To be naked. To feel that good everywhere.

Tugging the hem of his shirt higher, she dragged it up and off. In the moment when his arms left her, she instinctively moved closer, craving his touch again. Her gaze fell to his broad chest, hands splaying over the bared skin. She would have kissed her way along one flat pectoral muscle, but with a low growl, he took her hand and drew her deeper into the cabin.

Following blindly—gladly—Regina passed the kitchen island into a darker hallway. Devon pushed open the door to the master suite. A desk lamp glowed on the far side of the king-size bed at the center of the room, the tan-and-gold-striped quilt half concealed by a rich red duvet folded at the foot of the mattress. She had a vague impression of high ceilings and dark wood beams, but then Devon's arms were around her again and she forget everything except for his touch.

His kiss.

Her lips found his with new urgency. The dance of

his tongue along hers ignited a sensual shiver. Her hips arched against his. Seeking. Wanting.

His arms banded harder around her in answer, every inch of him steely and unyielding, making her melt. He stripped off her sweater and she shimmied out of her jeans, a new tension building inside her. She hadn't dressed for seduction, and for a split second, she wished she'd draped herself in sexy black silk instead of staid pink cotton.

Her gaze flicked up to his. He was taking her in with a frank male appreciation that sent any doubts fleeing. His focus narrowed to her breasts at the same time he slid aside the straps of her bra. Her breath caught as his eyes darkened, his fingers freeing the clasp just before his head lowered to capture a nipple between his lips.

A paroxysm of sensations coursed through her. Her head tipped back, and she gave herself up to the wicked skill of the kiss. He lifted her, depositing her gently onto the bed before his mouth moved to the other breast. She felt the delectable muscles of his shoulders and back flexing as he moved.

The ache between her thighs intensified. She lifted her hips, wriggling against him where his knee pressed into the bed. With a hungry groan, he lifted his head and shed his pants and his boxers. He retreated to the en suite bath for a moment and returned with a condom in hand, the packet already falling away in his rush to roll it into place. Heat and longing flooded her, her breathing fast and hard even though she'd done nothing more than kiss him. She thought she'd come right out of her skin if he didn't touch her soon.

Sitting up, she reached for him before he returned to the bed, her fingers trailing along the shadowed, incredibly sexy striations of his rigid abs. She didn't have long to admire him, though, because he slid his hands under her thighs before walking his fingers up her hips to draw down her panties.

The last garment between them finally removed.

He lifted her off the bed and she didn't hesitate to wrap her legs around him, her eyes on his. When he sat on the bed, she was on his lap. Straddling him. Trembling like it was her first time because the sensations were so intense.

She wrapped her arms around his neck, kissed him while he edged his way inside her. Joining them.

Pleasure crowded out everything else. Every touch, every taste, every stroke tantalized her, the passion building fast. She locked her heels behind him, holding him close while they moved in sync. Over and over.

Heat seared her. She closed her eyes again, wanting to focus on the sweetness of what he was doing to her. On his hands cupping her breasts, thumbs teasing over the peaks, his thighs flexing beneath her in a way that drove her right over the edge.

Her orgasm blindsided her, her feminine muscles seizing again and again, wringing out every shred of possible pleasure. She felt Devon go still beneath her for a moment before the same wave caught him, too, his body going rigid as his release pumped through him. It was impossibly good.

Pure and utter bliss.

And all she could do in the aftermath was tip her head to Devon's shoulder and cling to him because there were no words for what had just happened. Other people had sex. This?

She was pretty sure the earth had moved.

After long moments wrapped in each other's arms, he found a way to disentangle from her, pulling her back to lie beside him on the bed. He drew the spare blanket over their bodies while she tried to catch her breath.

Reason returned slowly, bringing with it new worries about what had just happened. As Devon smoothed back her hair, she was grateful for the long silence while she collected her thoughts. Tried to figure out what happened now.

Because no matter how good it had felt, Devon Salazar remained a potential enemy, as well as someone who had the answers to the puzzle of her shattered past. And she couldn't forget that, even for the sake of the best sex of her life.

"I can hear you thinking," he said finally, his voice a sexy whisper against her ear.

For a moment, she wished that this could be just a normal relationship where she could lean into him and savor what had just happened instead of thinking through her every move. But she hadn't come to Montana for romance. She needed to be careful around him, no matter how amazing he'd just made her feel.

While she debated her approach, Devon spoke again. "Before we try to figure out where things stand, why don't we put some clothes on and go have dinner?"

As he took another bite of a spiced scone with cinnamon glaze an hour later, Devon studied the woman across the table from him. She'd surprised him in so many ways tonight. First, when she'd come clean about her identity, it had rocked him. He'd imagined plenty of reasons for why she was pretending to be someone else, but it had never crossed his mind that Regina Flores had been born Georgiana Cameron, a woman caught in the crosshairs of the scandal created by his father's book.

Then, before he could wrap his head around what

that meant, there'd been the unforgettable sex. Even now, after they'd enjoyed companionable conversation over roast duck, coconut-ginger yams and risotto with mushrooms, Devon's thoughts kept returning to what they'd shared. The connection had been unlike anything he'd ever known, scorching away the suspicions and deceits until there was nothing but burning need. And she had seemed as taken aback by their chemistry as he had been.

Now, after devouring the last of his dessert, he slid the dish aside and wondered how to proceed with the beautiful woman full of contradictions in front of him.

"More wine?" He lifted the bottle of port while Regina scooped up a forkful of gingerbread shortbread, one of three choices the caterers had left for them.

"No. Thank you." Her dark hair curled in waves around her face, the strands tousled from his fingers. "I have to be a trail guide early tomorrow morning."

She had put her jeans and sweater back on, and had the sleeves of the bulky knit pushed up to her elbows.

"You're going to continue your job here?" He wondered why, since her cover was blown. "I mean, now that your identity is out in the open?"

"I'm enjoying the horses." She swirled her fork through the whipped cream dusted with tinted sugar. "I didn't realize how much I missed the Arabian of my youth until I got into the barns here. And, as it turns out, I really believe in the ranch mission."

"The sustainable ranching?" Devon had spoken to a few of the Mesa Falls owners about that when he'd first arrived. Creating public awareness of the green initiatives on the land was the number one goal of the launch event that Salazar Media had been charged with executing.

He was drawn to the authenticity in her voice as she spoke, the passion for a cause he felt strongly about, as well.

"Yes." Regina moved one of the red taper candles out of the way so they could see each other better across the small table. "I know the practices aren't feasible for all ranches yet, but the more we learn about what works, the more we can incorporate holistic ranching ideas into livestock management everywhere. Someone has to go first."

"Agreed." He sipped the rich red port from a dessert wine glass. "You sound as prepared as anyone on my staff to write the talking points for the launch party speeches."

She laughed lightly, the candlelight catching deep shades of cherry in her dark hair. "I studied hard to convince the ranch manager that I was the one for the job. And as for my identity being in the open, are you sure you want it to be?"

"What do you mean?" Defensiveness had him sitting straighter in his seat.

"Georgiana Fuentes being out of the public eye has allowed interest in A. J. Sorensen's book to fade away." She set her fork crossways on her plate and leaned back from the table. "Are you prepared for the renewed media focus?"

Was she threatening to expose him?

"No one knows my father wrote it," he reminded her, treading carefully. "So public attention would likely be more problematic for you than for me, unless you plan to reveal Alonzo's identity as the author."

"Right now, I'm more concerned with finding my own answers before media interest clouds the path," she explained. "So I won't be sharing that information—

for now. But if you feel the need to out me, I wish you would give me fair warning. Tabloid media can descend with shocking speed."

He could see her point. But she'd also skillfully reminded him that she could send *his* life into a tailspin at any given moment if she blew the whistle on the author. All the more reason he planned to stick close to her throughout his stay at Mesa Falls Ranch.

"I understand why you'd prefer to remain anonymous. I won't share your real name with anyone." He wanted to touch her, to draw her against him, but the conversation called to mind all the thorny issues between them.

The mistrust.

"Thank you." She wrapped her arms around her midsection, the watchfulness in her gray eyes mirroring how he felt.

Dammit.

He reached for her in spite of the wariness, drawn by the connection that remained even now. He dragged his chair closer, his knee bumping hers under the table.

"It wasn't my intention to remind you of something painful." Covering her hand with his, he squeezed her fingers. "I plan to share with you what I learn from my private investigator about my father's reasons for writing the book."

He hadn't pressed her about her endgame in coming to Montana, about deceiving him to get close to him. Was her goal simply to gain information, like she'd implied? Or was it revenge?

With her body close to his, her dark hair spilling loose over one shoulder, and her cheeks lightly pink from the warmth or the wine, Devon found it tough to imagine her setting him up for some kind of payback plot. Especially after the feverish way they'd come together earlier, like they were in the grip of something bigger than both of them.

"We could share our resources in that regard," she offered, taking a sip from her water glass while, just outside the windows beside them, the moon made an appearance above the trees. "The man I hired to find the author behind the pseudonym might have information that would help your investigator's efforts."

"I'm meeting her tomorrow. Should I ask her to contact you?" He hesitated. "For that matter, would you consider sharing your identity with her, if you trust her discretion?"

He could hardly renege on the agreement he'd just made, but no doubt Regina could help with April Stephens's efforts to follow the money trail from the book's profits.

She stared down at their joined hands for a moment before meeting his gaze. "As long as I can speak to her directly. Yes, that's fine."

He heard what she didn't say—that trust was going to come in degrees for both of them. It was the best he could expect, considering their tenuous relationship. He'd have to hope she didn't reveal his father as the author of the book—at least not in the weeks leading up to his mother's wedding. And she would have to trust him to keep her secrets and maintain her privacy under the new identity she'd worked hard to build.

"Of course." He let go of her hand and slid his arm around her shoulders, feeling the silky warmth of her hair as it brushed his sleeve. "I'll let you make the call on how much you feel comfortable sharing with her. Just know that whatever you can tell her will probably help speed things along."

"Believe me, no one wants answers as much as I do." The fierceness of the words matched the spark in her eyes. Perhaps she heard it, too, because she smiled belatedly, as if to soften the tone. "And now, as much as I hate to end our date, I really should get back to the bunkhouse for the night."

"You're more than welcome to stay here, if you prefer." He stroked her hair behind her ear so he could see her face better. "For that matter, there's a spare bedroom if you'd rather have your privacy."

There was a pale red mark on her neck, an abrasion from his cheek, he guessed. He smoothed a finger over it, regretting that he'd marred her skin while he'd been kissing her.

"Thank you, but my gear is at the bunkhouse. And it's surprisingly fun rooming with a bunch of women. Sort of like the summer camp I never had." She shrugged, a small grin playing at the corners of her mouth. "Besides, I've got an ear to the ground on what's happening around the ranch that way. And from what you said about your father's relationship with the owners of Mesa Falls, it sounds like there might be more to learn about him right here in Montana."

Devon stilled, realizing that he'd allowed sex to scramble his thoughts. He mentally rewound to their conversation on their horseback ride the day before when he'd told her as much. What else had he revealed about his dad before he discovered her true identity? Of course, he'd known to be cautious around her, so he hadn't said anything sensitive. Still, it caught him off guard how quick she was to zero in on a detail like that.

He kissed her cheek to try to hide his momentary surprise, still struggling to negotiate the balance between wanting her and maintaining his focus.

"Good thinking." He felt the small shiver go through her and wanted to explore it. To undress her all over again. But he would wait until they had more time. "The sleigh driver has returned to the ranch for the night, but I can bring you back in the all-terrain vehicle."

All of the cabins on the property came with the added convenience. But Devon's thoughts were far from the corporate retreat's luxuries as he retrieved Regina's coat and hat, and they dressed to back out into the cold.

He couldn't help remembering her last observation of the night—that she planned to key in on his father's relationships with the ranch owners. There was no doubt that Regina was sharp and quick-witted. And very committed to unearthing the truth behind his father's book.

As was he.

Selfishly, he hoped that whatever they found wouldn't destroy the tentative truce they'd made tonight. But more important, he needed to make sure the truth didn't implode on him before his mother's Christmas wedding.

Seven

Seated in a private meeting room at the Mesa Falls Ranch guest lodge, April Stephens reviewed her notes as Devon Salazar continued talking.

She'd purposely taken a high-back leather chair facing away from the spectacular view of the Bitterroot Mountains. She might not have time to indulge in the outdoors again during this trip, and she didn't want to tempt herself with the sight of those peaks. Instead, she grounded herself in the space around her, the warmth of the crackling fire in the hearth and the calming decor. The meeting room was sleekly understated in pale grays and cream, the furnishings not detracting from the real visual interest of the snowcapped mountains outside the wall of windows.

Her client was paying her firm well, and she wouldn't disappoint him. She'd been fortunate to have this opportunity to work with a powerful and high-profile figure like Devon Salazar in the first place. Her agency's senior financial investigator had a death in the family and her boss hadn't wanted to turn down the business. He'd offered April a serious incentive on this case.

Crack the secrets of Alonzo Salazar and she'd get a promotion. That meant more money, more travel and more opportunities to escape the responsibilities of the smothering home life weighing her down more every day.

April would not fail. She'd maxed out her credit cards buying a few high-end outfits to get through this week, needing to look the part of a senior staffer.

Had that been pathetically self-indulgent? Or a wise act of self-care that would put her more at ease with the well-heeled crowd that could afford to stay in places like Mesa Falls Ranch? She didn't know. But the buttery soft wool of the jacket she was wearing made her feel like a million bucks. And it was a good thing, because she dreaded sharing some of her findings with Devon. What if he didn't like what he heard? Would he put a halt to the investigation?

Now, as he brought her up to date about "Regina Flores"—the woman April had warned him about—she took notes by hand on a legal pad. Apparently he'd uncovered the woman's real identity: she was none other than the elusive Georgiana Fuentes, living and working right here in Montana. Which was most certainly not a coincidence, given that Devon was researching his father's book.

The book that had ruined Georgiana's life.

April remembered the sudsy read well. *Hollywood Newlyweds* by A. J. Sorensen had been a huge bestseller at a time when April read anything and everything she could get her hands on. She'd gobbled that book up, and had followed the tabloid headlines afterward when the supposedly fictional story turned out to have a basis in real life.

But no one in the media had seen Georgiana in years. So for her to pop up here, using a fake identity and trying to get close to Devon, was about as ominous as April could imagine. Unfortunately, her client didn't seem to share her concern.

"Georgiana invited me to contact her directly?" April asked him now, glancing up at him from across the small conference table.

He was uncommonly handsome, tall and well built, with light brown hair and attractive green eyes. He had an easy manner that made him a natural leader—the kind of man people would want to follow. Not that she was in the market for romance—far from it. But if she had been?

Yum.

The fact that he'd taken a marketing start-up founded by two brothers and grown it to a globally recognized leader in the social media environment appealed to her on an intellectual level, as well. Studying business accounting and working in financial investigations had given her an appreciation for the savvy it took to do something like that.

"She prefers to be called 'Regina.' And, yes." He slid a paper across the table toward April, and she noticed how the sleeves of his black button-down were rolled up. "We would like to keep her real identity private. The longer Georgiana stays out of the spotlight, the more likely my father's connection to the book will, too."

The "we" was not lost on April. Something in his tone gave her the idea that he felt protective of the woman. Guilt, perhaps, since his father's book had sent

Georgiana's life into a tailspin? Or was there something else at work?

She planned to proceed carefully with the woman.

"Certainly." She tucked the contact information into a file folder. "I'll reach out to her as soon as we're done here."

"So my father was paying for a nominee service to collect his royalties on *Hollywood Newlyweds*?" Devon asked, returning to the information she'd given him earlier in the meeting. He flipped through web search results on a tablet before spinning his screen to show her a few prominent agencies.

"Yes." She'd invested far more hours than she would bill him to confirm it. "He set up his pen name like a corporation and gave it a director. The company collected monies from the publisher, and the nominee service oversaw the transactions and made sure taxes were paid."

A nominee service was extremely expensive, but it provided an unparalleled level of privacy.

"But the service must have expired with my father's death?" Frowning, Devon set the tablet on the sleek birchwood table. "There was nothing about that in the will."

"The service was paid for in advance. Given the precautions Alonzo took in order to keep his name away from the novel, I suspect he left explicit instructions for the royalty income after his death." April had chased the lead as far as she could for now, but she wouldn't give up. "Arrangements for future disbursements may already be in place and you weren't aware because you aren't a beneficiary. The other possibility is that the nominee hasn't learned of your father's death yet."

"Months after the fact?" Devon sounded skeptical. He glanced up from his tablet, one dark eyebrow raised.

"It's conceivable your dad only needed to touch base with the service once a year at tax time." She hesitated before sharing her biggest concern, not wanting to give him any reason to shut down this job. "And while I'm prepared to keep searching for information, you should know that in my experience, searches like this uncover illegal activity about fifty percent of the time."

Even though she hadn't taken the lead on an investigation before this one, she'd been in the weeds on similar cases at her firm for two years. And although there were highly reputable nominee services, the industry attracted its share of the criminal element.

"I appreciate the warning." Devon shut off his tablet and leaned back in the chair across from her, the afternoon sun gilding his features. He templed his fingers together, propping his chin on them. "My father obviously had a secret life we knew nothing about, but I still hold out hope that he had more altruistic reasons for hiding that income."

"So you're certain you want me to keep searching?" she clarified, needing his blessing before she unearthed news that could be upsetting on a personal level, or that had the potential to stir legal interest in the case.

"Absolutely. Whatever my father was up to, I need to know about it. And the sooner the better, April, so if you are in need of additional resources, don't hesitate to come to me."

She felt the thrill of victory at his words. She still had the job. The doorway for that promotion remained open.

"Understood." Hope filling her, she closed the leather cover over her legal pad and laid her pen on top of it. "I'll contact Regina Flores first, then begin contacting the owners of Mesa Falls Ranch to explore their connection to your father."

"And you'll continue looking into the nominee service?" he prompted, his words reminding her that she was getting into dicey terrain.

That information was well protected.

"I'll do everything in my power to find answers for you," she vowed, knowing she had to make it work.

"Very good." Standing, he ended the meeting with a handshake. "I look forward to hearing from you."

As he left the room, April's gut knotted tighter. How would she shake information out of a nominee service that sold complete anonymity to its clients? Her better hope was prying answers from Regina/Georgiana. Or the owners of Mesa Falls Ranch.

As she packed the file and her pen in her bag, April's gaze veered out the meeting room windows toward the mountains. One day, she'd have the kind of life that allowed her the freedom of wide open spaces and fewer responsibilities. A life where she didn't need to constantly walk the tightrope between taking care of her mom and hiding her mother's increasing trouble from the world.

Until then, she would just keep her focus on the task at hand. Starting with Regina Flores.

Three days after her night with Devon, Regina was keeping her eye out for him in the great room at the main lodge, knowing he'd arrive soon.

She'd just finished a snowshoe trek with a group of new ranch guests. Her duties as a trail guide had quickly expanded from leading horseback rides to hosting other winter activities on the trails. With the huge influx of guests arriving for the launch event this week, all of the staff had been tapped to work extra hours. Now, as she transitioned her group of guests from the snowshoe activity to a whiskey tasting party in the great room, she would finally have her first evening free since the sleigh ride with Devon.

"The bourbons are on the bar and the scotches are on the buffet," she explained to an older couple puzzling over where to go next in the growing crowd.

Fires burned brightly in fireplaces at either end of the post-and-beam-style room. A huge antler chandelier hung low over a game table already filling with guests comparing tasting notes on preprinted cards. A solo guitar player sat in a high-backed stool near a stuffed grizzly bear. The scent of barbecue from the hors d'oeuvres being offered by passing waiters mingled with fragrant woodsmoke.

Regina took a bottled water from a silver tub full of ice near the whiskey display. Her cheeks were warm from the change in temperature after being outdoors for hours. She looked around the room, and somehow felt Devon behind her even before she turned to see him standing by the bar.

Her pulse quickened at the sight of him.

He wore dark jeans and leather loafers, but unlike most of the other men wearing flannel shirts or sweaters, he'd paired his denim with a white button-down and a gray tailored jacket. He didn't need a tie to appear like a man in charge.

Three days hadn't done anything to dampen Regina's hunger for him. But she'd spent every one of those days reminding herself that she needed to be wary with a Salazar. That she couldn't simply follow a compelling attraction to him; they had a far more complicated relationship.

But right now, seeing him again, she could only think about what it had been like to be bracketed in his strong arms. To feel the intense passion. To melt under his kiss.

By the time he arrived at her side, her breathing was fast and shallow.

He leaned closer to speak words for her alone. "If I'd known it would be three days before I saw you again, I wouldn't have been so quick to let you leave my cabin."

A thrill shot through her—both at his nearness and at the idea that he'd missed her. Wanted her.

Her skin tingled with awareness and he hadn't even touched her.

"Buildup to your launch event is keeping all the staff busy." She opened her water and took a cooling sip. "I had no idea the ride two days ago would turn into an overnight event."

His gaze lingered on her lips. "I didn't know, either, or I would have signed up for it myself." The heat in his green eyes distracted her. It made her forget what they'd been discussing, even quieted her years-old need for revenge. The strong reaction he incited both tantalized and worried her. She couldn't afford to let her feelings distract her from her goal.

Around them, the strains of a cowboy folk melody, the clinking of glasses and rumbled laughter faded until she could only hear her own breath.

"Are you free now?" he asked, his hand landing lightly on the small of her back.

"I planned to meet with—" She lowered her voice. "That is, I have a call scheduled from our mutual contact twenty minutes from now."

She'd been trying to find a time to speak to the private investigator, eager to get back on track with what she'd come to Montana to accomplish.

"Of course." He nodded, his hand still on her back. "She told me she'd been trying to reach you. Until then, maybe we could step out into a quieter spot."

Capping her water, she let him guide her through the crowded room. A pair of younger women stopped her to thank her for helping them with the snowshoe trek—or possibly to ogle Devon—but eventually she and Devon emerged from the great room to head toward the saloon.

He bypassed the bar and continued down a hall that led to the bowling alley and screening room. The sound of an old Western film filled the corridor for a moment before he steered her into a den that functioned as a small library. The three natural log walls were covered with floor-to-ceiling bookshelves, while the fourth wall featured a stone fireplace flanked by tall, narrow windows. A painting of one of the original homes on the ranch dominated the space above the fireplace.

Regina set her water bottle on a side table and wandered toward the hearth, her eye grazing the collection of photographs on the mantel showcasing the development of the property from small working ranch to corporate guest facility. She noticed Devon had closed the door behind them. Not that it would necessarily deter guests who wanted to drop in, but most of the activity in the lodge was in the dining rooms and bars by this time of evening.

He joined her by the fireplace, his gaze following the direction of hers briefly before returning to her. The scent of old books and pine hung in the air, familiar and welcoming.

"Are you all right?" He tipped her chin up so she was looking into his concerned green eyes. "I didn't know how to read your retreat."

Her belly flipped at his careful scrutiny. At the feeling she thought she heard in his voice.

No doubt she was misreading him, seeing a level of emotion that wasn't there. She was only valuable to him because he wanted to keep his father's deeds on lockdown.

"I'm fine." Steeling herself, she ignored the fluttery sensations his touch inspired. "I told you, I got roped into leading a longer tour than I'd signed on for. I hadn't realized that accompanying the group to a local ski resort meant I'd be stuck there until the ranch bus picked everyone up the next day."

He regarded her thoughtfully.

"You're putting in a lot of hours," he said finally, his hand falling away. "Are you sure this pursuit of my father's motives is worth so much of your time?"

Even as she missed the feel of his fingers on her cheek, she felt indignation straighten her spine.

"I thought I made it clear to you the other night that finding out why Alonzo mined my family's secrets for his own gain is my number one priority?" The words came out with more bite than she'd intended, but it frustrated her to think Devon couldn't see how deeply the book had affected her.

How it had *hurt*.

"You have every right to know." His voice hummed along her nerve endings, seemingly calibrated to soothe her. "My point is that I can help you now. You don't need to do this alone anymore."

His calm, easy demeanor only reminded her that Devon had lived without any knowledge of his father's actions until recently, whereas she'd been keenly aware of them her whole life, even if she hadn't known whom to blame for them.

"Are you suggesting I give up my quest and go home?" With an effort, she held herself very still, ignoring the physical need to be close to him and restraining the impulse to run. "Trust that the son of someone who tore apart my family will turn out to be an ally?"

Frustration vibrated through her, making her limbs shaky while the sounds of the Western movie in the room next door briefly blared louder. A gunfight, maybe, with swelling, suspenseful music that hummed through the hardwood floor.

"Is that the real reason you've been avoiding me these last three days?" The muscle in Devon's jaw tensed. Flexed. "Because you're back to thinking of me as your enemy?"

"I never said that." Wrapping her arms around herself, she turned from the hearth to stare out the dark window at the stars dotting the horizon.

She recognized there could be a grain of truth in his accusation. She had gladly accepted the extra workload, telling herself she might have a chance to learn more about the elusive ranch owners who had a close relationship to Alonzo Salazar.

But was that the real reason she'd filled her calendar?

"You didn't need to." He remained by the crackling fire, his broad shoulders outlined by the orange glow. "And I understand if you want to pursue answers in your own way. But my offer still stands to share information and resources. April Stephens is going to get to the bottom of this faster than you or I could alone."

Regina bit her lip to keep herself from responding impulsively. Angrily. Yet the injustice of the situation wouldn't let her stay quiet.

"Her allegiance is to you, because you're paying her." She'd had a lot of time to think about it these past few days when she'd buried herself in the work of entertaining guests. "And you have to recognize the extreme financial disconnect between our stations in life right now. You're running a successful business, possibly funded by your father's ill-gotten gains. I'm seasonal ranch help after being disowned by my father thanks to your dad."

"That's not fair." Devon stalked closer, taking a breath as if he was about to expound on the point, but she held up a hand to forestall him.

"I realize that," she conceded, her pulse speeding up again when he closed the distance between them. "Your business has grown because of your talent and commitment. I've meandered around without a solid career direction. That's on me."

A log in the fire slipped, spewing embers and hissing softly.

"But you feel robbed of opportunities, while they've been handed to me?" He shook his head. "If my father had access to hidden wealth, he never spent it on his sons."

"Yet he was an investor in Salazar Media." She'd looked it up and the amount was staggering. "It's a matter of public record."

Devon's lips flattened into a line for a moment as he studied her. She wanted to reach out and touch his shadowed jaw, even when she felt an unreasonable resentment.

"True." He nodded in a distracted way, his gaze sliding from hers to peer into the distance. "Though the amount was funded from his retirement account. I worried about him giving us that money because it meant he'd have nothing to live on while waiting for the company to start turning a profit."

Turning on his heel, Devon paced away from her, clearly caught up in his own thoughts. It seemed that he was speaking to himself more than her.

"What is it? Did you remember something?"

She knew he didn't have to tell her. But maybe she'd catch him in an unguarded moment. Hadn't he just been asking her to trust him to share with her?

She followed him toward the sofa table that held a stone statue of a bucking bronc.

"Dad traveled a lot." Devon slid a sideways glance toward her. "Friends who knew about those trips used to joke that he must be a secret agent on the side."

"Trips where?" Anticipation curled through her that she might learn something.

And yet, would discovering the truth about the father alienate her from the son forever? It shouldn't matter to her. Except after what she'd shared with Devon at his cabin, she couldn't deny that it would.

"We didn't know." Devon faced her, the warmth of his body suddenly close to hers. "Since finding out about the novel, I thought maybe he was just seeking out quiet places to write."

"But now you're wondering if he was financing a more extravagant lifestyle you didn't know about?" A piece of her hoped that Devon truly wasn't aware of that hidden income.

"Not necessarily." He withdrew his phone from his jacket pocket and tapped in a note. "It's occurred to me that the investigator would surely be able to track some of those travel dates. Perhaps his destinations on those trips would provide more insights."

Regina chewed on that idea while he finished typing. No doubt he had a good point. She felt uneasy that she hadn't spoken to the investigator herself yet. What if she held the missing pieces of the Alonzo Salazar puzzle?

Nearby a wall clock chimed the hour.

"Speaking of which, I'm scheduled to talk to her now." She needed to get her own read on April Stephens and decide how much she could trust the investigator. "I don't want to miss her again."

Devon deposited his cell into his jacket pocket. "If you'd like this room, I can give you privacy. I need to go over some particulars on the launch event with the ranch manager."

"Thank you." She retrieved her water bottle from where she'd set it on a side table earlier. "That would work well. If anyone comes in, I can always take the call outside."

"Can I take you out tomorrow night?" he asked quietly, his green eyes darkening.

An answering shiver ran up her spine as her body reminded her how much she'd like that.

"Because you want to see me?" she asked, tempted, but needing to keep a level head around this man. "Or because you want to keep an eye on me?"

"I could ask you the same question about why you spend time with me," he reminded her, angling closer in a way that made her heart skip a beat.

Or two.

When his lips closed over hers, she didn't hesitate to kiss him back. The kiss was slow, thorough and sensual. A deliberate reminder of what it was like between them. Her arms wrapped around his waist, fingers curling into his shirt as hunger returned with an aching insistence.

As her breasts tightened, her nipples peaked against the fabric of her bra. She almost forgot everything else until he pulled away, his breathing ragged.

"You decide what you want next, Regina." His hands slid away from her, and it was all she could do to remain upright. "I want you, but only when you're sure about this. About me."

She blinked fast, trying to think of a response, but he was already walking away. He closed the door to the den behind him, leaving her beside the hearth while the fire blazed.

Regina bit her lip until it hurt and waited for her thoughts to reassemble themselves. For reason to return. She was turned on. Confused.

And very, very alone.

Eight

An hour later, Regina sat in a deep leather barrel chair kitty-corner to April Stephens in the Mesa Falls Ranch den.

The investigator had asked to meet in person once she'd discovered that Regina was at the main lodge, and within five minutes of the call, the two of them had taken seats next to one of the tall windows flanking the fireplace.

April defied every expectation Regina had of a female PI. The willowy blonde's long hair hung in full curls around the shoulders of a suit that looked right out of the pages of a fashion magazine. From her stilettos to her French manicure, April appeared more apt to step out of a limo on Park Avenue than sit in a stakeout. But maybe that was because her investigative specialty was financial forensics.

Now, taking notes in longhand on a legal pad, April paused to peer up at Regina.

"Did your mother ever speculate about who in her life might have betrayed her trust?" The woman had listened without interruption while Regina recounted growing up as Georgiana Cameron, daughter of the prominent film star, before getting iced out of her "father's" life once the scandal broke involving *Hollywood Newlyweds*. She should have been numbed to telling by now, but sharing about the betrayal still left her raw and vulnerable, perhaps because she was still unsettled by her last conversation with Devon.

A burst of applause erupted in a room nearby, then died down again. The entertainment areas of the lodge had remained busy throughout the evening, but no one else had entered the den except for a passing waiter who'd asked if they needed anything. Regina sipped her water and set it back on the small round table with a wagon wheel painted on it, which sat between their chairs. Her hand trembled enough to give away her fractured emotions, and she yanked it back fast.

"She said the only people who knew about her affair with my birth father were her two best friends and their yoga instructor." Regina hadn't thought back to that in a long time, and she appreciated April coming at the story with fresh eyes. But would it help Regina in the long run, or only serve Devon? "Eventually, Mom decided it must have been my father who'd let it slip to someone, because she trusted all of those women implicitly."

"Have your mom's friends ever been questioned?" April shifted in her chair, the red soles of her shoes flashing for a moment as she recrossed her slim legs. "By a professional investigator, that is?"

"No." Regina felt a surge of hope that maybe something could still be unearthed from one of them. "I'm the only member of my family who has ever paid anyone to look into the matter, and I didn't have the budget for it that Devon Salazar does."

"Will it create discomfort for your family if I question your mother's friends now?" April asked, pen hovering in midair over her paper while she waited for an answer.

"Not at all." She withdrew her phone and started typing in names. "I'll send you their contact information, but I should warn you that I've spoken to all of them before." Although, looking back on those conversations, she remembered how emotional she'd been at the time. It had been shortly after her high school graduation, when the realization had settled in that her life would never, ever, be the same again. "Come to think of it, they were probably all hesitant to share anything with me based on how personally involved I was. Am."

April remained quiet for a moment while Regina looked up phone numbers and emails, drawing comfort in the task, feeling proactive for once, rather than just reactive. Once Regina sent April the text with all the info, the investigator spoke again.

"I'm going to get to the bottom of it," she said, blue eyes unwavering, voice certain. "We'll have answers soon."

In that moment, Regina saw beyond the pretty, carefully cultivated exterior to the fierceness beneath.

And she believed her.

"I look forward to that."

They spoke for another quarter of an hour, going over details of Regina's past before wrapping up the interview. She assured April she'd never met Alonzo Salazar or even heard of him before her own PI finally turned up the name earlier in the year. When the woman seemed satisfied she had enough answers, the two of them parted ways. April strode out of the den on her elegant high heels while Regina stood on shaky legs to return to the bunkhouse for the night. She wanted to believe it was just weariness from snowshoeing, but it more likely had to do with dredging up the past. She didn't know if she could trust her feelings for Devon. Or his for her.

Strangely, April Stephens had seemed like an ally even though she worked for Devon. That was only an illusion, though, and Regina would be foolish to think otherwise. The investigator would have allegiance to the man who'd hired her—end of story. Which meant Regina needed to stay close to that man if she wanted to know what April turned up.

That had been her plan all along and, pride be damned, she was going to stick to it because she was finally getting close to having answers about Alonzo Salazar and his book.

Regina told herself that was why she was seeing Devon again tomorrow night. It didn't have anything to do with being wildly attracted to him.

If Devon had been an oddsmaker, he would have put the likelihood of seeing Regina tonight at 50 percent.

After the way she'd avoided him for days, then danced around the idea of meeting, he feared her conflicted feelings about their relationship had overshadowed the attraction.

Then, in the middle of a meeting with his planning committee for the Mesa Falls launch event, he'd spotted her text asking if they could get together.

"This was a fun surprise." Regina's face glowed in the firelight as she passed him an old-fashioned tin star for the top of the Christmas tree in his cabin. "I never guessed you would choose tree-decorating for a date night. Where did you get the ornaments?"

They were seated on the couch in the living area. Instrumental Christmas tunes played over the room's built-in speaker system, and the white tree lights glowed on the fresh balsam, which was tucked in the corner between the bookshelves and a wingback.

Regina's red sweater had a V-neck that framed a necklace of tiny silver jingle bells, and a slim black skirt hugged her curves in a way that drew his eye every time she moved. Her dark hair was pinned back in a green-and-red plaid bow. She seemed more relaxed tonight than when they'd spoken in the lodge the night before. The jasmine scent of her fragrance wafted under the stronger smell of pine in the room.

"I ordered the box last week from a charity I work with in New York. They provide everything you need for themed trees, and half the cost goes to holiday gifts for people in need." He set aside the star to save for the end. "To be honest, I was going to have my staff decorate for a photo op to post on social media. But when you messaged me, I thought it might be fun for us to tackle."

She grinned as she pulled a straw cowboy hat ornament from the box. "You must have chosen the Western theme."

"The official name is 'Cowboy Christmas.'" He peered into the box on the coffee table, full of rodeo-themed decorations along with a garland made of twine and tiny reproduction horseshoes. "I thought it would work well with the cabin's design."

"Are they a client of yours?" She sipped the champagne cocktail he'd made for her. Her silver bangle clinked against the base of the flute as she set it back on the table.

His gaze lingered on the long spill of her dark hair on her shoulder as she moved. He wanted to touch the strands, to breathe in the fragrance of the silky mass. To taste the delicate column of her neck.

But he was trying his damnedest to give her some space. To let her set the pace tonight after the way she'd seemed skittish about continuing their relationship.

"You could say that." He stood up to keep himself from following the impulse to touch her. Digging the garland out of the box, he started wrapping it around the tree limbs. "From the inception of the business, my brother and I wanted to allocate a percentage of company resources to community giving. The organization that sells the ornament boxes was just getting started in New York at the same time we were, so we approached them to see if they wanted some help."

The holiday music switched to a country tune, with steel guitars and more folksy vocals. Devon stood back to see how the garland looked while Regina joined him near the tree. Growing up, he had never decorated a tree with his family. In his grandfather's palatial mansion, trees simply appeared one day, professionally trimmed. Even as an adult, he'd found his decorating opportunities were limited to office parties, as a way to connect with his staff. But something had made him want to share this with Regina tonight. Maybe a sense that her family holidays had to have been painful after her parents' well-publicized split.

"That was good of you." There was a wistful note in her voice as she slid a velvety quarter horse decoration onto a branch. "You've accomplished so much between growing your business and giving back." She straightened the ornament, so the horse dangled the way she wanted it to. "And during that same amount of time, I feel like all I've accomplished is chasing my tail."

Regret for what she'd gone through rained over him. How could his father have published that damned book and destroyed her family?

"This week is going to mark a turning point for you, though." He couldn't help but touch her then, needing to reassure her. His hand went to the space between her narrow shoulder blades. "Once you have the answers you deserve, you'll be ready to move forward."

Her angora sweater was impossibly soft. Even so, he remembered that it didn't compare to the texture of the creamy skin beneath it. Thoughts of stripping her naked forced him to move his hand away again.

"I hope so." She found more ornaments to hang and they worked in tandem for a few minutes. "Have you heard from April?" Her gaze flicked over to his.

Wariness crept through him.

Was this why she'd wanted to see him tonight?

But then, he told himself it was only natural she'd want to know. He'd just told her she'd have answers soon, after all.

"She took a red-eye to the West Coast last night." He met Regina's surprised gaze. "To follow up on leads you gave her, apparently."

Devon hadn't asked the PI for details. His workdays had been crammed with the logistics of the ranch's launch event. He had a sizable staff on hand in Montana now, but the event included satellite parties taking place simultaneously on both coasts in real time. This would allow Mesa Falls Ranch to reach more potential clients, even if the expenses were high up front. Bottom line, he needed staffing in both cities, coordinating everything.

"Wow. That was fast." Regina held a pewter ornament shaped like a pair of cowboy boots in midair, as if she'd forgotten what she was doing. "I'm grateful for your support in helping her get to the bottom of this."

Something about the way she said it rankled. He took the boots from her and found a spot for them on the tree, then cupped her shoulders in his hands.

"I need answers as much as you do. It's not just kindness. It's good business to work together." He didn't want her gratitude. And damn it, he sure didn't want to think that she was only spending time with him for the sake of the investigation.

Her brows knitted together as she frowned. "In that case, thanks for doing business with me."

He shook his head, letting go of her. "Are you always so prickly, or is it just me who brings out the defensive side?"

Her sudden burst of laughter smoothed over his irritation, the sound far more melodious than anything playing on the Christmas music station.

"Maybe a little of both. I definitely have prickly down to an art." She bent closer to the coffee table and retrieved her champagne flute for another sip of her drink, the bubbles glowing golden in the firelight.

"And why is that?" he asked, genuinely curious about her.

"After the whole debacle of the book—and losing my old friends—it became a protective measure, maybe. It was just easier to keep people at arm's length rather than let anyone close enough to hurt me again." She set aside the flute and studied the tree. "And I've only started to recognize that tendency this week, as I grow closer to some of the women in my bunkhouse. It makes me realize I've gone a lot of years without friends."

The acknowledgement of her solitary existence saddened him as she took time rearranging a few of the tree lights so they illuminated some of the ornaments from behind.

"Will you go home for Christmas?" He hated to think about her remaining at the ranch during a time most people spent with their families.

She shrugged in a way that shifted the neckline of her sweater closer to the edge of one shoulder.

"It depends how much progress I make in finding answers about your dad and the book." Spinning to face him, she seemed to notice his careful regard, and her cheeks flushed a deeper pink. "If I think that staying here over the holidays will give me opportunities to speak to any of the owners privately, then I will stick around."

He wanted to reassure her. To give her some concrete findings from April's investigation that would ease Regina's fierce desire for the truth.

But what if giving her those answers meant she would turn on him? Would she sue his father's estate for defamation or drag the Salazar name through the tabloids?

When he didn't reply right away, she leaned past him to retrieve a package of ornament hooks. "What about you?" she asked. "What are you doing for the holidays?"

"My mother is getting married on Christmas Eve." Tension pulled his shoulders tight, the way it had all week when he thought about the wedding. Because his meeting with the PI—her warning that Alonzo hiding his money could indicate illegal activity—made Devon worry how soon something would leak about his father's hidden life. "I'm flying to Connecticut to be with her right after the launch party."

"That should be fun, right?" Regina's jingle bell necklace chimed softly as she moved to decorate the left side of the tree.

His gaze followed her movements as the tree's golden glow lit up her features. Thinking about the wedding forced him to consider what his life would be like once he left Mesa Falls and Regina behind. And the vision made him feel suddenly empty.

"It would be more fun with a date." He articulated the idea the moment it came into his head. Because why not? He'd started this relationship to keep an eye on her.

Just because it had grown into more than that didn't mean that the need to keep her closer had dissipated. Far from it. If she had any inclination to drag his father's book back into the public spotlight for some sort of payback scheme, he'd prefer to know about it sooner rather than later.

"Are you asking me to attend the wedding with you?" She frowned, clearly surprised.

Because she was ready for their time together to end? Or because she hadn't expected this relationship to continue after he left Montana?

"I am." He stepped closer, breathing her in. "I can already tell I'm not going to be able to walk away after the launch event."

She licked her lips. "Can I think it over?"

"Of course." He wasn't going to press her, especially since the wedding would mean spending Christmas together. "I need to fly out right after the launch party for some pre-wedding festivities. But my mother gets married on Christmas Eve, so you could wait and join me the next day."

She gave a thoughtful nod, lips pressed in a flat line. "Do you like the guy she's marrying?"

"I don't know him that well," he admitted. That was partly his fault for not making more of an effort, but also because his grandfather had claimed all the family's face time with the groom-to-be in order to strengthen Radcliffe ties with the international banker. "But I think having someone marry your mother is like someone marrying a daughter—no one will ever be good enough for her in my eyes."

Regina bent to decorate a lower branch. "That's a touching sentiment from a son." Her expression turned strained as she straightened. "Or a father, for that matter." She busied herself, adjusting things she'd already tidied. "Did you spend much time with your father as a kid?"

"No." His role model had been his cold and distant grandfather, who'd made sure Devon knew he would never be good enough because he wasn't a Radcliffe. "I visited the West Coast a couple times to see him, but mostly my mother insisted he come back East if he wanted a relationship with me."

As a teacher—even in an elite private boarding school—Alonzo had never had much money when Devon was younger. Later in life, when Devon was in his late teens, his father had had noticeably more disposable income. Now Devon knew that was thanks to *Hollywood Newlyweds*.

"What was he like?" She wandered over to the side table, where Devon had put out the offerings from the chef to accompany the champagne.

Plucking a dark salted caramel from a small silver tray, she nibbled on it as she watched him.

"An inspiring teacher." Devon had heard it over and over again throughout his life, and especially after the funeral, when former students began sending condolences. "He wasn't an involved father to my brother or me, and he didn't place any importance on marriage as an institution, which hurt more than one of the women he loved." He watched Regina's tongue sweep away a tiny spot of caramel on her upper lip, the movement igniting a fresh blaze of desire for her. "But he made a difference in the lives of his students and that meant something to him."

He forced himself to focus on decorating the tree to keep from touching her. Tasting her.

He'd been so damned determined to let this night move more slowly. To allow her to dictate how things went. But he'd forgotten the potent power of Regina's appeal.

"I read about that boarding school online." She retrieved a Santa dressed in chaps and spurs from the box and went back to the tree, her curves drawing Devon's eye as she moved past. "Dowdon isn't all that far from Hollywood in miles, but it might as well be on the other side of the globe for how much the community differs from the social scene portrayed in his book."

Devon had thought the same thing. "One of the school's biggest selling points is the remote location in a national forest, close to a protected wilderness area."

As a kid, he'd thought it sounded idyllic. His father lived on the campus, and was part of the horse program, which offered a mount to every student for the duration of their time at Dowdon. Learning to ride, caring for an animal and competing in horsemanship activities were all central to the experience.

"I wonder if he could have met my mother somehow." Regina's silver-gray gaze locked with Devon's. "He obviously knew a great deal about her private life."

Devon heard the resentment leak into her voice, and hoped to reroute the conversation before it turned more divisive.

"What's your mom like?" he asked to distract her. "I remember some of her films."

For a few years, Tabitha Barnes had been the queen of romantic comedies, but she'd stopped making movies after her affair began dominating headlines.

"Bubbly. Sweet." Regina seemed to take the question seriously, a slow smile spreading over her features. "Not all that different from the characters she played during her filmmaking heyday. Davis—the man I believed to be my dad for the first fifteen years—fell in love with her when he was making his directorial debut. He starred in the picture that was her breakout movie, and he directed it, too."

Devon thought he detected a begrudging pride in those words, and he recalled that talk about Davis Cameron hurt her most. No doubt because the man had cut ties so completely.

"It was unnecessarily cruel of him to push you out of his life." How could a grown man purposely distance himself from a daughter he'd raised as his own? From what Devon could gather, Regina had been close to Davis Cameron—perhaps even closer than she was to her mother. "In all the years since he ended things with your mom, has he ever contacted you?"

"Never." The answer sounded like it came from a ripped-raw place, but she cleared her throat and moved purposely back toward the box of ornaments. "At least he's been consistent about not talking to the media, either. There was a small amount of comfort in the fact that he never commented on the situation."

"I'm sorry I brought it up," Devon told her sincerely, intercepting her before she could pull more ornaments from the box. "I can't imagine how painful it was for you to have your world turned upside down by that damned book. But I'm confident we'll hear from April soon with some more definitive answers."

He took her hand in his, folding her fingers into his palm.

"The mystery behind *Hollywood Newlyweds* has dominated my life for years." She shook her head and huffed out a sigh, sounding upset. "And I'm not very good at putting the frustrations out of my mind once I start thinking about it. The resentment just festers."

He drew her closer, wishing he could absorb the hurt and take away that pain. His father had no business tearing apart her family or making them the center of public speculation for years. Devon wanted to make amends.

And right now, he had an idea how he could help, at least temporarily.

"Maybe you should let me distract you." He lowered his lips to her ear to speak softly against her skin. "Give you something else to think about."

Already, his heart hammered with wanting her. When she sucked in a sharp breath, the need for her multiplied exponentially.

"I thought you said I was too prickly and defensive," she reminded him, arching a dark eyebrow as she gazed up at him. "Are you sure you want to tangle with me?"

There was a light, teasing note in her voice, but Devon suspected she'd put it there to mask a moment of insecurity and doubt. Not that he'd let her see he recognized it for what it was.

A vulnerability.

So he skimmed his hands around her shoulders and sifted through the silky dark hair.

"It would be the greatest pleasure I can imagine."

Nine

Every day that Regina had been without Devon felt like years, making her question how she'd stayed away from him for this long.

Winding her arms around his neck, she sighed into him, letting go of all the excellent reasons she had for not trusting him. Tonight, he'd showed her a new level of caring, a kindness even more compelling than the red-hot attraction between them.

She lost herself in his kiss, his tongue sweeping over hers in a way that made her forget everything but him. How was that even possible?

But she didn't want to ruminate or overanalyze. Right now, when she had the chance to forget all the old wounds, to shut out everything else but this moment with Devon Salazar, she would embrace it.

His hands skimmed her curves, stirring pleasure. She arched closer, remembering how he could make her feel. How good they were together.

She broke the kiss, determined to make her desires clear. Breathing hard, she stared up into his green eyes that were so intent. So hungry.

"I'll take all the distraction you can give," she whispered, her voice a husky rasp of sound, before she turned and led him toward the bedroom she remembered well.

He caught up to her in a half step, plucking her off her feet and lifting her in his arms like a groom carrying a new bride over the threshold. Squealing in surprise, she shoved aside the romantic thought. His hold on her gave her the chance to appreciate his broad chest, though. She ran her hand over one muscular shoulder.

He entered the master suite, kicking the door shut with his foot, his focus on the bed in the center of the room. Her focus was all for him as she trailed kisses along the underside of his neck. She traced with her tongue, for only a moment, the place where his pulse leaped, before he set her on the bed with a bounce.

She toed off her shoes while he raked his shirt up and off, his movements visible in the light from sconces on either side of the mantel. He was built like a swimmer, tall with wide shoulders and a body that tapered to lean hips. Her gaze dipped lower as he flicked open the fastening on his jeans. She couldn't concentrate on her own undressing in her desire to watch him. The narrow line of dark hair disappearing under the cotton of his boxers tempted her to touch him there. But when she reached for him, he caught her wrist in a surprisingly strong hold.

"I really like what you're thinking." He loosened his grip as he pushed her back on the mattress, her head sinking into a down pillow. The jingle bells on her necklace slid along her neck to fall onto the bed behind her.

"But it's supposed to be me who distracts you. Not the other way around."

"How do you know what I was thinking?" She tugged the bow from her hair, then smoothed her hands over his chest, savoring the warmth of his skin.

"I didn't. I only knew I liked it." He lowered himself enough to kiss the patch of flesh bared by her sweater, taking his time to taste the lowest point of the V-neck. "There was something a little bit wicked in the way you were looking at me."

He nuzzled her sweater off one shoulder, then clamped his teeth on one black silk bra strap, dragging it down. An ache started between her thighs as he let go of the silk and reared back on his knees to look at her.

Their eyes met. Held.

Was there more between them than heat and hunger?

A moment later, he peeled off her sweater and bra, letting them fall to one side of the bed. He cupped her breasts, tasting each one in turn, teasing the taut peaks. When he drew one into his mouth, suckling, the hunger for him grew unbearably. She arched her hips into him, needing more. Now.

He slid her skirt over her curves, and the rush of lust made her dizzy. His hands skimmed her inner thighs before dragging her panties down and off. She twisted the fabric of the duvet between her fingers, muttering wordless pleas for more.

By the time his lips covered her sex, she was so close to release she had all she could do to hold on another moment, allowing the intense, heady pleasure to build more as his tongue traced her.

She let go of the duvet as his shoulder dipped beneath her thigh, positioning her where he wanted her. The stubble on his jaw rubbing lightly against her thigh proved the tipping point, the feeling so exquisitely sensual she went hurtling into a lush, endless orgasm.

Ripples of pleasure pulsed through her, over and over. She let the sensations have their way with her as her whole body seized with bliss. While she gathered her breath, Devon moved over her, standing to shed the rest of his clothes. She soaked in the sight of him, her heart pounding madly while he found a condom and rolled it into place.

He stretched out over her just long enough for her to feel the thrill of anticipation all over again. When he entered her, she wrapped her legs around his waist. Holding him there. Moving with him in a rhythm all their own.

She streaked her fingers through his hair, kissing everywhere she could reach. Nibbling. Biting gently. Then he took over the kiss, his hips and tongue moving in a tantalizing sync.

They rolled over once. Trading the top position, letting each other lead the way. It was all delicious. Exciting. So much more than she'd ever experienced before in a relationship.

Devon's breath went ragged and she closed her eyes, feeling how close he was in the tension along his shoulders. His hips rocked hard into her, the pressure stroking a place inside her that unleased a fresh wave of release. Pleasure uncoiled, and her body quivered from it. She knew the movement pushed him over the edge, too, his spine arching, his breathing turning harsh.

After long moments, they collapsed side by side, limbs tangled. She tipped her forehead into his chest, feeling the comforting thunder of his heartbeat before it slowed by degrees. Eventually, her skin cooled. Her inhalations slowed along with her pulse. But through it all, Devon's arms remained wrapped around her, holding her close.

A long, shuddering sigh left her, and she knew she could gladly remain tucked against him the whole night through.

As long as she didn't let herself think about what had brought them to this moment. His promise to distract her. Her willingness—gratitude, even—for his ability to give her that.

Devon stroked her hair from her face, his touch soothing her before her anxieties could ratchet up again. She told herself she could remain here another minute to soak up the sensation that felt close to... tenderness.

It was wholly unexpected.

And simultaneously undeniable.

She sat up, knowing she didn't dare indulge something that could come back to bite her in the long run. Devon straightened beside her, his expression puzzled. But before he could ask her anything, his cell phone vibrated on the nightstand table.

Once. Twice.

She felt relieved when he turned to glance at it. But some of the relief faded as he punched a button on the screen.

"It's April," he informed Regina a moment before speaking into the device. "Salazar here. April, I'm going to put you on speaker so Regina can hear whatever news you have to share."

Devon didn't normally make impulsive decisions. But he needed Regina to start trusting him if he wanted to get to the bottom of his father's secrets. Sharing the PI's findings with her seemed like a way to show her he was serious about uncovering the truth. And that he was as much in the dark about his dad's motives as she was.

The surprise in her silver-gray eyes as she sat up in bed told him that she hadn't expected this kind of primary access to the private investigator. He hoped it was a step in the right direction to winning Regina over. Because as his gaze fell to her bare shoulders visible above the duvet she held to her chest, he felt a surge of protectiveness toward her. A need to make sure nothing else hurt her.

Now April's voice sounded through the speaker on his cell phone as he held it between them.

"I'm still searching for answers about how Alonzo got access to Tabitha Barnes's story in the first place," April told them. "But I have one more interview with her yoga instructor tomorrow before I fly back to Montana."

Devon studied Regina's profile as she listened. Her shoulders were tense. She chewed her lip, still pink from his kiss.

"Maybe that will yield something," he remarked, if only to reassure Regina. "Any other news?"

"Yes, actually." April's cool, professional tone gave nothing away. "I discovered Alonzo's destination for many of his secret trips."

Regina's gaze flew to Devon's. She reached to grab his wrist. Was she hopeful? Nervous? Maybe a little of both.

"And?" he prodded, even as his stomach rebelled at the idea of his father being implicated in any wrongdoing. It was bad enough he'd written the book that hurt Regina in the first place.

"He frequently visited a cabin in Kalispell, Montana, that belonged to a woman I believe was a romantic interest." April paused, and in that moment of quiet, his phone chimed with a new notification. "I just sent you her contact information."

More women in his father's life. No real surprise there, since Alonzo had once told Devon's mother that he thought marriage "killed the creative spirit." Alonzo had long considered himself a lover and admirer of women in general, but never one in particular.

And damn, but Devon needed to keep Alonzo Salazar's name out of the public eye until after his mother's wedding. His mom didn't need any of the old frustrations resurfacing now. His father's choices might have soured Devon on relationships, but that didn't mean he couldn't applaud his mother's ability to find faith in love.

Beside him, Regina let go of his wrist, and the loss of her touch frustrated him. It reminded him she was going to slip away, too, if he couldn't figure out how and why his father had written the tell-all book about her family.

He glanced down at the incoming text on his cell.

"Fallon Reed." Devon read the name aloud where it flashed on his screen. "I don't remember him ever mentioning her."

He looked to Regina, but she shook her head.

"The email I sent to her came back with a notification that the account no longer exists, but I'll drive to Kalispell to speak to her if I have to." The investigator shuffled some papers on her end of the call. "But Ms. Reed is significant because she's related to one of the owners of Mesa Falls Ranch."

"Which one?" Regina asked before Devon could. Her fingers clenched the duvet cover again, dragging it higher against her bare body.

Devon could feel her anxiety in the way her muscles coiled as she went still.

"My mistake. Make that a relation to *two* of the owners," April corrected herself. "Fallon Reed is an aunt to Weston and Miles Rivera."

"Is there any reason to think this woman profited from Alonzo's novel?" Regina asked, her voice tinged with worry.

Or was it defensiveness? Restrained anger?

Whatever the emotion behind the question was, Devon could tell it was intense. She bit her lip, breathing hard.

"Not as of yet." April's tone was cautious, as if she didn't completely rule the idea out. "Tracing the payments from the book is proving difficult, as I explained to Devon."

He felt Regina's gaze land on him. Was the look in her eyes accusatory?

Something about her expression struck him as frustrated, almost as if he'd betrayed her.

April went on to outline her next steps—interview the yoga instructor, return to Montana, then speak to Weston Rivera and possibly visit Fallon Reed. Devon only half listened as she bade them good-night, however. He was more concerned with Regina's reaction that he couldn't quite read.

By the time he disconnected the call, Regina was sliding out of bed, wrapping a chenille throw around her shoulders.

"Where are you going?" He grabbed his pants and stepped into them, wondering what he'd missed.

"I thought you were sharing the information from this investigation?" She lost no time retrieving her skirt and sweater.

"I am." He followed her until she disappeared into the en suite bath, where he stopped outside the partially closed door. "That's why I took the call with you, so you could hear what's going on."

What was she upset about? He could hear her rustling around in there while he searched for his shirt.

"Yet you never mentioned one word to me about tracing payments from the book, let alone why it was proving difficult." She flung the investigator's words back at him before she emerged from the bathroom with her clothes back in place.

Her hair fell loose around her shoulders now. He also thought her sweater might be inside out, but he said nothing about that, seeing the emotions blaze in her eyes.

She really thought he was hiding things from her.

"There was nothing to tell," he reminded her, trying to put himself in her position. Trying to understand how she could be so defensive so fast. "You heard that for yourself from April."

"I disagree." Pivoting on her heel, she stalked out of the bedroom and back into the cabin's living area. "You could have explained to me why there is a holdup," she said even as she barreled around the room, finding her bag to toss her hair bow into it. "We could have had a conversation about why it's difficult, or you could have shared the obstacles with me. But I am in the dark, Devon. As I always have been where your father's motives are concerned."

"Whoa." He saw her silhouetted in front of the Christmas tree where they'd been having fun decorating just an hour ago. "Let me tell you now—I understand how important it is to you."

It hadn't been his intention to hide significant parts

of the investigation. And it saddened him to see how carefully she needed to weigh his words. To test them for truth.

No question about it, Regina had been hurt before.

He reached out to brush a touch along her shoulder. Gently. Carefully.

"Give me a chance," he said, not sure when it had become so important that she let him in. But somehow, it had. "If you don't like what I have to say, I'll make sure you get back to the bunkhouse safely. Okay?"

Another interminable moment passed. In the end, she nodded.

He reached for the remote on the side table to shut off the holiday tunes. With the room quiet and Regina listening, he shared what April had told him about his father hiring a nominee service to collect the payments from the publisher to A. J. Sorensen. Briefly, he explained how they worked, based on the research he'd done since then.

"Apparently, Dad contracted a nominee through a lawyer, which gave him attorney-client privilege, as well." He'd read over April's notes more carefully after their meeting to discover that, learning how it gave his father's pseudonym an added level of privacy.

Regina folded her arms around herself, her brows knitting in thought. She paced past him, setting her purse back on the couch now that she wasn't heading out the door.

He was relieved about that. Grateful to have her stay. And damn it, he wanted to get to the bottom of what his father had been doing—for her sake and, yes, for his own, as well. He just wished the timing had been better since he couldn't afford for the truth to come out now.

"So the nominee service is still active," she mused.

"And still covered by the attorney-client privilege." Pausing by a painting of one of the ranch's studs, she met Devon's gaze. "Which makes you wonder how she learned about it in the first place."

"I didn't question her methods." He scrubbed a hand through his hair, frustrated. "With everything it's taking to get the launch event off the ground, I really need April to do her job so I can take care of mine."

Moreover, as much as he wanted answers for Regina's sake, he wasn't in that much of a hurry for the truth to come tumbling out before his mother's wedding.

Not that Regina would necessarily run to the tabloids to share the news. But what if she decided to do just that?

"Maybe it's time we give April some backup." She picked up her purse again, a new spark of determination in her eyes as she hooked the strap over her shoulder. She looked like a woman ready to head out the door again.

"What do you mean?" Wariness crept through him even as he grabbed his keys from a hook near the kitchen counter.

"April Stephens has the best lead yet on your father's secrets." Regina was already moving toward the coat rack to retrieve her parka and gloves. "And while *her* hands might be tied with how hard she can push her sources as a professional investigator, mine are not."

"Just because you ask her to reveal her sources doesn't mean she will." He took the coat from her to help her into it, tugging her hair from the collar. "That could be proprietary information."

He didn't want their evening together to end, but he didn't plan on standing in her way when she was on fire to get answers to her questions. Even if that meant he had to face more hard truths about his father, the man he'd never known as well as he'd thought. The facts needed to come out before either of them could find peace. He'd bring her back to the bunkhouse and then figure out his next move.

As much as he didn't want to call his brother in Paris let alone admit Alonzo's murky past was proving tough to investigate, Devon wondered if he should give Marcus a heads-up about what April had discovered so far. Devon's longtime rivalry with his half brother needed to end if they were going to present a united front when the truth about Alonzo was revealed.

He hadn't wanted to believe his father was involved in anything illegal, but considering the lengths Alonzo had gone to in order to keep his secrets, it sure made Devon wonder.

"If April has run out of options for shaking more information free from her source, she might be glad for a new approach." Regina tugged on her gloves and studied him with a level gaze. "I got the impression that April has a lot riding on this case, too."

Devon thought back to his meeting with April Stephens. She'd been professional. Thorough. Committed. But he hardly got the impression she had anything personal at stake.

Not like they did.

Regina reached for the door, but he put his hand over hers, needing to slow things down. The feel of her sent a bolt of desire through him, but he restrained himself for now.

"I'm not so sure about that," he told her. "But I can promise you we're going to have answers sooner or later."

He didn't miss the shadows that passed through Regina's eyes as she stared back at him.

"It has to be sooner." She threaded her fingers through his, her touch as urgent as her tone. "I've been waiting far too long for answers already."

Worry gnawed at him as he opened the door and escorted her out into the snow. Regina was desperate for her quest to yield information. Now.

And more than anything, Devon needed time. To get past his mother's wedding, for damn sure. But maybe more important, he needed time to figure out why Regina had so thoroughly rocked his world and what the hell he was going to do about it.

Ten

Regina retreated to her trusty laptop, the same way she had for years every time she heard about a new piece of information that might finally solve the puzzle of why someone would write a book that ruined her life.

After she'd said good-night to Devon, she slipped into the bunkhouse bathroom and changed into flannel pajama pants and a long-sleeved thermal T-shirt. Combing through her hair—tangled from lovemaking—she couldn't help but feel a twinge of regret that the need to research the clues had sent her fleeing Devon's arms for the night.

She'd had a good evening with him. No, that didn't do their date justice. She'd had a special, amazing time decorating the tree with him and then retreating to his bed, where their sensual connection had blazed into a bond she would have never expected to feel for her enemy's son.

And that left her feeling more than a little unsettled. Confused. Full of what-ifs... Most of all, what if they'd met on even, uncomplicated ground.

Turning from the mirror, she emerged from the bathroom to retrieve her laptop, telling herself not to dwell on a relationship that could never go farther than this time together in Montana. Devon's launch event and his mother's wedding were both less than a week away, and as soon as everything was over, he'd be on a flight back East.

Without her.

She tucked her brush into her toiletries bag and hung her wrinkled clothes in the nook near her bed, trying not to think about how much that might hurt. They hadn't known each other long, after all. And yet he'd become more important to her faster than anyone she'd ever known. Who else had taken up her cause for answers the way Devon had this week? He hadn't protested when she'd left his cabin tonight. He'd understood her need to dig deeper for answers about his father.

Her gaze went to her laptop in its neoprene case at the bottom of her drawer, and she withdrew it slowly, thinking about all the times *Hollywood Newlyweds* had robbed her of real-life experiences. She still ached over how the book had fractured her family life, robbed her of friendships and nearly cost her her life in the car wreck. Therapy had helped, but she still hadn't found the peace she so desperately needed. And now she was spending her time picking apart the mystery of the author and his motives when she could be lounging in bed with a gorgeous, successful businessman who genuinely seemed to care about her.

How much more would she let the book steal from her?

Behind her, she heard the floorboards creak and

turned to see Millie wander in with a steaming mug in one hand and a paperback novel in the other.

"Hey, hon," the older woman greeted her, laying the book on an unused bed. A kitschy reindeer cocktail ring clanked against her stoneware mug as she wrapped both hands around the cup as if to keep her fingers warm. "How was your date?"

Regina smiled over how Millie had remembered she was seeing Devon tonight and cared enough to ask how it went. Touched, she set down the laptop and leaned her hip into the ladder on the sturdy built-in bunks.

"It's hard to say." She breathed in the scent of hot cocoa, soaking in the joy of a friendship from an unexpected source. "We had a great time decorating a tree and…" Her cheeks warmed. "Um. Getting close."

A wicked twinkle glowed in Millie's eyes. "Sounds fun. Which begs the question, what are you doing back home already?"

Was it a burning need to do April Stephens's investigative work for her? Or was there more to it than that?

"I thought I had a good reason." She'd attended enough counseling sessions to identify an attempt to rationalize her choices. "But I'm wondering now if it was old trust issues that sent me running."

Frowning, Millie took a sip of her cocoa before responding. "It's always a risk trusting people—friends, parents, coworkers…romantic interests."

"There's a high potential for hurt in those relationships." Regina should know. She'd been kicked in the teeth by life enough times to have all the survival badges. "Is it so wrong to want to spare myself that pain? To just have fun?"

Mille tilted her head to one side, her steel-gray ponytail swinging down. "But are you having fun?"

No.

She was mostly having stress.

"Sort of," she said finally, smoothing her hand over the peacock blue quilt on her bed. Her maternal grandmother had given it to her long ago, and the pattern was "double wedding ring." A romantic name for a pretty design. A dream that seemed far out of reach for her, considering her parents' spectacular failure and her experience with rejection. "I mean, I had fun tonight."

"And maybe that will be enough." Millie patted her shoulder, a brief, comforting touch. But as the silence between them stretched, she added, "Just keep in mind that if you always play it safe with people, you might miss out on the chance for deeper connections that can lead to something really wonderful."

Regina knew she could never put herself on the line that way with Devon. There was zero chance that their out-of-control attraction would lead to something "deeper." It was amazing they'd already found as much common ground as they had. Because even if she ignored the way the book put them at odds, they were still very different people. Devon was an entrepreneur with a company on the verge of international expansion and she was drifting through different jobs while she chased her dream of payback.

Regina hadn't even really figured out what to do with her life once she put the ghosts of the past to rest. Devon had a family to go home to back East. She was untethered, isolated from the only family she had left. Her real father didn't have room for her in his life, while she and her mother had never really put their relationship back together again.

"Perhaps you're right." Regina wondered how she

could move forward with her mom. Put the past behind them for good.

"Just remember to take some risks now and then," Millie encouraged her, warming to her topic and gesturing as she spoke, the crystals on her reindeer ring flashing in the glow from a pendant light. "None of us goes through life unscathed. We're all going to get banged up and bruised now and then, but that's part of the ride, honey. You take the risks to reap the sweet rewards."

They talked a little longer before Millie went back to the front room with her book. But the idea of taking chances stayed with Regina.

Once she was alone in the bunkhouse, she retrieved her phone and stuffed her arms into the sleeves of her parka before stepping out of the building into the starry night.

A light snow was falling as she dialed a number she hadn't used in a long time. She began to wonder if she'd get an answer when she heard a recorded voice and a beep.

Regina took a deep breath.

"Hello, Mom. It's me." She closed her eyes, wishing things were easier between them. "Call me back when you get a minute."

She didn't know if Tabitha would return the message, but Regina hoped so. She might not be able to smooth over things with Devon the way Millie suggested, but at least she could start rebuilding her relationship with her mother.

For now, it would have to be enough.

April Stephens had stalked men in her line of work before. A couple of cheating husbands in the early days before she'd specialized in financial forensics. Later, she'd tailed some business types suspected of embezzlement. Sometimes she followed potential leads who simply didn't want to talk to her.

None of those men had ever looked like Weston Rivera.

For that, she was grateful on her first full day back in Montana after her trip to Hollywood. The Mesa Falls Ranch owner was so absurdly good-looking, she was distracted enough that she almost forgot why she was following him. She'd been trying to find the right opportunity to approach him as he finished up his work outside the stables, and somehow got caught up in watching him. Her gaze drank in the ruggedly handsome profile, the hazel eyes and longish dark blond hair, the powerful build and easy demeanor that let him handle the agitated mount he was leading around the snowy arena with a halter.

In the time he'd been working with the animal, the huge black draft horse had gone from pawing the ground and tossing its head to resting that same big muzzle on Weston's shoulder. She didn't know how he'd done it, but she felt as mesmerized by the man as the gelding clearly did.

When Weston broke the spell with a soft whistle, leading the equine into the state-of-the-art stables, April forced her brain back into gear. She wasn't here to ogle the man. Or to drink in the calming effect he had on her nerves as he moved around the arena. She needed to question him, since he'd refused to speak to her over the phone. And her professional pride demanded she have more information the next time she spoke to Devon. Although she'd uncovered something significant in her final interview on the West Coast, she knew it wasn't enough. Her client wanted the full story, and to nab that promotion she needed, she would have to provide it.

Now she waited a few moments before following him inside the building that housed the ranch's business office. There were stables on the main floor, with cobblestone floors and polished wooden stall doors. The place looked more suited to hold champion Thoroughbreds than working animals like the draft horse.

Brass lanterns hung at regular intervals on the heavy beams that lined a walkway leading from the foyer. April waited until Weston climbed the steps to the second floor, where double steel doors bearing the ranch name stood half ajar. Once he disappeared through that entrance, she trailed him, peering inside to where a reception area appeared empty. The scent of coffee hung in the air even though it was late afternoon, and she saw a pot percolating in the corner on a gray granite wet bar.

Beyond the vacant reception desk and a wall emblazoned with another ranch logo, a second door remained partially open. Weston must be in there. She could only see a glimpse of a conference table with gray leather swivel chairs.

She was sure she had him cornered now. He couldn't make excuses about his horse needing attention, or edge past her into the barn where guests weren't supposed to follow.

Striding into the reception area, she stuffed her gloves into the pockets of her long down jacket as she closed the office doors behind her. She was unwinding her scarf from her neck when Weston emerged from the inner office, his focus on a sheaf of papers in his hand.

"Hello, Mr. Rivera." She left her scarf dangling free around her neck, her jacket open.

He stopped short when he spotted her, his hazel eyes

all the more compelling when they were turned on her. He'd removed his shearling jacket and Stetson. His well-worn denim and pale blue flannel didn't begin to hint at his wealth. With his dark blond hair brushing his shoulders, he looked like a misplaced surfer, right down to the bristle of a jaw he hadn't shaved for days.

"Can I help you?" His voice was deeper than she'd imagined. Low and melodic.

The timbre of it reverberated through her, resonating on a pleasing frequency.

"Yes." She wished they'd met under different circumstances, and she could have enjoyed the warm thrum of awareness. But since this job was far more important than the fleeting pleasure of a handsome man's voice, she came to the point. "I have a few questions to ask you about your aunt, Fallon Reed."

The look in his eyes went from warm and inviting to glacial in an instant. She could practically feel the chill of it.

"You're the PI who keeps calling me." He said "PI" like it left a bad taste in his mouth.

His tone was dismissive, as if he'd just seen her childhood home and the disaster area it had turned into these last few years.

She swallowed hard before she started again.

"It will only take a minute—"

"I have no legal obligation to speak to you." He brushed past her and approached the coffee maker. Turning his back on her.

She watched him take a cup from an overhead cupboard and fill it from the stainless steel carafe of the high-tech machine. When the ceramic mug was full, he sipped it before striding back toward the inner sanctum like she wasn't even in the room.

Aggravated, she hurried to step between him and his office door.

"Is that really how you want to address this?" She suddenly stood too close to him, but she didn't think backing up a step would be a good move when she was trying to press him for answers. "Because if you're trying to protect someone you care about, don't you think a PI has more leeway keeping an investigation quiet than a police department?"

She was taking shots in the dark since she had no evidence that Fallon Reed had taken part in any remotely shady activity. But Weston's scowl at least indicated she had his attention.

Better she ticked him off than he ignored her.

"You have no idea what you're doing, do you?" He glowered down at her while tapping into her every last insecurity about her ability to do this job. "Or what's at stake."

Unease curled in her belly. Given his harsh tone, she wouldn't have believed he was the kind of man who could soothe a thirteen-hundred-pound beast if she hadn't witnessed it with her own eyes.

"I know enough to recognize that you won't want your ranch associated with a man like Alonzo Salazar once his past comes to light." She hadn't learned everything about her client's father, but what she'd discovered so far didn't paint such a pretty picture.

No one kept that many secrets without very good reason.

"He has a lot of friends who think otherwise," Weston assured her as he straightened. "And now, if you'll excuse me, I have work to do."

"You consider yourself a friend?" She stepped sideways to remain between him and his office. "Then why not set the record straight to maintain his reputation?"

Weston Rivera's eyes narrowed.

Later, she realized that should have been a warning. But for now, she watched him set down his coffee mug and his papers on the empty reception desk.

"I'm calling security to see you out," he informed her as he picked up the handset on a desk phone. Then he slanted her a sideways glance. "Unless you care to leave under your own steam?"

His gaze lingered on her a long moment. Long enough to make her feel a surge of awareness for him despite her frustration. Huffing out a sigh to hide that unwelcome feeling, she realized she wasn't going to learn anything from Weston Rivera today.

"I'm going to find out what Alonzo Salazar was up to one way or another," she informed him, wrapping her scarf around her neck again, if only to hide the rush of heated color she feared was climbing up her skin.

If he said any more, she missed it in her rush to leave the office. She retreated down the stairs and out into the chilly wind blowing off the mountains.

Where she could breathe again.

Drawing in shallow breaths of crisp air, she tried to slow her racing heart. She feared she wasn't cut out for this kind of work. It was one thing to trace a paper trail from the safety of her Denver office. Being on the ground and mired in real detective work was far messier. Upsetting.

She'd had Regina Flores calling her repeatedly for the last twenty-four hours, wanting to quiz her about the investigation. And she'd fielded a half dozen messages from her mother's neighbors back home, threatening to take legal action if she didn't get her place cleaned up. April could manage it. She absolutely would get on top of it all.

Starting today, with a drive to Kalispell to confront Fallon Reed in person. She needed to make some headway on this case, not just because the job and the promotion were mission-critical to keeping her mother under her own roof. She also needed to see progress in order to experience the therapeutic effects of peeling away someone else's secrets.

That aspect of the job kept her working even on the days she didn't like it one bit. And if that put her at odds with the mesmerizing ranch owner?

She just needed to remember that she couldn't afford to get close to anyone anyhow. Her own secrets ensured that. No matter how much she might wish otherwise.

Heading for her car, she dialed Regina Flores to start ticking items off her to-do list. She would take back control of this case. April had already sent the information she had to Devon, but she understood why Regina wanted to hear all the nuances.

The woman answered even before April heard the phone ring.

"Hello?" Regina sounded as desperate as April felt.

Maybe that was why she found it difficult to talk to the woman sometimes. She empathized a little too well with Regina's difficult journey. April remembered what it was like to have control of her life wrenched out of her hands.

"Hi, Regina." She hit the fob on the keys to her rental car as she approached the parking area outside the main lodge. "I have an update for you."

Regina had thought Devon's PI was trying to dodge her. But after a thorough phone briefing with April Stephens while the woman drove to Kalispell to interview Fallon Reed, Regina recognized that April had simply been too busy following leads to give updates.

Tucking her phone in her pocket, Regina went back to prepping for a bonfire happy hour down by the skating pond. She owed a giant thank-you to Millie and a few of her other bunkmates for pulling her share of the work during her phone call, but she was learning that was part of the employee code here. She'd covered for one of the ski concierges the week before when she'd ended up stuck overnight with a ski excursion. And in return, her coworkers had finished Regina's chore of lighting the antler Christmas tree they'd built out on the skating pond.

Setup appeared complete now, and the bonfire was lit even though the sun hadn't fully set. Regina could see activity in one of the dining rooms overlooking the skating pond. The waitstaff was preparing to bring cold and hot carts down to the ice so skaters could help themselves to cocoa, cocktails and appetizers. And, actually, as she peered up the hill toward the lodge lit from within, she spotted a conference suite where Devon was holding a meeting with the ranch higher-ups to finalize plans for the launch event.

Even at this distance, Devon was easy to recognize, from his broad shoulders encased in a custom-fitted suit jacket, to the way he leaned back in the leather swivel chair at the head of the table. His body was familiar to her. The way he moved. His gestures.

He would meet her at the bonfire afterward, and she was anxious to talk to him about the PI's revelations— that Alonzo had had an affair with her mother's yoga instructor, and the *yogini* had told him Tabitha's secret, effectively giving him all his story fodder. April hadn't yet figured out why Alonzo decided to write the story anonymously, but she'd asked Regina to weigh the possibility that he'd never meant for the story to be connected to the people it was based on in real life .

In other words, to consider the small chance that Alonzo had meant no harm with the book.

Boots crunching through the snow, Regina skirted the ice pond, remembering the unusual request, and how she'd rejected it out of hand. Why all the secrecy if he'd never meant for the truth to emerge? But the idea gnawed at her just the same, making her wonder what it meant if it turned out she'd chased down answers for years only to discover her life had been destroyed as collateral damage when Alonzo was only trying to tell a story.

But he'd done a poor job of disguising his sources of inspiration, and that felt damning to her. They'd know more about his motives, perhaps, once they could figure out where the profits of the book had gone, but April refused to share her information about the nominee service. Still, Regina knew they were getting close as her phone rang again. This time, her mother's number flashed across the screen, reminding Regina she'd been trying to reach her.

A mix of feelings washed over her. Nervousness. The old resentments. A tiny hope that one day they could have a relationship that wouldn't be overshadowed by the past.

Pressing the Connect button, she walked in the moonlight to the far side of the ice pond, where a gazebo provided shelter from the falling snow. She'd be able to see the skaters as they started to arrive. Devon had agreed to take a break from his work to meet her here later, too.

"Hi, Mom." Regina brushed some snowflakes off a picnic table under the gazebo before taking a seat on the wooden bench.

"Hello, Georgiana." Her mother's tone was cool. She sounded like she was in her car, or at the very least using her speakerphone. A rock tune played on a radio somewhere near her.

Regina bristled. "I'm not going by that name anymore, remember?"

"It doesn't change who you are, darling," her mom reminded her while a few car horns honked in the background. "And how's life in Montana? Are you honestly working at a horse ranch?"

Regina blew out a breath and tried to relax, remembering the whole reason she'd reached out to her mother in the first place. Hadn't Millie suggested she take more risks to build better relationships?

"I am." She'd imparted that much information in the message she'd left for her mother. Staring out across the ice pond lit with white lights strung from tree to tree around the perimeter, she couldn't imagine a more beautiful place to be right now. "It's peaceful here. I feel like I can think."

She hadn't realized how suffocating her life in Los Angeles had been back when she'd been trying to hold the threads of her unraveled life together. Back home, there had been reminders everywhere of all she had lost. The stores and restaurants she couldn't afford anymore. The parties that she didn't get invited to. And, of course, the tabloid interest in her story that made her feel like she was always running from questions.

"You needed *more* peace?" her mother asked drily. "I thought that's what counseling was for." There was a biting edge to her tone, reminding Regina how much her mom had resented the discussions of her daughter's therapy. Then her mother sighed, and some of the bitterness eased when she spoke again. "I was under the impression you'd forgiven me."

Regina closed her eyes, trying to remember the things therapy had taught her about her family relationships. She had traveled this road with her mom before, and was unwilling to fall into the same conversational traps.

Her mom's answer to the upheaval from *Hollywood Newlyweds* had been to retreat. Ignore. Move on. But that had never worked for Regina.

"I meant a different kind of peace, Mom," she clarified gently. "It's really beautiful here."

In the long, awkward pause that followed, she could almost hear her mother debating her response. Finally, she said, "What drew you there?"

Encouraged that maybe her mother was going to work on establishing a new peace between them, Regina decided to be forthright. She spotted a camera crew setting up to take footage of the bonfire party as it began. It was bound to be crowded, since the ranch's lodge was now full to capacity as guests and media convened for the coming launch event.

"I think I'm getting very close to finally putting the scandal and that damned book in the past, Mom." Her thoughts had been all but consumed by the new developments since April Stephens had taken the case. Or—perhaps more to the point—since Devon had decided to spare no expense in looking for the truth.

His contribution toward uncovering his father's motives only added to his undeniable appeal. If only she could trust what she felt for him. Or trust *him*. She'd been putting up barriers with people for so long she wasn't sure she knew how to relate to a man any other way.

"That would be good news. But why do you sound so sure?" Her mother switched off the radio, a drum solo ending abruptly. "What did I miss?"

The curiosity in her mom's voice reminded Regina that this wasn't just about *her own* past. The scandal and aftermath had affected her mother, too. Had devastated her, even. Tabitha Barnes had never returned to Hollywood. She'd never acted in another film.

Alonzo Salazar had stolen Tabitha's secrets and profited off them, wrecking her life in the process. Wasn't it only fair for Tabitha to know the truth? She might have put her anger behind her—and the hunger for answers that haunted Regina—but that didn't mean she didn't deserve to know the truth.

"If I tell you, will you keep it between us?" she asked, needing to keep the information out of the tabloids. Not just for Devon's sake, but for her own.

"Of course," her mother agreed. "I learned the hard way not to share my secrets," Tabitha continued, a hint of bitterness giving an edge to her voice.

Relaxing a bit, Regina told herself it hadn't been a mistake to reconnect with her mother. They could mend their relationship, couldn't they? Maybe Millie had a point about taking chances. Deciding to start with her mother, Regina brought Tabitha up to speed on what she'd learned so far, confident that her mom understood the hellish ramifications of having the tabloids involved in their lives.

"Who the hell is Alonzo Salazar?" Her mother interrupted midway through the story. "Hold on, Geor— Regina," she corrected herself. "I need to pull off the interstate so I can give you my full attention."

Waiting while her mother swore softly under her breath a few times, conceivably crossing multiple lanes to find an exit ramp, Regina's gaze traveled back to the window where Devon was still in his meeting in an upper-level conference suite. Seeing him there, remembering how supportive he'd been of her journey—with no thought to the consequences for his own family—made Regina realize that the progress she'd made in her quest for answers wasn't as exciting as she'd hoped it might be. Somehow, nailing Alonzo wasn't bringing her the peace she'd expected because he'd just exposed problems that were already there just under the surface of her family dynamics. She just hadn't known about them.

Like it or not, Alonzo Salazar had only spoken the truth.

"Okay." Her mother's voice sounded sharply in her ears. "I'm in a parking lot and I'm ready to hear it all. Spare no detail, Regina. I need to know all about the bastard who destroyed my family."

A twinge of worry passed through her that her mother sounded so serious about a topic Regina thought she'd put behind her long ago. Could her decision to share the news with her mom dredge up old unhappiness that Tabitha had put behind her? That hadn't been her intention. Maybe she'd just really needed to share the information with someone else—someone who'd been as affected by the scandal as her—because it was eating away at her inside to know the truth and not be able to talk about it.

"I'm telling you this in confidence, Mom," Regina reminded her. "I won't have the tabloids hounding us again."

"I know, sweetheart," her mother assured her. "I understand."

Satisfied, she took comfort in the words. "Thank you."

While she finished filling her mother in on the new developments in the investigation, Regina watched the camera crew film a few laughing ice skaters on the small pond, trying to reevaluate her feelings about the book and her family. It occurred to Regina that she was finally in the perfect position to unmask the author of the book that had ruined her life. She had a captive media audience. The storyline would be relevant since Alonzo Salazar had been a frequent guest at Mesa Falls Ranch, and his son was working with the ranch.

As tabloid news went, it seemed like a slam dunk.

It was an opportunity she'd been waiting for ever since she'd found the front door to her childhood home locked, her life as a pampered heiress—a beloved daughter—over forever.

Except, seeing the snow globe beauty of this place, seeing how her previously empty world had filled with friends and a warm, generous lover, Regina didn't feel the same thirst for revenge she once had. Because while she still wanted more answers about Alonzo Salazar's motives and where the profits from his book had gone, they no longer felt like the most important things in the world to her.

She'd placed all her anger on that one man—and things were more complex than that. *People* were more complex. Time to quit thinking of the past in terms of black and white and to see the nuances beneath. Her gaze flicked back up to the conference suite window, where Devon was passing his tablet to a colleague, pointing out something on the screen. He'd been so kind to her this week.

Even when she'd been spying on him and trying to wheedle information from him, he'd been supportive. So no matter how many issues from her past she dragged into this relationship, she knew he deserved better than what she'd given him in the past.

By the time she wound up her phone call with her mother, sharing more with her than she had in years, Regina felt ready to take a new kind of chance. A new risk.

And it had Devon Salazar written all over it.

Eleven

Devon's meeting ran long, making him late for his evening with Regina. He hadn't bothered to return to his cabin to ditch the business attire, or trade his overcoat for a parka, but at least he'd had a pair of boots in the utility vehicle he'd used earlier in the day. Now, as he trudged through the packed snow to where they'd agreed to meet, he could see the bonfire happy hour must have ended. The white lights over the skating pond were still lit, but the ice was empty except for a couple of antler trees twinkling in the dark.

He pulled out his phone to text Regina to apologize and see if he could still salvage some time with her. But before he could remove his leather glove to key in his password, a snowball pelted him between the shoulder blades.

Feminine laughter followed the ambush.

Tucking his phone back in his pocket, he turned to

see Regina peeking from behind a tall ponderosa pine. She stood mostly in shadow, but the glow from the skating pond let him see her smile. The red ski jacket she wore was different from the dark duster she favored for riding. A white knit hat covered her dark hair. Seeing her stirred him so much that the feeling stopped him in his tracks. It made him nervous that she had that kind of power over him. He pushed aside those sensations to greet her.

"Hello to you, too," he said, closing the distance between them. "I'm going to let you get away with that since I'm late."

He wrapped her in his arms, pulling her against him for a taste of her lips, grateful to lose himself in the feel of her. This, he understood. He just needed to keep things simple. Enjoy the physical connection.

Even with the wind blowing off the mountains and a light snowfall swirling around them, he was all in for this kiss. More than any wind or snow, he simply felt the arch of her spine toward him, the give of her soft mouth under his.

"Very late," she reminded him as she broke away to look up into his eyes. She didn't sound upset, though, for which he was grateful. "I might need to throw a few more rounds at you to even the score."

"I'm sorry." He brushed another kiss along her forehead, wondering how she could feel so right against him. "With the party day looming, we had a lot of details to finalize. I didn't feel like I could rush through the conference call with the staffers doing the heavy lifting."

"I understand." She slid one arm around his waist and ended up tucked under his arm, subtly steering him toward a couple of Adirondack chairs flanking a firepit.

"The one positive thing about being late for the party is that we've got a bonfire all to ourselves."

He'd rather have her in front of the fireplace at his cabin, where they could be alone, but he liked seeing her this way. She appeared happier than the last time they'd been together, when she'd rushed out of his cabin to dive deeper into April Stephens's latest findings.

"Sounds good." He followed the path around the perimeter of the ice. The catering staff was hauling the food carts back up to the dining area on the hill overlooking the pond. "Were you able to speak to April?"

He figured it would be better to dispense with the dicey subjects first so they could move past them. As they reached the stone firepit, he swiped off the snow from one of the seats for her.

"Yes." She dropped into the chair and leaned forward to warm her hands by the fire. "She was on her way to Kalispell to interview Fallon Reed and she got me up to speed while she was driving."

"I heard she didn't have any luck speaking to Weston Rivera." Devon had been receiving regular updates, too, and that one frustrated him. He took the seat beside her. "Which makes me wonder if the Mesa Falls Ranch owners are more tightly connected to my father than I first realized."

Peeling off her gloves, she laid them on the chair arms and held her bare fingers out to warm in the heat from the blaze. "I'm wondering if Weston said something to make April revisit her perspective on Alonzo. Because she asked me to weigh the possibility that your dad wrote the book without any intention of connecting to my family."

That was news to Devon. The idea sure as hell had

appeal. He grabbed a nearby stick and poked at the logs in the pit, stirring the flames higher.

"What do you think?" he asked, dropping the stick to study her expression in the brighter orange glow.

"At the time, I said 'no way.'" She gave him an apologetic smile. "But I've been thinking about it ever since. And I know that it's wrong of me to pin all the blame on your dad when it was my mother who betrayed my family."

The pain in her words was unmistakable. He reached to touch her, to soothe her somehow, his hand skimming her back through her parka.

"But it wasn't his story to tell," Devon assured her, empathizing with how much it hurt to realize the people you loved didn't share your moral compass. He'd struggled his whole life with forgiving his father for how much he'd hurt his mom. "I understand that. Though I guess the book wouldn't have experienced the level of fame or sales that it did without that gossip columnist getting involved and going public with her idea that the story was based on real people."

"No one made the connection to my family for eight months." Shifting in her chair, she turned toward him, shadows chasing through her eyes in the moonlight. "Maybe no one ever would have if not for that columnist."

He wanted to comfort her for all the ways her life had spiraled out of control. He stroked her back, wishing his father had left more clear answers in the paperwork he'd left behind at the ranch.

"No matter what his intentions," she continued, dragging in a deep breath, "I feel like the time has come for me to put it behind me."

As the light snowfall picked up speed, she lifted

her chin a fraction, and he saw the determined glint in her gaze.

"Really?" he said, feeling wary. He wondered what that involved.

"The biggest transgression was my mother's," she said firmly. "I've always known that, and that's why I started counseling, to try and work through my resentment at her. And my father was at fault, too, for just walking away. But even though I thought I'd gotten past it, I'm still here, spinning in circles looking for a way to blame my lack of family on someone else—anyone else—besides me."

"You've never been at fault—"

"Not moving on *is* my fault." From her pensive tone, she seemed to be at peace with the idea of taking full ownership. "I've seen that more clearly in my time here than I did in all the months I spent dragging myself through counseling sessions."

Weighing her words, he gazed at the skating pond, where the falling snowflakes sizzled softly when they met the bonfire's blaze. Then he turned back to her and searched her eyes, hating what she'd been through. His hopes for an uncomplicated evening together got more and more remote by the minute.

"That much I can understand. Being in Montana has given me a serious dose of perspective, too." He peeled off his gloves and threaded his bare fingers with hers. "As much as I want to support my mother at her wedding, I'm in no hurry to return to my grandfather's world, where everything is an excuse to network and get ahead in business."

Regina stared down at their joined hands for a long moment before raising her gaze to his. "Maybe it will be easier for you if I accept your invitation to be your date."

His heart slugged harder inside his chest.

"Are you sure?" He hadn't pressed her about continuing their relationship after this week, but he'd damn well been thinking about it.

A smile curved her lips. "Yes."

The light in her eyes called to him, making him realize how much he wanted to be alone with her. To spend more time with her. No matter what happened during the rest of their stay at Mesa Falls Ranch, at least he had that to look forward to afterward.

Edging forward in his seat, Devon captured her lips in a kiss. She sighed into him as her free hand wound around his neck, slipping under the collar of his overcoat to his bare neck just above his shirt.

She hummed a pleasurable sound against his lips, the vibration echoing through him and ratcheting up his need for her. It could be below freezing and he would still burn when she touched him.

"Come home with me," he urged her, scarcely breaking the kiss.

"Yes," she murmured back as the snowfall renewed its intensity.

Sensual hunger firing through him, he rose to his feet, lifting her with him, then peeled himself away. Blinking through the fog of red-hot attraction, he saw the same lust—or could it be more than that—mirrored in her eyes. Whatever was happening between them was moving fast.

As he led her to the utility vehicle on loan from the ranch, he told himself that as long as the fire remained purely sensual, there was no need to worry about it consuming them both.

But even as he opened the passenger door to help her inside, Devon wondered if he was only fooling himself.

* * *

Waking up beside Devon the next morning, Regina became aware of two things simultaneously.

First, she'd never felt this level of happiness in her adult life. Every cell in her body seemed to sing with contentment to be naked and lying next to this endlessly sexy man. He'd adored her from head to toe the night before, lingering in all the best places in between, until she'd drifted into deep, blissful sleep on a raft of happy endorphins.

Her second realization as the light of dawn streamed over the bed was that she'd never spent a full night with another man.

And as she examined that idea more closely, she acknowledged that was both strange and messed up. Somehow, she'd always found a way to distance herself from romantic interests, telling herself those guys in her past were never "the one," so it didn't matter. After the way her father turned on her, it wasn't easy to trust men. Yet her subconscious had quit blocking her from Devon, allowing her to enjoy the whole night in his arms.

Now, here she was. Naked. Happy.

And then realization number three hit: her heart was suddenly vulnerable.

Amazing how quickly realization number three could torpedo the first two.

Slipping from the covers, she retrieved her clothes to dress, worry spiraling out from that one thought like ripples in a pond. Millie had told her no one went through life unscathed. But was it so wrong for Regina to feel like she'd already had her cuts and bruises? She wasn't ready to take on more just when she was starting to let go of the need for revenge that had been driving her for too long.

She dug in her purse for enough toiletries to comb her hair and put herself back together, taking her time to try to steady her nerves, too. By the time she was ready to head out of the bedroom, she smelled the heady scent of coffee brewing and bacon cooking.

This man was too good to be true.

The feeling was confirmed when she first spotted him from the doorway of the kitchen. "How do you like your eggs?" he asked over the brim of a white coffee mug, the steam drifting up to caress his handsome features as he drank.

His flannel shirt was unbuttoned over his naked chest, his jeans low on his waist. Even after the supreme fulfillment of the night before, her gaze got stuck on the center ridge between his abs that ended in a sprinkle of dark hair above the top button on his jeans.

With an effort, she set aside some of the morning panic and uneasiness to enjoy his well-meaning offer.

"Over easy." Setting her purse on a chair in the living room near the cowboy-themed Christmas tree they'd decorated, she padded on stocking feet into the kitchen and helped herself to a cup of coffee from the pot on the breakfast bar. "You look decidedly comfortable in the kitchen for a man who grew up in a life of privilege." She realized how that sounded after the words left her lips. "No offense meant. I know I never learned to cook anything for myself until after my dad cut off my mom and me."

He grinned as he cracked the eggs into the skillet. "No offense taken. I had a brief notion that my father would let me visit more often if I was independent and didn't behave like a trust-fund kid." He shrugged as he tossed the eggshells in the trash. "So when I was about eight or nine, I asked our cook to teach me some stuff. And while my father never discovered my culinary skills, I've never regretted the lessons."

Eight or nine years old? She hadn't thought before about how his father's defection must have hurt at such a young age. Her heart ached for the boy he'd been... And the weight that he must still carry with him now.

"Consider me grateful to your cook." She helped herself to the cream and sugar he'd left on the counter. "And it must have been hard having so little of your dad's time growing up. As much as it hurt when my dad cut me off completely, at least I had him in my life until my midteens."

Devon shook his head while he dug in a drawer to retrieve a spatula. "I don't think anyone would say that the teens are an easy time to go through that kind of loss."

His words were yet more proof that Devon was a thoughtful man. Butterflies fluttered in her belly. She sipped her coffee to quiet the feeling while his phone rang. He silenced it with one hand and flipped eggs with the other.

"Do you have a lot of work obligations today?" She wondered about the schedule for the launch event. And their flight out afterward.

Last night she'd agreed to attend his mother's wedding with him, extending their relationship after the event ended. Her stomach knotted a bit at the memory. Not because she didn't want to be with him, but because of how very badly she *did*.

What if this risk exploded in her face?

Her belly tightened painfully.

"Yes. Although that message was from my mother, who's thrilled I'm bringing you to the wedding." His green eyes met hers for a moment before he plated the eggs and bacon he'd already cooked. "She's excited to meet you."

Her pulse raced at the realization that this was really happening. She was genuinely taking the next step with Devon, no matter that their relationship had started in such strained circumstances. Should she come clean about how she'd rifled through his jacket on purpose that first day?

She didn't want her first effort with a man who mattered to her to be marred by a lie going in. If she allowed that, she wasn't all that different from her mother.

The toaster popped near her elbow, startling her.

"You okay?" Devon asked as he set a plate in front of her and passed her a slice of toasted golden wheat bread.

"Sure." She nodded too fast. "Just realized I'm cutting it close to lead my first trail ride."

"I'll drive you back soon. I know we both have a lot of obligations today and tomorrow, but the day after that, you're all mine for the launch party gala." He took the seat beside her at the long breakfast bar, his green eyes turning a shade darker as his gaze smoldered over her.

She went from worried to keenly aware of him in the space of a heartbeat. How did he do that?

"I'd better start the search for a dress," she admitted, thinking how long it had been since she'd attended a black-tie event.

"I'm already on top of it," he assured her, straightening to dig into the meal.

"On top of dress shopping?" She gave a surprised laugh and nibbled at the bacon.

"You'll need a dress for the wedding, too, and I can't have you bearing the cost of that when I invited you so last minute." He tapped a screen on his phone to show her a web page for a well-known couture house. "So I messaged one of Lily's designer friends from New York to send you some samples."

Lily Carrington was his good friend and the COO of Salazar Media, who'd departed Mesa Falls Ranch after falling for Devon's brother, Marcus. Regina knew, because she'd spied on Lily and Marcus, too, in her quest to find answers about Alonzo. And despite the guilt that memory brought with it, she couldn't quite suppress a purely feminine rush of pleasure at the idea of wearing the gorgeous clothes he showed her on his phone. It had been so long since she'd had access to those kinds of garments.

"That's so kind of you, but—"

"I insist." He leaned over to kiss the back of her hand before returning to his breakfast. "I know the ranch has you booked for too many tours the next two days to give you enough time to shop. And for what it's worth, I appreciate your role in making this event a success."

She murmured her thanks before finishing her meal, trying to sort through all the feelings swelling like an incoming storm. Was she moving too fast in taking new risks? She'd been so sure she wanted to pursue this relationship with Devon, but the closer she got to him, the more she realized how devastated she was going to be if things fell apart.

And no matter how much she tried to focus on the positives of what was happening between them, she had the weight of a lot of frustrating years riding on her back, whispering that it would never work out. Even with the launch party to look forward to—surrounded by friends in a place she'd come to care about—Regina couldn't shake the fear that she was one step away from screwing it all up.

Twelve

After all the hours he'd put in the last two days, Devon was more than ready for his night with Regina. The day of the launch event, Mesa Falls Ranch looked like a scene straight out of a kids' picture book. The holiday decorations were heavy on the greenery and red bows. Even the four-rail fences were decked with pine boughs, and white lights were strewn along the private drive that led to the main lodge.

An event space simply called "The Barn" was a historic reproduction in turn-of-the-century style, with a giant wreath decorating the cupola. The whole building was lit with landscape lighting in addition to the Christmas lights, making it easy to photograph for the wealth of camera crews present.

Fat snowflakes fell from the sky, giving every photo a snow globe touch. Dark draft horses in full dress tack pulled the sleighs conveying the guests from the lodge to the party venue, dropping them off on a red carpet that led through the huge double doors.

Inside, Devon had checked and triple-checked the logistics of the social media tech. He'd done all he could to make this night a success, and he wanted the reward of time with the sexy woman who'd dominated his thoughts all week. He walked past the massive screen over the dance floor already broadcasting live video feeds from the simultaneous party events in New York and Los Angeles. Here, the focus was on traditional black tie, but in the other cities, there were ranching gurus on hand to narrate programs about sustainable ranching. They'd flown baby lambs and sheep across the country in both directions to make ranching issues more real, combining petting zoo opportunities with social media content moments.

The intent was to drive awareness about the benefits of making ranch lands greener and establishing greater harmony with the animals—both the livestock and the native species. Marcus had brainstormed it, but Devon had executed the bulk of the events. Now, with everything running smoothly, he could focus on finding his date.

Leaving the barn, he stalked out into the snowy night again, checking his phone for messages. There were none. He'd called Regina ten minutes ago, thinking she was just running late, but now he was concerned since they were supposed to have met half an hour ago. He hated not being able to pick her up personally, but he felt it was important to be on site before the event kicked off in case the ranch owners had any concerns. Three of them were here tonight: Weston Rivera, Gage Striker and Desmond Pierce. Two others were attending the party in Los Angeles, and one had flown to New York.

Frustration spiked that this event had required so much of his time during a week he would have enjoyed devoting to Regina. And while he understood his brother's wish to take time with Lily Carrington this week, Devon knew it was past time to confront Marcus about the simmering rivalry between them. He refused to let it destroy their company. He'd worked almost nonstop since starting Salazar Media, expanding the business during explosive growth in the field. What was the point of all that work—all those profits—if he couldn't take the time to enjoy what really mattered? Maybe Marcus had already figured that out for himself.

Even as the thought crossed Devon's mind, he tried to push it aside. Because if he admitted that Regina really mattered, he would have to confront the fact that his father's behavior had soured him on relationships. That he didn't trust himself, considering what kind of male role model he'd had. He'd always avoided serious relationships because he didn't want to put any woman through the hell that his father had wrought for his mother and other women, too.

He looked up, straining to see who the passenger was in an approaching sleigh. It wasn't Regina. Then he scanned the crowd for her face. He didn't see her, but as the sleigh pulled up in front of him, he glimpsed April Stephens in a dark blue gown with a high neck and long sleeves.

"April." He went to the sleigh to personally help her down. "Have you seen Regina?"

April's blond curls fell in artful ringlets around her face. Other men turned to look at her. She was a lovely woman, and yet she left him cold because the only female who captured his attention was a dark-haired beauty with quicksilver eyes and fierce determination.

"I saw her at the spa earlier today." April smiled as she smoothed her long skirt and rushed to the temporary canopy to protect guests from the snow. "One of her bunkmates had a couple of openings in her schedule at the pedicure station, so Regina invited me to get my toes done with her."

"Did she mention her plans for the evening?" He couldn't imagine why she wasn't here. Had she backed out?

He'd sensed she'd been nervous about attending his mother's wedding even after she'd agreed to be his date. At the time, he'd told himself that was only natural, since going to weddings and meeting families were traditionally big steps in a relationship and he'd catapulted them straight into both arenas when he'd invited her to his mom's nuptials.

"Of course." April laughed, a dimple appearing in one cheek. "She seemed excited to go with you. She showed photos of her gown choices and let me help her choose."

Devon frowned.

So if something had gone wrong with Regina, it must have been after she'd seen April.

"Okay," he muttered distractedly, already straining to see if another sleigh was on the way. "Thank you, April."

Worried now, he was ready to ask one of the grooms about finding him a ranch utility vehicle when he saw one more sleigh headed toward the barn, horses trotting out in front.

She had to be in that one.

Waiting for the vehicle to arrive, he heard a commotion inside the barn—a subtle uptick in crowd noise as if they were reacting to a new band on stage. Or a speaker.

Which was curious, only because there was no change in entertainment scheduled for twenty more minutes.

He turned toward the barn, where one of the doors stood open despite the cold, thanks to the enormous heaters warming the space. A handful of people were moving purposefully toward the entrance as if something inside had captured their attention.

Curiosity turned to a bad feeling that something was going wrong inside. But he forced his feet to stay rooted outside for another minute so he could check if Regina was in the last sleigh. He waited until the horses pulled under the lights, where he could make out the faces of the occupants more clearly.

Regina wasn't there.

He began to feel downright dismal.

Had she blown off their evening together? Changed her mind about going to Connecticut with him for the wedding? Confused and still worried, he couldn't take time to hunt for her yet. Not when there was something clearly happening inside the barn.

As he jogged toward the entrance, he realized a hush had fallen over the crowd. In fact, as he stepped into the gala venue, he saw hundreds of guests in black tie all standing still, listening to a woman at the podium near the dance floor. Devon didn't have to crane his neck to see her; his company had installed a closed-circuit video system that was playing live footage from the three parties on a big screen.

Thirty feet tall, in full color, actress Tabitha Barnes—Regina's mother—had commandeered the microphone. She stared out at the crowd while she spoke, her gray eyes so like her daughter's.

"...and the author behind the book *Hollywood*

Newlyweds, which ruined my life, has been unmasked at last."

Devon's gut sank to his feet.

Not just because an audience in three cities was about to know the truth that would ruin his mother's wedding. But because he couldn't deny how the woman had learned this secret.

Regina had betrayed his trust in the cruelest way possible. No wonder she was nowhere to be found tonight. She'd been too busy orchestrating the revenge she'd craved for years.

The sweet smell of balsam and cedar turned sour as he took a ragged breath. He stalked toward the control board, edging through rapt listeners to turn off Tabitha's microphone and the overhead screen and switch the channel to any other feed.

It didn't take him long to attract the attention of the logistics coordinator. He gave her the "cut" sign that would kill the audio, but it didn't really matter. Because Tabitha Barnes was already dropping her bombshell.

"His name was Alonzo Salazar, father of the social media moguls who run Salazar Media—"

Tabitha's audio dropped. For a moment, there was silence, heavy and thick with the shock that could only precede an eruption. His gut twisted in anticipation a second before the burst of reaction came from the crowd. Just then, the image of the actress on the big screen switched to a feed from the Los Angeles party, where a rock star known for his philanthropy was arriving to support the party. But the damage had already been done.

A moment later, the chamber musicians scheduled to play during the welcome hour returned to their instruments. The violins blanketed the buzz of gossip, muffling the details somewhat but not nearly enough.

"Salazar" was the name on everyone's lips. He heard it over and over like an audio recording on repeat as he moved through the crowd to confront Tabitha.

And, more important, her daughter. Because he knew without a doubt where Tabitha had gotten her inside information about Alonzo, and it sickened him. He was mad as hell—and yes, hurt—to think how easily he'd been played and betrayed when he should have known better. He would find Regina and tell her exactly what he thought of this stunt and her.

After that, he would focus on tying up his business in Montana so he could put this piece of his life—and her—behind him for good.

"How could you do this to me?" Regina wheeled on her mother in the hallway outside the restrooms at the back of the event space. Framed photos of the ranch's public buildings covered the wall, and there was a black leather bench tucked into the far corner.

Her mother had never messaged her that she was on her way to Montana. She'd simply texted Regina five minutes before her date to say that she was going to use the launch event as a way to "set the record straight" about Alonzo Salazar.

Regina had been devastated. Hadn't she explicitly asked her mother to keep the information confidential? Her mother had agreed. And still, Tabitha had betrayed that trust. Even as Regina had scrambled to stop her mom, she'd assumed Tabitha would attend the party in Los Angeles since that was right in her backyard—the family's old stomping grounds.

In a panic, Regina had called and texted her mom

and her mom's friends. Then, when she'd gotten her first inkling that Tabitha had actually flown to Montana, Regina had raced around Mesa Falls Ranch like a madwoman in heels to try to stop the train wreck before it happened. Her feet were still freezing from tromping through snow in stiletto pumps, heedless of the need to walk on the red carpets laid out for guests. Her beautiful shoes and gown were ruined after she'd spent all day primping for this night, eager to see the look on Devon's face when he saw her. Instead of savoring that moment, however, she'd arrived with the hem of the plum-colored velvet sheath rigid with ice from her trek through the snow. But despite her best efforts to stop her mom, she'd failed miserably, not locating Tabitha until she was at the podium.

When it had been too late to protect Devon.

"How can I do this to *you*?" Her mother turned on her, narrowing her gaze. "Do you think you're the only one who has been affected by this nightmare? My life was stolen from me, too."

Tabitha paced the narrow hall in a floor-length emerald dress that was a size too small, a couture gown from a long-ago film premiere that Regina had once paraded around in as a child. Her mother's breasts swelled over the bodice, her now softer physique straining the side zipper. Poor dress choice aside, she was still incredibly beautiful on the outside.

On the inside? Clearly, she still wrestled with dark demons.

Regina could see that now with the perspective of time and distance. Funny how much she'd gained of both those things in her brief stay at Mesa Falls Ranch. Especially since she'd met Devon. She understood now that her mother's lies had hurt them both immeasurably.

Not just recently, in breaking the promise to keep the information about Alonzo confidential. The pattern of lies was more deeply rooted, dating all the way back to Tabitha's decision to pass off another man's child as her own. Alonzo Salazar had done a great wrong in revealing a story that wasn't his to tell. But he'd been able to tell the tale because of Tabitha's decision to live a lie in the first place.

"Mom, I thought we were going to try to rebuild a relationship." She thought back to that phone call when she'd shared the information about Alonzo with her mother. She'd really thought it was a turning point for them, an opportunity to share the hurt and move past it. "But that requires trust, and after what you just did, I don't—"

"You're a surprising person to tout the merits of trust." The masculine voice behind her was familiar, but the tone bore an iciness she'd never heard.

"Devon, I'm so sorry." She turned toward him, knowing this was her fault. Hating that she'd hurt him.

Desperate to fix it.

And yet the remote expression on his face gave her pause as he stared her down. Dressed in a custom-fitted tuxedo with a sprig of holly pinned to one lapel, he looked achingly handsome. But the coldness in his gaze sent a chill curling through her. Behind him, two burly ranch hands dressed in tuxes and cowboy boots stood at attention.

"Ms. Barnes." Devon's gaze flicked past Regina, landing on her mother. "There are still reporters out front. If you'd like more media attention tonight, I suggest you seek it outside the barn to avoid being escorted from this private event."

Her mother gave a harrumph of disapproval as she

brushed past them both. Regina noticed how the ranch hands followed in her wake, no doubt tasked with ensuring she didn't return to the building. Not that Regina could blame Devon for that. Her empathy with her mother ended tonight. She felt only guilt that she hadn't stopped her.

"I had no idea she would show up here—" she began before Devon cut her off.

"We can speak more privately back here." He pointed down the hall, toward a small cloakroom located near a back entrance.

She noticed he didn't touch her as they moved together toward the coat check, and that made her tense with worry. A quick glance into the main area of the barn showed the gala proceeding normally, although a few heads turned their way as they walked past. She overheard "Salazar" spoken behind someone's hand. She could see the way Devon's movements—already brittle—tensed even more.

Dread for what her mother had done multiplied.

Devon spoke in quiet tones to the young woman working the station, and she stepped aside to let him pass behind her into the coatroom. Regina followed him, stepping behind three rows of coatracks to see an assortment of folded tables, chairs and catering carts. The buffer of the coats filtered the noise from the party, making the space feel private. The scent of pine from the log construction permeated the room.

"You have every right to be furious," she said as soon as they were alone once more, her nerves wound past the point of tight.

And maybe it was easier to speak to his back since she was intimidated by the coldness in his eyes.

"Perhaps I do." He turned to face her, his face a neutral mask. "But since anger won't fix the situation, I have no intention of indulging useless emotions."

She drew in a breath, needing to explain what had happened. To apologize. But he continued before she could gather her thoughts.

"Since my mother is about to be besieged by tabloid reporters looking to feed off this story, I need to be at her side for damage control." His gaze narrowed, coldly assessing her. "And to personally apologize for my poor decision to trust you with sensitive information gleaned by my private investigator. How much does she know, by the way? Everything?"

Regina closed her eyes for a moment. She couldn't bear to see his disappointment in her. She knew he was hurt, and she hated that she'd been the cause. She ached to realize how badly she'd messed up. She'd been so resentful of his father for tearing apart her family. But now she was the one to cause pain.

"Yes." She wrenched her eyes back open. "I thought it would provide her the same closure as it has brought me." She had gained more than self-awareness these last weeks. She'd gained forgiveness. And that had been a beautiful gift she'd hoped to share with her mom. "I really believed we could put it behind us finally."

Devon's right eyebrow twitched, but his expression did not change. "Or else you believed you could finally have the revenge you've sought for years."

Crushed he would think that of her, she sensed there were far more emotions at work inside him, no matter what he said about not indulging them. She feared he was slipping away. That she wouldn't be able to fix this.

"I wouldn't do that to you." She'd grown deep feelings for him in a short span of time and she wouldn't just throw them away like that. She pressed her case, needing him to listen. "I didn't even know my mother had come to Montana until a few minutes before our date tonight. I panicked, but I thought I could stop her. With the benefit of hindsight, I can see I should have called you to help, but I didn't know she was *here*, in this state, let alone what she was planning. At the time, I was just so fixed on intercepting her."

When she paused in her diatribe, she peered up into his eyes and saw his expression hadn't changed.

A slow, dawning realization blindsided her.

"You really think I could stab you in the back that way, after everything we've shared?" Unshed tears pricked at her eyes as disbelief washed over her.

The anger at her mother stopped mattering. The frostbite in her toes from running around the ranch in the snow ceased to be a problem. Because the only thing she felt was a pain knifing directly into her heart.

Devon said nothing. If anything, his expression hardened a fraction, his lips compressing in a thin line.

"You're cutting me off." The realization struck her as she quietly said the words out loud, and she felt the ground wobble under her feet. She reached for the closest coat rack to steady herself, her hand falling on rough wool and cashmere. "Just like my father did."

"No." Devon's eyebrows scrunched together as he shook his head slightly.

But it was crystal clear to her. Her grip tightened on the wool coat and the wooden hanger underneath it, her reality rocking along with the seesawing garment.

"You might not lock a physical door to bar me from your life. But you're shutting me out just as effectively with the coldness and unwillingness to listen." The strategy hurt her so much more this time. Maybe because she'd believed Devon was a better man.

"That's not true," Devon responded finally. Starkly. But since he didn't have any follow-up to the statement, she took it for what it was.

A knee-jerk reaction.

"It is, though," she said softly, straightening herself despite the pain in her chest, desperate to hold onto her tattered pride. "And I'm more sorry than I can say. For both of us."

Awkwardly pivoting on her heel, she headed to the closest exit, knowing they were done. She'd taken the risk and put herself on the line like Millie had suggested, but it hadn't paid off, because Devon didn't love her the way she loved him.

And she didn't have any idea how she was going to recover from that.

Thirteen

How could it hurt so much watching Regina walk away when she'd betrayed his trust?

Devon stood immobile as she strode from the cloakroom, achingly beautiful in her deep purple gown, half of her dark hair piled on her head while the rest cascaded in curls around her neck.

Maybe it pained him so much because she might be telling the truth? Had her mother acted independently of her? Had Regina only been guilty of confiding in someone she should have been able to trust?

And the most painful truth of all? That Devon had been no better than her heartless father, blaming her for something she couldn't control.

Except she could have controlled this situation. She'd even admitted to telling her mom about the PI's report. Although if he could trust her reasons, Regina had said she did it in order to put the book in her past. For good.

Had she been ready to move forward with him?

Devon couldn't afford to dwell on the knot of questions or the cavernous ache in his chest. Not when he had an event to get through. And, far more important, he had to reach his mother's side to help her weather this latest Salazar scandal two days before her wedding, no less. Forcing one foot in front of the other, he began making his way back out to the party.

Swearing to himself, he paused near a stack of unused folding chairs to check his phone before he departed the privacy of the storage area. He'd already missed a video call from his mother.

His foreboding grew. Out on the dance floor he could see a few couples two-stepping, since the country band had taken the stage. He had to trust that his staff was keeping the event on track. Maybe his presence would only serve as a distraction since—inevitably—some of the media outlets would want a statement on the book.

He tapped the button to return his mom's video call, waiting in the shadows until the device connected. When the feed came through, he could see his mother on the other end. She appeared to be in the passenger seat of a vehicle wearing what looked like a cocktail dress with a heavy winter coat over it.

"Devon, I'm so glad you saw my message," she said in a rush, her phone unsteady in her hand and making the image shake. "I wanted you to be the first to know what's happening."

He ground his teeth together, hating that she had to deal with the stress of his father's mistakes. And Devon couldn't dodge that he'd been a part of the cause for her pain by sharing the PI's information with Regina.

"Mom, I'm so sorry about that—"

"Sweetheart, there's no need for you to apologize."

His mother cut him off. "You can't control the choices your father made. Besides, I think it's going to be for the best."

"For the best?" Devon asked, confused as hell. He tucked deeper into the storage area to focus on the call, gladly letting the gala event unfold without him.

A secretive smile curved her lips as she slid a glance to the driver's side of the car. In the background, Devon recognized her fiancé's voice.

"Damn right, it's for the best." At the man's gruff pronouncement, his mother laughed and glanced back down at her phone.

"Bradley and I have decided to elope. Tonight." She sounded genuinely excited. "We were getting ready for yet another one of Granddad's parties that turn into glorified networking opportunities when we heard about that actress's announcement."

From the other side of the car, Devon heard his mother's fiancé say, "And I said, to hell with it!"

Devon couldn't believe his ears. His mother was eloping? His grandfather would be furious. But if his mom was happy, that was all that mattered to him. Some of the knot in his chest eased a fraction.

His mother laughed again. She sounded sort of giddy. Full of joy. "I think Bradley was only too glad to have a reason to skip town. So we're going to Greece."

"I've said all along we should get married by a ship's captain," Bradley added, leaning into the frame quickly to kiss his future bride's hand. "We met on a yacht, right? This was meant to be."

Even when Bradley shifted out of the image, their clasped hands remained on screen, a silent testament to their solidarity. Trust. It made Devon glad because it showed how much this guy understood his mom.

Loved her.

Of course Devon was happy about that. But at the same time, seeing the way Bradley stood by his mother made him realize how much he'd just screwed up with Regina by not giving her that same kind of support when she needed it most. He'd shut her out. Refused to listen.

The pain in his chest worsened, a surefire sign that he had feelings far deeper for her than he'd been willing to admit.

"Mom, I'm thrilled for you," he said finally, grateful that she had someone looking out for her.

"I knew you would be." Her expression turned serious. "And I wanted you to know that there was no need to rush home to Connecticut for Christmas. Unless you really want to, of course."

She knew he'd never been close to his grandfather. And he appreciated the heads-up. If he didn't need to help his mother navigate the renewed tabloid interest in her ex, he could stay in Montana for Christmas.

He had to apologize to Regina. Make her see how sorry he was for being so rash in pushing her away. He would do whatever it took to show her how wrong he'd been. He could be a better man than her father.

Or his.

Especially when it came to the woman he loved. The realization pierced through the muddle of his thoughts, the one, clear, burning truth.

"I think I'm going to stay right here." Devon was already moving toward the exit. He didn't care about the gala party without Regina at his side. Right now, he needed to find her and do everything in his power to make this right. "I look forward to celebrating with you both when you get home."

"Thank you, Devon. I love you, son." His mom blew him a kiss. "Merry Christmas."

The video disconnected and he shoved the phone in his pocket. He had to find Regina so he could share everything in his heart with her. Tell her how wrong he'd been and how much he loved her, how much he wanted her in his life.

And pray she would hear him out even though he hadn't given her that same courtesy. Just thinking about it made him realize how much he'd need a Christmas miracle to pull this off.

After changing out of her party clothes, Regina found herself back in the stables at Mesa Falls Ranch. It was quiet there, with all the draft horses in their stalls for the night now that the sleigh ride portion of the launch event was done. The grooms had cleaned up well in the tack room, replacing the fancy dress tack on the hooks where it belonged. The scent of leather polish hung in the still air along with the sweet scent of hay. She'd been drawn here for the comfort of the horses after the heartache of the night.

After the betrayal of discovering that her mother was more interested in a media spotlight than in resurrecting a relationship with her. And the even more formidable pain of losing Devon.

She dragged in a sharp breath, stopping herself from dwelling on the memory of his cold rebuff. But the agony was still so fresh. The heartbreak so devastating. She caught sight of her reflection in a shiny halter plate bearing one of the horse's names. The woman's face staring back at her was growing more familiar as Regina Flores became more real to her.

For all the hurts she'd experienced tonight, Regina

was still standing. Not fragile Georgiana Cameron, the pampered Hollywood princess who'd lost the man she believed to be her dad. Not Georgiana Fuentes, whose birth father hadn't wanted anything to do with a daughter who reminded him of his mistakes.

But Regina. The woman who awoke from a car crash with a different face and a need for a name to go along with it. *That* woman was strong. And she was taking full credit for conceiving her, and for loving her. Because it would take all that strength to get over a heartbreak worse than she could have imagined. The heartbreak of losing a man who'd swept her off her feet in such a short time.

Leaving behind the tack room, she shuffled back into the stable to stroke the nose of Evangeline, the Appaloosa mare she'd saddled for Devon that day she'd taken him on a tour of the ranch. Memories swamped her, making her wonder how she'd ever sleep tonight without sobbing her eyes out.

She'd finally healed her past, only to be brought low by loving a man who didn't return her feelings.

"There you are." The voice startled her and Evangeline, too.

Hand falling away from the mare's soft muzzle, she turned to see Devon standing in the stable door. A tidal wave of complicated feelings threatened to knock her off her feet and drag her under. She tipped her forehead to the horse's cheek, taking strength from the animal's calming presence.

Devon cast a shadow over her since the only light she'd flicked on was a lantern near the entrance. He still wore his tuxedo from the party, though he now wore boots and a long duster over it. Snowflakes dusted the dark coat, and he stamped his boots to free them of icy bits.

"Here I am." She smiled sadly, unsure why Devon would seek her out but hoping she could hold back her emotions and save her pride if not her heart. "In the last place I thought I would see you." She hadn't wanted to run into him again before he left for his mother's wedding. Especially since she was supposed to have been accompanying him. She'd told all her bunkmates that she was leaving for the Christmas holiday. "You're going to miss your flight if you don't hurry."

"I'm not going to Connecticut." He hovered near the entrance, not getting closer, but not leaving, either. "My mother decided to elope instead."

Regina exhaled hard, twinges of guilt stinging her over the woman losing out on her special day. The news did little to alleviate her guilt. But then again, she hadn't been the one to hold an impromptu press conference during the launch event, so why should she bear that weight? She'd done her best to stop her mother.

"I've already apologized, but please know if this elopement has to do with my mother's announcement, I'm sorry for—"

"I know." He hung his head for a moment before taking a step closer to her. "And I'm sorry I was too much of a stubborn ass to listen to you then."

Now that caught her attention.

While it was hardly enough to soothe a broken heart, she liked to think maybe he knew how hurtful he'd been. She leaned on the wall between stalls, not trusting her shaking legs to hold her upright. "I'm listening."

"Regina, it was wrong of me to assume the worst of you." Peeling off his gloves, he took another step closer.

Close enough that she could see what looked like genuine anguish scrawled across his handsome features. "You gave me no reason to doubt you, and I got defensive right away."

She folded her arms across her chest to hold in the pain of the memory, needing to hear more from him before jumping in with both feet again.

"I'm done being judged based on the actions of my mother." She had thought she'd moved past the old tensions with her mom after the counseling sessions, but apparently, she'd needed this reminder to understand that sometimes you couldn't trust people who were supposed to love you. "I really thought she and I could resurrect a relationship, but tonight proved to me how wrong I was. And that hurts."

"I hate knowing that I only added to your grief after that painful realization." He stepped closer once more, bringing him within reach. He lifted a hand to touch her shoulder, his grip gentle and warm. "I don't expect you to forgive me for the way I behaved, but I had to find you to tell you how much I regret it. How sorry I am."

Hearing the heartfelt apology eased her misery a little. The physical contact helped, too, although she didn't dare let herself think there was anything more at work here than just that olive branch. She'd been through enough tonight.

"I appreciate you finding me and telling me that," she said, the words sounding stiff and formal since she couldn't let her guard down. Her gaze landed on his boots, which she now realized looked frozen. Her attention shifted back to his face. "How *did* you find me?"

"By looking everywhere. This was the last building on my list, but I saved it for the end so I could get a horse and start riding the trails if I didn't find you anywhere else. That was my next guess—that you took off on horseback."

"I thought about it," she admitted, feeling begrudgingly moved that he'd searched the grounds for her personally.

In a tuxedo. In December.

His hand on her shoulder was softening her defenses, his caress reminding her how much this man affected her.

"I should have come here sooner. I remember you saying how much you missed the Arabian of your youth, and that's why you wanted to keep this job." He shook his head. "But I ignored my instincts, thinking I should search the ranch more methodically."

It heartened her that he remembered her talking about the horse she'd had as a teen. She felt herself melting, hoping.

"You're a good listener," she acknowledged. "Most of the time. And, for what it's worth, I do understand what it's like to be so rattled you make poor decisions. I know it had to be awful to hear my mom at the podium tonight."

His green eyes tracked hers as he lifted his hand to her face.

"Nothing was as awful as losing you." The words stroked over her as tenderly as his touch. "Nothing else even came close."

Her heart pounded faster at the admission, a fragile hope taking root while Evangeline nuzzled the back of her shoulder.

"You seemed content enough with your decision when I left the gala." It had taken all her strength to walk away with her head held high. Where was he going with this?

"I never gave myself a chance to trust a relationship, in light of the twisted role model I had." His thumb brushed her cheek and she couldn't bring herself to pull away. "I told myself our connection was just physical, even when my heart knew there was far more to it than that."

She knew it, too. But hearing him say it, seeing the truth in his eyes, swept away the last of her pain and opened her heart to beautiful possibilities she hadn't dared to entertain before now. Before Devon.

"What made you change your mind?" she asked, still needing to hear the reasons.

He sounded more certain of himself this time. Outside the stables, a gust of wind battered the windowpanes, reminding her how cold the night had turned.

"My mother and I had a video chat." He reached to stroke the horse's muzzle as the Appaloosa nosed closer to them. "She told me she was eloping. She was already in the car with her fiancé, and they were going to catch a plane to Greece to get married by a ship's captain."

"That sounds wildly romantic." She was happy for his mother. Relieved that her mom hadn't totally wrecked the wedding plans with her ploy for media attention.

"It is. Even though the wedding plans were going up in smoke, she still seemed so happy they were together, because her fiancé turned a tough situation around for her." His brow furrowed as his focus turned on her, the truth of his emotions plain to see. "Seeing that bond, the unshakable connection, really slammed home how I'd failed you when you needed me."

Her throat burned with emotions as he shared the memory with her. She blinked through the feelings, not quite sure where it was all leading, but hoping desperately that his being here meant he wanted to fix things. Try again. She couldn't speak over the lump in her throat.

"More than that, Regina," he continued, his eyes locking on hers in the shadowy light cast by that single brass lantern, "it made me realize how much I wanted to bring you that kind of happiness. It made me understand that I love you."

The words reverberated as if he'd shouted them, even though he'd never raised his voice. The echoes of that simple, incredible statement burrowed deep into her heart. Her soul.

Unable to hold back another moment, she flung her arms around him and buried her face against his chest to feel the warmth of him against her. The scent of the holly berry sprig on his tuxedo lapel mingled with a hint of his aftershave, familiar to her after the nights spent in his arms. In his bed. She breathed him in along with his love as he kissed the top of her head.

When she had soaked up his strength, and reminded herself he was real—that all of this was real—she edged back to look up at him.

"Does that mean you forgive me?" he asked, his voice a raw whisper that revealed how much he meant what he'd said.

"Yes." Knowing how important this was to him soothed every hurt in her soul. "It also means that I love you, too, and it stole my breath that you feel the same way."

He bent to kiss her lips. The long and lingering kiss stirred her more than ever with the strength of this love firing through them.

"Everything else we can fix," he vowed as he pulled

back to look at her. "I promise I'll never hurt you like that again."

"I'm trusting you." She remembered how Millie told her that you take risks to reap the sweet rewards. She couldn't imagine a sweeter feeling in the world.

"I'm going to make sure you never regret it." He wrapped her in his arms, making her feel safe. Loved. Desired.

She arched up to kiss him again, her heart and thoughts full of joy over how she could look forward to repeating the pleasure.

"What are you doing for Christmas?" she asked, ready to have him all to herself for the night. "Because I have some free time I could spend with you before I have to be back at work."

"The cabin is mine for the rest of the week," he mused, a glint in his eyes. "And the tree is already decorated. I have an excellent idea for how we should spend the holidays, just you and me. Together."

"Perfect." Contentment curled around her. She would be able to see her friends, who'd become like family. But most important, she could be with Devon to plan for a future. "We can have a cowboy Christmas."

Epilogue

Two months later

"This view is so gorgeous."

Devon heard the awe in Regina's voice as she emerged from the bedroom to peer out the living area's bay window in the luxury cabin he'd rented them for the week. Glacier National Park sprawled before them, the cloudless blue sky making the mountains stand out in sharp relief above Saint Mary Lake.

"I'm looking at an even better one," he assured her, rising from the sofa where he'd been waiting for her to dress for an early dinner.

She took his breath away, the same way she had since they'd first met. For the last two months, she'd allowed her hair to return to its natural color, a pale blond that made her gray eyes all the more dramatic. She didn't seem concerned with hiding who she was anymore, even with the media's renewed interest in her family.

But she also seemed content to leave her identity as Georgiana behind. Tonight, with a diamond ring in the pocket of his jacket, he hoped she would consider taking a new last name, as well.

She'd chosen an amethyst-colored sweater dress that hugged her curves and sky-high gray heels that showed off beautiful legs. But the best part of this outfit was her contented smile, a radiant happiness he liked to think he'd helped to put there.

The investigation into his father's past continued—privately, thanks to April Stephens—but Regina seemed content to wait for answers about why he'd written his book and where the profits went.

"You are completely biased," she teased, turning toward him. A pair of heart-shaped diamonds that he'd given her for Valentine's Day dangled from her ears. "But thank you just the same."

"I'm a lucky, lucky man." He folded her in his arms, drawing her against him to savor the feel of her.

In the months since Christmas, they'd never gone more than three days apart, even though she'd wanted to stay on at Mesa Falls Ranch for a while to find her footing again. He'd respected that, knowing how much she enjoyed the horses and the sense of family she'd gained from the friends she'd made there—something she hadn't experienced since her youth.

But he'd brought her to New York on her days off, showing off the city to see what she thought, since his work was based there. His mom adored her, and had lobbied for her to move closer so they could see each other more, an invitation Regina seemed to be seriously considering. He'd move anywhere to make her happy, and find a way to do his job wherever he was now that he and Marcus had decided the only path forward for

Salazar Media was to keep the company together. To continue to run it as a team. The decision felt right now that they both understood brotherhood didn't have to be a competition. They could succeed together.

So Devon could work on the West Coast or in New York, and it didn't matter to him. Yet Regina genuinely enjoyed Manhattan, delighting in the luxuries that the city could provide. Tonight, he was going to see what she thought about a farm upstate where they could keep horses and he could commute in a few days a week.

If she didn't love that idea, he could see about setting up a presence in Montana, because this place would always hold a piece of his heart for bringing this woman into his life.

"I hope you still feel lucky now that your girlfriend is officially unemployed." She arched an eyebrow at him. "It seemed strange to pack up my things from Mesa Falls yesterday."

"I know it wasn't easy." He understood that she was more attached to the friendships than anything else. But he also wanted her to find whatever path in life brought her the most joy, and he had the feeling she was getting ready for her second act now that she'd put her past to rest. "But Millie said she'd come and see you no matter where you end up."

They'd talked about taking time off—together—to travel for the next two months. See new places. Explore the world. Find out what made them happiest. Marcus—already a married man since he'd tied the knot in Paris on New Year's Eve—had been supportive, assuring him the company would survive without him for eight weeks.

Devon hoped he would be as fortunate as his brother. He couldn't wait to ask Regina to be his wife.

"I know." Regina rested her head against his shoulder for a long moment, gazing out the window with him. "It's up to me to figure out what to do next."

"Are you okay with that?" He tipped her face up to his. "I know there's been a lot of change in the last few months. But I'll move mountains to make you happy."

He'd already helped her navigate a meeting with her father—the actor who'd raised her and then shut her out of his life. The guy had reached out twice after Tabitha's announcement at the launch event, expressing his regret that he'd handled his wife's betrayal so poorly. But Regina had been open to talking to him again, and Devon had hope that the two of them—not related by blood, but by a shared bond and obstacles—would heal.

"I know you would." Her gray eyes met his, her fingertip grazing his lower lip. "And I love you so much for that, Devon. Thank you for giving me a chance to find myself again."

"You're the woman I've been waiting for my whole life." He felt it deep in his heart. In his soul.

He never questioned the direction of their path. All that mattered was that they took it together.

* * * * *

RED CARPET REDEMPTION

YAHRAH ST. JOHN

To my husband and best friend,
Freddie Blackman,
for helping keep me grounded.

Prologue

"We have to clean up your image, Dane," his publicist, Whitney Hicks, informed him while they sat in his trailer in Mexico, going over Dane's public appearances for late July. It was blazing hot and he'd come in to get out of the heat.

"It's not my fault," Dane Stewart responded, leaning back on the sofa and propping his legs on the sofa arm. "I had no idea Lia Montgomery was taken. I pride myself on having one relationship at a time and being a one-woman man."

"Who according to tabloids can't stay with one woman."

Dane shrugged his broad shoulders. "Can I help it if a woman can't manage to hold my attention?"

"You're going to have to learn," Jason Underwood replied. Jason had been his manager and agent for years. He was tall, lean and always in a suit. "Negative publicity could damage your image as America's Sexiest Man Alive."

"I beg to differ. I think it shows what a hot commodity I am," Dane said with a smirk. He was thirty years old and in his prime.

"Thanks to your shenanigans, the studio wants you to do some damage control. They don't want this kind of publicity attached to what essentially is your best acting work. You could get a best actor nomination for your latest film. Think of how this would catapult you into the stratosphere."

It had taken Dane years of callbacks and tending bar to be in the position he was in now. He didn't have to act in the big budget action flicks or romantic comedies anymore. Instead, his success in Hollywood had finally allowed him to choose a passion project like the film he'd just wrapped. Dane was proud of the work he'd done and didn't appreciate the press making him out to be some Neanderthal who couldn't keep it in his pants.

"Although I think this is all a load of hogwash," Dane responded, "I agree now isn't the most convenient time for this to blow up. I want my work to define me, not what I do behind closed doors."

"Good. Then you'll agree to the publicity I have scheduled?" Whitney inquired.

Dane trained his eyes on her. "Depends on what it is."

"You'll like this one." Whitney reached for the remote to turn on the television and start a recording.

Dane watched as a local newscaster talked about a young boy, six-year-old Jayden Turner, who was in need of a bone marrow transplant. The camera panned to the cute boy with a mop of curly hair and dark brown eyes. The doctor talked about Jayden's acute lymphocytic leukemia in which the bone marrow made too many white blood cells. He went on to say the best form of treatment was a bone marrow transplant. Then the camera zoomed in on Jayden's mother, Iris Turner, a tall, slender woman with a beautiful smile.

Iris pleaded with the public to register to have their bone marrow screened. Dane immediately sat upright and listened to her impassioned plea. He admired her quiet strength. There was a tranquility to her he was drawn to, even though she wasn't a dazzling beauty like many of the models and actresses he usually dated.

"Let me guess. You want me to be screened?" Dane asked over the hum of the television.

Whitney beamed. "Great minds think alike." She walked toward him and he scooted aside, making room for her. "This is exactly the kind of positive press you need."

"I won't make a mockery of what that mother is going through," Dane stated vehemently.

"And we're not asking you to," Jason chimed in. "Just a photo op after the screening. Your involvement will be a huge help raising awareness for Jayden's cause."

Dane inhaled deeply, staring at the screen. The mother was staring back at him and he could see how desperate she was for a chance to save her son's life. "I'll do it."

Whitney grinned. "I'm glad that didn't take too much convincing. Now here are my other ideas."

Dane listened as Whitney rattled off several other appearances, including late-night television, a morning talk show and a stop at the local food bank, but all he could see was the haunting eyes of Iris Turner. Dane hoped his presence at the hospital wouldn't disrupt her and Jayden's life.

One

Iris Turner was praying for a miracle. She didn't know when or in what form it would come, but she knew God wouldn't be so cruel as to take away the precious gift He'd given her six years ago. Her son, Jayden.

"Do you think it will help?" her mother, Carolyn, asked as Iris sat at her parents' kitchen table, wringing her hands. It had been several days since the news story about Jayden had aired, and there was still no bone marrow match.

"I don't know. I hope so." Iris glanced down the hall to where her father and Jayden were playing in the living room. To the outside world, he looked like a normal kid; now all of Los Angeles knew how sick he was.

"It will." Her mother reached across the short distance to squeeze her hand.

Her family had thought Iris had lost her mind when she'd decided to become a single mom. Her mother had discouraged Iris, telling her Mr. Right would come along one day, but Iris had known it wasn't true. She was damaged goods and no man would want to sleep with her—let alone make a baby—if he saw her body in the dark.

Eight years ago, when she was twenty, she'd gotten mixed up with the wrong crowd, dating a musician who liked to drink and have fun. One night, he'd had a little too much fun and wrapped his car around a tree with Iris in it. She'd suffered severe burns to her arms and thighs. Iris had lost count of the reconstructive surgeries she'd had since then to help with the disfigurement. Her arms had been transformed almost back to their original state, but after many painful procedures, Iris had finally given up and accepted she wouldn't be completely healed.

She'd attempted dating, but once the evenings had become intimate, men had shuddered, making a speedy departure. Some were more direct; one outright told her she was a monster. Iris hadn't dated since.

"Let's not dwell on it." Her mother went over to the stove and removed the kettle she'd turned on earlier. "How about a cup of tea?"

"Sounds great, Mom." Iris offered a smile. Her mother was not only her best friend but an excellent cook and homemaker. She'd always been there when Iris needed a shoulder to cry on or someone to accompany her to the endless medical treatments. Iris had wanted to be just like her, and part of that was having a child of her own to love and being the best mom she could be like her mother.

Six years ago, she'd decided the only way she'd become a mother was through artificial insemination. And it had worked! She'd become pregnant on the first try. Nine months later, she'd given birth to a beautiful baby boy. Recently, she'd learned her precious boy had a rare leukemia that couldn't be treated with chemotherapy alone. The doctor had suggested that a bone marrow transplant could be Jayden's best chance.

Iris accepted the cup of tea her mother handed her and

took a tentative sip. Chamomile always had a way of making her feel calm, and she was summoning all her inner strength for the fight ahead.

Her cell phone rang and she answered after several rings. "Hello?"

Iris listened intently to the caller on the other end before hanging up the line. "You will not believe it, Mom. It was the hospital. Their phones are being flooded with callers who want to know how they can help Jayden and if there's a GoFundMe page."

"I told you it was going to work out, Iris. You just have to believe."

Iris was beginning to think her mother was right. Maybe there was a miracle waiting around the corner for Jayden.

"So what's this I hear about you dating another man's girl?" his sister, Fallon, asked Dane over the phone that day.

"Not you too," Dane said, padding into his kitchen in his bare feet. He removed a beer from the fridge, unscrewed the cap and took a generous pull.

"I've never known you to do anything so underhanded."

"Then you have to know I didn't think she was seeing someone."

Dane loved being single and the freedom it gave him. He'd always done uncomplicated sex but now this disaster with Lia Montgomery had blown up in his face.

"All right, so what now?"

"Damage control," Dane said, drinking his beer. "I'll put in some appearances, be contrite and do some charity stops. Actually, I'm kind of excited about the one tomorrow."

"Oh really? What's it about?"

"There's this young boy who needs a bone marrow donor and I'm going to have myself tested."

"Dane! That's wonderful and very selfless."

Dane shrugged as he walked to his patio door and slid

it open. The balmy ocean air wafted into the room, filling his senses. He loved his Venice Beach house, which he kept in addition to his mansion in the Hollywood Hills. It had cost him a mint, but the view of the Pacific out his back door was worth every penny.

"Yeah, well. I'm being tested. There's no guarantee."

"It's the thought behind it."

Dane wished he could take credit, but it was Whitney's doing. "So," he said, changing the subject, "when are you, Gage and that good-looking nephew of mine coming down for a visit? You haven't been here in ages." Fallon had recently married Gage Campbell, a wealthy financier who'd help save the family business and she'd given birth to a son, Dylan.

"I'm sorry, Dane. Getting Stewart Technologies back on its feet took a great deal of time. With Gage's influx of cash, I've been able to get new research in the works to put us back on the map but that's taken a while. I promise we'll come soon."

Dane never understood Fallon's devotion to their father's company and her sense of responsibility for its survival considering their parents had run it into the ground with frivolous spending. He'd offered some financial resources over a year ago when it appeared the company was on the brink of failure, but she'd turned down his offer, determined to save the company on her own.

"Good. 'Cause I miss you, sis."

"Back at you."

From his patio, Dane stared out over the darkened horizon and thought about his family. Ever since he'd been able to read, their father, Henry Stewart, had talked to Dane about taking over the company, but it hadn't been his dream, and when he was old enough he'd run as fast as he could. Fallon had taken up the mantle and Dane was glad because, quite frankly, he'd never lived up to his father's expectations. The rumors of Dane's scandalous behavior had only added fuel to the fire.

But what did he care? Dane didn't need anyone. Or at least that's what he told himself. As long as he had a winning smile and there were beautiful women around, he would never be alone for long.

The next morning, Dane arrived at Cedars-Sinai Medical Center and was immediately engulfed by a large, noisy crowd of fans, mostly women. Some were holding banners with his picture; others screamed how much they loved him and wanted to have his babies. Dane reminded himself this was all part of the price of fame.

After climbing out of the low-slung seat of his Ferrari, several bodyguards surrounded him as photographers flashed cameras and journalists shot questions at him. Dane waved and signed a couple of autographs as he strode into the hospital entrance.

Whitney came toward him. Her bouncing blond hair hung in luxurious curls down her back and she was wearing her customary dark pantsuit. Dane appreciated her professionalism.

"Come with me." She led him down a long corridor to an elevator that within seconds had them disembarking onto the pediatrics floor.

Whitney moved ahead of him, and they soon stopped in front of two glass double doors leading to a room with brightly colored walls. "It's a play area for children in the hospital. I thought it would be a good place to start, but Ms. Turner isn't here yet."

Dane glanced into the room and his heart clenched. There were several young children in the room. Two were in wheelchairs and the other three were at low tables coloring. He vowed at that moment to give a donation to the hospital; it was the least he could do.

He heard the chime of the elevator and the hairs on his neck stood up. Dane knew Jayden Turner and his mom had arrived. He turned around in time to watch Iris Turner walk toward him. She was a lot taller than she appeared on television and every bit as slender in a pencil skirt and ruffled blouse. She was much prettier in person.

There was a youthful glow to her unblemished caramel skin, big brown eyes and dark brown hair, which fell in soft waves past her shoulders. His body tightened, reacting to her beauty, and Dane tamped the feeling down. He didn't mess around with single moms—that was borrowing trouble he didn't need. But he couldn't deny he was drawn to her.

"Dane, I'd like you to meet—" Whitney began, but he interrupted her.

"You must be Iris Turner. Pleasure to meet you."

"You, as well." She offered a hesitant smile. "Thank you so much for doing this. To have someone of your stature…" Her voice trailed off as Dane's focus shifted to her son. "I'm sorry." She blushed. "This is Jayden. Jayden, say hello to Mr. Stewart. He's here to see if he can help you."

"Help me?" The little boy looked up, and Dane froze.

With his tight black curls, dark brown eyes and bushy eyebrows, Jayden bore a striking resemblance to Dane when he'd been young. Dane shook it off. He must be projecting because he felt sorry for him. He kneeled down. "I'm here to see if I'm a match to help you get better."

"Why would you do that?" Jayden asked.

The innocent question caused all the adults in the room to laugh. "Because it's the right thing to do." Dane responded.

"Do you mind if we get a few photographs?" Whitney inquired from behind them. Dane had been so engrossed with meeting Iris and her son, he hadn't noticed that a photographer had entered the room and was snapping away.

Iris glanced at Whitney and then back again at Dane.

"Only if it's okay with you," Dane said. He sensed fear in her eyes, and he didn't want to take advantage.

Iris nodded. "Yes, of course."

"You mind if I pick you up?" Dane asked Jayden.

Jayden immediately held out his arms and Dane eased him into his embrace and stood.

The photographer asked Iris and Dane to move closer together into the frame. "Yes, like that. Smile, please. Heck, if I didn't know any better I'd say you guys looked like a family."

Iris quickly glanced up at Dane, but he merely laughed.

Within minutes, the photographs were taken and the nurse led Dane away for the cheek swab test that would register him as a bone marrow donor. Due to Jayden's aggressive leukemia, they would have the results back within a week. The entire process was over with quickly, and Dane realized Iris and Jayden hadn't needed to be there. It was merely a photo op to show America Dane wasn't some lothario who couldn't be trusted, but for him it was more. It was a chance to shed light on the issue of bone marrow transplants.

When he was done, Whitney was waiting for him in the corridor. "That's it for today. For the next couple of days, you'll have a full calendar of appearances and events, which will hopefully bring up your approval ratings."

"Am I being rated?" Dane inquired.

"Well, no, but we do informal polls on your image," Whitney replied. "It's my job to ensure you have the right kind of press."

"I appreciate it. Now if you'll excuse me." Dane headed for the playroom. He could still make out Iris's form through the glass doors. He was curious to know her story.

"Where are you going?" Whitney inquired.

Dane didn't answer. "If the PR stunt is over, you can

leave. I'll see you on the plane tomorrow." He spun away and went inside the playroom. He found Iris huddled over the blocks with Jayden. As he approached, he noticed a wariness come over her and it made Dane nervous. "Hey."

"Hi."

"The testing didn't take long, so—I was wondering if you wanted to grab a cup of coffee and maybe a cocoa for the little man." Dane looked at Jayden, who was oblivious to them, too caught up with building a large tower with the blocks.

"Just us?"

Dane grinned. "You mean, you don't want my entire entourage?" He glanced behind him to find the bodyguards were guarding the door. "Yes, just us."

She nodded. "Okay, sure."

Dane lent his hand and helped Iris up from the small chair. He was surprised when an electric shock surged through him at merely touching her. He was aghast at having a reaction when Iris was here with her sick child, and quickly stuck his hands in pockets.

Iris swallowed and tried not to show how hurt she was by Dane recoiling from her. When he'd touched her, she'd felt the zing low in her pelvis, awakening sensations she had almost forgotten. Her heart had fluttered, making her breath catch in her throat, but it was clear Dane was disgusted. Since he had no idea about her injuries, his reaction had to be because he found her lackluster. In comparison to his latest dalliance that she'd read about online, Lia Montgomery, Iris was sure she was. She'd perked up when he'd asked her to coffee, but now she understood it for what it was: pity.

It didn't stop her from staring at Dane from underneath her lashes. He was startlingly good-looking. With his hair cut short, his face was a marvel up close, all creamy tapioca skin, strong clean jawline, dark brown eyes, bushy ebony brows and tempting mouth. Dane was movie-star handsome and downright sexy without even trying. Take what he was wearing today, for example. The leather jacket, T-shirt and faded jeans were what any joe on the street would wear, but a woman could forget herself completely in his smile and would be thankful she had.

Impossible images flashed in her head of Dane without any clothes on. Each one was more inappropriate and more unlikely than the last. She blinked to clear her thoughts.

They made it to the cafeteria with the two bodyguards flanking them. After the two men had surveyed the place, she, Jayden and Dane were allowed to make their way to a four-seater table.

Iris was surprised when Dane pulled out her chair and scooted it underneath her before sitting across from her. When Jayden began to get fidgety in his chair, she reached inside her purse and fished out her iPhone. She handed it to him and watched with amusement as he found his favorite video game.

"Regular coffee okay?" Dane asked. "Or are you one of these LA women who drinks a soy latte with no foam or something?"

His low, rich voice washed over her like a caress and her body melted. "Nothing fancy for me," Iris said. "With Jayden's illness, I've gotten quite used to regular ole coffee from the hospital cafeteria."

"Two regular coffees coming up," Dane said, rising again to his feet. "And what about you, Jayden?"

"He'll have milk."

Jayden glanced up at Dane. "You promised cocoa."

A broad smile spread across Dane's sensuous lips. "So you do listen when you want to," Iris teased, ruffling his curls affectionately. She looked at Dane. "A cocoa it is."

"One cocoa and two coffees coming up." Dane sauntered away and Iris couldn't help but watch him. The man had swagger. Lots of it. And a great behind to boot. She couldn't believe someone as famous as he had the time to spare for her. Iris was nobody's fool. She understood part of today's exercise had been to garner good press for Dane. But if seeing a famous A-list actor like Dane registering to become a donor could help Jayden, she would take a hundred pictures with him.

Dane returned several minutes later carrying two steaming cups of coffee and a cocoa with whipped cream on top for Jayden. "How did you manage that?" Iris wondered aloud.

"I have my ways," Dane said with a smirk, his dark eyes gleaming.

Jayden immediately began drinking his cocoa and got a white mustache. "Go wipe your face, Jayden," Iris said, laughing as she watched him get up to find napkins.

"So tell me, Iris—is it all right if I call you Iris?"

"Yes."

"Where's Jayden's father?"

Iris frowned. "That's a very impertinent question to ask."

"I'm sorry. I wondered where he was in all this and why he wasn't here supporting you both. I'm sorry if I overstepped."

"No, I'm sorry," she apologized. "I suppose I'm overly sensitive. It's just me and Jayden. Though my parents have been wonderfully supportive since he was diagnosed."

"How long ago was it?"

"About three months," Iris replied. "Jayden wasn't gaining any weight and was weak and lethargic, so I took him to the doctor. They ran a battery of tests that were initially inconclusive, but I knew something was wrong."

"A mother's intuition?"

"Something like that. I refused to give up so they kept

digging and eventually Jayden was diagnosed with a form of acute lymphocytic leukemia."

"Had to be hard hearing the news. I mean, he's so young."

"Yes, it was very difficult, especially when I learned how hard it would be to find a donor. And then here you are."

"Don't make a saint of me just yet," Dane responded. "I'm only registering."

Jayden returned with the napkin and Iris used it to wipe his face, catching the spots he'd missed. "But you're doing something and that means so much to me," she said, meaning every word as she glanced up at Dane. Whether he was a match or not, or had just come to the hospital to boost his image, he was here, and it could mean the difference between life and death for her son.

"What else can I do to help Jayden?" Dane glanced down at her son with genuine concern. "I feel like getting tested seems so small in the grand scheme of things."

"It isn't. I wish more people like you would register. I think there's a stigma attached to bone marrow donations because people have seen it on TV and heard it can be painful. But they've made advances and there's more than one way to donate now."

"I'll certainly make sure to talk about registering when I make the rounds on the morning and late night shows."

Iris's eyes grew large. "You would do that?" She gulped a large amount of coffee in an effort to steady herself and not think about why Dane Stewart would help her, a nobody.

"Of course. Anything to help this little guy." He glanced down at Jayden. "He should have his whole life ahead of him and if there's anything I can do to prolong it, I will. Matter of fact…" He reached inside his leather jacket and produced a business card, handing it to Iris.

Her eyes filled with tears and instinctively she reached for Dane's hand on the table to squeeze it. "Thank you."

This time he didn't pull away. Instead, he let her hold his hand a moment longer than was necessary. Iris's heart bounced like a ball in her chest as she relived the excitement from his touch earlier. Her tummy fluttered and she could feel her breasts becoming taut as awareness flooded her entire being. She bit down on her lip, but when she glanced up at Dane, raw primal lust was etched across his face.

Dane took in the glorious brown eyes staring back at him. Sensation galloped in his chest from the shocking contact and enveloped him like wildfire. He'd felt it earlier too and it made him want to touch her shiny dark brown hair. Their gazes clashed and mingled and something unspoken fizzled in the air between them. Something Dane couldn't define. Was it lust?

He was taken by surprise because there was an answering hunger in her quiet gaze. Dane reminded himself he was repairing his public image, and to even consider messing around with Iris at a time like this would be low. Yet he couldn't stop himself feeling this pull toward her and the boy. He wanted to be there for her, comfort her, *protect* her.

With his self-discipline vanishing, Dane abruptly rose to his feet. "I have to go."

Iris did the same, and he noticed how she nearly matched him in height. "Of—of course. I'm sorry to have kept you." She blushed alluringly as if she shouldn't have been caught looking at him.

"You didn't, but I have an early morning tomorrow."

"Thank you again for registering."

Dane crouched down to say goodbye to Jayden, who'd already finished his cocoa. "I hope you get better, Jayden. I'm rooting for you."

Jayden glanced up. "Thanks, Mr. Stewart."

The young boy's smile in spite of all he'd been through broke Dane's heart, and he quickly made for the exit without looking back at Iris. He couldn't. Instead, he pulled out his cell phone, made a call and snapped out instructions.

The bodyguards followed him to the lobby and out through the main entrance, where his car had magically appeared, along with Whitney, who was now by his side barely keeping pace with him.

"What was that about?" she asked.

"What?" Dane was disconcerted. He was still thinking about the beautiful woman he'd left upstairs whom he'd given his private number to. It was something he never did, but Dane felt like he could trust her.

"Iris Turner. You asked her to coffee."

Startled, Dane glared at her. "I'm not sure what you're implying, Whitney. I was merely being nice. I would think you'd appreciate the positive press instead of twenty-questioning me." He didn't wait for a response as he hopped in his sports car.

Adrenaline, sleek and sure, pounded through him as he revved the engine. Had the truth been written on his face? Could Whitney sense his interest in Iris? Her hand was so delicate, yet strong. He could *still* feel her touch as if she'd branded him, which was ridiculous. She was going through a lot and for some reason Dane wanted to help her. And if it was in his power to assist, he would.

There was nothing more to it than that.

Two

One week later

"You're a match," Dr. Lee said.

It was early on a Monday morning, and she and Dane were seated in the conference room at Cedars-Sinai. Dane had flown in last night from New York after the premiere of his latest film. It was a departure from his usual body of work and would finally elevate him from heartthrob to serious actor. Early reviews were positive and Dane had left on cloud nine.

He hadn't expected this news.

"Really?" Dane asked, stunned. He'd registered and done the test when he'd been trying to repair his bad boy image. It had worked. The press began to focus on Jayden's illness and the media lost interest in his supposed affair with Lia. He'd been so busy doing damage control, he hadn't contacted Iris. It was just as well because he couldn't act on his attraction to the single mother.

This was an unexpected wrinkle in his plans. "How is that possible? I thought chances were rare I would be a match." He stared in disbelief.

"It's difficult to match the needed tissue type between donors and patients, so this is quite a surprise. Seventy percent of all bone marrow donations do come from people unrelated to the recipient, so only 30 percent come from matches with family members able to donate. And when I compared your genetic markers to Jayden's, there was no doubt—you're related."

Dane sat back in his chair. "Pardon me?"

"If I was a betting man..." Dr. Lee began, then paused for several beats. "I would say that you're Jayden's father."

"No," Dane shook his head and jumped to his feet. "That can't be. I never met Iris before last month. You've got this all wrong, Dr. Lee. There's no way Jayden could be my kid. You need to run your tests again." His mind raced to recall a moment he could have met Iris. A drunken encounter he could have forgotten maybe? But no—that wasn't possible.

Dr. Lee sighed. "Well, that's why I wanted to bring you in. Quietly, of course." He looked out the glass partition at Dane's two bodyguards waiting outside. "I wanted your permission to run a DNA paternity test."

Dane stopped pacing. "A DNA test?"

"Yes, it will give us irrefutable evidence and set the record straight."

"That depends. Do I have your word you'll treat this with absolute discretion? I can't have this leaking to the press."

"Understood. And you absolutely have my word I'll keep this confidential. But in the meantime, I need to know if you're willing to donate your bone marrow to Jayden. Whether you're his father or not, you're a match. I'd like to take a sample of your blood and confirm the human leukocyte antigen match. Once I confirm, you'd meet with a counselor to talk about the procedures, benefits and risks of the donation process. And then you can decide whether you're comfortable with donating."

Dane wiped his hands across his face. This was surreal, but he was sure of one thing. "Of course I'll help. That was never the question. Jayden is a very sick little boy and from what I've heard he doesn't have much time. But I need to know if he's my son."

Dr. Lee rose from his seat. "Excellent, Mr. Stewart. Ms. Turner will be so relieved but probably shocked once she hears of the connection."

"She can't know," Dane replied.

Dr. Lee frowned. "What do you mean? I need her permission to run a DNA test."

"I understand that, but," Dane pronounced, "under no circumstances am I going to rip that family to shreds and have the press crawling through their lives if this is merely a case of mistaken identity. This has to be kept under wraps until we can run a test."

"I understand you're apprehension about the DNA test, but it's more of a formality for legal purposes. I'm certain the additional blood test you're required to undergo will further confirm you're Jayden's father," Dr. Lee replied.

"I don't know. Let me figure this out. What I need from you is discretion. Promise me, Dr. Lee, you will keep this between us until we know more."

"All right. I'll keep your genetic connection to myself, but I'd like to give her some hope and at least tell her you're a match. Let's reconfirm the match."

Dane nodded his acquiescence. "I'm here, so let's do this."

Two hours later, Dane slid into the back seat of the SUV waiting for him outside a secluded section of the hospital. For once he was grateful to be alone with his thoughts, so he could absorb the bombshell Dr. Lee had dropped on him.

Dane had reacted on autopilot throughout the testing, not caring one bit about being poked and prodded. Now that he was done, he was finally free to feel, well, dumbstruck.

Jayden Turner could be his son!

But how? He'd never met Iris until that day a month ago. And since then he'd pushed all thoughts of the slender beauty out of his mind. Until now. One thing was certain: if they'd ever met, Dane was sure he'd *remember* her.

Then it came to him.

Eight years ago, he'd arrived in Los Angeles to make a fresh start. Considering he'd snubbed working for his father, Dane had been determined to live on his own without any help from his family. However, he'd quickly learned how expensive it was to live in the city and after toiling at two, sometimes three jobs he'd barely made ends meet. A year in, he'd had a particularly rough patch, when he'd blown off work to go on some auditions. Dane knew he'd be discovered. He hadn't been. Instead, he'd found himself without a job. Desperate to pay the rent, he'd taken the advice of several other starving artists and gone to donate at a sperm clinic. They'd happily accepted him since he fit certain criteria and he'd signed a contract for a few months. He'd never thought it would come to anything, but he had been selected once. And apparently once was all it took.

It was highly possible Iris had used his donation. Jayden could very well be his.

Dane felt like he couldn't breathe. He didn't need Jason or Whitney to tell him the fallout over this decision could be massive. They'd finally gained momentum for the movie and now…now he had a son? And a son who was fighting for his life, no less. Dane didn't even know how to comprehend the barrage of emotions hitting him. Iris had been handling Jayden's illness all alone for months. Heck, she'd been a mother and father to Jayden. If Dane was truly the father, how would she react to his sudden appearance in their lives?

It was all too much to contemplate. He was so lost in thought that he was stunned when the SUV came to a stop in front of his Hollywood Hills home and his bodyguard Doug opened the door for him. He was already home.

"Thanks, Doug." He nodded at the three-hundred-pound former college linebacker as he strode inside. He was hoping for some time alone, but instead found his assistant, Morgan, along with Whitney and Jason, lounging around on the couch in the living area.

Morgan was a twenty-four-year-old film school dropout who'd been working for him for over a year. They'd met on the set of one of his films, and she'd begged him to give her a job, any job. At first, Dane had been reluctant. Five feet six with long, silky black hair and hazel eyes, Morgan could have been trouble. But Morgan had never looked at him as anything other than a big brother and typically dressed in gender-neutral clothing. She was a godsend and kept his life on track.

"There you are," Jason said from his perch. "We were starting to think we were going to have come get you. How'd it go?"

"I need the room," Dane said, directing a look at Morgan and Whitney, who took the hint and made a speedy exit. He headed for the bar and quickly produced two glasses and a bottle of aged brandy. He poured generously and pushed a glass toward Jason, who'd come to join him at the bar. Even though Jason was his business manager and agent, Dane considered him a friend. For years, Dane had been able to rely on Jason's advice and he prayed he wouldn't fail him now.

"What's going on?" Jason asked, sitting across from Dane who'd remained standing behind the bar. "What did the hospital say?"

Dane stared at the brandy in his hand for a moment and then took a large gulp. It burned on the way down.

"Easy now, Dane. Whatever it is, spit it out and we'll deal with it." Jason reached for his brandy and sipped.

"Jayden Turner could be my kid."

Jason spluttered as brown liquid spilled from his lips. "What did you say?"

"He could be mine. Jayden could be my son."

"That's impossible." Jason quickly snatched a napkin from the countertop and wiped up around him. "If there's one thing I know about you, Dane, it's that you practice safe sex. Whatever this Iris is saying about you is a lie. I don't know if she sensed your interest in her or what, but it's fabricated. Don't worry. We'll fix this."

"You don't get it, Jason. There's nothing to fix," Dane responded. "I donated sperm seven years ago and Jayden is probably the result."

"You did what!"

Dane rolled his eyes. "Don't look at me like that. I was low on cash and rent was coming due. It was a high-end clinic with a very selective process. I was only selected one time."

"One time that could be Jayden?" Jason inquired.

"Ding-ding-ding! You're finally getting it. And I have no idea what to do."

"We need to confirm it," Jason stated, "so we can get ahead of the story before the truth gets out. Spin it."

"Jason, if he's mine, there's no spinning. I will claim him," Dane responded. "I'll do what's right. And if he's not, I'll still donate."

"This is big, Dane. Are you sure you're ready for the heat this could bring? Not just for your career, but personally? To my knowledge, you've never wanted to be a father."

Jason was right. Dane didn't see himself like his brother and sister, settling down and having a family. He'd always been the odd bird and that had been fine with him. His career had always been his central focus, but now he could unwittingly have a ready-made family waiting in the wings.

Iris was on cloud nine.

Earlier today, Dr. Lee had called and informed her there was a match for Jayden. For months, she'd thought it was a pipe dream. She'd gone on television and begged people to register to donate, but she'd never actually thought anything would come of it.

"Are you sure?" she'd asked him, and she'd given her an unequivocal, resounding yes. But nothing could have prepared her for her next words when she'd asked who the match was. It was none other than Dane Stewart, the man who haunted her dreams day and night.

Since their meeting, Iris had found herself searching out his movies and watching them, either on television or Netflix. She'd become obsessed with seeing him on screen, with his sexy good looks and killer abs. Maybe it was to remind herself how strictly off-limits a man like Dane was. And she'd done a good job. She'd convinced herself she'd imagined the connection between them in the cafeteria because Dane had better options than a harried single mother.

Iris had just put Jayden to bed, and was finally ready to retire for the evening. But as she went into her bedroom, she decided there was one more thing she needed to do. Reaching for her purse, she pulled out the business card Dane had given her. Iris had never thought she'd have the opportunity to use it, but she felt compelled to thank him. Dr. Lee had told her donating was much easier these days and that they could do a peripheral blood stem cell donation, but it was still a procedure that might have some recovery time. Dane was a working actor, so it meant a lot that he was willing to make the personal sacrifice for Jayden's benefit.

Without thinking, she grabbed her iPhone and dialed his digits. *He's not going to pick up*, she told herself, *he's not going to pick up*. But he did.

"Hello," a deep masculine voice said from the other end of the phone.

"Dane?"

"Yeah?"

"Hi, um, it's…it's Iris Turner. Jayden's mother," she began. "I hope it's okay I called. You gave me your cell at the hospital—"

"Iris," he interrupted her, "relax. It's fine. You're not bothering me. I was hoping you'd call."

"Really?"

"I assume you heard the good news. I'm a match for Jayden."

"Yes." She breathed a sigh of relief. He wasn't upset she'd phoned. "Dane, I'm so thankful you're willing to donate."

"Of course I'll donate. Jayden has his whole life ahead of him. I want the best for him."

"You do?"

"Yes. I'll clear my schedule whenever I'm needed."

"Thank you. Will you let me know when the procedure is? I'd like to come if that's all right with you."

"Absolutely. It's going to be okay, Iris. Jayden will pull through this. We'll see to that," Dane said.

"You make it sound like we're in this together."

"We are. I now have a vested interest in Jayden's recovery."

"Is that all?" The moment the words were out of her mouth, Iris wanted to take them back, but she couldn't. They lingered, floating on the air.

There was silence for several beats, and Iris was wondering if she'd overstepped when Dane said, "No, it's not all, Iris. I've thought of you often since our meeting."

"You have?" Nervous excitement raced through her veins. Had her initial intuition been right? Dane was interested in her?

Dane chuckled. "Don't sound so surprised. You're a beautiful woman, Iris. I'm sure you know that."

"It's been a while. We single moms don't get very many compliments, especially not from America's Sexiest Man Alive."

"Aw, don't believe the hype, Iris. I'm a man like everyone else."

"Yeah, but you always have a beautiful woman on your arm."

"Those are hookups," Dane admitted. "I don't date. Not really. Because I don't know if they're after my money or if they really want me, you know?"

"That's terrible, Dane. How do you live with it?"

"Not very well. I'm the actor everyone wants in their movie, but sometimes the whole machine of my reputation and brand swallows up the real me. Yet when I talk to you, all the chatter melts away and I feel like myself."

"I'm glad, but what about your family? Aren't they there for you?"

"No, not really. They have their lives and I have mine, but I do check in with them from time to time."

"I don't know what I would do without my family," Iris replied. "They keep me grounded."

"Then you're lucky indeed," Dane said. "Hold on a minute, Iris. What's that?" Iris heard voices and realized he was talking to someone in the room with him, but couldn't make out the conversation. When he returned, he said, "I have to go, Iris, but I'm glad I have your number now. I'll save it in my phone. I'll be seeing you soon."

"All right. And Dane?"

"Yes?"

"Thank you. You're a lifesaver."

Dane sucked in a deep breath as he ended the call with Iris. Morgan had called him on the intercom and he'd used it as an excuse to get off the phone. Leaning back in the executive chair in his study, Dane stared at the ceiling. He hadn't anticipated hearing her sweet voice again so soon, but he supposed he shouldn't be surprised. Iris wanted to thank him for agreeing to donate his stem cells. What she didn't know was that Jayden could be Dane's son too.

All that was left was the additional blood work and a DNA paternity test, but Dane didn't need that. He'd felt an instant connection to Jayden from the start.

But it was six years too late, in his opinion. He had a son who needed bone marrow. And *his* would save Jayden. Fate, the cosmos or something was sending him a message. He hadn't figured out what it was yet.

All he knew was that if he was going to be a father, he didn't want to be like Henry Stewart. But was he being premature? Would he even be able to carve out a parenthood agreement with Iris? It was entirely possible she would fight him on any visitation arrangement, given that he was just a sperm donor.

But perhaps the even bigger question was…how would this affect his career?

Three

Fallon, it's Dane. I really need to see you. I'm flying into Austin tomorrow. In the throes of a full-blown panic attack, he'd called her in the wee hours.

Now, as Dane boarded the private jet he'd anonymously booked to fly him to his hometown that morning, he thought back on recent events. He knew the voice mail he'd left for his older sister was cryptic, but he needed to talk to someone who knew him. Who understood him. Who would listen without judging. Iris was right. He needed his family. Fallon had always been his sounding board, so here he was, on his way to Austin.

The flight was smooth. After renting a nondescript SUV, Dane drove through the city toward Fallon and his brother-in-law Gage Campbell's home, which wasn't far from Stewart Manor. No matter what, he couldn't keep his mind from spinning.

Deep in his gut, Dane knew he should tell Iris the likelihood that they shared a son, but quite honestly, he was afraid of her reaction. What if she refused to let him see Jayden? She might think he'd set all this in motion as a way to get closer to his son when that was far from the truth. He'd had no idea of Jayden's existence until a two weeks ago, but that might not stop her from thinking the worst. He was already a scoundrel for the feelings he had for her.

When she'd called him last night, they'd shared such an easy rapport. Dane hadn't been able to talk to someone like he was just a normal guy in ages. Maybe it was the novelty factor. Iris wasn't the kind of woman he usually dealt with. She wasn't trying to flatter him or cozy up to him because she wanted a role in his next film. She just wanted to talk to him and it made Dane feel like everyone else, which had been sorely lacking in his world. Was that her appeal?

When he arrived at the Campbell residence, he punched in the security code and the black wrought-iron gates opened. There was a long driveway leading up to a château-style mansion with a well-manicured lawn and tall topiaries. Immediately upon exiting the vehicle, the front door opened and his sister came running out and into his arms.

"It's so good to see you, Dane," Fallon said softly.

He was in his usual casual attire of faded jeans, T-shirt and worn leather jacket. The jacket had seen better days, but it was the one item of clothing he'd bought with what he'd earned from his first paid acting gig and he'd kept it ever since. "You too, sis." He squeezed her back. Eventually, he pulled away and gave her the once-over.

Fallon was still an absolute stunner in her cape top and slender trousers. She wore her honey-blond hair in its natural curly state rather than straight the way she usually did for her job as CEO of Stewart Technologies.

"You're looking good, girl. How's Dylan?"

Fallon beamed, which caused her hazel eyes to sparkle.

"He's doing fantastic. C'mon inside and see for yourself." She slid her arm through Dane's and walked him inside.

"I'm surprised you're home. I would have thought you'd be out conquering the tech world instead of playing happy homemaker."

Once in the foyer, Fallon came to a halt. "First off, I will never be a homemaker," she responded. "I have a great staff here to help. Plus, I doubt Gage would let me. He and Dylan demand all my attention."

Dane laughed. "So married life is going well? I know you and Gage got off to a rocky start."

His sister hadn't married Gage for love. It had been a marriage of convenience to help save Stewart Technologies. Dane and their older brother, Ayden, had offered to pitch in monetarily, but Fallon hadn't accepted. She'd chosen to marry Gage in exchange for his funding instead.

Dane had worried about the union, but he supposed he shouldn't have. He and Fallon had grown up with Gage while Ayden had lived apart with his mother who raised him. Ever since her teens, Fallon had had a huge crush on Gage and had never really gotten over him. It turned out the feeling had been mutual, so what had started as a temporary arrangement ended up becoming a real marriage.

"That's all in our rearview," Fallon replied. "I hope one day you can find what Gage and I have, not to mention Ayden and Maya."

"How is that older brother of ours?" Dane inquired.

"He's right here," Ayden bellowed from several feet away.

Dane spun around and was surprised to see his older brother, casually dressed in jeans and a pullover sweater, holding Dylan. "What are you doing here?" The question came out harsher than he'd intended.

"Well, since you barely ever come home, I had to get in where I can fit in," Ayden replied, bouncing the eleven-month-old baby in his arms. "I'd like to get to know you better, Dane, but you don't make that easy."

Dane shrugged. "I'm sorry. Life's been…challenging."

"Care to fill us in?" Fallon asked, folding her arms across her chest.

"Sis, that's exactly why I'm here."

A half hour later, Dane had had brought Ayden and Fallon up to speed on the details, including his hard times that had led to his donation to a sperm bank. He confessed his sample had been used once and Jayden Turner was most likely the result. Fallon was so bowled over, she called the nanny to come get Dylan so they could discuss the matter in private without interruption.

"Wow!" Ayden scrubbed his jaw and leaned back in his chair. "Are you certain he's yours?"

Dane nodded. "When I registered to become a bone marrow donor, I took some tests. When the results came in, Dr. Lee was surprised Jayden and I shared genetic markers. She asked me to come in privately to talk about it. Initially, when she suggested I could be Jayden's father, I thought she'd lost her mind, but upon reflection I recalled the sperm donation. So it makes sense that Dr. Lee's hypothesis is true."

"Have you taken a DNA test? Are you ready to be a father and all that it implies?"

"Hell no!" he said, jumping to his feet. "I'm not ready for any of it. But I'll know more soon after the additional blood test results come through."

"The press is going to have a field day with this." Ayden had just spoken Dane's worst thoughts aloud.

"I know. I can handle them ripping me to shreds. I'm used to it. But Jayden and Iris? They don't deserve what's in store. Jason and I have been figuring out a way to protect them."

"You told your *agent* before you told us?"

Dane heard the censure in Fallon's question. "I did. And I'm sorry, but I'm here now. Don't I get credit for that? Do you have any idea of the media storm that's about to rain down on me?"

Fallon stood and walked over to him, grabbing his hand. "I do. And you know Ayden—" she glanced at their big brother "—and I will be here for you. We can't wait to meet Jayden and his mother."

"Iris."

"You're on a first-name basis with her?" Ayden inquired.

"Yeah, we've talked a couple of times and I met her when I registered to become a donor. She is an amazing woman. Beautiful, strong and a dedicated mother."

Ayden's brow rose. "Is that right?"

Dane hated that his brother could tell he wasn't being completely forthright. "What's it to you?"

"Nothing, Dane." Ayden shrugged. "But I suspect there's more to you and Iris than you're telling us."

Fallon's gaze clashed with Dane's. "Are you two involved? Because if you are, it will only compound the problem. Being attached to you carries a huge spotlight."

"Well, thanks a lot, Fallon. And for your information, we are not involved," he responded.

"Not yet," Ayden offered. "But if you can't be honest with your family, who can you be honest with? You came here because you needed to unload. Do that. I know I'm not as close as you and Fallon, so if you need me to leave, I will."

Dane glared at him. Ayden was right, but that didn't make it easier to hear. "All right, I'm sort of interested in Iris. I gave her my private number and we spoke the other night, but I haven't acted on my attraction to her."

"But you want to?" Fallon deduced.

"Yeah, but I know it's not good for either one of us. I'm keeping my distance, but when she learned I was a match for Jayden, she offered to come to my procedure for emotional support."

"And you agreed?" Ayden asked.

Dane nodded. Why were his siblings ganging up on him? "Is that so horrible?"

"Of course not, but you could have called either of us," Fallon glanced in Ayden's direction. "We'd hop a flight and be there in a heartbeat. The truth of the matter is, you didn't want us. You want *Iris* to be there."

Fallon had hit the nail on the head. "You may be right," Dane finally admitted. "But I can't let her do that without telling her the truth."

"But you're afraid of how she may react?" Fallon asked.

"Can you blame me?" Dane asked. "This whole situation is bizarre. I want to do what's right and help save my son…"

"But you also want his mother," Ayden surmised. "I'm not sure it will be quite so easy to have your cake and eat it too, Dane. Iris is going to be extremely conflicted. On the one hand, you're saving her son's life, but on the other, you bring an entire media firestorm."

"Which is why I've been trying to figure out how to insulate her and Jayden from the fallout."

"Is that really possible, Dane?" Fallon said. "I mean, you might be expecting too much."

"I'd expect to hear that from the pessimist over here—" Dane motioned to Ayden "—but not you. You're supposed to be the optimistic one."

"I am, but I'm also a realist," Fallon responded. "I've had to be."

Dane knew what Fallon meant because they'd always understood each other so well. She'd been levelheaded about business, a pragmatist who'd saved Stewart Technologies. But she also blamed herself for letting their father's mismanagement and their mother's spending habits wreak havoc on the family company. "It wasn't your fault, Fallon."

Ayden peered back and forth between the two of them. "What wasn't her fault?"

"She thinks she let Father ruin the company."

"You didn't *let* him do anything," Ayden responded hotly. Dane smiled because it didn't take much for his brother to pick up the torch. There wasn't any love lost between Ayden and their father. "Henry is responsible for his actions. And Nora too."

"I know you are not a fan of our parents." She glanced at Dane and then at Ayden. "And justifiably so considering how our father treated you, so let's agree to disagree on this, okay? Dane…" She turned to him. "You need to tell Iris. If you wait too long, she'll resent you for keeping this from her. Tell her. And tell her soon."

He stayed with his siblings for the remainder of the afternoon. He didn't intend to stay long. Dr. Lee was rushing the blood test and Dane wanted to be back in LA in case he learned Jayden was indeed his. Fallon suggested visiting their parents, but Dane was in no mood for Henry to gripe about him throwing his life away to be an actor. Instead, he met up with his old friend Jared Robinson for a beer. Jared came from a wealthy family and was a rabble-rouser like Dane had been back in the day. They reminisced about old times when chasing women was their number one hobby, but those days might soon be behind him.

The next morning, Dane hadn't forgotten Fallon's advice to tell Iris and he intended to tell her Dr. Lee's suspicion when he landed. His plans, however, didn't fall into place like he wished. When he'd arrived home, Morgan filled him in on his new schedule and he'd been annoyed. Instead of time to meet with Iris, Dane found himself the following day at a photo shoot in downtown Los Angeles warehouse.

"Don't be mad," Whitney said as a stylist trimmed

Dane's perpetual five o'clock shadow early that afternoon. "We have to take advantage of every opportunity to plug your movie. You want a blockbuster, right?"

Dane stared at her crystal-blue eyes in the mirror. "I wouldn't make it a habit of going against my wishes, especially when I give you a directive to clear my schedule."

"Of course. I'll get with Morgan and make sure your schedule is clear for the next couple of days."

"Thank you."

Dane was desperate to talk to Iris about Jayden. *His son.* The words still sounded foreign. Probably because he hadn't gone through the normal process like most people where you had nine months to prepare for becoming a parent. Dane was being thrown in the deep end of the ocean without a life jacket. On the jet ride home last night, he'd downloaded several books on parenthood and was reading them voraciously. He understood he had a lot of catching up to do.

Jayden might even be angry at him for not being there and Dane would have to accept that, even though it would hurt. When he'd signed up to be a sperm donor, he hadn't thought about the consequences. If he could go back, Dane was certain he'd make a different choice, but he couldn't regret he had a son. Someone with his genes. His DNA coursing through his veins. He would do anything to help him, even putting aside promotion of his new movie, which had been his baby from the moment he'd signed on to play the role. Because Jayden's health now took precedence over everything else.

When the photographer signaled he was ready, Dane walked over to the set. He was in the same attire he usually wore, except this time the jeans and T-shirt were supplied by the stylists. He went through the motions, striking the requisite poses.

When Dane finished an hour later, Morgan was wait-

ing for him with her tablet in hand. "I have the car to take
you to the beach house."

Dane smiled. Morgan was a saint. She knew exactly
what Dane needed after a long day trip to Austin. "Thanks,
Morgan. I'll check in with you later." He waved at the photographer, thanked the stylists and left.

Within minutes, he slid inside the Bentley waiting for
him outside in the alley. Thankfully, security had surrounded the warehouse, preventing the press from getting
in. Several paparazzi shouted his name as he did, but Dane
was weary and quickly closed the door. Within seconds the
vehicle took off blessedly toward home.

They arrived at his Venice Beach house nearly an hour
later because of traffic. After punching in the code, Dane
closed the door and sagged against it. He was dog-tired.
Plopping down, he drifted asleep. It was nearly 5:00 p.m.
when the ringing of his cell phone woke him up. "Hello?"
he said without looking at the caller ID.

"I'm sorry. You sound like you were taking a nap. I must
have woken you up. I'll call back later."

Instantly, Dane bolted upright. "Iris?"

"Yes."

"Is everything okay? How's Jayden?" Dane was surprised how quick he was to think about the boy.

"I'm fine. He's fine. It's just... I—"

"You what?" He could tell she was hesitating.

"I made a rather large pan of baked ziti and... I don't
know, it's silly, but I thought you might like to join us for
dinner if you weren't too busy."

Dane felt the broad grin spreading across his face. "It's
not silly at all. I can't remember the last time I was invited
for a home-cooked meal. I would love to come, but it'll
take a minute to talk to my security detail so they can help
me lose the paparazzi. I'll take my bike, but I'll be there
within the hour."

She let out what sounded like a sigh of relief. Did she think he would turn her down? "Okay, great. We'll see you then. I'll text you my address."

Dane stared down at his phone. He was actually going to get to spend time with his son. This was beyond great, but it was also an excellent segue for him to talk to Iris. He hoped he could find the words.

Four

Iris smoothed down the one-piece V-necked jumpsuit she'd changed into. It was casual enough to wear around the house on a Wednesday evening, but was nice enough to entertain in. She didn't want Dane to think she was trying too hard.

She'd been surprised when he'd accepted her invitation to dinner. Since their talk, she hadn't been able to forget him. Despite his fame and obvious good looks, he was approachable and she'd found the connection between them wasn't one-sided. Dane could have said no, he was too busy, but instead, he was coming to her humble abode.

The roar of the motorcycle engine brought Iris over to the window in time to catch Dane swinging one muscled leg over the bike and onto the sidewalk. Iris's heart thumped loudly in her chest. Dane Stewart was about to walk over the threshold of her house. It was almost too much to process. *Almost.* Instead, she took a deep fortifying breath and opened the door. Dane stood on the other side, looking hot and holding up flowers and a bottle of wine.

"Can I come in?"

"Of course." She motioned him inside and blatantly stared at him. "It's kind of surreal having you in my living room."

"I couldn't turn down a home-cooked meal from a beautiful woman."

"Dane…" She blushed. He was a charmer.

"You're nervous," Dane observed, taking off his leather jacket and throwing it over the arm of her sofa. "Don't be. I *wanted* to come." He handed her the flowers, an assortment of peonies. "I brought these for you." He placed the bottle of wine on the cocktail table.

"Thank you." And she was nervous. It had been years since she'd been on a date, much less had a man in her home. It was nice to feel young and carefree and revel in the fact she was with a gorgeous man like Dane. "I'll put these in water."

She made for the kitchen and once there, leaned against the sink trying to regain her composure. "Get it together, Iris." She placed the flowers in a vase and brought them into the dining room. On her way, she grabbed two wineglasses from her cupboard and the corkscrew from the drawer.

She found Dane standing by the fireplace, looking intently at the pictures on the mantel. There were various photos of Jayden and a family portrait of the Turner clan. There were none of Iris before her accident; she couldn't bear to see how she *used* to look because she would never look like that again.

"Would you like to open the wine?" Iris inquired and noticed he jumped as if she'd caught him doing something he shouldn't.

"Uh, yeah, I can do that." Dane accepted the corkscrew and set about opening the bottle. "Where is the little fella?

I was hoping to spend some time with him." Dane sat on the sofa while Iris chose the adjacent love seat.

"For now, it's just me," Iris responded. "I hope that's okay? Jayden's at tae kwon do. I wanted him to have an activity that develops good character. They teach self-esteem, courage, courtesy, self-respect, focus and discipline. If you knew what it was like wrangling a six-year-old, you'd understand. Anyway, he should be here soon. My neighbor's son also takes tae kwon do, so we rotate picking them up from class each week. It allows me to get dinner started so Jayden isn't eating too late."

"That's great. I'm glad you have a support system. I'd hate to think of you doing this all alone." When he released the cork, he poured them each a glass and handed her one.

"Thank you, but I'm not alone. My parents, my sister, Shelly, my neighbor—they're all part of the village it takes to raise Jayden. Cheers." She tapped her wineglass against his.

The front door of the bungalow sprang open and Jayden bounced excitedly into the room.

"Mommy, you should have seen me tonight!" Jayden rushed over to her, not even noticing Dane on the sofa. He was still wearing the standard white *dobok* uniform consisting of a top, elastic-waistband pants and a belt. "I did a better ax kick than TJ."

Iris smiled broadly. "That's great, Jayden. Say hello to Mr. Dane. You remember him, right?"

Jayden spun around and hazarded a glance at Dane. "Yeah. You're the man who is going to be my donor." And without her asking, Jayden threw his arms around Dane's neck. "Thank you."

Tears sprang to Iris's eyes as Dane held Jayden in his arms. He seemed as overcome as she was by Jayden's spontaneous affection. "You—you're welcome, Jayden." Dane patted his back and just that quickly, Jayden was moving on.

"I'm hungry. What's for dinner?"

Iris rose to her feet and picked up his book bag, which he'd left in the middle of the floor. "Your favorite—baked ziti and garlic bread. Go wash up. Dinner will be ready shortly." Jayden scampered out of the room, leaving the two of them alone again.

"Sorry about that. Jayden can be a bit extra if you're not used to him."

"Extra?" Dane appeared distracted, then shook his head. "No, he's fine. Is he always that affectionate?"

"I guess. Why?"

"No reason. He's a really special little boy."

Iris grinned. "I think so. C'mon, grab your wine."

Dane followed Iris down a small corridor into a farm-house-style kitchen with a table big enough for four, but with place settings for three. He sat down in one of the chairs and watched Iris. She busied herself taking garlic toast from the freezer and putting it in the oven.

Dane couldn't recall when he'd witnessed anything so domestic except when Gage's mother, Grace, had lived at Stewart Manor and worked as their cook. She hadn't minded him and Fallon being underfoot. Lord knows his mother, Nora, wouldn't be caught dead cooking; that would require putting in effort. The only thing Nora was good at was keeping herself well preserved with Botox and frequent trips to the gym and salon.

Iris spun around and faced him. "Is something wrong?"

"No. Why?"

"You're frowning," Iris answered. "I'm sorry dinner's not ready. I know your time is very valuable. The garlic bread will be ready in five minutes."

Dane gave a mirthless laugh. "It's not you, Iris. I was thinking about how my mom never cooked for us. She's never been all that interested in me or my sister."

"Really? What mother doesn't care about her kids?"

"The kind of mother who stole our father from his first wife and made sure to get pregnant so he wouldn't leave her."

"Surely she isn't as bad as you say?"

"Worse, but I don't want to talk about my mother." He sipped his wine.

"What do you want to talk about?"

Her question was innocuous. She had no idea of the undercurrents about to sweep her away. Dane figured the conversation could wait until after dinner. So he used his charm and changed the subject. "How about how good you look in that…" Dane tried to think of the word for the contraption she was wearing. All he knew was the difficulty in getting a woman out of one. *But not impossible.*

"Jumpsuit?" Iris offered, glancing down at her outfit. "This is really nothing."

"I don't think so." He ran his gaze over her body and the attraction he felt sizzled. She was aware of it too—that subtle shift in the atmosphere. He noticed how her nipples suddenly thrust against the fabric.

Dane stood and walked over to her, forcing Iris backward against the sink. Lifting his hand, he ran the tips of his fingers experimentally over her hair. He felt Iris tremble at the action. "Your hair feels like silk."

Iris looked up at him, and Dane felt an overwhelming urge to kiss her. He told himself to resist. He hadn't come clean with her about his discovery he was Jayden's father. Until he did, it wouldn't be right. But Jesus, he was sorely tempted. "I want to kiss you so bad." He didn't realize the words were out of his mouth until they hung in the air.

"Then why don't you?"

"Mom—" Jayden's voice startled them, forcing them to quickly step away from each other "—is dinner ready?"

"Yes. I think it is," Iris said.

* * *

After dinner, Iris didn't recall how the baked ziti and garlic bread tasted. She'd been too caught up in the illicit feelings Dane had evoked when he'd backed her up against the sink and stroked her hair. It had felt so good. It had been so long since she'd felt desire. It was as if he'd drugged her with his words and she wanted more.

Someone, however, had taken Dane's attention away from her. Who would have thought it would be her six-year-old son? The two of them were like peanut butter and jelly. They meshed. Iris was surprised at how easily Dane conversed with Jayden and vice versa. They had a natural ease around each other. Dane was very inquisitive about Jayden's likes and dislikes. Iris loved that Dane was taking such an active interest in her son, because they were a package deal.

Iris suspected he was probably bored with the women in his circle and wanted to branch out. As a single mother, Iris knew she couldn't go too far down this rabbit hole with Dane, but it was sure nice to feel wanted.

Eventually, Jayden went to bed, but only after Dane agreed to read him a bedtime story. Iris tried to talk him out of it, but Dane insisted he was fine. And so, Iris had watched from the doorway as Dane sat by Jayden's bedside in his Spider-Man–inspired room and read him a bedtime story about a prince with fire-breathing dragons until eventually Jayden's eyes closed. Dane softly crept out of the room, meeting her in the corridor.

She glanced up at him. "Dane, you really didn't have to—"

Iris didn't get another word out. His arms came around her and her chest collided with his. And any past doubts she may have had about herself ebbed away when he pressed against her. He was hot and hard, and deliciously male. He wanted *her*. That much was obvious. She glanced straight up into those dark brown eyes of his and lost the battle.

Everything exploded at the first touch of his mouth on hers. Dane took control of the kiss and one of his hands wrapped itself in her hair, so he could angle her head for a better fit. And then he simply...*took*. He kissed her deeply and Iris loved every minute of it. She shivered against him uncontrollably as a rich, heady desire stole through her body.

The passion between them was so strong, it obliterated everything else, making Iris forget they were in the hall outside her son's bedroom. So when Dane shifted to haul her against the wall, Iris didn't care; the only thing she could do was kiss him back like she was a starving woman and he was her only sustenance.

Nothing existed but the two of them in this moment as their lips and tongues tangoed in a sensual rhythm as old as time. She circled her arms around his wide, powerful shoulders, curved with muscles honed by what she was sure were many hours in the gym. When he leaned in harder, pressing his hips against hers, it forced her small breasts into closer contact with the hard wall of his chest, and Iris moaned. Heat gathered low in her belly, making her feel hot, hungry and ready—

Jesus, she was losing her mind. She hadn't behaved this way in a long time, since...since the accident. Thinking about that and what might come next was like having a bucket of cold water poured over her and Iris slowly stopped engaging in the moment.

Sensing the change, Dane pulled back. His breathing was ragged and heavy. "I'm sorry. I shouldn't have done that."

Iris lowered her eyes and shook her head. "It's not you. It's me."

Dane snorted. "If ever there was a line from a movie..."

Glancing up, Iris offered a small smile. "I don't know what came over me." She moved away from him and started toward the living room.

"Would it help if I said I didn't expect it either?" Dane said. "I didn't come over to seduce you, Iris. I genuinely care about you and Jayden."

"I can see that."

His brows furrowed. "Can you?"

"The way you were with him tonight was amazing," Iris said, turning around to face him. "Makes me realize he's missing not having a father in his life."

Here was his opportunity to come clean. To tell Iris he could be Jayden's father. By some stroke of fate, life had led them to this moment where he would be able to save his son's life, the son he never knew he had.

But Iris was still speaking and he didn't want to interrupt her. He followed her to the sofa where she'd made herself comfortable and sat down beside her. He was going to try to keep his hands to himself, but after that explosive kiss in the hall, it was going to be difficult.

"I've tried to be both mother and father to Jayden," Iris said, "but it's hard sometimes, ya know? Was tonight his way of telling me he needs more male companionship in his life? As his grandpa, my dad does his best to pitch in, but I wonder if I made a mistake."

"A mistake?"

"I don't know who Jayden's father is because I had Jayden through artificial insemination." When Dane remained quiet at her revelation, Iris asked, "You don't want to know why?"

"Only if you want to share." He had wondered. Iris was a beautiful woman. What would make her decide to take such a drastic action? But he couldn't ask that. He had no right to judge her, considering he'd been a sperm donor himself.

Iris shrugged. "I... I wanted to be a mother," she admitted. "And I wasn't sure it was going to happen for me. My family was dead set against it. They tried to talk me out of it, but I was determined. And wouldn't you know, I got pregnant on the first try! What are the odds? Anyway, that's the long and short of it. I thought I understood how hard it was going to be, being a single mother." She glanced down the hall. "But I guess I was wrong."

He had to say something. This was the perfect opportunity. He wasn't going to get another one, but where did he start? "Iris, I—"

"Mommy, I'm thirsty." Jayden appeared in the living room in his Spider-Man pajamas, looking sleepy eyed.

Iris was immediately on her feet. "I'll be there in a minute, honey. Go on back to bed."

Rubbing his eyes, Jayden didn't argue and went to his room.

"It's going to take me a minute to put him back to bed." Iris glanced down at Dane. "I should walk you out."

No. This couldn't be happening. She was asking him to leave now, when he was on the cusp of telling her he was Jayden's father? "Iris, we should really talk," he began.

She nodded. "I know, but it's late and I should get Jayden back to bed. Can I take a rain check?"

Dane couldn't push his luck. The conversation they needed to have was too important to be rushed. "Of course." He grabbed his leather jacket off the sofa arm and followed her toward the door. "Thank you for having me over tonight. I can't remember when I've had such a great time."

Iris laughed aloud, and the sound was melodious. "No need to lay the charm on so thick, Dane. I highly doubt baked pasta with a single mom and her six-year-old is a barrel of fun. Not with the movie premieres, travel and stars you get to meet."

"You'd be surprised, Iris Turner. You'd be surprised."

The glow of being a movie star had worn off a long time ago. Luckily, he still enjoyed the craft of acting.

Iris walked him to the door and when he got to the threshold, Dane leaned in and brushed his lips tenderly across hers. "Don't sell yourself short, Iris. Tonight was amazing." Then he was running down the stairs toward his motorcycle. He turned and caught Iris in the door watching him. He could feel her blush all the way from where he stood and she immediately closed the door. Dane remained outside for several moments, staring at the house. Inside was his son and the mother of his child, a woman who was quickly becoming so much more.

Five

Dane wished time would slow down for once and allow him to catch his breath. Since his dinner with Iris a week ago, he felt as if someone had pressed the gas pedal to the floor. Dr. Lee had rushed the results as anticipated. Now Dane knew with 100 percent certainty that Jayden was his. He was both excited and overwhelmed. Rather than tell his family and friends, Dane was taking time to digest the news.

One thing was taking longer than he'd expected, though. He'd thought that the procedure for Jayden would be in a few weeks, but once he went to the information session about acute lymphocytic leukemia, he'd quickly realized his error. It would be at least a month before Jayden was ready to accept his bone marrow. Dr. Lee explained Jayden would have to have daily chemo treatments before his immune system was wiped out. Only then would he be able to receive Dane's healthy stem cells.

Meanwhile his team ran full steam ahead with his normal slew of activities. When he wasn't promoting his new film, he was reading scripts for his next project and working through callbacks for his next leading lady. He wasn't excited about another big blockbuster, but the only way Jason had gotten the film studio to agree to his passion project was if he agreed to do a sequel to a megahit he'd done two years earlier.

Competition was stiff for his new leading lady but so far the readings were ho-hum in his opinion. Dane supposed that was why his mind was always drifting to Iris and that one incredible evening they'd shared.

Iris haunted him.

Her taste. The sounds she'd made when she'd moaned out her enjoyment during the heated kiss in the hall. The sweet scent of her fragrant perfume. He found it impossible to concentrate on running through the scene with the myriad women the casting director brought in. Instead, Dane went through the motions. Apparently it hadn't gone unnoticed because one day Jason pulled him outside the warehouse during a break.

"Are you all right?" Jason inquired. "You're a little distracted."

"I have a lot on my mind."

"Well, snap out of it. The studio head is here and he might forget you're the star if you don't show them who's boss." He stared at Dane for several moments and then asked, "Is this about Iris Turner?"

Dane grabbed Jason's arm and pulled him farther away from the warehouse entrance. "Keep your voice down."

"Are you still hung up on this kid thing?" Jason asked. "You know, you don't have to *do* anything. You can donate your bone marrow and she can continue raising him without you ever telling a soul he's yours."

Dane stared back at him incredulously. "Do you honestly think I can go my entire life knowing I have a kid," he whispered, "and do nothing? Is that really the sort of man you think I am?"

"I'm giving you an out, Dane. In case you were looking for one. I've known you a long time and I'd hate for this situation to derail your hard work."

"And your cash cow?" Dane replied. He was Jason's biggest client and that was fine, so long as they were honest about his intentions.

"This is not about the money, Dane, and I resent you saying so," Jason responded. "I care about you. You're like my kid brother. I'm looking out for you and maybe telling you something you're afraid to think, much less say out loud. But if you need me to be the fall guy, then fine, so be it."

Dane sucked in a deep breath. "I'm sorry, Jason. This whole situation has me on edge. I should have told Iris when we had dinner."

"When did you have dinner? Did you sleep with her?"

"No!"

"But you came close," Jason surmised.

"We kissed after she'd invited me to share a meal with her and Jayden. Can you blame me for wanting to get to know my son?" His voice was low, nearly a growl. He didn't want anyone hearing their conversation.

"Of course not, but you have to be careful, Dane. You're not an average guy who can have dinner with a woman you're interested in. You're Dane Stewart."

Dane nodded. "I realize that. But she still has to know."

"Ultimately it's your decision, but in the meantime, I need you to get your head into this reading."

Dane followed him inside, but Iris and Jayden were not far from his mind. He had to figure out a way to ease into releasing the bombshell and pray Iris didn't explode when she found out.

* * *

Iris wanted to cry. Over the last couple of months she'd watched Jayden go through physical exams, blood tests and a monthly bone marrow test. But today was the worst, when the nurses put a PICC—a peripherally inserted central catheter—in his arm. It was a thin, soft tube inserted into a peripheral vein in his upper arm. It would facilitate the pretreatment for the transplant and allow prolonged and safer access to Jayden's veins to draw blood and administer chemo.

The line would stay in his arm the entire treatment. It was hard to hide and needed to stay bandaged to prevent infection, but the team at Cedars-Sinai was so great. They were making it fun for Jayden. They'd given him a Spider-Man sleeve cover to put over the bandage. Most kids would probably screech at the top of their lungs at seeing a needle, but Jayden had taken this and the battery of tests he'd been subjected to the last several months like a pro.

After the procedure was complete and they'd just gotten to the car, Iris had a suggestion. "How about some Moose Tracks ice cream?"

"I can have some before dinner?" Jayden asked.

"You absolutely can!" Iris said with a smile.

She'd buckled Jayden into his seat and closed the rear door when she felt a presence behind her. She spun around and found Dane there. "Dane! You nearly scared me to death." She swatted him with her purse.

Dane held up his hands in defense. "I'm sorry. Guess my lame attempt at surprising you wasn't the right move."

Iris placed her hand over her racing heart. "I appreciate you coming, but you could have warned me. What are you doing here?"

"Well, I was bombing at a reading for my next movie and I hadn't seen you in a couple of weeks so I figured I'd see how you both were doing. I remembered you mentioned Jayden's visit, so I took an Uber over." He glanced in the back seat and waved at Jayden, who responded with an enthusiastic flap of the hand.

"We just finished getting his PICC line in. Jayden was a real trooper."

"But it was hard seeing it." Dane said what she couldn't. Tears welled in her eyes and she nodded.

"Come here." Dane pulled her toward him and wrapped her in his arms. Iris allowed herself to accept his embrace. There was something about the comfort she received from Dane that was unlike anyone else's. He made her feel special. So special it scared her and made her worry this thing between them couldn't possibly be real. For God's sake, he was a superstar.

Was she imagining he cared for her because she wanted it to be true? She breathed deeply, inhaling his heady masculine scent. Eventually, she tried to push him away, but he held on tightly.

"Don't treat me like a stranger, Iris," he murmured. His eyes were blazing with some emotion she couldn't read. When he cupped her face and kissed her, she wound her arms around his neck and his lips crushed her mouth. He invaded her senses, tasting her and teasing her with his tongue. Iris was so deep in the kiss she barely registered a knocking on the window. It was Jayden and he was staring right at them.

Iris blushed, stepping away from Dane. "I have to go. I mean, we're going for ice cream."

"Can I join you?"

One of Iris's brows rose. "Do you want to? I mean, you could be recognized and there would be a mob."

"It's why I brought this." Dane produced a baseball cap from his back pocket. "No one expects me to walk into Baskin-Robbins. I can hide in plain sight."

"All right, if you're game, then so am I."

"Good, because I wasn't taking no for an answer anyway." Without waiting for an invitation from her, Dane hopped in her Camry and they were soon taking off down the road.

On the way to the ice cream shop, Dane realized he was in way over his head. The more time he spent with Iris, the more he couldn't keep his hands off her.

Since their dinner, they'd talked on the phone a few times. Sometimes the conversations were long, sometimes short, because Iris would be exhausted from working all day and taking care of Jayden. And every time they spoke, Dane told himself he would tell Iris the truth about Jayden, but he pulled back. If he didn't tell her soon, it would be too late. She would be so upset by his deception she might not ever forgive him or allow him to see Jayden. And she had every right as his sole guardian.

Last week after Dr. Lee called him with the blood test results, he'd gone to see a custody attorney, who made it quite clear he didn't have any rights as a sperm donor. But given Dane's name and stature, the attorney thought it might be interesting if Dane did take her to court because it would set a precedent. Dane didn't want that. Iris was a great mother, yet he wanted a place, a small one, in Jayden's life. And he was certain with his help, Iris and Jayden could have a better life.

"We're here," Iris announced, pulling into a space across the street from the ice cream shop.

Dane immediately put on his baseball cap and turned around to Jayden. "You ready for some ice cream?"

"Yes," Jayden said.

Dane came around to the rear door and helped Jayden out of the booster seat. He saw Iris glance over at him, surprised by his behavior, but he'd done what a parent was supposed to do. And when Jayden grabbed both his and Iris's hands to walk across the street, Dane beamed with pleasure.

Despite the mild evening, there weren't many people inside. Jayden rushed toward the displays.

"Thank you for coming," Iris said.

"Who doesn't love Rocky Road?" Dane said with a smile.

When the cashier came over, they placed their orders: Moose Tracks for Jayden followed by a Jamoca Almond Fudge for Iris and a four-scoop banana split for Dane. While the cashier took care of their order, they found a booth. Iris and Jayden sat on one side and Dane on the other. His trainer would kill him for cheating on his strict high-protein diet. It was worth it, however, when Jayden's eyes lit up at his banana split.

"Want some?" Dane inquired. "Dig in."

Jayden sank his spoon into the gooey chocolate mixture and let out a sigh of pleasure. "It tastes better than my Moose Tracks."

"Have some more," Dane encouraged.

"Dane, he has his own ice cream," Iris admonished.

"I know, but there's plenty for everyone. Why don't you dig in too?" Dane said with a smirk. He doubted Iris could resist the sinfulness of the banana split.

And she didn't. Minutes later, she was plunging her spoon in and licking it off. Dane's libido stirred to life watching her tongue lick and flick the spoon. He wondered what it would be like if she used it on him in places aching for her mouth.

Iris glanced up at him, and Dane had to mask his desire.

"So does kissing make you and Mommy boyfriend and girlfriend?" Jayden inquired as he took alternating spoonfuls of his ice cream and Dane's banana split.

The unexpected yet innocent question caught Dane off

guard and he looked to Iris. When she shrugged, he said, "It means we like each other an awful lot. Does that help?"

"Doesn't kissing make babies?" Jayden asked. "My friend TJ said when he caught his parents kissing, a baby popped out of his mom's belly nine months later."

Dane couldn't resist letting out a loud, rambunctious laugh. "Jayden, has anyone ever told you how funny you are?"

A wide grin came across the boy's face. "Nope. But you just did."

Dane continued laughing while making eyes at Iris and eating his split.

Eventually it got late. To go along with the strategy of hiding in plain sight, he called a Lyft to take him home.

"Are you sure? I could drive you," Iris offered.

"No, it's fine. I don't want the paparazzi to get used to seeing your vehicle. So it's best if you keep a low profile."

"All right."

When they were done, Dane slid a twenty into the tip jar and walked them to their car. Once he'd settled Jayden into his booster seat, he gave him a fist bump. "You were a big boy today. Keep it up. And if you need me, your mother has my number."

"Okay," Jayden said.

Shutting the door, Dane turned to Iris. That was when he noticed the Lyft driver pulling up outside the store. "That's my ride."

"It was fun. Thank you for coming, Dane." Iris glanced behind her. "But I don't want you to make promises you can't keep."

He frowned. "What do you mean?"

"You're Dane Stewart," Iris replied, "and you're going to be pulled in a million different directions. I don't want Jayden's hopes getting high that you're going to be permanently in his life."

"Because I'm transient, passing through, is that it?" Dane asked. The Lyft driver honked his horn. "Be right there," he yelled over Iris's shoulder. "Listen, I get it. I know this thing—" he motioned between the two of them "—came as a surprise, but I'd like to be a part of Jayden's life if only for the simple fact I'm giving him my bone marrow and I want to see him live."

Iris blushed. "Dane, I'm sorry. It's just... I—I don't know—"

Dane bent forward and kissed her to silence her fears. It was a sweet, soft kiss and didn't last long because the driver was honking again, letting him know he was getting impatient. He lifted his head and said, "Stop thinking so much, Iris, and just go with the flow."

He waved, ran across the street and hopped inside the waiting car.

"Ready to go?" the driver inquired, but Dane couldn't answer because Iris was still standing there. It made him want to leap out of the vehicle and take her back home where he could make love to her until the sun rose, but instead he gave the driver his address. "Yes. Take me home."

Six

"Wake up, Romeo," Jason yelled into Dane's ears on Tuesday morning. "We've got some damage control to do."

Dane rolled over on his bed in his master suite and glanced at the clock. It read 7:00 a.m. "You know I'm a night owl and don't like getting up until at least nine."

"Well, today is not your day because you couldn't keep your hands—oh, wait, excuse me, your *lips* off a certain single mother. It's now front-page news."

Dane bolted upright, letting the covers slide away. "What did you say?"

Jason leaned forward and placed a local tabloid in his face. A picture of him in the baseball cap kissing Iris at the ice cream shop was sprawled across the front page.

"What the hell?"

"Didn't I ask you to give her a wide berth?" Jason responded. "But no, Dane's going to do what Dane wants to do."

"Don't berate him." Whitney strolled into his bedroom

even though Dane was bare chested and wearing pajama bottoms. She handed him the mug of coffee in her hands. "Thought you might need this."

"I could use one myself," Jason stated cheekily.

"Not a chance, Underwood. Get your own," Whitney responded, sitting on the edge of the bed as if Dane had invited her there. "Dane and I need to have a chat."

Jason rolled his eyes. "Fine. I'll get my own coffee." He left the room.

Dane rubbed the sleep from his eyes. "Where's Morgan?"

"Morgan is downstairs," Whitney replied.

Dane threw back the covers and rose from the bed. "I'm not in the mood, Whitney." He walked to his en suite bathroom and began brushing his teeth. His publicist didn't accept his boundaries and came to watch him from the doorway.

"You broke the internet, Dane. The tabloids put two and two together and realized Iris was the mother from the photo you took at the hospital after your donor registration. Did you give any thought to the consequences of your actions?"

Dane spit out the toothpaste and wiped his mouth with a nearby towel. Then he rose to his full six-foot-three height. "Don't think you're going to school me, Whitney, like I'm some naughty little boy. I can hire you and I can fire you." He strode from the bathroom and opened the door of his oversize walk-in closet. He searched the rows of clothing, which were color-coded and in order of length, until he found some sweats. When Whitney made as if she was going to join him, he gave her an evil eye and she remained outside.

"Might I remind you," Whitney said from the doorway, "you hired me to extricate you from one media disaster and here you go creating yet another. Are you a masochist?"

Dane didn't respond until he came out of his dressing room fully clothed. Jason had returned with a mug of coffee. He seemed equally floored by Whitney's audacity.

"Whitney, you should remember *Dane* is the client," Jason said.

"I do remember," Whitney nearly growled. "I just need *you*—" she glared at Dane "—to help me help you."

"Who's the actor here? Being melodramatic?" Dane inquired, raising a brow. At his lighthearted response, Jason let out a guffaw and even Whitney smirked.

"Jesus, Dane. What am I going to do with you?" Whitney asked.

"Protect my son," Dane said fervently. He glanced in Jason's direction. They'd kept the news of Jayden's existence from Whitney, but now it was time to fill her in.

"Your son!" Whitney exclaimed. "Since when?"

"It's a long story," Dane began, but Whitney shook her head.

"Oh, no, you don't." She wagged her finger. "You don't get to dismiss this out of hand. I need the entire story so I know how bad this is going to get."

Fifteen minutes later, Whitney sat in silence. "Did you hear me?" Dane inquired. He'd shared his sperm donation story and that Jayden was his son.

"Okay. So now you've got to give me some time to absorb the news. I can figure out how to control the fallout."

Dane resented the fact they had to do damage control because he had a child.

"He's your son," Whitney said. "We can't change that, but we show what you're willing to do for your son. Maybe do some interviews about how much you can't wait to be a father. If we can get Iris on board, maybe even have the three of you on camera." At Dane's glare, she doubled down on her argument. "C'mon, from the looks of it, you two are getting along swell if that lip-lock is anything to go by."

"Present them as one happy family?" Jason added, sipping his coffee. "I don't know, Whitney. We've always sold Dane as the sexiest man alive every woman or man wants to bed. And now he's suddenly father of the year? I don't buy it."

"I need to speak with Iris first. Tell her the truth before this blows up in her face," Dane interjected.

"No, absolutely not." Whitney shook her head. "Once she knows and tells her family and friends, the story goes viral. We need to have a narrative in place before then."

"I don't like it," Dane said. "It's dishonest."

"It's protecting your brand," she responded. "Plus you've kept the secret this long, so what's another few days?"

She was right, but Dane hated continuing to keep this secret from Iris. She deserved to know what was going on before her life change irrevocably. Because once the press caught wind of their true connection, all bets were off. "All right, let's talk this through again..." Though Dane doubted it was possible to sort it all out. They were between a rock and a hard place, and there was no easy way to tell a six-year-old you'd been MIA from his life because you'd never wanted to be part of it to begin with.

"You've been holding out on me," Shelly said when she stopped by Iris's bungalow later that evening. It looked like she'd come directly from work because she was in a business suit.

Iris frowned. "What are you talking about?"

"Don't you play innocent," her sister responded. "I was on the treadmill when a picture of you kissing Dane Stewart popped on the screen. Apparently TMZ is trying to figure out how the single mother with a dying child caught Hollywood's hottest actor."

"What?" Iris rushed to the cocktail table and grabbed the remote. She flicked the television on and found an entertainment channel. And there it was in bright Technicolor: apparently she was Dane Stewart's latest squeeze. "Omigod!" Iris placed her hand over her mouth. "This can't be happening. He thought he was being so careful."

"So it's true?" Shelly said, forgoing the couch and sitting directly on the cocktail table. "You're seeing Dane?"

"No," Iris denied. "It's nothing like that. We just…"

"You just fell into his arms?" Shelly offered. "I'm not buying it."

Iris twisted her hands in her lap. The flirtation and kisses with Dane were supposed to be harmless. Something just between the two of them. It had been so long since anyone had shown interest in her. Dane didn't even have any idea about her injuries because it hadn't gotten that far between them. *Yet.*

Had she allowed the kiss to get out of control when he'd been at her home for dinner, Dane might have discovered the horrible truth. She shouldn't have allowed her attraction to Dane to interfere with Jayden's care. Dane could walk away at any time. No, she couldn't let that happen. Whatever this was between them couldn't go any further. "All right, I'll admit Dane and I have been friendly."

Shelly glanced at the entertainment channel, which seemed to be running the picture of their kiss on a continuous loop. "I beg to differ."

"We've been talking on the phone and he showed up yesterday to Jayden's appointment for the PICC insertion."

"How'd that go?"

"Jayden's a trooper, but all this—" Iris motioned to the television "—is more than I'm ready to deal with."

"I'm sorry to tell you, Iris, but you should have thought about that earlier. You can't date someone of Dane's stature without repercussions."

"Date?" Iris's voice rose. "It wasn't a date, for Christ's sake. He took us out for ice cream."

"And then he kissed you for the entire world to see."
Iris huffed.

"Listen, sweetie." Shelly reached for her hand. "I'm not saying you shouldn't grab every bit of happiness you can find. I know Jayden's illness has taken a toll on you, but you also have to be realistic. Any involvement you have with the man could threaten Jayden's transplant. Think about it, sis—Dane is a superstar and the media is interested in his every move. And if you're with him, your every move."

"I didn't sign up for this."

Shelly shrugged. "But here we are. You need to talk to him right now. Come up with a plan of attack."

Iris pulled her hand away and jumped up. "When do I have time to do that? I'm busy taking care of Jayden, making sure everything is all wrapped up at school so he can finish out the next few weeks before we have to homeschool him." She sighed and took a deep breath. "I'm sorry, Shelly. I don't mean to jump on you. I'm overwhelmed."

"That's why I'm here. To help out any way I can."

Shelly was right. She needed to call Dane because her and Jayden's anonymity were about to be obliterated.

Iris didn't have to wait long. Shortly after Shelly's visit, her cell phone rang. The display read Dane.

"Iris, I'm so glad I reached you." Iris loved hearing his deep, masculine voice. "How are you? How's Jayden?"

"We're fine," she replied. "For now."

"So, you know we've been discovered?"

"Yes."

"I'm sorry, Iris. I should never have…" His voice trailed off.

"Should never have what?" Iris was curious what he was about to say. Was he regretting spending time with her? "Whatever it is, Dane, just tell me."

"I should never have gone to the ice cream shop without my security properly vetting the place. Someone must have recognized me and alerted the press."

Iris breathed a sigh of relief. She'd anticipated Dane saying he wished he hadn't gotten involved with her. She knew it was naive to hope someone like Dane would stay interested in her for the long haul, but it had been nice the last fortnight having someone to talk to, sharing her fears and concerns.

"I wish I could tell you I knew how to handle this," Iris responded, "but this is way out of my wheelhouse."

Dane chuckled. And she was glad he could laugh and didn't blame her for any bad publicity. Or was that an oxymoron? Was publicity bad? Lately notoriety was as equally sought after as praise. "Of course I wouldn't expect you to know how to deal with this," Dane said. "It's why I hire people."

"And do they have any suggestions?"

"They do, but I'm not sure you're going to like them."

"That sounds ominous."

"Didn't intend it to be," Dane replied. "But if I'm putting all my cards on the table, you should know I had a bout of negative publicity. I turned it around over the last month after the hospital photo shoot with you and Jayden, but the paparazzi are still out for my blood. They're going to try to put a negative spin on this."

"Why would they do that? You're donating your bone marrow to Jayden and helping save his life. That's a good thing and somehow that message is being lost."

"The tabloids are always looking to spin the story and make it seem tawdry. Make it more about us."

"How can they? We're just friends," Iris said.

"Is that all we are, Iris?" Dane said softly.

Suddenly, her throat felt dry and constricted and she knew somehow she wasn't going to like what came next.

"If I'm honest," Dane said, "I think we're *more*. But

more in my world comes with a lot of challenges. The media will want to know everything about you and Jayden. They'll be relentless in researching you. They may even try to find dirt to make what's between us feel sordid, but I don't want that to happen. Call me selfish, but you've been a breath of fresh air and I don't want to lose you."

"Did anyone ever tell you you come on strong? We've only known each other a short time and I'm expected to answer you now?"

"Yes. I have to know where you stand, so I can protect you and Jayden. Even if we don't continue, there will be some heat if the media thinks there's some teeth to the story."

"So I'm in this either way?" Verbalizing it was scary, but she appreciated Dane's honesty. She had to state her answer.

Dane was nervous. He didn't know what Iris was going to say. He knew Whitney felt presenting a happy family for the press was the best play, but Dane didn't want Jayden or Iris to be subjected to their scrutiny this early on. He had to shield them for as long as he could. "Iris?"

"I've enjoyed our nightly phone chats."

"So have I. You have no idea how hard it is to find someone who's genuine in my world. I find you fascinating."

"Dane…" Her soft sigh came through the phone.

"I know it seems crazy I'm asking if you're in this with me when we've barely gotten to know each other, but that's the only way I can protect you. Protect Jayden."

"I'm his mother. I should be protecting Jayden."

Dane wanted to spit out the truth that he was Jayden's father. It was his job to protect him too, but instead he went with the status quo. "Of course you are, but I can help. I have a lot of resources at my disposal that can help make your and Jayden's life more comfortable. Please let me."

"Exactly what are you asking me?"

This conversation wasn't going exactly how he'd envisioned. He'd assumed Iris would go along, not be a protective mama bear looking after her cub. "Be my girlfriend. We can announce we're seeing each other. Tell them that after meeting at the hospital, it was love at first sight and let them take the story from there."

"G-girlfriend? That will make them more interested in me and Jayden. And neither one of us wants that. I think if we lay low, maybe not see each other for a bit, this will blow over. I'm not the story—you are."

"I don't think this is the right play here, Iris."

"And your objections are noted," Iris replied, "but this is my and Jayden's life you're talking about. We're not chess pieces your PR team can move across the board. I need time to think about this."

"Time is running out, Iris." He was desperate for her to see how bad this situation could get. The paparazzi could be vicious.

"I have to go, Dane. We'll talk soon." Iris ended the call before Dane could get another word in edgewise. It was the first time one of their chats ended so abruptly and he was perturbed. He paced the terrazzo floors of his balcony and wondered how he was going to get Iris to listen to reason. At the end of the day, Dane realized, he didn't have a choice. He had to tell her *he* was Jayden's father. Only then would she see his way was the only way out of this mess.

Seven

Iris was on edge. She had been since last week when she'd spoken to Dane. She'd thought giving herself some breathing room would make it easier but it hadn't. And Dane had been persistent. He'd left voice mails and texts for her to call him. He wanted to see her, but Iris wasn't ready. She wasn't ready for any of it.

Every morning when she'd dropped Jayden off at school or left to go to work or the grocery store, she'd waited for a reporter to jump out of the bushes and ask about her relationship with Dane. But it hadn't happened. She and Jayden had been able to go on with their daily lives. They'd regularly gone to Dr. Lee's office and Jayden had started his pretreatments for the transplant.

Dane's stem cells were an incredible gift. But was she grateful enough to act like his girlfriend? Not that she would have to do much acting—she liked Dane. But she was scared of the world he lived in. She wouldn't want to subject Jayden to it when he was fighting for his life. And what were Dane's expectations anyway? Would he expect intimacy from her? Because no matter how much she might want to, she would die inside if she had to see a look of disgust or pity in Dane's eyes if he ever saw her scars. She'd have to say no.

But everything changed this morning when she and Jayden left the bungalow only to be surrounded by members of the press. She saw the news truck parked at the curb. Reporters yelled at her and bulbs flashed brightly in her eyes.

"Iris, how long have you been seeing Dane?"

"How long have you been lovers?"

She wanted to wring their necks. How dare they yell such things around a six-year-old boy? Iris shielded Jayden as best she could by pulling him closer and whispering for him to lower his head.

"Please let me pass," she yelled, but they wouldn't stop. It was the last question tossed her way as she was settling Jayden in the back seat that got her attention.

"How long have you known he was your sperm donor?"

Somehow Iris closed the rear door, but she was sure the media got what they were looking for in her stunned reaction. She sat in the driver seat and didn't start the engine. Her mind was swirling with their questions. Could it really be true that Dane Stewart was the sperm donor she'd used for her artificial insemination? No. She shook her head. It couldn't be true. She went to a reputable clinic whose donors were anonymous. Dane couldn't be Jayden's father, could he? If he was, it would explain why Dane was such a great match for Jayden—*they shared genes.*

If this was real and not all just a dream, the question was, did Dane know? Was his interest in her some elaborate cover-up to conceal the truth that he was Jayden's biological father?

* * *

It was too early in the morning to drink, but it was Friday somewhere so Dane went out to his living room and poured a stiff one at the bar. He had to. His worst fear had materialized when he'd rolled over in bed and reached for his iPhone. News of him being Jayden's father was on every major social media and news site. *Damn.* He'd turned on the television and several channels were showing footage of Iris leaving her home and being besieged by the press. He wished she'd agreed to his protection days ago when he'd offered it. The reporters had barely given her room to enter her car. But what Dane couldn't forget was the stunned expression on her face when one of the reporters rudely yelled out asking how long she'd known Dane was her sperm donor.

Dane sipped his brandy and waited. Iris had called. Her voice had been clipped, strained when she asked if he was home. He knew why and had given her the address to his place in the Hollywood Hills. She'd told him to expect her within the hour, and Dane wasn't looking forward to the conversation. He drank more because he felt guilty. He could have prevented this, if he'd been honest with her as soon as he'd found out. Instead, he'd waited and they were paying the price.

The doorbell rang and Dane bolted upright on the sofa. Slowly, he placed the tumbler down on the table and stood. With leaden feet, he walked toward the door. The moment of reckoning was here.

He just wasn't prepared for what greeted him.

A slap.

"How dare you, Dane Stewart!" Iris strode past him into his home. After calling in sick to work, it had taken Iris nearly an hour to get to his house. She'd steadily had to dodge reporters who'd been in pursuit of her from the moment she'd left her bungalow. They'd followed her to Jayden's school, where she'd had a serious talk with the principal, informing the rather flustered woman under no circumstances should anyone be allowed to speak to or take Jayden off campus without her express consent. She needed to get her mind around what was happening, but the more she drove, the less Iris felt in control of her life.

Dane was Jayden's father. She was fairly certain of it. How else to explain his sudden interest in her in the weeks after the photo op? He'd known the only way to get close to Jayden was through her. She not only felt diminished but angry she'd allowed herself to be used. Why hadn't she seen the signs? An A-list Hollywood superstar wouldn't look twice at her. Yet she'd fallen for his charms hook, line and sinker. She felt like an idiot. And she'd come here to tell him what she thought of his deception.

Eventually, she spun around to find Dane had followed her into what could be described as a room worthy of an Italian palazzo. It was enormous, with high ceilings, marble floors and furniture that must have cost a fortune. Iris tried not to act like a country bumpkin with her mouth hanging open. Instead, she glared at him.

Surprisingly, Dane showed remorse and lowered his head.

"Do you have anything to say?"

He glanced in her direction, "What would you like me to say, Iris? That I'm sorry all this happened and you and Jayden were pulled into the circus? Then hear me—I'm sorry."

"Are you sorry for lying to me?" she queried, folding her arms across her chest.

His brow furrowed. "What do you mean?"

"Really, Dane. Are you honestly going to play dumb?

How long have you known? How long have you known Jayden was your son?"

He didn't answer. Instead, he walked past her, barefoot, in the same loose-fitting jeans and T-shirt he liked to sport, and reached for his tumbler on the table. She watched him take a sip and nearly asked for one herself. She was so tense she was about to explode, but she needed to keep her head on straight. "Well? I'm waiting for an answer. And I'm not leaving here until I get one."

Slowly, Dane turned to face her. "I've known there's a possibility for a while. After I registered, Dr. Lee called me in a week later and told me I was a match. I was happy, Iris. I could help a little boy. But then she hit me with the news Jayden and I shared certain genetic markers that were too close to be coincidental. He told me it was likely I was Jayden's father. A follow-up blood test all but proved it."

"Dr. Lee knew and didn't tell me?"

"I implored her to keep it confidential until we could take a paternity test."

"And exactly when did you think that was going to happen? Were you going to go behind my back to obtain some of Jayden's hair or saliva?"

Dane snorted. "Nothing so melodramatic. I was going to ask you and tell you the truth that there was a chance Jayden was my son. I tried calling you the last couple of days, but you ignored my calls and my texts."

"Are you blaming me for the mess we're in? You had plenty of time to tell me but you chose not to. Why did you let me believe you liked me, wanted something m-more?" Iris's voice cracked and she moved so he couldn't see her face.

She felt Dane's hands on her shoulders moments later as he turned her around. "I never lied to you, Iris." He looked into her eyes and Iris had to remind herself not to read too much into it. But her body betrayed her; she felt the sudden thrust of her nipples against the silk of her button-down shirt. "Not about us." One of his large hands reached out and his fingers drifted through the strands of her brown hair.

How was it that one touch from him made her senses jangle? The familiar desire she always felt around Dane was making her breathless in a way she didn't want to be. Iris pushed her hands against his chest to get some breathing room. "Yeah, yeah, yeah. You found me fascinating. The plain Jane who needed a sperm donor so she could get pregnant. How you must have laughed about me to your team."

"Stop it, Iris. Stop putting yourself down. I won't have it."

Iris laughed. As if he could stop her from the downward spiral she'd felt since the moment she'd woken up in the hospital after the car accident to find out she'd been disfigured, most likely permanently.

Dane clearly didn't understand the change in her. "Why are you laughing?"

"Because. This situation is so contrived. It's like something out of a bad Lifetime movie of the week." She did her best impersonation of a voice-over. "'Famous actor falls for single mother with dying son.' Except this time the joke is on me because the actor in question also happens to be his father."

"Iris, I had no idea of Jayden's existence. If nothing else, believe that."

"Oh, I believe it," Iris said. "I doubt someone like you purposely wanted to make a baby."

He winced at her harsh words. "That's not fair, Iris. You don't know the situation. It's not fair to judge me."

"Well, then, enlighten me." She moved over to a chaise and plopped down. She eyed him as he walked to the couch adjacent to her and sat down.

"I was a starving actor. Low on cash. A friend of mine

told me a clinic was looking for the cream of the crop to use as sperm donors. He said with my looks, I would be a shoo-in. Of course it wasn't as easy as it looked. There were lots of exams, blood work, questionnaires and the like, but eventually the clinic used me. And I just forgot about it because I was discovered and my career was blowing up. I vaguely recall getting a letter once about being selected, but it didn't register until after I left Dr. Lee's office. That's when I realized Jayden could be mine."

Iris sucked in a deep breath. "Thank you for the backstory. It helps me see exactly where we stand."

"And where is that?"

"You said it yourself—you never wanted to be a father. You never gave a thought to the possibility of a child."

Dane's face turned red, and she could see she'd struck a nerve. "And so in your opinion, I'm disqualified from being Jayden's father? Who are you to judge me, Iris Turner? You're the one who went to a sperm clinic and got artificially inseminated."

"Because I wanted to be a mother," Iris railed, "and all that entailed. *I* have been in Jayden's world from the moment of conception. *I* carried him in my womb for nine months." She pressed her hand to her stomach. "*I* gave birth. *I*'ve raised him the last six years."

"I know that," Dane responded, "and I'm not discounting any of it. You're an amazing woman, Iris. I've said so from day one. But I know Jayden exists now. He's real to me. And he needs me. He needs his father."

"Does he? Because up until now he has done quite fine without one," Iris responded. But she knew she was lying to herself; she'd seen how different Jayden was when Dane was around.

"I disagree."

"Does it matter now? You've brought down hellfire on

all of us because you're in his life, in my life. I don't even know what to do next."

"I would like to take the paternity test."

"No."

"Iris, you're being unreasonable. You may want to deny this is happening, but the truth is already out there. Kids are going to talk. We need to explain to Jayden what's going on."

"*We* don't have to do a darn thing," Iris replied. "*I'll* talk to him."

"When?"

"Don't press me, Dane. Jayden is my child."

"And he's probably mine too. You can't cut me out."

"After all your lies and deception, I can do what I please. You could have just told me the truth and left me out of this entire debacle, but you had to come in and play hero like in one of your movies."

Dane stared back at her for several long moments before saying, "What's got you more upset, Iris? My being Jayden's father or not knowing whether my interest in you is genuine or not?"

"Oh, no, you don't." She wagged a finger at him. "You don't get to turn this around on me."

Dane scooted closer to her until he was only inches away. "Yeah, I do. You're laying down all these edicts but I know you're not this woman. All angry and breathing fire. It's not who you are. It's not the Iris I've come to know."

"Don't presume you know me, Dane. You have no idea what I've been through."

"Well, what I see, I like," he responded. His eyes darkened even further until they were black as midnight. "And the feeling is mutual." When she attempted to shake her head, he called her out. "When we've kissed, you've responded. *Passionately*."

Iris could feel a blush creeping up her skin.

"You've wanted me as much as I've wanted you," Dane responded. "You still do."

"I shouldn't have come here." Iris went to move away, but Dane's reflexes were lightning fast. He curled his fingers around her forearm and pulled her toward him, like an expert fisherman reeling in his catch of the day. She let him tilt her chin with those strong fingers and allowed his mouth to travel toward her in what felt like slow motion. Iris tried to hold back, but the minute their lips touched, she felt a flash of connection, so intense she released a moan of joy.

Dane's mouth explored hers with a thorough familiarity that had her mind racing. He plundered her lips until there was no oxygen left in her lungs and she had to draw back and suck in a breath of air. "Dane," she whispered.

Dane's chest tightened as he abandoned any thought of going slow. Instead, pure instinct took over and the kiss became hungry, hot and hard. He could hear the thud of his own heartbeat, especially when she pressed her soft curves against him. She was sweet and so responsive. He felt her nipples harden into pebbles through her blouse. He broke the kiss to lower his head and close his lips around one peak. He drew it into his mouth, making a wet patch on the shirt as he laved and teased the bud before moving on to the next one.

He wanted more of her. His hands crept lower until he found the waistband of her slacks. He slipped his thumb beneath them until he came into contact with bare skin. He felt her clench, but his intent was to keep going until he could caress her where she was surely hot and wet for him. The way she'd been wiggling signaled she was ready for a lot more, but when he went to move lower, she stopped him. Her eyes were hooded, but she just shook her head fervently, then moved to the other side of the couch.

"Iris, what's wrong? Did I move too fast?" Words were

spilling out of his mouth because he didn't know how to react to the look of terror on her face. Had he misread her signals? He hadn't thought so. "Baby, what's wrong?" he asked again when he saw unshed tears on her lashes like morning dew on the leaves of a flower.

"I'm sorry. I can't." She started for his front door, but there was no way she could leave in the state she was in.

"Iris, please stay. I promise I'll keep away from you if that's what you want." He held up his hands. "Just stay. Please. You're in no condition to drive. You've already had one fright this morning. I'm sorry. I shouldn't have come on so strong."

"It's not you, Dane," she cried, and the tears that had been threatening began to fall. "We can't be involved. Not now. Not ever."

Iris continued to move away from Dane. If things had gone any further, he would have discovered the truth. Felt the scars from the accident that, no matter how many surgeries she'd had, wouldn't go away. She should have resisted, but the pull she felt toward him was strong.

"I won't apologize for kissing you, Iris," Dane said softly behind her, "because I wanted to, but I will say I'm sorry if I moved too fast. Why don't we put what's happening between us aside for a moment and talk about Jayden? It's out in the public now. We have to get in front of it and I'd like us to not be on opposite sides."

Dane had a point. She was way out of her depth in handling the kind of media attention she got today or would get in the future. Her feelings didn't matter right now. She—*they*—had to do what was best for Jayden. "All right, what would you suggest we do?"

"I'd really like to have a paternity test," Dane repeated. "I can get the test expedited and have results within twenty-four hours, if you're willing. I'll leave it to you on how best to tell Jayden what's going on. Even though I would love to be there when you did."

Iris noticed how soft his voice had become. It was as if he was speaking to a frightened horse needing cajoling. He didn't need to coddle her; she was much stronger than she looked. She'd already been through more pain than anyone could endure and come out on the other side. "It's best I speak to Jayden *alone*. And after that?"

"I release a statement to the press on how happy I am to have discovered my son and request privacy during this difficult time as we deal with our son's health."

"Do you honestly think it will be enough?" She didn't think the reporters she faced today were going to accept a simple press release.

Dane scrubbed his jaw with his hand. "Probably not. My team thinks we should do a televised interview with one of the major news outlets."

"*We*, meaning you and me?"

"Yes. If we present a united front, it could put some of the rumors to rest."

"Or spark more," Iris returned. "They could think we're an item and camp outside my house. I've heard the horror stories about the paparazzi. Is this really what you want for Jayden?" *For me*, she wanted to add, but kept herself out of the equation.

"No. But we don't have a lot of options here, Iris. However, I can help with securing your home and provide protection for you and Jayden."

"Is that really necessary?"

He nodded. "Please don't fight me on this. I *have* to do something. It killed me seeing the two of you besieged this morning without any protection."

"All right."

"To what?"

"To the paternity test and the security. I'd rather have

someone there who is looking out for me and Jayden. But as for the interview, that's a no."

"Of course, I understand."

"I'm going to go now." She needed to leave because the air between them was still crackling with unresolved sexual tension. "Call me with the details for the test, okay?" She walked to the front door, and Dane followed behind her. She sensed he wanted to say more, but instead, he watched her leave. She was venturing into an unknown world she was ill-equipped to handle and she feared what was coming next.

Eight

"Dane, are you okay? We saw the news reports in Austin this morning," Fallon said.

It was well into the afternoon and Dane was still at home. He was in no mood to deal with the media and all the questions they would pepper him with. He was letting the initial dust settle when he got the three-way call from Fallon and Ayden.

"It looked like poor Iris was under fire," Ayden said, "and a bit stunned by the news you were Jayden's father. You didn't tell her your suspicions, did you?"

"No."

"Why not?" Fallon asked. "At least she could have been prepared."

"Please don't beat me up, Fallon. I feel guilty enough. I left her open to be blindsided today and you can best believe Iris let me have it already."

"How'd that go?" Ayden inquired.

"Better than I'd hoped," Dane responded. "Initially she

was upset with me, justifiably so, but after she calmed down and listened to reason, we were able to come to a consensus."

"And what was that?" Fallon asked.

"She agreed to the paternity test. She's taking Jayden after school to a private facility that will handle the test with absolute discretion. Iris will talk to Jayden and explain what's going on. I wanted to be there, but she thought it best she handle it alone."

"Wise move," Fallon stated. "Iris probably already feels like her entire world is spinning off its axis, but telling her son—"

"Our son," Dane corrected.

"Telling *your* son gives her some of that control back. I think you're going about this the right way. How are you planning to handle the furor over this news, though?" Ayden asked.

"I suggested an interview with one of the reputable networks. It would allow us to set the record straight and stop any speculation. But Iris disagreed."

"And what about you and Iris?" Fallon inquired.

Dane clenched his jaw. "I'm not ready to talk about that right now."

"It's okay, Dane. I was just curious. You have our support. We're here for you if you need us. Once you have the official proof Jayden is yours, we'd like to come visit if that's okay with you?"

Dane's mouth curved into a smile. "I have no doubts what the results will show," he replied, "and I would love that. Let's plan on it soon. It's time Jayden knows the other side of his family."

After he'd hung up with his siblings, Dane thought about Iris's reaction to their intimacy earlier today. One minute they were kissing and in the throes of a heated bliss and the next, she was pushing him away. Her response was way over the top and he wanted to understand why. Because Dane knew he wouldn't be able to keep his hands off her for much longer.

Iris ignited a hunger in him. Over the years, he'd grown cynical about women, especially the marital ambitions of the single women he encountered. Most of them bored the hell out of him. But when it came to Iris, she rocked him to his core and made him believe that maybe, just maybe, there *was* someone out there who could truly get him. Up until now, Dane thought he'd remain single forever. He hadn't seen many happy marriages. He certainly didn't count his parents' marriage as the epitome of happily ever after.

He'd suspected his father married his mother because she'd been pregnant with Fallon, tossing aside his first wife—Ayden's mother, Lillian—because Nora demanded it. Dane was certain he wasn't too far off the mark.

He was determined not to make his father's mistakes when it came to women. What was happening with him and Iris was so precious. She was a fierce mama bear, yet sweet and humble and oh so craveable. He would get to the bottom of her fears and whatever was holding her back because he didn't just want moments with Iris. He wanted all of her. *In his bed.*

After leaving Dane's, Iris planned to speak with Jayden. She wasn't relishing the idea, but it had to be done. Lord knew what kids were saying at school.

When the school day ended, Iris was waiting for Jayden outside of his classroom.

"Mommy, what are you doing here?" Jayden asked, walking toward her with his backpack around his little shoulders.

"I wanted to talk to you." Iris grabbed his hand. "Come with me." She led him to the principal's office, who'd graciously allowed Iris to use the room after she'd told her the situation. Iris nodded at the receptionist who motioned for her to go inside.

"Why are we going into the principal's office?" Jayden asked. "Am I in trouble?"

"No, honey, you're not," Iris said, closing the door behind them. "I need to talk to you about some important stuff."

"You mean about Mr. Stewart being my daddy?"

Iris swallowed the lump in her throat. There was no burying the lead in this conversation. "What have you heard?"

"Some kids at lunch showed me some video. Why is everyone saying that? You always told me I didn't have a daddy."

Iris sighed. She'd known this conversation wasn't going to be easy, but hadn't quite anticipated it being this tough. "I didn't lie to you, Jayden. Mommy would never do that. Usually mommies and daddies love each other so much, they make a baby together, but I wanted to have you so much that I used a medical procedure to have you."

Jayden frowned. "I don't understand."

"I know, honey, and I'm so sorry," Iris said.

She did her best to explain, but in the end Jayden was still confused. "We need to take a test to find out for sure if Mr. Dane is your father."

"What if Mr. Dane isn't my daddy?" Jayden asked.

Iris pressed her lips together. "Let's cross that bridge if we come to it, sweetheart. In the meantime, there's a lot of people who like Mr. Dane because he's in the movies and they want to know all about you, so we're going to play a game of hide-and-seek. We're going to hide from them, but they'll be seeking us out and asking questions. We're not going to answer them, okay?"

"Okay, Mommy."

Iris wrapped her arms around Jayden. She knew it was

a lot for him to process and hated the position they were in. They were playing defense when they should have been playing offense. "C'mon, honey." She rose to her feet and grabbed him by the hand. "We're going to go out the rear entrance so no one sees us."

According to the receptionist, the press were now parked outside, hoping to catch a glimpse of Jayden, but Iris had switched cars with Shelly. When she'd called her sister at work, Shelly had been more than willing to help out. Iris couldn't believe she had to be so stealthy in order to ensure their privacy.

Dane had already texted her the testing facility's address. They were expecting her, and when she and Jayden arrived, they were whisked right into an examination room. After completing a cheek swab, they were back on their way. Next she was headed to her parents' house. Iris knew they and her sister would want to know what was going on.

Pulling into the driveway, Iris turned off the ignition but didn't go inside.

"Mommy, why aren't we going in yet?" Jayden asked.

Iris released a long sigh. "No reason. I just needed to catch my breath." Within seconds, Jayden was bounding out of the car with no thought of whether they were being watched. It was Iris who glanced around the quiet tree-lined street looking for paparazzi, but there were none.

Jayden had already pushed the front door open and rushed inside when Iris made it up the front steps and into the foyer.

"Iris, thank God you've come over." Her mother, Carolyn, pulled Iris into the hug. She grasped Iris's face in both her hands. "Are you okay? I saw the news and, oh my god, I just can't believe it. Is it true?"

Iris stepped out of her embrace. "Where's Jayden?"

"He went to get some freshly baked chocolate chip cookies and some milk. I told him to do his homework while me and you have a serious talk."

Iris moved into the living room and glanced around. Her mother's taste was rustic; several antique pieces gave the room a cozy vibe. "Where's Daddy?"

"He's on his way home from work but he's called me several times asking if I'd heard from you."

"Well, let's sit," Iris said, sliding onto the comfortable microsuede sofa while her mom sat beside her. "I'll tell you everything you want to know."

"Is Dane Stewart Jayden's father? I mean, how is this possible? You were artificially inseminated."

"It's a crazy coincidence," Iris said.

"Are you sure, sugarplum?" a deep tenor voice said from the doorway. "Because I find in life there are no accidents."

"Daddy!" Iris popped to her feet and rushed over for one of his signature bear hugs. He wrapped her in his arms and gave her a gentle squeeze before setting her away.

"All right, girl. I'm here now." He took off the jacket he'd been wearing, hung it in the closet and joined them in the living room. "I left work because your mama told me you'd be coming over. Where's that grandson of mine?"

"He's in the kitchen, Charles," her mother replied, "eating cookies."

"Good. It will allow grown folks to have grown folk conversation." Her father sat down in his favorite reclining chair. "So, Iris, what in the hell is going on?"

Iris sighed and started over. "You know exactly what I know, Daddy. I went to a reputable doctor and was artificially inseminated. I got pregnant on the first try and nine months later, I had a beautiful baby boy."

"Where does Dane Stewart fit in this scenario?" her father inquired.

"Unbeknownst to either of us, it appears as if he was my sperm donor. He was a struggling actor looking for some serious cash and he was well paid for his donation. He'd forgotten the one time his sperm was used."

Her mother clutched her chest. "Do we have to keep saying that word?"

"Aw, Carolyn, don't be such a prude," her father chided. "Go on, Iris."

"He went about his life and I went about mine. Until Jayden's diagnosis. When I went on-air and pleaded for people to register as bone marrow donors, Dane's camp heard about it. He'd had a bout of bad press and needed to clean up his image. For him, registering was only supposed to be a feel-good story and he'd move on."

"Then what happened?" Her mother seemed as enthralled with the story as the rest of the country.

"Dr. Lee told Dane that he and Jayden were most likely related, but did he tell me?" Iris's voice rose. "No, he chose to keep that little bit of information to himself. Instead, he charmed his way into our life, by giving me his private number."

"And?" her father pressed.

"We started talking and he came over for dinner and spent time with me and Jayden."

"I knew it," her sister stated, storming into the house like a nor'easter. "You've been holding out on me."

"Where's my car?"

"Sitting in your driveway," Shelly said. "I took an Uber over here."

"Shelly, have a seat, please. Your sister was just sharing this bizarre tale of events," her father said. He turned to Iris. "So how did the press get wind of your relationship? I would imagine someone like him knows how to retain his privacy?"

"He thought he had it covered. Someone must have recognized him at the ice cream shop where we went after Jayden's PICC was inserted and alerted the media. Anyway, does any of it matter now? Reporters are going to be crawling through my and Jayden's life now and I hate it. We didn't ask for any of this."

"No, but you did choose to use a sperm donor, which has inherent risks," her father stated matter-of-factly.

"C'mon, Dad, not even you could have predicted my sperm donor would be a famous Hollywood actor," Iris responded.

Her father smiled. "No, I suppose not. And what about Dane? Does he want to be a father?"

"I think so. And in the meantime, while we get this sorted out, he's offered to give us a security detail to protect us from the media."

"You're going to need it," Shelly chimed in. "The Uber drove by your house on our way here. The television crews were swarming your neighborhood."

"This is all too much." Her mother stood and began pacing. "You already have so much on your plate with Jayden's illness. And now you add the press breathing down your neck. How are you going to handle it all?"

"One day at a time," Iris said. "I can't worry about what people think of me, Mom. Jayden comes first."

"From what you've said," her father replied, "sounds like Dane sees it the same way. I'd like to meet him."

"I dunno, Daddy."

"He's the father of my grandchild and has his sights set on my daughter. I darn sure want to meet him." Charles Turner puffed out his chest and Iris knew when she was beat. It was better to give in than to fight.

"Fine. I'll ask him."

"Good. Now come and get a bite to eat," her mother said. "I have some beef stew cooking on the stove."

Iris followed her parents into the kitchen and watched them and Jayden from the doorway. They were such a close-knit family with everyone looking out for each other.

What was going to happen bringing Dane into the mix? Was she really ready for the changes ahead?

"You're going to wear a hole in the floor," Jason said, "if you don't stop pacing."

"Do you have any idea how I'm feeling?" Dane asked. "I've been in this mansion for twenty-four hours while the entire world gets to comment and Tweet on my life as if they had a right to. And what do I do? Nothing. Instead I have to listen to Whitney give me the business. Iris, who's in all likelihood the mother of my child, railed at me for keeping secrets and lying to her, when all I want to do is take her up to my bedroom and have my way with her. And then there's Jayden. He could be my little boy and he's suffering from a life-threatening illness. I'm all set to give him my bone marrow so he can get better, but I can't until he goes through debilitating chemo. Do you have any idea how inept I feel?"

Jason leaned back. "Okay, I think you must have needed to let that out. And I'm sorry, Dane, if I've made light of this whole situation. It's just extremely unusual, ya know."

"No kidding. I'm living it, Jason."

"When will you know the results of the paternity test?"

"Within the hour. A courier will be delivering the results to both Dane and Ms. Turner simultaneously," Morgan chimed in from her position in the corner of the room. His assistant always seemed to be nearby when Dane needed her.

"Well, no wonder you're all wound up," Jason said. "Why don't you come with me to the gym? We can spar a bit and you can release some tension."

"I don't think that's a good idea," Dane said. "I'm in a foul mood and could hurt you."

"I can handle you, Stewart," Jason said. "C'mon, no sense in clock-watching."

Ten minutes later, both men had changed into sweats and were in the gym going through the paces. Dane hadn't realized how much he needed to relieve his stress until he took the first jab. Soon he and Jason were going toe-to-toe, with a jab here and quick punch there. It was exactly what Dane needed, so by the time he noticed Morgan in the mirror, hovering in the doorway, Dane was feeling good because endorphins were rushing through his veins.

Morgan held up the envelope and walked toward them. "The results are in."

Dane took off his boxing gloves and stared at the envelope for several seconds before accepting it. "Thank you."

"C'mon, Morgan. I'll buy you a Gatorade." Jason wiped the sweat off his brow with a towel from the nearby towel rack, and then they left Dane alone in the gym.

Dane's heart was beating fast because the contents of the envelope would change his life forever. The DNA test would officially set the record straight once and for all that Jayden was his son.

Sliding his forefinger through the flap, Dane pulled out the report. He wasn't interested in all the mumbo jumbo of how they arrived at the result; he wanted only to know unequivocally if he was a father. Scanning down the page, Dane found his answer.

Jayden was his son.

Nine

The driver pulled the SUV up to Dane's Venice Beach home a couple of hours later and Iris hopped out. Like him, she'd received the test results confirming he was indeed Jayden's father. Now Dane was going to be a permanent fixture in their lives because, knowing the truth, there was no way she would deny her son the chance to know his biological father. Although Dane hadn't been a part of Jayden's life from the start, he'd been prepared to donate his bone marrow. Had it initially been a media ploy? Yes. But he was a good man.

After reading the results, Iris had called her parents. They took the news in stride, as did Shelly, who thankfully agreed to come over and babysit so Iris could talk to Dane alone in person. But when she'd called him, Morgan had answered his cell. She'd informed Iris that Dane had taken off on his bike. Morgan figured he'd gone to his Venice Beach house and suggested sending a driver so Iris could dodge the paparazzi. Then Morgan gave her the gate and key codes.

Iris had been surprised when three identical SUVs pulled up outside her home ten minutes later. Immediately, the news reporters sensed activity, especially when a beefy security guard got out of his vehicle, knocked on Iris's door and escorted her to one of the SUVs.

"Why three cars?" Iris asked as she got in.

"Subterfuge, ma'am. They won't be able to figure out which one has you." And with that, he closed the door and the SUV pulled from the curb.

An hour later, she was standing outside Dane's home. The paparazzi hadn't been able to follow her, but they were staked out at the gates of his beach house, desperate for a glimpse of Dane. No lights were on and it appeared that no one was home. Had Morgan gotten it wrong? Iris started walking toward the back of the house. Using the code Morgan gave her, she opened the side gate, which opened to a narrow alleyway that led to a private stretch of beach. The sight before her was spectacular. There was the Pacific Ocean in all its majestic glory, the sunset tinting the sky in various shades of orange, pink and purple. She could see why Dane liked coming here.

Toeing off her sneakers, she tucked them under her arm and walked in the sand. That was when she caught sight of him. Dane was standing outside on the terrace with a drink in his hand. He didn't appear to see her; she could tell he was deep in thought. Iris understood why. She'd had nine months to prepare for Jayden's arrival. Dane had had less than two months to deal with impending fatherhood, but like it or not, it was here.

"Permission to come up?" Iris yelled to him.

Dane glanced down at her and blinked as if to make sure she wasn't a mirage. "What are you doing here? How did you get here?"

She smiled. "Morgan gave me the info. Now can I come up?"

"Of course." Dane quickly went to unlatch the gate leading up to his terrace. He opened it, and she walked up the few steps until she was standing in front of him. He was barefoot, and looked more handsome than ever in his usual outfit of T-shirt and jeans.

She offered him a small smile, and then reached inside her back pocket and produced a cigar. "Congratulations!"

Dane chuckled, but he accepted her gift with one hand, his tumbler of dark liquid in the other. "Thank you. I was outside watching the sunset. Do you mind?"

"Not at all."

She sat beside him on one of the loungers and together they watched the colors change on the horizon in silence. When it was over, he finally turned to her. "Before when I thought Jayden might be my kid, it was an idea, you know? But now—"

"It's different," Iris finished. "He's your son and knowing means you would do anything for him. Go to any lengths to protect him. Because you *love* him."

Dane nodded and if she wasn't mistaken she saw a hint of tears in his eyes. "Yeah, I would. But it's also frightening because I don't want to mess up. I don't think I know how to be a father."

Iris chuckled. "Do you think I knew what I was doing?"

"No, but you chose to be a mom."

"You're right," Iris nodded. "I did. But listen to me, Dane. No one has some magical book that shows you how to be a good parent. We just have to do the best we can to love them and help them grow into good people."

"Thank you for the wise words. Now I don't know about you, but I'm starved," Dane said, heading toward the sliding glass doors. "You staying for dinner?"

"Am I invited?"

"As long as you can chop veggies, you are. When I got here, the fridge was already stocked. I thought I could whip up some pasta primavera. Maybe grill some chicken. How's that sound?"

"Heavenly." Iris kicked off her shoes and followed him inside, walking barefoot on the hardwood floors into Dane's killer beach pad. There was floor-to-ceiling glass that brought the ocean right into the home's open-concept main room. A cream sofa, ombré blue rug and azure chairs were in the classic white-and-blue seaside color scheme. The kitchen was fully equipped with a gas stove, spacious breakfast bar and state-of-the-art appliances.

"This place is amazing," Iris said. "And here I was thinking that nothing could top your mansion in the hills."

"I come here for privacy. And space when the world gets a little too claustrophobic."

Dane walked over to the fridge and pulled out boneless, skinless chicken and veggies before getting the pasta and sauce from the pantry. Iris didn't wait to be told what to do, opening several cupboards until she found the chopping board and some knives. They worked in tandem, cutting vegetables and chicken.

Eventually Dane uncorked a bottle of white wine and set about starting the grill. She followed him outside and watched him heat it up. "I never took you for a chef," she said, leaning against the rail.

"I'm not one." Dane laughed. "I know enough to get by and keep myself fed."

"I would think you'd hire staff."

Dane shook his head and placed the chicken on the grill. "I don't like all those people under foot. As it is, I have Morgan, Jason and Whitney and that's more than enough. They're always trying to get me to have a stylist, but that's not me. The only time I take fashion advice like that is for an awards show."

"Like when you won the Golden Globe. You must have been so excited."

"I was actually quite inebriated," Dane replied. "They keep the drinks flowing at that party. I like it best because everyone's more relaxed than at any other awards show."

"I suppose you want to win a golden statuette."

"What actor worth their salt doesn't?" Dane replied with a grin. "And maybe my last film is the answer and maybe it's not, but I'll never stop trying to get the brass ring. But you—you've stopped trying to find that special someone, Iris. Why?"

Her brows bunched together. "How did we segue from your career to my love life?"

"Because I want to learn more about you," Dane responded, turning the chicken over on the grill.

"I thought we were going to keep this about Jayden?"

"We are," Dane said, placing the tongs down on the grill's counter. He turned and looked into her eyes. "But there's something going on between us, Iris. And I want to explore it."

"E-explore it?" Her pulse quickened and the breath caught in her throat. His words had been spoken quietly, but the deep timbre of his voice could not be mistaken. She saw something in his dark, long-lashed eyes that made it impossible to tear herself away.

"That's right. I can't wait to have you in my arms again, so you can come apart."

Iris swallowed. "I'm going inside to check on the pasta." She knew she was being a chicken, but Dane's hungry gaze was making her overheat. After testing the pasta to ensure it was al dente, she busied herself in the kitchen by adding the vegetables to the cream sauce and taking out place settings for dinner. She was avoiding going outside and they both knew it.

Dane wasn't just any man—he was sophisticated,

charming, skilled and, she was sure, very experienced in the bedroom. She wasn't a virgin, but it had been a long time since she'd been intimate with a man.

She reminded herself she wasn't sleeping with him, no matter what.

Dane returned to the kitchen several minutes later carrying the platter of grilled chicken. Iris had finished making the pasta, but it wasn't food that he was hungry for.

The jeans Iris was wearing skimmed her tush and made her waist look slender. And he liked her tank top and plaid shirt because they hugged her curves in all the right places. He was eager to explore what was underneath. He'd had only a taste of those delicious buds. Now he wanted the whole meal.

"Smells delicious," she commented. "The pasta and vegetables are ready."

"Hmm…"

"Are you listening to me, Dane, or ignoring me like your son does?" Iris said as she tossed the chicken in with the pasta, veggies and sauce.

Dane chuckled. "Does Jayden tune you out at times?"

"Sometimes when he doesn't like what I'm saying."

"Oh, I like everything you're saying," Dane countered, and watched Iris scurry to the other side of the counter.

"I thought you were starved. I know I am. I was on pins and needles waiting for the results to come in." Iris leaned over so Dane could scoop a healthy portion of the chicken and pasta primavera onto her plate. Then he dished some out for himself and they walked over to the dining room to eat their meal.

"What did you want the answer to be?" Dane said. "Were you hoping it wasn't true?"

Iris took a forkful of pasta and didn't answer right away. "When I first found out there could be a chance, I was angry at you for keeping it from me, but the more I thought about it, the more I realized it would be a good thing for Jayden. Not just because you're his donor match, but because of all the things I hadn't taken account when I decided to have him. About Jayden *needing* a father." She reached for her wine and took a sip.

Dane nodded. "Thank you. It means a lot to hear you say that. I thought you might resent my role in Jayden's life."

"No, I'll champion it, because I want what's best for him, even if it isn't convenient for me." She continued tucking into her meal, avoiding his gaze.

"I understand. Being part of my world has its challenges. And if we go public and I acknowledge him as my son, the media frenzy will whip up around you. Are you sure you can handle it?"

"Do I have a choice?"

"You do," Dane said. "If you want me to, I'll deny I'm his father." He would do anything to protect his son and the woman he was coming to care for.

"I wouldn't do that to you or Jayden," Iris replied. "He needs you."

"Do you need me?" He took in how she was sitting too far away from him, and he wanted her closer, much closer.

"I need to get home," Iris said, wiping her mouth with a napkin and abruptly standing up. "It's late and my sister is watching Jayden. The driver Morgan sent for me has been kind enough to wait outside."

He glanced down at her plate. She'd eaten about half her meal even though he knew she was enjoying it. She was running away like she always did.

She made it as far as the foyer before he caught up and stopped her. "Iris—"

She tilted her head, barely acknowledging him. "Good night, Dane." Her voice was low and faint. She started forward, but he put his hand on her shoulder, stopping her. She turned and he moved closer, allowing his hand to slide from her shoulder and fasten onto her arm. He felt her muscles tense as he drew her toward him. Time seemed to stop, and it was nothing but him and Iris.

Slowly, his mouth covered hers. She tasted like nectar sweeter than honey. She gave herself over to this moment of bliss and Dane took it, moving his lips over hers ever so softly and slowly. Dane kept his response measured. When he lifted his head, he said, "Stay with me tonight, Iris. I promise you, I won't hurt you."

She shook her head. "You don't understand—"

He didn't let her get another word out. Instead, he grazed his lips along the beautiful caramel skin of her neck and collarbone. Then with featherlight touches, he skimmed the curve of her breasts and felt them swell at his touch. He couldn't wait to touch his lips and finger-tips to those stiff peaks until she released her husky cries like before. "Whatever it is, baby," he whispered, "what-ever your fears, I promise you, we'll go as slow or as fast as you want."

He sensed her hesitation. Slipping his hand around the nape of her neck and cradling her head, he kissed her again, deeper this time. He wanted to make her wild with desire for him, to tantalize her with the promise of the sensual pleasure that awaited them.

And he did. Her arms slipped around him instantly, her lithe body, melting and twisting, pressing against him.

"Yes," she murmured. It was the sweetest word he'd ever heard. Not wanting to waste another moment, he lifted Iris into his arms and carried her upstairs to the master bed-room.

He set her down on his bed, cast aside the multitude of pillows to the floor and tugged her to him. Then he ran his hand from her neck to flank, urging her legs to open up to him. Careful not to box her in in case she decided to run for the hills, he slid his fingers through her hair, tilting her head until she could meet his kiss. Her entire body shivered, but instead of running, she moved closer, settling herself against him, causing a delicious friction against his hard erection. Oh, they were going to have a lot of fun tonight.

"I want you so much, Iris," he murmured. "Tell me you want me too." Because he couldn't wait to peel the clothes from her and rip his own off.

Her answer was to return his kiss, increasing the depth and pressure with her lips and tongue. Dane could feel her blossoming like a flower given water.

"I want you too," she moaned.

Iris couldn't believe this was happening. Dane had taken over her fantasies almost from the moment they'd met, but all along she'd pushed them aside. Now she was allowing this to happen. Although she was fearful of what Dane would find, perhaps it wouldn't be so bad with the lights off and the moonlight streaming in. Maybe…

He must have sensed her pulling away because he intensified the kiss, teasing and tracing her lips before plundering deep again. Her tongue sought his and she reveled in the heat between them. Her body was awash with sensation and she was mindless with delight. She'd never expected to feel this way, let alone with someone like Dane.

All inner protestations fell silent as she gripped his shoulders, pressing her body against his muscled chest and powerful thighs. He tugged the shirt down her shoulders and arms, revealing the cami she wore underneath. With his gaze on her, he cupped her breasts, grazing his thumbs over the peaks. Iris shuddered.

"You like that?" he asked, and when she nodded jerkily, he reached between them to pull the cami swiftly over her head, leaving her breasts bare to his gaze. She knew her breasts were small, but Dane didn't seem to care. He went lower, and Iris arched off the mattress when his mouth closed over her breast. She gripped his head, because she wanted to anchor him in place as he brought her dormant nerves to life.

He moved over to the other breast. His tongue swirled around her nipple while his mouth created a vacuum, sucking her in harder and harder. Iris felt herself tighten down below, but then he was moving past her breasts, placing lazy kisses on her stomach and teasing her navel as he went farther still. When he came to her jeans, he easily unzipped them and began sliding them down her legs. That was when Iris halted his hands.

"What's wrong?" Dane asked.

"I—I..." Iris faltered. How did she tell Dane she was damaged goods? That she wasn't like any of the beautiful starlets he'd been with? She didn't have to. Her jeans were already to her knees and Dane was looking down at the scarred, mangled flesh of her thighs. He glanced up at her with questions in his eyes she couldn't answer.

Then he finished removing her jeans. And instead of expressing disgust, Dane came closer. "I don't know what happened, Iris," he whispered, palming her face, "but I understand why you were nervous. You don't have to be. I think you're beautiful."

"You don't have to say that, Dane. You know the truth now."

"I know you're the sexiest woman I've ever had the pleasure to have in my bed. And I know that I've been thinking about you day and night."

"You have?"

He grinned devilishly "Will you let me love you tonight, Iris?"

She merely nodded, afraid to speak. She feasted her eyes on Dane as he shrugged out of his own clothes and joined her on the bed. That was when the fun began. Their bodies came together, skin on skin, and it felt so intensely intimate. But it was okay because all she saw in Dane's eyes were lust and hunger. A hunger for her.

So when he returned to where he'd left off and nudged her thighs apart, Iris was nervous. She nearly bolted off the bed when she felt his warm breath near her center and when he kissed her intimately, she let out a long moan. He explored her with his tongue and then added his fingers to her core, teasing and stroking, rubbing her slick heat. His intensity increased and Iris heard a low moan and realized it was her.

Her thighs shook and she planted her feet on the mattress, but his tongue and fingers continued penetrating her. "Dane…" she sobbed. Her back arched off the bed as a powerful orgasm roared through her. Dazed, she collapsed backward on the bed.

Dane coaxed every last spasm from Iris until she was flushed and bathed in a light sheen of sweat. Never had any other woman tasted so good. He slid up her body and they kissed again. It was deep and heady, and this time Iris didn't hold anything back. She was an active participant. Her hands drifted to his shoulders and then skimmed his back and hips. He liked that she was touching him and getting over her fear of intimacy.

Dane was curious about her injuries, but he wasn't going to let that stop him from making love to her. And when Iris moved her hand from his hip to curl her fingers around his pulsing arousal, he let out a hiss of air between his teeth. Then she took one pebbled nipple into her mouth, all the while stroking his length. He was bewitched; his breath left his mouth with a whoosh and his head dropped back on the bed.

Iris wasn't done. She climbed over him and had her

way with him. He wasn't surprised when he felt her warm mouth teasing the tip of him. With gentle licks and flicks of her tongue, she whipped him into a frenzy, so by the time her mouth closed completely over him, Dane bucked. But Iris held him down with her palms, all the while working magic with her mouth. Now a sheen of sweat covered his brow and he wanted, no, *needed* to be inside her.

Flipping Iris onto her back, Dane took over. He slid his finger inside her core. "You're ready for me, sweetheart," he said. As she closed her eyes, he reached for the drawer by his bed, grabbed a foil packet, ripped it open and sheathed himself. Then slowly, he slid inside her, but she was very tight. Dane sensed it had been a while and he gave her time to accommodate him. He brushed a tendril of hair from her forehead and looked down at her. "You okay?"

Her big brown eyes looked up at him and the trust there was a gift. "Yes."

"Good, because I don't want you to have any regrets."

"I won't."

Only when she began to wiggle her hips and relax into him did Dane begin to move. He slid in deeper, all the way in, and it felt sublime to finally make love to Iris. She put her arms around his taut shoulders, bringing him in closer.

"Please," she whimpered, clearly needing more.

So he drove deeper and she let out a moan, then another when he wrapped her calf around his thigh, pushing in farther, opening her up to him. Then he slowly began thrusting, setting a rhythm while their mouths fused, tongues twisting and dancing in a frenzy of need. Her inner muscles clenched around him and she clutched at him, her fingers digging into his back.

"Yes, yes…" she panted. He changed the pace to rapid thrusts and Iris met him stroke for stroke. When she cried out, it was a glorious sound that sent him crashing into the atmosphere as his body shuddered above hers.

* * *

A half hour later, Iris was feeling wonderful and more confident. Dane lay beside her, sprawled across the bed, asleep. They'd just made love and her mind and heart were full. Dane hadn't cared about her condition. He'd been gentle when he needed to be and eager when she'd wanted more. Iris hadn't thought it was possible she would ever find someone who could look past the physical. Dane Stewart could have any woman in America, but he'd *chosen* to be with her. It was a heady feeling.

But she mustn't forget herself. She glanced down at him. A real relationship with this man was unlikely but she could enjoy the moment. Tiptoeing from the bed, she found her jeans and retrieved her smartphone. Glancing around the room, Iris saw Dane's T-shirt and swiftly pulled it over her head and then went into the master bath to place a call to her sister. She wanted to check in on Jayden and make sure he'd had a good night.

Shelly answered on the first ring. "Iris? Are you okay? I was beginning to worry. You left hours ago."

"I'm sorry," she said. "I didn't mean to make you worry. I'm at Dane's."

"How did he take the news?"

Iris's mouth curved into a smile at the question. "He's excited to be Jayden's father, but understandably he was a little shook up by the weight of the responsibility falling onto his shoulders."

"I'm glad to hear it. When are you coming home?"

"I'm, uh, I'm…" Iris stuttered, trying to find the right words.

"Did something happen between you and Dane?"

"What are you talking about?" Iris's voice rose.

"Omigod, you're getting busy with Dane, aren't you?" Shelly didn't wait for a response. "Don't bother trying to deny it. It explains why we didn't hear from you."

"I can come home."

"I wouldn't," Shelly replied. "Enjoy him tonight, but I want all the details later."

Iris chuckled. "All right. Thank you, Shelly." She ended the call and opened the door only to find Dane standing buck naked in the doorway. Iris swallowed hard. "Hey…"

"Hey…" Dane gave her a winning smile that captured many a young woman's heart on the movie screen. "What are you doing in here? I reached for you and you weren't there."

Iris got a kick Dane was still thinking about her and not showing her the nearest exit. "I called my sister to check in on Jayden."

Dane sighed. "Of course you did because that's what mothers do. I should have been thinking about that, instead of keeping you away from him all night."

Iris could see the self-recrimination in his eyes and stepped forward, wrapping her arms around his waist. "Don't beat yourself up, Dane. I've had years of practice putting Jayden's needs before my own. You'll get used to it."

"I have a lot of catching up to do," Dane said. "How's our son?"

Our son.

Iris still couldn't believe those words. They shared a child together. "He's already in bed, so I didn't get to tell him good-night, but he's fine."

"Good." Dane walked her backward to the bed and they both came tumbling down onto the mattress. His hands framed her face as he looked into her eyes. "When do you think you'll tell him about me? I'd like to be there when you do."

"Tomorrow."

Dane nodded, and Iris could see he was worrying about Jayden's reaction. "Don't fret," Iris stated. "When I told Jayden there was a possibility you could be his father, he took it well. All we can do is be honest with him and how we intend to move forward."

"And how *do* we intend on going forward?" Dane asked.

Iris surprised herself when she circled her arm around his neck and brought his mouth back down to hers. "How about we think on that tomorrow?"

Ten

The next morning Dane didn't want to get up. He and Iris were in a safe cocoon as long as they were in bed, but as soon as they left, the real world would intrude on the precious time they'd shared together. They'd made love two more times last night and Iris had surprised him with her eagerness and utter abandon. There was nothing she wouldn't do for him or let him do to her. He'd been with lots of women over the course of his life. Since he was in his teens, his easy charm had made him a magnet for members of the opposite sex. But no one made his libido soar like sweet Iris Turner.

When she'd straddled him last night, he'd held on to her bottom, allowing her to rock against him. As she'd taken her own satisfaction, a low growl had escaped his lips. Every emotion had felt heightened. And when her mewls of pleasure turned into cries, he'd pumped upward to meet her, taking them both to a place Dane had never found before.

And now, knowing they shared a child together seemed

only to further cement the growing feelings Dane felt for Iris. And Jayden had stolen his heart from the very first moment he'd seen him on television. Dane was looking forward to getting to know his son even though he'd sprung from very unusual circumstances.

He knew Jason, Whitney, Morgan and any number of people on his team were probably trying to reach him. But right now, all Dane wanted to do was be a man and a father.

Iris stirred from sleep and rubbed her hands over her eyes. She glanced up at him and blushed furiously. Was she remembering how many times he'd made her come and scream out his name?

"Good morning."

"Good morning. What time is it?" She sat up and reached for the duvet to cover herself.

"A little after eight."

"I should go." She made to move, but Dane halted her.

"Stay with me for the day. Then we'll tell Jayden together."

"Dane, there's no way we can go out together and not get caught. We tried that before and everyone knows you," Iris said. "And hell, with every media outlet running the story, they recognize me now too."

"Okay, you have a point, but don't you want to live a little?" If there was one thing he hated about being a celebrity it was being boxed in. "I want to spend the day with you and walk around like everyone else for as long as we can. And we can keep security nearby. How about it? Are you willing to walk on the wild side with me?"

"All right, let's do it."

Iris was glad she'd allowed Dane to convince her to escape the confines of his beach pad—even after an incredible shower together when Dane had gotten down on his knees and spread her thighs to pleasure her. Iris still colored thinking about the experience. Although she'd loved the morning and night they'd shared, it would be nice to get out together and have some fun. And that was exactly what they did.

Since she had no other clothes, Dane had loaned her a T-shirt that was huge on her. Iris had knotted it around her waist, showing off a little skin. Dane's eyes had gleamed with lust and she'd had to shoo him outside before they ended up horizontal again. Eventually, they made their way out of the beach house with Iris in a wig and Dane in a baseball hat and fake beard from one of his movies.

A dark SUV dropped them off near the beginning of the Venice Beach boardwalk. They held hands as they meandered the streets. Iris had a blast people watching. It was an eclectic mix, from mimes to musicians to jugglers. She loved the way the saxophonist played some old-school Kenny G and the way the street performers did some B-boy tricks. Along the way, she and Dane stopped for a hot dog and drifted into shops to look at the cool artwork on display. They even had their fortunes read. It had been very insightful: the woman had said big, life-altering changes were ahead for them.

That woman didn't know the half of it.

After leaving the fortune-teller, they found themselves in front of a bathing suit shop. Dane suggested they go in, but Iris hesitated. Why hadn't she discussed this last night? Because she hadn't wanted to. It had been different when it was just the two of them alone in bed. He'd made her feel invincible, but now that she was in public, it was a whole other story and her insecurities were kicking in big-time. She hated bathing suits because when she wore one, there was no way to hide her injuries. Anyone could see her scars.

"What about this?" A saleswoman came up holding a revealing high-cut one-piece, and Dane nodded in agreement. Maybe the models or actresses he dated would look great in it, but not her.

She shook her head.

"How about this one?" The salesclerk was trying to be helpful, but she was grating on Iris's nerves.

"Not my style." Iris stayed at the front of the store, fingering the wide-brimmed hats. She would need one to block out the sun and keep from getting freckles. If she stayed in the sun too much, she got a slew of them across her nose.

Dane sidled up beside her, holding the most revealing swimsuit yet. "I think you would look great in this one."

"Dane! Did you not see me last night?" Iris let out in a burst. "I would never wear this, or any of it." She motioned toward the racks of bathing suits and then rushed out the store.

He met her outside. "C'mon." He pulled her away from the shop toward the Hotel Erwin, which was a stone's throw away.

Iris was quiet as they went up to the rooftop lounge and settled onto a comfortable cushioned divan underneath an umbrella, a beautiful view of the Pacific stretching out endlessly in front of them. After a few minutes of silence, Dane finally ventured to bring up what occurred at the shop.

"I'm sorry," he said, hanging his head low.

"Why? It's not your problem," Iris responded bitterly. "It's mine."

Dane studied her and when she didn't say anything else, he asked, "Are you ready to share what happened with me?"

Iris knew she'd been unfair, but it was how she felt. "I'm sorry."

"For what?"

"Sniping at you."

"You had every right. It was incredibly insensitive of me to take you into a place like that. It's just that I don't see your scars, Iris. I only see you. Call me foolish or tell me I have it bad, but it's the truth."

His honest and sincere apology took the wind out of Iris's sails. "I'm hypersensitive about my body. You saw how I ran away the moment things started heating up between us."

"But I wore you down," he said with a sly grin.

"You didn't have to try very hard. I wanted you, Dane. I still do. But you have to understand I'm never going to be comfortable showing off the lower half of my body. The car accident eight years ago changed me. It transformed my life and all the hopes I had for the future. It's why I did something as drastic as artificial insemination."

"Go on," he prompted.

"I'd been dating Mario. Your typical bad boy musician who liked to drink and have fun. My parents hated him, which of course only made him more appealing. So I broke curfew and did all the stupid things a young girl in love does. Until one day that bad boy drank and drove and wrapped his Ford Mustang around a tree with me in it."

"But you survived."

"Did I?" Iris asked. "I suppose, but I took the brunt of the impact while Mario walked away with only scratches. After the crash, the car caught fire, causing severe burns to my arms and thighs."

"But your arms…" He glanced down at them.

"I know you're thinking, 'How can that be?' Well, I endured countless reconstructive surgeries hoping to be my old self again. They worked on my arms. But after two years and many painful procedures, I just had to accept it—I was no longer the pretty girl I'd once been."

"Like hell you aren't! You're beautiful, Iris. Inside and *out*."

"Thank you for saying that, but I know what I see when

I look in the mirror. And it's taken me a long time to accept who I am. Do I think I'm a monster anymore? No."

"Why would you say such a thing?"

"Because when I tried dating, a man told me I was, and after that I couldn't risk putting myself through rejection again. Until you came along."

Dane reached for her then, pulling her into a hungry, possessive yet masterful kiss, sending white-hot bolts of desire shooting through her. Without a second thought to where they were, she responded, kissing him back.

A discreet cough from a nearby waiter alerted them to the fact they were still in public. She looked up to see a man wearing a button-down shirt standing nearby. "Today was lovely, really," Iris said, "but—" she glanced down at her watch "—it's time Jayden learned the truth."

"You're right. It's time."

Dane was in a foul mood. After spending a leisurely day with Iris, enjoying all that Venice Beach had to offer and winding down on the rooftop lounge, they'd come outside only to be bombarded by questions from the press. Their day of being inconspicuous was over and now reporters were in full attack mode as Dane and Iris ducked into the SUV waiting at the curb. His security team had gotten wind of the crowd forming outside and ensured the vehicle was ready.

He didn't answer any of the questions. *Are you and Iris now a couple? When's the wedding?* And most importantly: *Are you Jayden's father?* He and Iris owed it to their son to hear the truth from them, not some muckraker.

The drive was slow, but eventually they made it to Jayden's school. Iris went inside without Dane because she didn't want the fanfare. As if that were possible. He'd already caught a handful of photographers lurking nearby.

Iris appeared several minutes later with Jayden at her

side. He was dressed in khaki pants and a plaid button-down shirt and carrying a book bag. He looked like a little man.

One of Dane's security team opened the SUV door and Jayden's brow furrowed because he was surprised to see him. "Mr. Stewart?"

"Hi, Jayden." Dane scooted over on the back seat to make room for them. "I hope it's okay I came?"

Jayden nodded. "I suppose. It's just that kids at school are saying you're my daddy and if they see you picking me up from school, they'll think it's true."

Dane looked to Iris for guidance because he was tongue-tied. He was thankful when she stepped in. "How about we talk about it when we get home? Tell us about your day."

When the SUV stopped in front of Iris's house a half hour later, reporters swarmed the vehicle. Jayden glanced at his mother and then at Dane. "Why do all these people keep coming to our house?"

"We'll explain everything inside," Iris said.

As soon as the doors opened, the bodyguards were right there, preventing cameras and microphones from being shoved in their faces. Iris and Jayden disembarked first with Dane following suit. It was a melee, but eventually they made it inside.

Dane leaned against the door and watched Iris help Jayden with his belongings. He followed them into the small living room and waited. Standing by the mantel, he felt like a wood statue because he didn't know what to do. How was he supposed to tell a six-year-old boy he was his father?

"Come here, baby," Iris said, lowering herself to the sofa. "Sit with me." She patted the seat beside her and Jayden came over and sat down.

Jayden's eyes grew large. "Have I done something wrong?"

"No, no, of course not," Iris smiled. "You've been a good

boy and I've proud of you for giving your lunch money to help a friend. Remember that test we took the day before yesterday?"

He nodded.

"We got the results back." Iris glanced over at Dane. "And well, the kids at school are right, honey. The tests showed that Mr. Stewart... Well... He's your father, Jayden."

Jayden looked at Dane standing there. "You're my daddy?"

A lump formed in Dane's throat and he forced himself to sit down and scoot over next to Jayden. "Yes, I'm your father." Dane finally said the words aloud to the most important person in his world other than Iris.

Jayden leaned toward him and swept his tiny arms around Dane's middle. Dane looked to Iris and saw tears swimming in her eyes, undoubtedly over Jayden's unexpected show of affection. He hugged Jayden as tight as he could. He'd never thought he would be accepted with open arms by the child, and it meant the world to Dane.

"I've always wanted a daddy," Jayden said. "I thought I wasn't normal like other kids."

Dane pulled back from Jayden slightly, but didn't completely let go. "You are normal. You may not have been conceived like other boys and girls, but there's nothing wrong with you. Don't ever let anyone make you feel less than." While it was true he was saying the words to his son, he hoped Jayden's mother would hear them too.

"You're squeezing me too hard," Jayden managed to eke out before Dane released him. "What does it mean?"

"It means I'm going to be a part of your life. You'll be seeing a lot of me."

"Are you coming to live here with us?" Jayden asked. "Are we going to live with you because you're rich?" He turned to his mother.

"It's not quite like that, Jayden," Iris responded.

"I don't understand. Other mommies and daddies live together."

"And you know some of them don't," Iris replied. "Like your friend Amy. Her parents share custody. She spends half her time with her mom and half her time with her dad."

Jayden frowned. "But I don't want to spend half my time with both of you. I thought you liked each other. You were kissing."

Iris chuckled. "I know it's confusing, honey. And yes, your dad—" she used the phrase for the first time and Dane's heart turned over in his chest "—and I do like each other, but we're still getting to know each other."

"So you could get married?" Jayden asked.

Dane interrupted his barrage of questions. "Not so fast, sport. I know you're excited and I am too, but your mom's right. We have to spend time with one another. I have to find out your likes and dislikes."

"That's easy. I don't like veggies and I like the color blue," Jayden answered.

Dane couldn't resist laughing at his son's forthrightness. "That's good to know, but your mom probably needs to get dinner ready and you probably have some homework."

"Not for much longer," Jayden said. "Once I get the transplant, I'll be out of school."

"That's definitely a plus. Iris, will you walk me out?" Dane stood up. "I'll be back soon, Jayden, and we can talk as much as you like."

Iris stayed behind with Jayden for a moment and then met Dane at the door in the foyer. "That went better than expected."

Dane nodded. "I thought it was going to be a lot harder, but he was so accepting." He felt his heart seize up in his chest. "I'm, I'm…"

"It's okay." This time it was Iris's turn to hug Dane.

Dane leaned and brushed his lips across hers. "I enjoyed last night and today, but it's only going to get crazier once I officially announce Jayden is my son. Are you sure I can't convince you to come stay with me for a while?"

Iris shook her head. "This is Jayden's home. We won't be run out. Eventually, they'll get tired of the story and move on."

"But they'll be a nuisance."

"I know. And we'll deal with it."

"Thank you for including me in that 'we,'" Dane responded. With another kiss on her forehead, he opened the door and let his security guards and the crowd swallow him, taking him away from his son and the woman he was falling for.

Eleven

"So are you finally ready to talk strategy or is your head still in the clouds after blowing off me and Whitney?" Jason asked Dane later that evening when Dane summoned him to the Hollywood Hills mansion.

"Yeah, I am," Dane responded evenly, ignoring Jason's jibe.

"Good. Because while you were spending the day gallivanting in Venice Beach with your new ladylove, you were being crucified in the media," Whitney scolded. They were all sitting around the kitchen table while Morgan ordered some takeout.

"What are they saying about me now?" Dane asked. He was completely bored by the media's misrepresentation of the entire situation.

"They are calling you reckless," Whitney informed him, "since you willfully donated your sperm without a thought to the consequences."

"Untrue," Dane stated. "As I recall, donations help infertile and same-sex couples, so I would beg to differ."

"Some outlets are stating this was all an elaborate media ruse."

"So what—I could vilify myself and put my sick child and his mother in front of a national audience? I don't think so."

Whitney held up her hands. "Don't shoot the messenger. I'm merely letting you know what people are saying so we can be prepared should you choose to make a statement."

"I plan on acknowledging Jayden Turner as my son," Dane stated. This was not up for discussion or debate.

"You realize your image as America's favorite heart-throb is toast?" Jason responded.

"I will *not* turn my back on my son in order to maintain people's false expectations or some fantasy they have about me. My boy is sick and I don't know how much time I could have with him. What if this bone marrow transplant doesn't work? I could lose him when I've only just found him." Dane jumped from his seat and walked out onto the terrace. The night was dark and there were no stars in the sky.

"We're not going to think like that," Morgan said, coming outside and handing Dane a beer. "He's going to get better because you've got great genes."

Dane smiled at his assistant. "Thanks, Morgan." Over the last year, he'd found her to be loyal and reliable.

"Dinner will be here in a half hour. I'm going to head out, unless you need me?"

"No, I'm good, Morgan. Have a good evening." Dane returned to the kitchen to find Jason and Whitney staring at him.

"What?"

"I have never seen you like this before," Jason said. "You truly love that kid."

"It's true. I hardly know him, but he's my son."

"Then we release a statement of how overjoyed you are at your newfound fatherhood," Whitney said. "And that you intend to be a fully involved parent, sharing duties with Jayden's mother, whom you admire for taking care of your son during these formative years. You're excited to be a 100 percent match with Jayden, and you'll be taking time off to spend time with Jayden and prepare him and yourself for the transplant."

"Time off?" Jason inquired. "We're getting offers left and right for Dane. We can't take our foot off the pedal."

"You don't honestly expect me to be off shooting a movie while my son is fighting for his life," Dane said.

"But his mother is here. She's been taking care of him this entire time without any help from you."

"Jason, are you daft?" Whitney asked. "I know this is a shock to us all but there's no way I can spin it if Dane continues to be absent from his son's life. It would do more harm than good. Now here's the plan. We do an interview with your favorite anchor. And…" Her voice trailed off before resuming excitedly. "We could even film your journey of becoming a transplant donor to help more people register. What do you think?"

Dane nodded. "Now you've got your thinking cap on, Whitney. I love it. Let's do it."

Whitney beamed with pride. "Thank you. I'll get right on this." She rose to her feet. "We'll talk tomorrow."

After she'd gone, Dane and Jason sipped their beers. Dane sensed his manager had something on his mind. "What's up?"

"Don't you think you're moving too fast? You hardly know this woman and now you're so entrenched in her life—"

"My son's life."

"Iris's too. Don't act like there's not something going on between you two. I know she spent the night with you last night."

Dane glared at him. "And how the hell do you know that?"

"Because I went to your beach pad and security refused to let me in. Said you had company and were not to be disturbed."

"I'll have to talk to them about being more discreet with my business."

"They didn't tell me who it was. They didn't have to. You have besotted fool all over your face. The pictures of the two of you today at the Hotel Erwin were all over social media. You don't need to be a genius to figure it out."

"Are you always this cynical, Jason?"

"I'm only looking out for your best interests."

"Then I would suggest you tread lightly, Underwood," Dane responded. Because there was no way Jason or anyone else would stand between him and his son. Or between him and Iris, for that matter. Speaking of, even though it had been only a few hours since he'd left them, it was time he checked in.

"How's this going to work?"

"Are you going to share custody with him? You get the weekdays, he gets the weekends?"

"Or just visitation rights and summer break?"

Iris covered her ears. She was having Sunday brunch with her family and they were firing questions at her left and right. She didn't have all the answers. She was still wrapping her brain around the fact that Dane Stewart was Jayden's father. And she'd had the best sex of her life with the man.

Dane had made a point of calling Jayden every night

since they found out the truth last week. And just two days ago, Dane had come to Jayden's pretreatment. Jayden had lit up when he saw his father.

"Listen, guys," Iris said, taking a deep breath. "I don't know what's going to happen. Dane and I are taking it one day at time."

"With the statement and the televised interview coming up, Dane seems to be taking steps to solidify his position," her father countered. "You have to protect yourself, sugarplum."

"Dane would never do anything to harm Jayden."

"Or you?" her mother ventured. "I can see the stars in your eyes, Iris. Your father and I just want you to be careful."

"I need some air." Iris left them in the dining room. They were suffocating her with all their questions.

"Are you okay, sis?" Shelly asked from behind her.

"Yeah."

"I know they came on a bit strong, but they love you. As do I."

"I understand that, but is it so wrong for me to believe in someone again? To count on someone besides myself and my family to care for Jayden? You haven't seen the two of them together. They complement each other. Dane has a way with Jayden I haven't seen before and I want that for my son."

"No matter the cost to you?"

"What do you mean?"

Shelly shrugged. "I'm glad Dane has broken through the barrier you've had around yourself for years. That he sees the beautiful, sexy woman that you are. But I'm also urging you to be careful. He's an actor. A superstar, for heaven's sake."

"And I can't compete?"

Shelly shook her head. "No, but a lot of women throw

themselves at him. There's always going to be temptation for a guy like him. Guard your heart."

Tears slowly made their way down Iris's cheeks. "It's too late, Shelly. I'm already in love with him."

"Oh, Iris."

"Please don't pity me, okay? His feelings may not be as strong as mine yet, but I believe he cares for me."

"Then bring him here to Jayden's birthday party. Let us meet him and see for ourselves the kind of man he is."

"You know the kind of man he is. He was the man who agreed to a transplant before he knew Jayden was his. If nothing else, trust that."

"I will."

"Jayden's birthday is coming up," Iris told Dane in bed the next evening at her home. He'd come over after his interview with Robin Roberts from *Good Morning America*. He'd chosen Robin because she'd been in Jayden's shoes with her transplant and understood why he wouldn't want to leave Jayden's side. She'd flown to Los Angeles for the interview. It had gone surprisingly well.

With the questions planned in advance, Dane had spoken candidly about his sperm donation, the reason for joining the bone marrow registry and finally his joy at discovering that not only was he a match for Jayden but Jayden was his son. Dane proudly claimed Jayden and welcomed him into the Stewart family.

The curveball came when Robin asked him about his relationship with Iris. He'd answered honestly, speaking of his respect and admiration for the mother of his child, but Robin hadn't taken the pat answer. She'd asked him about the images of them kissing and their day out in Venice Beach. Dane didn't want to attract more scrutiny to Iris, so he'd stated they were exploring a relationship.

Immediately after the interview, his cell phone had

blown up with Tweets, IMs and Instagram pics of women's devastation because he'd finally found love. Jason texted him angry-face emojis while Whitney stood enthusiastically behind the cameras giving him the thumbs-up signal. He was increasingly glad he'd hired her.

And now tonight, he and Iris were celebrating his media victory in the best way he knew possible. In her bed.

"Are you throwing a party?" Dane asked, gently caressing her cheek with his hand. "Do you think he'll be up for it?"

Jayden had started the chemo treatments and become increasingly lethargic. Dr. Lee had suggested he not return to school due to increased risk of infection. Despite the chemo and losing his hair, somehow his son still managed to smile each day. Jayden was a fighter. He took after his mother.

"Yes. Jayden has been looking forward to it. I'd hate to cancel. Plus, I already have something in the works, just family and friends."

Dane wanted to suggest inviting his family or at the very least his siblings, but he didn't want to be pushy. Iris was allowing him to be a father to their little boy. He wanted her and Jayden to be comfortable with his presence before introducing the entire Stewart gang.

Or maybe not the entire gang. Lord knows his mother hadn't been happy when she'd found out. Although they weren't close, he had FaceTimed with her and his father to share the good news they were grandparents again. Nora Stewart had been horrified over how Jayden was conceived.

"You donated sperm?" she asked. *"Why would you do such a thing, when you could have asked us for money?"*

"Because I was determined to make it in LA on my own two feet."

"Well, now you're saddled with a baby mama," his mother retorted.

He was annoyed by her response, to say the least. Why had he even bothered informing her? "I don't feel that way, Nora. Iris is a wonderful woman and if you're ever fortunate enough to meet her you'll treat her with respect."

"Of course we will," his father chimed in. "You know, this now makes Jayden our oldest grandchild."

"I'm not old enough to be a grandmother and now I hear you made me one before my time," Nora bemoaned. "Since he's old enough to talk, let Jayden know he can call me Mimi, because I refuse to be called Grandma or Nana."

"Duly noted," Dane returned. "Anything else?"

"When can we meet him?" his father asked.

"Soon," Dane responded. "Soon."

"Earth to Dane." Iris cut into his thoughts and he caught her wrists as she waved her hands in the air before his eyes. "Have you heard a word I've said?"

"Words? Hmm…" He leaned in and dragged his lips along her shoulder to her neck. Then he closed his mouth over the tender flesh there and sucked. He was pleased when he heard her whoosh of breath, and moved from her neck to her jaw until he returned to kiss her lips. Her eyes became heavy lidded, and she closed them. She trusted him with her body, and he didn't waste time undressing her, quickly tugging her nightie over her head. For him, it was pretty easy: rip off the boxers and he was naked.

Iris's eyes widened and traveled south to the mighty swell of his arousal. He wanted her panting underneath him, so he pushed himself back on his heels, pulled down her panties and discarded them. Then he was moving her legs apart to position himself between them.

"Dane…" Those were the last words he heard as he lowered his head and used his tongue, mouth and fingers to bring Iris to the peak. He licked, tasted and nudged, over and over again, alternating speed and pressure until he felt her quicken and she raced to the edge. Only then did he sheath himself with a condom and slide home. It took only a few final strokes for them to shatter into a million pieces, crying out each other's name.

Twelve

"Iris, I want to thank you so much for inviting the Stewart clan to Jayden's birthday party," Fallon said when she, her husband and son, along with Ayden Stewart and his wife, arrived at the Turner family home the following Saturday. The party hadn't yet started; they were an hour early. After making the introductions to her parents and sister, they were all sitting on the veranda.

"I want Jayden to know Dane's side of the family and you're his aunt," Iris responded. She'd secretly gotten Fallon's info from Morgan and called his sister. Iris sensed Dane wanted to ask her to invite them, but was afraid of stepping on her toes. But that wasn't possible. Jayden could never have too much love.

And the Stewart family had brought it in abundance. It was supposed to be a small party, but they'd literally come with a delivery truck and unloaded box after box for Jayden. All his gifts were overflowing on the table in the backyard.

"What can I do to help?" Fallon asked when Iris rose to get them some refreshments.

Her mother and Shelly were already in the kitchen putting the finishing touches on the meal. Dane had ordered the birthday cake, which had been Jayden's only request. Dane had wanted to do something and she'd seen no reason not to let him. Morgan had brought the cake with her, telling Iris she was under strict orders to ensure the cake arrived in one piece. Iris had invited Morgan to stay for the festivities too.

"Not a thing," Iris replied. She looked at Fallon. Dane's sister could easily be a supermodel with her café au lait skin, hazel eyes and slender yet curvy body. While Iris had small breasts and narrow hips, Fallon had curves perfectly suited to her. She wore a wrap top and skinny jeans and looked like she hadn't seen a mop or a broom in her lifetime. "I want you to get to know your nephew. Plus you might want to keep an eye on your son— he's pulling out Mom's roses."

"Omigod!" Fallon jumped and rushed off to get Dylan, who was into everything. "Gage, help me… Please."

Gage was dreamy if you went for the tall, dark and handsome corporate type in trousers and a button-down shirt. Iris preferred Dane's rugged style. Gage wore his hair neatly cropped like he went to the barber weekly. His warm caramel-toned skin complemented his brandy-colored eyes. Eager to help his wife, Gage sprang from his chair and sprinted after Dylan.

Iris smiled. She remembered that age when Jayden was a Tasmanian devil and had to touch anything not bolted down. She was glad those years were behind them. She just hoped Jayden would be allowed to get the chance to grow up. A well of emotion surged through her and she could feel her eyes becoming misty.

"You okay?" a deep masculine voice asked from behind

her. Iris turned to find Dane's older brother, Ayden, standing by her side. He appeared equally amused as she to see sophisticated Fallon and Gage being bested in a running competition by a toddler.

"I'm fine, just a little nostalgic." Iris sniffed.

"Time goes by fast, doesn't it? It's hard to believe I only connected with Fallon and Dane nearly two years ago. It seems as if I've known them forever."

"Was it hard gaining a family so suddenly?" Iris wondered if Jayden would be overwhelmed or excited by the prospect of so many aunts and uncles.

Ayden cocked his head to one side. "Not really. I'd always known they existed, and was kind of jealous of them at first. But I know now that it wasn't quite roses and sunshine for them either."

"I appreciate your candor," Iris said. "Thank you."

"You're welcome. So when is my nephew getting here?" Ayden inquired, glancing around. "I'm eager to meet the little fella."

"Dane took him for a haircut and a new outfit. He wanted some father-son time alone. They should be here any minute. They'll both be surprised to see you."

Thirty minutes later, Dane couldn't believe his eyes when he saw his siblings and their spouses and children milling around in the Turners' backyard. He looked around until he found the person he wanted to thank—Iris. He'd had no idea when he stopped by Iris's earlier to pick up Jayden that she'd planned this.

The day hadn't started out great. Jayden hadn't wanted to go shopping, but once Dane told Jayden he could select his birthday outfit, his son had been thrilled. Jayden claimed his mother never let him wear what he wanted because it didn't match. They'd settled on jeans and a Puma T-shirt. Jayden was looking smart and hip. The most important thing for Dane was that Jayden was happy. It was why they'd kept the birthday party a secret from everyone except family and Morgan who was quickly becoming like a baby sister to him.

But when they left the store, the trouble started. They were mobbed by a large crowd eager to get their first look at Dane and his son together. The store manager had to usher them through the back door to leave and get back in time for the party.

"Jayden, c'mon. I want you to meet your aunt Fallon." Dane rushed over to his sister. She met him halfway, and he hugged her tight. He didn't realize how much he needed his family until they were here with him.

"It's okay," Fallon whispered so only he heard her. "Your big sister's here."

He squeezed her tightly one more time before letting her go. He shook Gage's hand, kissed his sister-in-law and gave his big brother a one-armed hug. "I can't believe you all kept this secret from me."

"Trust me, it wasn't easy," Gage said. "Every time Fallon talked to you I thought she was going to spill the beans."

"Hey, hey, I know how to keep a secret."

Dane crouched down to Jayden's height. "I'd like you to meet the other half of your family, Jayden. This is my sister, Fallon, and brother, Ayden. They're your aunt and uncle."

"Pleasure to meet you," Jayden said formally.

"And this is my husband, Gage." Fallon kneeled down, looking into Jayden's eyes as she spoke. "So I guess that makes him your uncle Gage and Ayden's wife, Maya, your aunt Maya and then there's Dylan running around here."

"That's a lot of names to remember." Jayden scrunched his face.

"It's not a test, Jayden," Dane said. "In time, you'll remember their names."

Jayden nodded. "Is that all my gifts over there?" He eyed the mound of wrapped presents sitting on the table.

"All for you, nephew," Ayden replied. "We couldn't come empty-handed."

"You guys are the best!" Jayden ran to the table.

Dane stood and watched Jayden shake each gift, trying to figure out what was inside. "He's awesome, isn't he?"

"It's hard to believe he's sick," Maya said quietly.

Dane glanced at his sister-in-law. "I know. You'll be able to tell as the afternoon progresses. He'll become more and more tired. He gets drained from doing normal activities."

"How long before he can get the transplant with your bone marrow?" Fallon inquired.

"A few months. He's going through the pretreatment chemo first to wipe out his immune system. Then he'll get the transplant and have to stay in the hospital for months to ensure he doesn't reject my bone marrow."

"I'm sorry Jayden has to go through this," Fallon commented.

"My son is strong." Dane glanced across the yard at Jayden. He'd seen their resemblance from the start, but as time went on, he'd seen a resilience in Jayden that reminded him of Iris.

Fallon smiled when her gaze connected with his. "Your son."

"Who's ready for some lunch?" Iris yelled from across the yard. "Come and get it!"

"Isn't she amazing?" Dane said aloud to no one in particular. Dane couldn't get enough of Iris. They'd made love twice this morning and he was still excited about being with her tonight. "I love that woman!" The words were out of his mouth before he realized he'd said them.

Dane glanced at his siblings and they were both looking back and forth at one another. He laughed nervously. "I didn't mean that how it sounded. It's just she's so thought-ful, bringing you all here."

"Sure, bro," Ayden said, patting him on the back. "That's exactly what you meant." He smirked as he walked off with Maya toward the picnic table laden with fried chicken, po-tato salad and a fruit-and-veggie tray. Gage scooped Dylan up in his arms and walked off, leaving Dane and Fallon alone.

"C'mon, sis." Dane stepped farther away from the group. "No need to give me that look. It was a slip of the tongue."

"Who are you fooling, Dane? Certainly not me, but maybe yourself. I saw the way you looked at Iris when you realized she'd pulled off this surprise for Jayden's birthday party. You were touched. *Deeply.*"

"I'm attending my son's birthday party for the first time. Of course I'm affected, Fallon. I never thought I was going to be a dad—parenthood wasn't in the cards. That was going to be something only you or Ayden did. But this, this came out of nowhere and blindsided me, but in a good way, ya know?"

Fallon nodded. "I do, so I'm going to give you a piece of sisterly advice and you can do with it as you like. Leave the past in the past. Mom and Dad don't have the perfect marriage. So what if they aren't madly in love? That doesn't mean true love can't exist. You can be happy, the three of you. You, Iris and Jayden, as a family. Don't rule it out."

She left him standing there, watching her as she walked away. Was she right? Was he projecting his misconceptions about love and marriage onto him and Iris? He'd thought he came to the table with a clean slate and they had only Iris's insecurities to face, but perhaps she wasn't the only one who needed to heal. He was afraid to admit to Fallon and maybe even to himself…that he was in love with Iris. It scared the living daylights out of him, because he'd never been in love. Until recently, he didn't even know what it was. All he had to go by was his parents' train wreck of a marriage. But seeing Fallon and Gage and Ayden and Maya gave him hope that love was worth the risk to his heart.

"I'm impressed," her father told Iris when she went into the kitchen to top off the beverages.

"With what?" Iris asked.

"Dane and his family. Considering he's famous and they're rich, they're down-to-earth people."

"I told you, Daddy."

"Yeah, you did, but I had reservations," he replied. "But seeing how Dane is with Jayden and how he looks at you has made me realize I misjudged him."

"How so?"

"He's an actor, Iris. I thought he was snowing you, but I can see he really does care for you both. And if I'm not mistaken, I'd say the young man has stars in his eyes when it comes to you."

"Oh, Daddy. There's probably something wrong with your eyesight."

"I know what I saw. I haven't seen you light up this way in years, baby girl." Her father stopped her from adding bottled waters to her tray. "I'm happy to see that spark in your eye. After the accident, you lost it, and I thought you'd never get it back. But Dane—he's the reason, isn't he?"

Iris shrugged off his question. She wasn't ready to talk about her tender feelings for Dane aloud to anyone, at least not yet. "Dane coming into our life has brought us so much joy, especially because Jayden has such a long road ahead."

"C'mon." Her father nodded his head toward the terrace. "Let's go make this a birthday Jayden will always remember."

"You go on." Iris handed her father the tray filled with drinks and watched as he left the room. "I'll be there in a minute."

Her father's words had reminded her of Jayden's illness. If he couldn't withstand the treatment or if the stem cells from Dane's bone marrow didn't take, this could be her last birthday with him. The sadness Iris had been keeping at bay washed over her, and she covered her mouth with her hand.

"Iris?"

Dane's voice brought her back to reality and she quickly brushed the tears away from her cheeks. Taking a deep breath, she turned around to face him.

"What's wrong?" Sensing her distress, Dane immediately came forward.

She sighed. "I was so happy and then it dawned on me, Jayden might not—"

Dane reached for her and grabbed her by the shoulders. "Don't say it, Iris. Don't even think it, okay? You have to stay positive. Jayden is *going* to pull through this."

"How can you be so sure?" The odds weren't in their favor. She would never forget when Dr. Lee had first shown her the graphs and charts of Jayden's life expectancy if he didn't get a transplant. It had been frightening.

"Because…he's a fighter like his mom and dad."

Iris couldn't resist a small smile forming on her mouth. "How is it you know exactly the right thing to say to keep me from being a Debbie Downer?"

"Because I have bucketloads of charm."

Iris chuckled and looped her arm through his. "You're so arrogant, but I adore you." She glanced up at Dane. She'd nearly said the *L* word but caught herself in time. They weren't in a place to have *that* particular conversation but it was coming. Sometime soon.

"Happy birthday to you,
Happy birthday to you,
Happy birthday, dear Jayden,
Happy birthday to you."

Jayden's blended family sang to him. Dane was so grateful Fallon and Ayden had made the trek to LA. Being here with Iris and her folks along with his made the moment more poignant, because Dane hadn't felt this way about family in a long time. Was he getting soft?

"Make a wish," Iris said.

Jayden closed his eyes and then blew out his birthday candles on the Transformers cake Dane ordered. Dane had made sure Morgan had found the best baker in all of Los Angeles because only the best would do for his boy.

Dane laughed when his nephew stuck his finger in the icing. "Dylan!" Fallon reprimanded him, but he didn't seem to care. He'd already gotten what he wanted and was licking his fingers.

"Are you ready for one of those?" Dane asked Ayden, who was a couple of feet away.

"Yeah." Ayden nodded. "I actually think I am."

Dane pulled him aside. "You know, it's a lot harder than it looks. I've been getting a crash course on fatherhood."

"I know, but I'll have the next six months to prepare."

Dane glanced up at his big brother. "Are you saying…?" He let the words trail off because the goofy grin on Ayden's face was a dead giveaway. "Have you told anyone yet?"

"Naw, man, you're the first. We were waiting until the second trimester, but Maya's nearly there and I've been dying to tell someone."

"Congratulations." Dane pulled Ayden toward him and they embraced. "I'm happy for you both."

"Thank you, thank you." Ayden glanced behind him and when he laid eyes on Maya his entire demeanor changed. Dane wondered if that was how he looked when Iris was around. "I'm a lucky man. I'm so thankful she came back to Austin. If it hadn't been for Maya coming home for her niece's baptism and her mother's cancer treatments, I may have never seen her again."

"How is her mother doing?"

"Thanks for asking. She's in remission," Ayden said. "It was touch and go there for a while, but she pulled through. It even brought Maya and her sister, Raven, closer."

"Adversity will do that," Dane responded. He glanced at his son, who was devouring a piece of the chocolate cake. Icing was all over his face, but he looked content.

"He'll be okay."

Dane looked up at Ayden. Though they'd reconnected two years ago, they hadn't seen each other much. Lately, however, their bond was becoming stronger. "Thanks, Ayden. I appreciate it."

"Before I forget to ask you… Your assistant, Morgan. Who is she?" Ayden inquired.

"A film school dropout who is working for me. Why?" Dane inquired.

Ayden shrugged. "I don't know. There's something familiar about her."

"I'm sorry to break up this bromance," Fallon called out as she said her goodbyes to the Turners, and Iris and made her way toward them, "but we're going to head home."

"Back to Austin?" Dane asked with a frown. "You just got here."

Fallon stroked his cheek. "And we'll be back. Now that we've met our nephew and Iris, you're going to be seeing a lot more of us. Maya tells me she has a doctor's appointment she can't miss tomorrow."

Dane smiled knowingly. "Of course. Thank you all for coming." He squeezed Fallon in a tight hug. "Gage." He shook his brother-in-law's hand. "Take care of my sister."

"Always," Gage responded.

When Maya came over to him to say goodbye, Dane hugged her close and whispered, "Congratulations."

"Ayden Stewart." Maya turned her full gaze on her husband. If it was possible for a grown man to tuck his tail between his legs and run, Ayden would have done it right then. He had guilty written all over his face. Maya smiled at Dane. "We'll see you again soon."

"Today was fantastic, Iris," Dane said once they'd put an exhausted Jayden to bed. On the way home, he'd talked incessantly about the party, all his gifts and his new aunties and uncles. He'd even taken a shine to Dylan, who'd followed him around like a puppy dog.

And they hadn't even had too much trouble with the paparazzi. When they'd arrived at Iris's, a few tabloid reporters had yelled happy birthday to Jayden, and one had asked if having Dane as his father was the best birthday gift. Dane wanted to deck him, but knew the best approach was not to ignore him and not feed into the mania.

Now Dane and Iris were going to bed. Dane had gotten rather used to spending the night over at Iris's. At first, they'd been worried about how Jayden would react. They needn't have bothered. When Dane had come out of the bathroom wearing his boxers one morning, Jayden merely said, "Hey, Daddy," and went back into his room. It was the first time he'd called him that and Dane had been overjoyed. Iris had still worried about the impact on Jayden. But over bowls of cereal later that morning Jayden had told her he liked having Dane around, saying he felt safe. And that was that. Dane began staying over more often.

"You really enjoyed it?" she asked, smoothing hand cream on after brushing her teeth and removing her makeup.

"Couldn't you tell?" Dane asked, pulling the covers back. "I was touched you included my family in Jayden's birthday celebration. And better yet, you managed to keep it a surprise from me. *You and Fallon.*"

Iris rubbed her hands together. "We were great coconspirators."

"Yeah, you were," Dane said. His fingers clamped down on her arm and hauled her down onto the bed with him. He'd already undressed to his boxers, which he didn't intend to keep on for long. He lowered his head and she accepted his invitation readily, allowing his seeking tongue entry into her mouth. Her kiss gave him life when for years he'd been a wasteland. Unfeeling, emotionless, not allowing another person in. But Iris changed all that. She gave him hope and the promise of so much more.

His hands skimmed the nightie she wore. It was a piece he'd bought for her after seeing it in a shop on Rodeo Drive. He'd thought it was beautiful and delicate, just like Iris, and purchased it. When he'd presented it, Dane loved how Iris had blushed like a schoolgirl. It was one of the many endearing things he loved about her. And so he continued his languid exploration of her mouth while his hands eased over her curves. He didn't care about the scars. Did he know they were there? Yes, but he no longer saw them. *Only Iris.*

When he lowered the strap of her nightie and placed his mouth over one breast, she shuddered in his arms, arching her back. His teeth tugged at her nipple while his hands dipped to the backs of her knees. Finding the edge of the nightie, he lifted it by the hem over her head, so he could feast his eyes on her incredible body. He groaned when he saw the dark curls of her womanhood and immediately his erection swelled. That was what Iris did to him: she made him hot and eager. He reached for the nightstand and after donning protection, thrust inside her, filling her completely, leaving no space for anything but him. He drove into her purposely, before withdrawing, only to surge in again.

He couldn't stop the overwhelming force that was lifting him, higher and higher, as he thrust inside her. Iris moaned her appreciation and Dane lost himself, coming apart with a deep guttural cry.

"Iris, I…"

Words were on the tip of his tongue, but he didn't set them free. Instead, he shuddered into her, which prolonged her release and sent them both hurtling into space.

Thirteen

The next few weeks flew by for Dane. Every other day he was going to the pretreatments with Jayden and Iris. And each day, he could see some of the vitality drain from Jayden's face.

Meanwhile, he and Iris's relationship bloomed. He took her to his favorite barbecue joint, where she dug into the meat platter full of ribs, smoked sausage and chicken and licked the sauce from her fingers.

"Delicious," she'd said, and he couldn't resist taking her fingers into his mouth and licking the sauce off.

Yes, it is, Dane had thought.

He took her to a Los Angeles Clippers game and secured much sought after tickets to a Beyoncé and Jay-Z concert. They needed these stolen moments to help deal with caring for their sick child. Of course, their outings brought much fanfare with the entertainment shows commenting on each date and what Iris was wearing. Surprisingly she took it in stride. It helped that Dane had hired Iris a stylist for such occasions to ensure she felt comfortable. She'd even convinced Dane to attend *Hamilton* in New York over a weekend while Shelly babysat. He knew it was all the rage, but he could have had a V-8. He loved being with Iris, though. Loved having her in his life...

And he loved making love to her. Sometimes it was fast and furious with no time for foreplay. Other times it was slow, with Dane making every kiss, every stroke, sweeter and longer than the last. Tonight, however, was going to be different.

He and Iris were attending a Friday evening premiere for one of his acting buddies. His team had been involved in every step, including selecting their attire to ensure they complemented each other. Morgan hired a stylist and hair-and-makeup team for Iris to ensure she looked her absolute best. In Dane's eyes, Iris was already perfect and didn't need a makeover team. Although she hadn't said anything, he suspected Iris was nervous about the appearance and wanted to give her as many tools as she needed.

Iris had arrived at his Hollywood Hills home a couple of hours ago. Her parents were babysitting Jayden so they could have a night out on the town. They'd been great, always supportive and willing to lend a hand if Dane and Iris wanted some alone time. He wished he could say the same for his parents; they'd yet to make an appearance to meet Jayden, though they had sent him a birthday gift.

"I have your diamond cuff links," Morgan called out, disturbing his thoughts as she knocked on his open bedroom door.

"Thanks, Morgan." Dane took the pieces from her. "These will work well for tonight. What would I do without you?"

"I don't know. I think you'd kind of miss me."

"Having you here is like having the kid sister I never

had," Dane said. A weird look came across her face, but it was fleeting and quickly replaced with a smile.

For Dane, the premiere was one of endless events he'd attended to keep his name out there. He also gave back to a number of charities, which meant he frequented hospital fund-raisers, gallery openings and galas. Dane could care less about the Hollywood elite or crème de la crème of society, but he recognized the importance of nights like this.

Once he'd showered and dressed in a black suit with a black shirt and tie, Dane was ready for the evening. Morgan whistled when he came down. "You look great. I'm sure Iris will be pleased."

"I certainly hope so," Dane replied with a smirk. "'Cause I certainly wasn't doing it for you."

"This is a very big deal," Morgan said. "Your first official appearance as a couple. Are you ready for the brouhaha?"

"Iris and I have been out many times."

"But not with the fanfare of attending a movie premiere where all the world's press will be in attendance," Morgan responded.

"I'm not worried. Iris will be great."

"I don't know if I can do this." Iris nervously paced across the plush carpet of one of Dane's guest bedrooms. "I mean, do I look okay?" She glanced down at the sparkling white floor-length gown. Four spaghetti straps were asymmetrically located across her shoulders, dipping in a V at her cleavage. The stylist had teamed it with simple black pointed heels, a sparkly clutch and large black shades.

"You look fabulous, Iris," Whitney gushed. She was here for moral support.

"You don't think it's too bold?"

"It's attention grabbing," Whitney stated, "and that's what we want. This is the public's first chance to get a genuine look at you all glammed up, so we want them to know you're proud to stand at Dane's side. Your hair and makeup are flawless." She gave the hair-and-makeup artist a thumbs-up.

"Thank you." Iris's normally wavy hair had been roller set and she now had big curls touching her shoulders. Add her scarlet lipstick, and it was a very 1920s glam look.

"C'mon, I'll take you downstairs. I'm sure Dane is eager to see you." Whitney propelled Iris toward the door. Navigating the sweeping spiral staircase in four-inch heels wasn't easy. Iris breathed a sigh of relief when she made it to the living room in one piece. Dane and Morgan were already there along with a couple of his bodyguards.

A large grin spread across Dane's face when she walked in the room. The look of searing heat he gave her caused everyone else to fade from existence. He held out his hand to her and Iris walked toward him. She gave him her hand and he kissed it. "You look stunning."

"Hearing you say it, I believe it," she whispered.

"You ready to get going?"

She nodded.

"All right, folks, we're heading out." Dane led Iris toward the foyer. "And might I suggest you all be gone by the time we get back?"

Iris blushed as she headed outside with him. It was a warm, pleasant evening and she didn't need a wrap. She slid into the limousine and Dane joined her.

"Don't be nervous." He patted her thigh.

"Easy for you to say. You won't have the entire world looking at you waiting for you to mess up. It's why I agreed to the makeover to begin with."

"Is that really what you think?"

Iris turned to give Dane an incredulous stare. "C'mon, Dane. I'm not that naive. I know your team." She motioned with her thumb toward the mansion they were pulling away from. "I know I'm not your type."

She'd seen the type of women Dane dated in the past. Sophisticated and poised, with money and opportunities to spare, they'd probably never had a day of uncertainty in their entire life. Iris wasn't that woman. Maybe she could have been if it weren't for her accident. As it was, she'd asked for privacy when it had come time to dress. Her scars were no one's business but her own.

"*I* don't care about any of them. The only people who matter are in the back seat of this limo. Me—" he pointed to himself and then to her "—and you."

That was easy to say, but did he really believe it? Iris looked away, but Dane tipped her chin to face him.

"I mean it, Iris. I've always been upfront and honest with you. Don't doubt that and let anyone poison what we have. Don't doubt us. If you do, then they win."

Iris nodded and tried to keep the tears that were threatening to fall at bay, but in the end a single drop trickled down her cheek, and he wiped it away with the pad of his thumb. Then he leaned in and softly kissed her. It was sweet and poignant and did the trick to settle her nerves.

She gave him a tremulous smile and before she knew it, they were at their destination. Maurice, one of their bodyguards, turned around to face them. "It's time."

"You ready?" Dane asked, and Iris nodded.

Then Dane was sliding out of the limo. From her position, all she saw were flashes of light. Dane was in front of a big spotlight being photographed by tons of news media outlets. Iris was unprepared for the near frenetic energy surrounding the red carpet, but she placed one high heel tentatively on the pavement, and Dane took her hand, ostensibly to help her out of the limo. All the while cameras continued to flash in her face.

Iris smiled as best she could, reminding herself this

wasn't real. On any given Sunday she was in her pajamas watching the red carpet for the Oscars or some other Hollywood award night. Instead, tonight she was with Dane as he waved at his screaming fans, who held up signs with his picture and yelled they loved him.

Dane bent his head and placed a kiss on her cheek and the crowd went wild. Reporters were yelling questions from all angles. Dane answered he was excited to have Iris on his arm tonight and they looked forward to a great movie.

In the end, the movie was a complete dud, but Iris had never had more fun. Once she allowed herself to relax, she found celebrities were like everyone else with their own fears, insecurities and quirks. She and Dane stayed long enough for him to wish his friend luck at the box office before they departed for a late dinner.

Instead of going out the front where Iris was sure the press waited, Dane led her out a side entrance to his SUV. "When did you arrange this?" she asked, giving him a sideways glance.

"I gave the fans what they wanted at the beginning of the evening," Dane said. "The rest of tonight is for us."

"I like that. I like it a lot." She'd worried unnecessarily because in the end Dane was so thoughtful and cared about her needs. Something about him drew her closer and it was more than the powerful lust they shared, though they had that in spades. It was more. It was the tingle in her belly every time she saw him. It was the sensation galloping through her like wildfire when he touched her. It was the fireworks she felt when they made love.

It was love.

Fourteen

"I'm thinking of asking Iris to marry me," Dane told Jason when they met up for a meeting that Monday morning. Jason had asked Dane to come to his office because he wanted to talk shop with no interruptions. And that was fine with him. It gave Dane time to go ring shopping and find the most exquisite and unique piece he could for a special lady.

"You're what!" Jason bolted from his seat and came around to face Dane. His agent was in his customary dark suit and tie, wearing designer loafers. "Are you mad?"

Dane stepped back and glared at him. "What's your problem, Underwood?"

"You're a star, Dane. A bankable Hollywood sex god. It's what we've sold you as for years. It's been your calling card. Now suddenly you want to flip the script?"

"I'm not the first A-list actor to get married," Dane responded evenly, "and I certainly won't be the last. My marrying Iris won't change my popularity."

"Why are you doing this?" Jason asked incredulously. "Out of guilt? Because you haven't been there for your son? Out of some misconceived notion of responsibility? You weren't responsible for Iris choosing to get herself knocked up by a sperm donor."

Dane shoved Jason against the desk and bore down on him. "Don't you dare speak ill of Iris. Not only is she the mother of my child, but she's a damn fine woman. You have no right to judge her, Underwood, especially considering some of the things you've done."

Jason's eyes narrowed. "Are you really going to turn on *me*? On me? After everything I've done? I made you into a star."

"And you got paid handsomely," Dane responded. "Don't act like it was altruistic on your part. You've benefited from my success."

"And I've been like a brother to you, more than your own family," Jason countered.

"Do you think that gives you the right to tell me what to do?" Dane yelled. "Don't get it twisted, *Jason*. At the end of the day, you're my manager and agent. And I thought you were a friend, but I'm beginning to wonder if all you care about is your own best interest. But guess what? This is *my* life. I get to choose. Not you. Not the press. Not the general public. You got that?" He poked his index finger into Jason's chest.

"Fine. Do what you want. Throw away your life. Just don't cry to me when it needs fixing because you've screwed yourself."

"I'll remember that and take my leave before I say something I can't take back," Dane said. He started for the door and then turned around. "Why did you call me here anyway?"

"I thought you might want to know George Murphy is interested in you for the next biopic he's directing. His first pick, Kevin Brady, pulled out at the last minute after he'd gotten studio approval. He's in a real pickle to cast in the next few months and you're on the short list. Since you've always wanted to work with him, I was under the impression you might want to talk strategy on how to bring your name to the top of the list. But since you have other priorities, I'm going to fight for other clients who want it bad enough."

Dane wanted to strangle Jason. He didn't appreciate his tone, but he'd been right to call him. George was *the* director he wanted to work with. Dane never thought he'd get a chance to read for him because he'd been seen as the pretty boy for years. But his latest film had shown all the doubters that he had some acting chops. However, he and Jason both needed a time-out to let cooler heads prevail. "I'll call you later." Dane swung open Jason's door and stormed out.

Once he was in the car, Dane wondered if he was a fool for considering making such a leap. He and Iris had known each other for only several months, but it felt as if he'd known her a lifetime. Iris wasn't like other women who saw only his face and physique, or were only after him for his money and fame. Dane was under no illusion that if he didn't have his good looks and the money to back it up they'd ever come near him. None of them wanted to get to know *him*. It was why he didn't allow people to get too close. Jason was right about that. He didn't trust easily.

But Iris was special. She wasn't just a selfless mother. She was a good listener, a caring daughter and… Well, when it came to the bedroom, they were very compatible. He loved her responsiveness. To his touch. To his kisses. He loved her little moans when he was deep inside her. After Jayden's party, he'd almost said he loved her but thankfully caught himself in time. It was cliché to say those three little words while in the throes of passion. When he said them aloud, Dane wanted them to be real and meaningful.

The question was whether she would say yes to his proposal. And there was only one way to find out: he'd have to ask.

"So you and Dane are officially a thing," Shelly said to Iris later that afternoon. Her sister had come to Jayden's chemo appointment to show her solidarity. "Who would have ever thought it?"

Iris shrugged. "I'm just as surprised as you are." When he'd asked her to attend the movie premiere a few days ago, she'd been on cloud nine. It had been exciting and scary being part of Dane's world. The lights, the cameras, the questions shouted at him. Women had begged for his autograph and worn T-shirts printed with Dane's face. He was a superstar, but he was *with* her. It had seemed surreal that at the end of the night, she got to go home with him.

"When I met Dane that day in the hospital, my mind was on Jayden and finding a donor. I—I never thought my search would end up with me not only finding his match, but his father too."

"And someone for you?" Shelly finished. "Admit it, Iris. You've fallen for Dane."

Iris hadn't chosen to fall in love with Dane. She'd thought it was a crush because he was good-looking and famous, but if she was honest with herself, she had to admit she loved him. "Yes, I have."

Shelly beamed with pleasure. "I'm so happy for you, Iris. You deserve it and so much more."

"Dane and I haven't really talked about where this is all going. I mean, we've talked about Jayden and his future, but never ours. We've been so focused on Jayden. He caught a cold, I don't know from where. I've been so careful. Anyway, Dr. Lee is pushing back the transplant date. She wants to be sure he's healthy enough to receive the stem cells.

"Sis, I'm sorry to hear that. You must be outta your mind with worry."

"I am. Worrying about Jayden and now this thing with Dane—I have no idea what he wants."

"Don't you think it's time you asked?"

"I don't want to smother him or seem needy."

"I understand, but you also have to tell him how you feel and what *you* want," Shelly admonished.

"What if he doesn't want the same thing?"

"Then you'll co-parent Jayden and get him through this crisis."

"You make it sound so easy," Iris responded, when she knew it was far from that. There were so many variables.

"Love never is," Shelly said. "I only hope to find the kind of love you've found with Dane one day."

Iris smiled and hoped the fairy-tale ending her sister was envisioning would really come true.

Once Jayden was settled in at home after his treatment, her doorbell rang. It was one of Dane's security guards. "Ms. Iris, I have Jason Underwood here to see you."

"Yes, I know Jason." Iris nodded in Jason's direction. "But I'm afraid Dane isn't here."

"Yes, I know," Jason responded. "I'm here to speak with you if you have a few minutes."

"Jayden and I were about to eat dinner, but I suppose I can spare some time. Come in." She motioned him inside. "Can I get you anything? Water, tea, coffee?"

Jason shook his head. "Nothing for me. I won't be staying long."

Iris's ears perked at the comment. Yet, he'd come all this way to speak with her. "All right. Please have a seat." She waved him in the direction of her couch and sat in a nearby armchair. "What can I do for you?"

"Well…" He sat down, making a big production out of

unbuttoning his jacket to avoid wrinkles, and then looked her directly in the eye. "I was hoping you would let Dane go."

"Pardon?"

"Iris, I know Dane cares a great deal about his son, and you for that matter..."

"But?" Because she suspected that word was the next on this man's tongue. Why else would he have come to her home unannounced and without Dane? Was there something he didn't want Dane to know?

"Your relationship has caused Dane to lose focus. He's tanking his career and blowing off projects when he's at his prime."

Iris swallowed the lump in her throat. "And you think that's my fault? I have no power over Dane."

Jason stared at her incredulously. "C'mon, Iris, you and I both know that's not true. You have his heart." He pointed toward the bedroom. "In there. His son. A son Dane never knew anything about or asked for, quite frankly. For years, he's been focused on becoming an award-winning actor, maybe even directing. But since he's discovered Jayden's existence, Dane hasn't committed to his next project and barely picked up a script."

Iris released a long sigh. "And what would you have me do, Mr. Underwood?"

"Let him go. He didn't ask to be a father. Never wanted to be one from what he told me," Jason responded. "Yet he has a ready-made family in you and Jayden."

"And we're the albatross around his neck, dragging him under?" Iris finished for him. When Jason looked down at his designer loafers, she knew that was what he'd meant. "You don't think I'm good enough for him, do you?"

Jason shook his head. "It has nothing to do with that."

"Bull crap!" Iris jumped to her feet. "I know I'm not

some Hollywood starlet who can keep Dane's name in the papers, but I care. Probably more than anyone ever has."

"Then if you do, you'll do what's best for him," Jason responded smoothly, rising to his feet and buttoning his suit jacket. "And let him do what he does best—get in front of the camera and act."

She folded her arms across her chest. "I think you should go, Jason."

"I realize what I'm asking you to do isn't easy, Iris." Jason stood and walked toward her, but she stepped backward. Since their first meeting, Iris had gotten the distinct impression Jason didn't much care for her or want her in Dane's life. "But if you do what's right, I'll ensure Dane always provides for Jayden. You will want for nothing."

"Because everything comes down to money for you, doesn't it?" Iris countered. "Well, it's not the be-all and end-all for me, *Jason*. I don't want Dane for his money. I never have. All I've ever wanted is for that little boy—" she motioned toward the bedroom "—to be happy and healthy. Meeting Dane was…" Her voice trailed off and she walked to the front door and held it open.

Jason peered at her for several seconds. "You love him. I can see that. And if you do, you'll let him go." And with that statement, he gave her one final glare before leaving.

Iris slammed the door after him. How dare he come into her home and tell her what to do. He had no right! He was one of the many people who wanted something from Dane while she—she just wanted to love him. But was it enough? Would it ever be enough?

On some level, despite his protests to the contrary, Dane loved the glitz, the glamour and the fame. Why else would he continue to do what he did year in and year out? Yet she was certain he'd found an inner peace when he was with her and Jayden. Or was she fooling herself because she was so in love with him?

Perhaps she was a fool for believing they were building something strong and enduring. Maybe Dane had sent Jason here because he was too afraid to tell her that all *this* was too much. A new son who needed a bone marrow donor. A new lover with her hang-ups. His future would be golden if he didn't have her and Jayden bringing him down. And she would never want to get in the way of Dane reaching for the stars. Because when you loved someone, you were willing to sacrifice for them.

And she loved Dane. But was she prepared to show him how much? Was she strong enough to let Dane go so he could soar?

Dane used the key Iris gave him to enter her small bungalow later that evening. He hated that he could no longer stop by without being accosted by the press. Several of the paparazzi had taken to camping out at Iris's home in the hopes they'd catch him stopping by. Social media was always abuzz with his comings and goings and how often he visited his son, but he wasn't going to let that stop him.

He wanted to see Iris. Hear her teasing laugh and, if Jayden had been put to bed, turn it into a quivering sigh. Sex with Iris was intensely gratifying and by far the best of his life. And when they were together, he wanted to stay with her forever and damn if that didn't amaze him.

She greeted him at the door, brushing her soft lips across his and sliding her arms up his back. Dane's chest tightened and his lips sought hers in a purely carnal kiss. A sultry moan escaped Iris's lips. He lost his head completely and swept his hands over her. Desire stabbed hard through him and he hauled her closer, cupping her behind until she was up against his body and the clear evidence of his need pressed between them.

He drew his head back a fraction. His breathing was ragged and choppy, but he managed to speak. "Hello."

She laughed. "Hello to you too."

His eyes darted around the room, but the lights were muted. He could tell she'd been reading in the armchair because a book was lying face down next to a glass of red wine. "Where's Jayden?"

"Already in bed. Chemo drained him and he couldn't wait up for you. I'm sorry."

"Don't be. I got delayed with some errands and meant to be here sooner," Dane said. "So it's just us?"

She grinned. "Yes."

"Why don't we head to the bedroom?" Dane suggested. He was eager to get Iris naked so he could do all sorts of wicked things to her.

Iris's room was a third of the size of his master suite in the Hollywood Hills, but Dane didn't care. He didn't care that her bed was a queen size compared to his California king that could sleep several people. The cozy room was all Iris. It even smelled like roses and sunshine, because that was how he thought of her.

"Come here, you." She pulled him toward her and reached for his belt. He bent and kissed her again, meshing his lips with hers and slowly sweeping his tongue inside her luscious mouth. She quickly helped him out of his clothes while he took his time stripping her bare. He touched every part of her with soft, tender kisses. She trembled, arching against him. In her eyes, he saw the need he'd felt all day. He used his fingers and mouth to tease, tempt and stretch, keeping her pleasure just out of reach.

Iris fought back. Her mouth went to his throat and her lips danced a wild tango on his neck. It made him feel raw and exposed. "Iris…"

She smiled and rolled atop him. Having her skin on his inflamed him and he murmured words of encouragement as she took him in her hand and lined him up against her wet opening. Her searing gaze burned into his as she sank onto him. Then she rocked her hips, undulating against him, taking him deeper and deeper until she had him to the hilt. It was searing, slow and sublime. They were so close, nothing could come between them. If this wasn't love, Dane wasn't sure what was.

A wave of emotion clogged his throat and Dane knew he wanted to be with Iris forever. He looked into her eyes and gripped her hips tightly as he bucked underneath. "Yes, Iris. *Yes. Give me all of you.*" He rammed upward and Iris clung to him, riding him as they both hurtled straight to the stratosphere.

Afterward she fell forward on top of him, and he wrapped his arms around her. She'd never been more beautiful to him than she was at this moment, glowing from his lovemaking. He whispered the words he could no longer keep contained. "I love you, Iris."

But when he glanced down, Iris was sound asleep on his chest. He grinned. There would be plenty of other times to tell her he'd fallen madly and deeply in love with her.

Fifteen

Iris was up early the next morning. She was already showered and dressed when Dane wandered into the kitchen bare-chested and wearing pajama bottoms. He looked sleepy eyed and sexy as hell. Last night after they'd made love, he'd told her he loved her. *And she'd heard him.* But she'd feigned sleep because she'd been so overwhelmed. She hadn't been the only one feeling this way. Dane loved her too!

But Jason had got in her head yesterday by telling her Dane was throwing away his career and his future if he stayed with her and Jayden. Iris didn't need Jason to point out that she wasn't beautiful like the models and actresses Dane usually dated. She saw it herself every day she looked in the mirror and saw the disfigured flesh from the accident. If they stayed together, Dane might regret being with her, he might wish he'd held out for someone more beautiful and without all her hang-ups. He deserved better than her, but Iris had finally found happiness. Was it so wrong to want to hang on tight to it? It's why she had told him she loved him back.

If she stayed with Dane, it would hurt him, but if she didn't, he'd be hurt just as much. Would he think she'd been using him for Jayden or for healing herself in some way? Because she had.

For years, Iris had been afraid to put herself out there. She'd been content to live in the shadows and raise her son, never knowing the depth of emotion she could feel for another human being until Dane came along. He was everything she'd been waiting her whole life to find.

And she had to let him go.

Sometime around dawn, Iris realized she was holding Dane back. He was America's Sexiest Man Alive, but he was also a damn fine actor who was destined for greatness. He needed someone who could be in the limelight with him.

Plus, if he stayed with her, his focus wouldn't be on his craft, but on her and Jayden. Jason had been right. Jayden had come down with a cold a few days ago and they'd had to push back the transplant for a couple of weeks until he was fully recovered. Dane had been by her side for days. And she loved him for that. Truly she did. Dane had taken to fatherhood much more easily than anyone thought he would.

Everyone had expected he'd be one of those see-you-on-the-weekend kind of dads. Not Dane. He was invested. And not just because he was giving his bone marrow. He came to all Jayden's treatments. He picked up Jayden from school even if that meant his entire entourage, press included, followed him. Dane was determined to be a better father than his own had been, and he was. That was what made what she *had* to do so hard.

"Good morning." Dane brushed a kiss across her forehead as he moved toward the coffeepot and poured himself a cup. She didn't have a fancy Keurig, just an old-school coffeepot she preprogrammed each evening so she could take a very large YETI mug with her on the way to work.

"Good morning." She avoided his gaze as she set about pulling out cereal and a bowl for Jayden's breakfast. She wasn't sure he was going to eat it. He hadn't had much of an appetite these days due to the chemo treatments.

"You're up early," Dane commented as he sipped his coffee. "Didn't I sufficiently wear you out last night?"

"I have to get to work," Iris said.

"Doesn't your job understand you have a sick child who might require more of you and give you a bit of leeway?"

"It's not needed. Jayden is in the shower and I'm already dressed to get him to chemo," Iris replied tightly. She'd ensured they were on track because she didn't dare spend any more time alone with Dane than was absolutely necessary. Otherwise, she wouldn't have the guts to do what needed to be done. "Some of us can't play around all day. We have to actually make a living."

Dane's dark brown eyes stared at her, clearly disturbed by her tone. "Wow, okay." He scrubbed his jaw. "I guess someone woke up on the wrong side of the bed this morning. I didn't realize it was take-a-shot-at-Dane time."

Iris shrugged. She hated doing this but she saw no other way. "I'm just saying. I have to make a living."

"I could easily take care of you and Jayden. You'd never have to worry about anything but staying by Jayden's side and being there for him when he needs you."

Damn him. He was going to make it harder for her to walk away. "As kind and generous as that is, I don't take handouts, Dane."

"It wouldn't be a handout!" he spat, slamming his coffee cup onto the kitchen table and splashing it all over.

"I'll clean it up." Iris went for a dishrag, but Dane grabbed her forearm.

"Jayden is my son too and I'd like to do my part in taking care of him and supporting you."

"You're doing your part by donating your bone marrow," Iris stated. "But as for me? I've got this and so does my family. We've been doing it for nearly seven years before we knew about you. Please just go back to your life. I'm sure there's plenty of things you should be doing other than getting mired in the muck of our lives."

Dane frowned. "What the hell, Iris? Where is this coming from? We had an incredible night last night and…and this morning you're acting cold and distant. What's going on?"

"Don't you get it, Dane? I'm letting you go. I'm giving you a free pass to go back to your life and do whatever it was you were doing before you met me."

Hurt was etched across his face, and Iris hated that she was the one putting it there.

"What if I don't want a free pass?"

"That's too bad because I'm giving it to you," Iris responded. "It's over, Dane. You and me. I won't stand in the way of you having a relationship with your son. I wouldn't do that, but…" Her voice trailed off.

"It's not easy giving someone the brush-off, is it?" Dane asked. "Trust me, I know. I've done it. And you know why, Iris? Because you don't want to do this. I have no idea what's got into you, but perhaps it's best if I leave."

He started for the door, but Iris said, "I would like my key back."

Dane spun around to face her, and Iris nearly lost it. His deep brown eyes were filled with despair. She was breaking his heart as well as her own. It was a risk, letting Dane go, but if he was the man she knew him to be, he wouldn't abandon Jayden. He'd still donate his bone marrow and be a father to Jayden. He just wouldn't be with Iris. But in the long run, she was doing what was best for both of them.

They were from two different worlds and he needed to be free to pursue his passion.

"I knew you had issues, Iris, but I thought we'd addressed them. I thought you trusted me, but clearly I was wrong. They go much deeper than even I imagined."

"Don't you dare bring my scars into this." She pointed at him. "You don't get to put this on me like I'm the one with the problem!"

"Aren't you?" Dane asked. "You're the one who out of nowhere is turning tail and running as fast as you can from a good thing. Am I getting too close, Iris? Is that the problem? Is being in the light with me too much?"

"Oh, that's rich coming from you. You *have* to live in the limelight. You feed off all the adoration of your fans. I saw you the other night when we went to the premiere. You were eating it up with a spoon."

"It's my job!" Dane responded hotly. "All those people stood in line for hours for a glimpse or picture of me and, God forbid, an autograph. So yeah, I played my part, but it doesn't mean I'm a narcissist."

She knew he wasn't self-absorbed, but she had to push him away. "No, Dane, you're just doing the right thing like you always do."

"What the hell does that mean?"

"C'mon, let's be honest here. The only reason you're with me is because I'm Jayden's mother. And I get it, okay? You want to make sure our son has a better home life than you did growing up, but I'm releasing you of your obligation."

"That's a low blow, Iris. My family has nothing to do with why I'm with you."

Iris shrugged. "Does it matter now anyway? I've said my piece, Dane, and now it's time for you to leave."

"Just like that?" he asked incredulously.

When she didn't answer, he merely turned and left her standing in the kitchen staring after him. Several minutes later, he returned and she was still standing in the exact same place. He didn't look at her. He merely placed her front door key on the table between them, then he strode out of the room. She heard the door slam moments after.

Iris grabbed the top of the nearest chair and crumpled into it. Tears stabbed at her eyes and she tried to blink them back, but she couldn't. She let them fall.

A door opened and Iris heard the pitter-patter of feet and looked up to see Jayden. "Did I hear the front door? Where's Daddy?" He glanced around and then behind him.

Iris wiped the tears away. "He had to leave a bit early, but I'm sure you'll see him soon." But she wouldn't. Iris doubted she'd ever see him again.

Dane shook his head in disbelief as his driver drove him to his Venice Beach house. He still couldn't believe it. Why was she turning her back on him? On the family they'd been creating?

All his life, he'd desperately wanted to feel like he was a part of the Stewart family, but he'd always felt he was an outsider among his own kin. Fallon and their father had always had a special relationship and as for Nora, theirs wasn't the typical mother-son connection. He and his mother couldn't be more different. It was why he'd left Austin to come to Los Angeles. It was here he discovered he belonged in front of a camera. He could come alive and become somebody else. Was it because he'd never truly liked who he was to begin with?

With Iris and Jayden, Dane felt like he finally belonged. He had a family to call his own. He hadn't even realized he'd needed that until the thought of not being part of one left him cold and empty inside. Since he'd found he had a son, Dane hadn't felt trapped. Instead, a scared yet wondrous joy had taken root inside him and he'd felt happy. Happier than he'd been in a long time. Of course he was angry life had dealt Jayden a raw deal with his disease, but Dane felt strongly the bone marrow transplant would work and if it didn't, they'd try everything until his boy was healed.

And then there was Iris. Beautiful, sweet Iris. It had been only several months, but in their short time together, he'd felt comfort and ease, as well as laughter and sorrow—not to mention desire and passion. When he was with her, he lost total control and rather than scaring him, he'd given in to it. He'd allowed himself to feel whatever he was feeling because Iris wasn't like any woman he'd ever met. She wasn't trying to *get* anything from him and because of that, his feelings had grown.

At first, he hadn't been able to identify them because other than Fallon he'd never really loved anyone, but Iris was easy to love. And now that he'd finally found *the one*, he was afraid of losing her. But what could he do? She'd all but kicked him out of her home.

Eventually the SUV came to a halt and Dane hopped out and punched in the code. His bodyguards knew better than to come in. He was in a surly mood and he needed to be alone to lick his wounds in private. Once inside, he slammed the door and immediately began stripping off his clothes. A punishing swim in the ocean was exactly what he needed to take the edge off.

An hour later Dane felt no better, even after letting the waves wash over him. He was angry. Angry with Iris for turning her back on him. Even though he'd never thought about having a family, he'd thought they were going in that direction. Instead, he felt as if he'd been sucker punched by the woman he loved.

After showering and dressing, Dane reached for his phone and used FaceTime to call the one person he could turn to.

"Hey, Dane." Fallon's image appeared on the screen.

"To what do I owe the pleasure of a call at this time, and on a weekday, no less?"

"Iris dumped me and I have no idea why."

"What?" The stunned expression on Fallon's face must have been exactly how Dane looked when Iris delivered her harsh words this morning. "Dane, what are you talking about?"

"This morning, after we'd had such a wonderful night together, Iris started a fight. Told me she didn't have time to spend cuddling with me. Pretty much acted as if I was insignificant in her or Jayden's life. I don't understand any of it, Fallon. Why would she do something like this?"

"This makes absolutely no sense. The Iris I met clearly adores you. She was so excited to surprise you with our visit. It showed me how invested she was in your relationship. I can't believe she'd cast you aside so easily."

"Well, she did," Dane stated, running his hand over his head. "And for the life of me I don't know why. I've tried to be the best father I can for Jayden."

"And you have been, Dane. I mean, you never expected to become a father after being a sperm donor, but I've seen you rise to the occasion. No pun intended."

"Thanks, Fallon."

"No, I mean it. When I was there I saw how much you loved your son and that you'd do anything for him. And for Iris."

"Then why did she push me away as if I was nothing to her? Do you have any idea how humiliating and embarrassing this is? I've risked everything to be with her, Fallon. My reputation, my career, my *brand*, because I thought we were building a future together. And now I find it's made of sand."

"Don't say that, Dane. Don't give up on her. There has to be an explanation for Iris's actions."

"If you can find one, I'm listening. Because all I hear

right now is my team telling me to take it slow. 'You don't have to have a ready-made family, Dane. You can be a father to your son without being Iris's husband.' But no, I had to go all in, guns blazing."

"Wait a sec." Fallon was silent for several minutes. "Did you say *husband*?"

Dane rolled his eyes. He'd been hoping to gloss over that part, but Fallon had heard him. "Yeah, I was seriously considering asking Iris to marry me."

"Marry you? Omigod, Dane, that's wonderful!"

"Like hell it is," Dane roared. "She wants no part of me, Fallon, and I'm not going to sit at home spinning my wheels trying to figure her out. I'm going to take charge of my life and do what I do best—make movies."

"Oh, Dane, running away won't solve the problem."

"Really, Fallon? As I recall, you kept Gage at arm's length for months when you were pregnant with Dylan."

"Hey…that's not fair. And that situation was different. Gage lied to me and violated my trust. We had a lot to work through. You and Iris can overcome your issues if you just give it a chance."

"No," Dane said definitively. "I'll be there for Jayden, but me and Iris are done."

Dane ended the call with his sister minutes later, but he didn't feel any better. The thought of starting another movie left him cold, but what choice did he have? Iris didn't want him. He could go back to the life he had before, when he had an endless selection of willing bedmates. But the thought of sleeping with anyone else made his skin crawl and he couldn't stomach thinking of Iris with another man.

All he wanted to do right now was call her and make sure she was okay. He was a fool. She'd probably felt only gratitude to him for reintroducing her to sex. He should be flattered and move on, but he couldn't. And once it was time for the bone marrow transplant, he would have to see

Iris more frequently. How was he supposed to navigate being beside her but not with her? There was an ache in his chest that wouldn't go away and he was beginning to realize what it was.

He was heartbroken.

Sixteen

"I want you to arrange a meeting with George Murphy," Dane told Jason when his manager stopped by the following day.

"What brought on the change?" Jason inquired. "I thought you were going to focus on 'your family.'" He made air quotes with his hands.

"If you're talking about my son, I'll be there when I can for his treatments and certainly back in enough time for the transplant."

"Actually no, I wasn't talking about Jayden. Correct me if I'm wrong, but weren't you going to ask Iris to marry you?"

"Iris and I are over," Dane said, turning away to face the massive infinity pool in his backyard. He didn't see the look of pure joy cross Jason's face.

"Oh? When did that happen?"

"Does it matter?" Dane asked, turning back around. "All you need to know is I'm taking your advice and focusing on my career."

"I'm ecstatic you're heeding my advice, but are you okay?"

"I will be once I get back to work, so find me something. Anything at this point, but I need to get the bloody hell out of Los Angeles."

"I'm on it," Jason said and then walked toward him to place his hand on his shoulder. "For what it's worth, I'm sorry this happened. I know how much you cared for Iris."

Dane was thankful when Jason had finally gone. He couldn't bear to see the smug look on his face that he was right about Iris and him. How could he have been so wrong?

"Dane, I don't mean to interfere, but are you sure you don't want to take some time, ya know…?" He heard Morgan's voice trail off behind him.

"To mope around and feel sorry for myself that my girl dumped me?" Dane inquired. "No thanks, Morgan. It's better if I get back to work as soon as possible."

"What about your family? Maybe talking to your dad might help. Henry Stewart, right?"

Dane frowned. "Yeah, that's him, but I don't have those kind of parents. Thank you for caring, though."

"You're welcome."

He appreciated his assistant trying to help, but the more he thought about Iris's behavior, the angrier he got. He wanted to go over there and give her a piece of his mind, but in the end it would solve nothing. He'd still be back where he was in this purgatory where his mind and heart were at war. His mind told him to move on, focus on his career, while his heart…his heart told him to fight for what he wanted and never let go.

His mind won out.

It had been seven days, four hours, thirty-eight minutes and five seconds since Dane had walked out her door. Iris recalled to the minute detail the look of utter hurt that crossed his beautiful face when she'd told him to leave his key and get out.

She'd done it for all the right reasons. Because she *loved* him and would do anything for him, including give him up for the greater good. Dane was tanking his career to be with her and Jayden and she couldn't let that happen.

But why did it have to hurt so hard?

She missed sleeping beside him night after night, missed cuddling close to the rock-hard wall of his chest. She craved the intimacy they shared. She missed rousing him from sleep with a kiss on his sensuous mouth and the intoxicatingly addictive passion Dane brought out in her. Somehow he'd seen through her—to the loneliness she'd carried with her for years.

Another part of her was angry too.

Why hadn't Dane fought harder to save what they had? Iris knew it was irrational to think this way when she was the cause of the breakup. Somewhere deep down, Iris wanted Dane to fight for her, fight for them. Show her he wouldn't give up on her so easily when times were tough. But he hadn't. He'd accepted the easy way out and left, leaving her shell-shocked.

The pain was so excruciating, Iris hadn't wanted to get out of bed. If it hadn't been for Jayden coming to wake her up, he would have been late for his chemo treatments. Jayden was starting to suspect something was wrong because he'd never seen her in the dumps. The only time Iris had been like this was after the accident. She hadn't wanted to leave the house then because she'd felt ugly. It wasn't healthy for her to stay in this headspace and Iris knew it was pointless to wallow in the grief, but she couldn't seem to help herself.

So it was no surprise on the eighth day when her sister made an appearance. "Iris?" Shelly called out as she let herself inside the bungalow. "Where are you?"

"In here," Iris called out from her bedroom.

Minutes later, Shelly appeared in the doorway. She was dressed for work in a knee-length skirt, silk blouse and pumps. "Why are you still in bed? It's the middle of the week, for Christ's sake."

"I'm tired," Iris said, sinking lower into the covers.

"That's not what my nephew tells me." Shelly came into the room and opened all the blinds before sitting on the bed.

How was it that, in just a short time, Iris had come to think of the right side as *her* side of the bed? Why? Because Dane favored the left side, that was why. "Did Jayden rat on me?"

"If you mean did he call his auntie to tell me his mother won't get out of bed and has missed the last week of work? Then yes, he ratted you out."

Iris leaned backward against the pillows. "I'm sorry he did that. I'm fine."

"No, you're not fine." Shelly pulled back the covers so she could see Iris's face.

Iris shuddered to think what she must look like. After crying on and off for days, her eyes were probably swollen and puffy, her nose red from constantly blowing it. "Go home, Shelly, and leave me be."

"I can't do that, Iris. Jayden needs you to be on top of your game, especially if his father is MIA these days. And two, whatever it is, whatever is going on between you and Dane, surely it can be fixed."

Iris shook her head. "Don't you get it, Shelly? It can't be fixed!" she wailed. "Don't you think if it could, I wouldn't be in this state?"

Shelly clutched her chest. "What on earth could have happened? Last time I saw Dane was at our parents' for dinner a couple of weeks ago, and the man was walking on cloud nine."

"We broke up," Iris blurted. "Correction. I broke up with Dane."

Shelly's eyes grew large. "Why would you do such a thing?"

"Because— Look at me, Shelly. I'm nothing special. I'm not like the beautiful starlets with the perfect bodies he's used to being with."

"You're not giving yourself enough credit. You're more than just your looks."

"But I'm bringing Dane down. He's worked so hard to get to where he is and he's turning down movies because of me."

"And Jayden," Shelly clarified. "Let's not forget he has a son."

"A son he had no idea he had. And now all of a sudden, we've blown through his life like a tornado, leaving nothing but damage in our wake."

"That's not true, Iris. I *saw* how happy Dane was. How happy you were. *Together.* I'm not wrong about that. You told me yourself you were in love with him. Why would you break up with him?"

"To set him free. I don't want him to feel obligated to be with me."

"So he could be America's Sexiest Man Alive? Did you for once think that maybe, just maybe, Dane might want more in his life than the superficiality of Hollywood? That having you and Jayden in his life has grounded him?"

Tears slid down Iris's cheeks. "If—if I allowed myself to think that, Shelly, then I've just made the biggest mistake of my life."

"I'm sorry to tell you, sis, but you did," Shelly stated matter-of-factly. "You're not holding Dane back. You've given him so much more. A son, love and a family. Sure that's worth fighting for. So my question to you is, what are you going to do to fix it?"

"I can't fix it."

"Au contraire," Shelly said. "I know how stubborn you can be when you put your mind to something. Remember how adamant you were about no more reconstructive surgeries? Because I do. Be that determined again. Show Dane that woman. Tell him you love him and I promise you he'll take you back."

Was Shelly right? Should she try to repair the damage she'd made of their relationship? As for Jayden, she was certain Dane would still donate because he'd been willing to do so before he knew he was Jayden's father. However, their relationship would be strained and she didn't want to do anything that would jeopardize Jayden's well-being. Not to mention he'd miss having his father in his life day-to-day. She had to do whatever she could to repair the rift she'd caused between her and Dane. Because they deserved love and happiness for themselves and their son.

"What if it's too late? What if he turns me away?" Iris was scared that she might have done irreparable harm.

Shelly smiled. "You showing up to fight for him should be more than enough to melt the ice. But you'll have to take a risk and lay yourself bare and be completely honest with him."

Iris threw back her covers and stood. "All right, you've talked some sense into me. I'm going to get my man back."

"'Atta girl!" Shelly cheered.

Iris just hoped Dane would forgive her and if he didn't, she'd keep trying until he did.

"Can't you get anything right? I asked for a Perrier," Dane snapped at Morgan the following day.

"Of course. I'll get right on that," Morgan said before rushing away.

Dane leaned back in the director's chair and sighed. He should never have agreed to this movie. It was like the romantic comedies he'd done early in his career when he was trying to make a name for himself. The last couple of years, he'd been more selective about the projects he chose. He wanted them to have range for him to showcase his acting muscles. Instead, he'd taken what he could get to keep his mind off Iris, and was faced with memorizing bland clichéd dialogue. It was driving him crazy.

He hadn't meant to snap at Morgan. It wasn't her fault he was in a bad mood. He'd been this way since he'd left Iris's home that fateful morning over a week ago.

Staying in Los Angeles hadn't been an option. There were too many reminders of the places they'd gone or things they'd done. Even his beach house wasn't an oasis anymore because all he could think about was the first time he'd made love to Iris. How beautiful and intense it had been.

Dane doubted he could ever go back there now. It was too painful. So when Jason told him this movie was teed up and ready to go in Kitty Hawk, North Carolina, he'd jumped on the opportunity to get out of town. He'd regretted it almost immediately. Despite the scenic beachside location, he was miserable. His heart wasn't in the role; he wanted meatier, grittier material. But most of all he wanted his life back. He wanted the life he'd created with Iris and Jayden.

His cell phone vibrated and Dane answered. "Hey, sis."

"Are you being mean to Morgan?"

Was he being filmed on *Candid Camera* or something? Dane jumped up from his chair and glanced around. That's when he saw a honey blonde walking toward him on the sand.

"Fallon? What are you doing here?" Dane asked, ending their call.

"Saving you from yourself, it would seem," she stated with one hand on her hip. She was wearing a maxi dress and holding a pair of strappy sandals. "When I called your house to check on you, I was informed by your maid you'd left to work on a film in North Carolina. After you called me last week, I'd already planned to come to you. I just needed to get childcare arranged. But then Morgan called me and told me you'd been a tyrant all week and thought you might need your big sis to give you a kick in the rear, so here I am."

Dane grinned. "Morgan called you?"

"She cares about you. She's been your assistant for over a year now. And she gives a crap about you despite how you treat her."

"Yeah, she's a good kid."

"She's twenty-four years old."

Dane chuckled. "I don't know what it is, but now that I'm a father, I feel older. Wiser somehow."

"Wiser?" Fallon raised a brow. "I don't know about that." She looped her arm through his. "Walk with me for a bit."

"All right." They walked in silence for several minutes before he said, "I'm surprised Gage let you out of his sight."

"Gage has mellowed, Dane. I admit when we were first together he was rather dark and intense. But he's grown. We both have. And I can see you have too."

Dane's brow furrowed. "You can?"

"Oh, yes. I may have joked with you back there, but you've matured greatly, Dane. You no longer think about just yourself. You put others' needs ahead of your own."

"Well, being a parent kind of forces you to do that."

She nodded. "It does. But that's only part of your growth. You've grown because you've finally opened yourself up to love."

Dane shook his head. "No, you're wrong. I might have fancied myself in love, but it was one-sided. Iris doesn't love me."

"I don't believe that. And neither do you. Otherwise

you wouldn't be so angry and biting everyone's heads off. Besides, I know a woman in love and Iris has been bitten by the love bug."

"What would you have me do, Fallon? She sent me away."

"Fight, Dane. Fight for what you want. Don't let anyone, anything or any career—" she motioned around them to the set "—get in your way. I took a private jet here and it's waiting to take you home and back to Iris."

"What if she sends me away again?" Dane inquired.

"Maybe she ran scared," Fallon suggested. "But if you coming back doesn't show her that you're absolutely made for each other, nothing else will."

Dane pulled Fallon into his arms and gave her a squeeze. "Thank you, sis."

He was going to extricate himself from this movie and get back to Los Angeles. This time he would tell Iris how he felt. He would tell her and show her exactly how much he loved her and their life together. And this time, he wasn't taking no for an answer.

Seventeen

Iris was nervous as she drove to Dane's set in the Outer Banks of North Carolina that afternoon. She'd never been to the state before, much less to the East Coast, so she was way out of her comfort zone. But she had to do this.

On the nearly seven-hour flight from Los Angeles to Norfolk, Virginia, Iris had had plenty of time to think. Shelly was right; she'd made a big mistake listening to Jason and giving in to her fears about whether she and Dane truly had a shot. How would she ever know, if she gave up on them at the first sign of adversity? She was guilty of the very same thing she was accusing him of.

Dane had been shocked when she'd told him they were over. He'd told her he loved her, for Christ's sake! And if there was a chance, any chance they could be happy together, have a family, then she had to be willing to risk it all, including her own embarrassment at coming to Dane's movie shoot. She owed him and herself that much.

Iris was thankful when she phoned Morgan that Dane's

assistant hadn't hung up on her. In fact, she seemed ecstatic to hear from Iris. She'd shared that Dane had been miserable since he'd left her over a week ago and was ripping everyone to shreds. No one was off-limits. Iris knew Dane wasn't that person, but he was hurting and she was the reason. She apologized profusely to Morgan and hoped her coming would change things. Morgan understood and gave her all the details on where to find them, and said there'd be a set pass waiting for her.

When she arrived, Morgan immediately came to meet her. "I'm so glad you're here," she said. "I think *you* are exactly what, or shall I say *who* Dane needs to see."

"Do you really think so?" Iris asked. "He's probably really upset with me."

"And he may not be happy with my interference either," Morgan said with a snort, "but I had to do something. You guys are so cute together." She looped a lanyard over Iris's head. "He's down that way." She pointed toward the set.

"Thanks, Morgan." Iris gave her a nervous smile and started walking toward her future.

Dane walked briskly with Fallon through the sand to get back up the embankment to the main road. He needed to get his wheels. He was anxious to get home to Los Angeles as fast as he could.

Dane came to a stop by the stairs leading to the parking lot. "You don't mind traveling to Los Angeles and then back to Austin?"

"Not at all. I'm here to help, but it looks like I don't need to…"

Dane glanced up. Surely his eyes were deceiving him. Iris couldn't be standing at the top of the stairs leading to the beach—here in the Outer Banks of North Carolina? He blinked several times to make sure she was real and that he hadn't imagined her. But when he looked again, she was smiling down at him and his heart swelled.

"Iris?"

She nodded.

"I'm going to go now," Fallon said, backing away from Dane. "I think the two of you—" she used her index and middle finger to point at them "—have a lot to say to each other and don't need an audience."

Dane looked back at his sister and mouthed the words, "Thank you." He watched her for several beats as she walked down the beach until her figure became a speck on the horizon. Then he looked up, only to realize Iris had beat him to the punch. She had descended the stairs and was standing in front of him.

"What—what are you doing here?" He couldn't get the words out. He was tongue-tied.

"I had to see you," Iris replied. "I—I had to tell you I made a mistake and I was fool to let you go."

A lump formed in Dane's throat and he wasn't sure he could speak, so he listened.

"I thought I was doing what was best for you. Jason said that—"

"Jason?" he interrupted her almost immediately. "What does Jason have to do with any of this?"

"He came to see me. He said you were tanking your career by being with me and Jayden, giving up good projects, and it was going to ruin everything you'd worked so hard to build. I couldn't let that happen."

"So you told me to go?"

She nodded and an errant tear fell from one of her eyes. She wiped it away with the back of her hand. "Yes. I said horrible things to you that day. Words I deeply regret. I wish I could take them all back because I didn't mean any of them, Dane. I only said them because I knew if I didn't hurt you, you would stay and I needed you to go so you could be happy."

"Happy?" His voice rose. "Iris, don't you get it? You and Jayden make me happy," Dane responded. "You're my world."

"We are?"

"Of course you are. Haven't I told you from the moment I first met you? It's always been you. I don't want anyone else. Because none of them, none of these actresses or celebrities—" he pointed behind him toward the set "—are *you*. You're the woman I'd measure every other woman against anyway, and they'd be severely lacking."

"You don't have to say that."

"Damn it, Iris. When will you get it? It's you I love. It's only you." Dane hadn't intended to blurt out his feelings, but seeing Iris so unexpectedly gave him hope. She hadn't traveled cross-country to his movie set just to say hello. She'd come for a reason. He just prayed and hoped she felt the same way about him.

A shadow of a smile crossed her face and it filled him with such joy. He'd been missing *this* for the last week. It had felt like the sunshine had gone from his life and there was nothing but dark storm clouds left.

Her next words were softly spoken, but he heard them all the same. "I love you too, Dane."

Dane released a long sigh because it was a balm to his aching heart. "You do?"

"Yes, I came all this way to tell you. I was a fool for listening to the haters and the doubters who don't believe in us and I'm done with it. If you can forgive me, if you can accept my most heartfelt apology for hurting you and putting us through this week of agony, then I'm yours. Mind, body and soul."

"Oh, Iris." Dane swept the woman he loved into his arms, anchoring her to him while his mouth lowered to kiss hers. Iris's lips immediately opened under his and she accepted his invitation, fusing her mouth with his as they sought to get closer together. Her kiss rocked his soul and promised him a lifetime of happiness.

"We should get out of here," he said. His breathing was ragged and edgy, and he was hungry for her. He couldn't wait to run his hands all over her.

"Please," Iris murmured. "I can't wait to be alone with you too."

Taking her by the hand, Dane led Iris away to start the next phase of their journey.

It wasn't too late. Dane could and would forgive her. Iris had never been so grateful in her entire life, except when Dr. Lee had told her they'd found a donor match. When she'd seen Dane in dark jeans and a navy T-shirt standing at the base of the stairs just now, she'd nearly lost her nerve, but when he'd looked at her and given her one of his signature devastating smiles, she'd seen the truth there. She'd been right to come. He'd wrapped his arms around her, and it was exactly what she wanted—what she needed. She needed him more than words could ever express. And she could see he needed her too.

Hand in hand, Dane led her to an SUV that was his to use for the duration of the movie project. The drive to the vacation rental house on stilts where Dane was staying didn't take long. When they got there, they quickly exited the vehicle and rushed up the stairs, eager to be alone together like two love-crazed teenagers.

They didn't make it to the bedroom. Dane tumbled her back onto the couch. He knelt over her, his hand slipping behind her head so he could loosen her topknot. Her hair was free within seconds and he sat back on his haunches to wrench his T-shirt off. Iris stared up at him and inhaled his delicious, rich, woodsy scent she loved so much.

His gaze caught hers and he smiled wickedly. "I've missed you, Iris."

"And I've missed you."

He began unbuttoning her blouse and before she knew it, both that and her bra were tossed to the floor beside the couch. Then he kissed her long and hard until she was breathless and she didn't care. She wanted to hold his mouth prisoner against hers forever.

Hot, all-consuming desire enveloped them and they fell onto the rug, laughing. But that didn't keep them from their kiss. They greedily feasted on one another. She was holding on to his muscular shoulders while his arms molded to the shape of her. She could feel him all around her and Iris welcomed his dominance because only Dane could make her feel so alive.

Her legs naturally splayed to accommodate him and he obliged, moving from her mouth to her breasts. And when he fastened his mouth on her tightly budded nipple, a flame of excitement shot straight to her belly and she moved her hips instinctively to *feel* him.

"I want to do things slowly," Dane murmured against her bosom. "I want to savor you."

The sweep of his lips against her skin was like a hypnotic swirl against her flesh. Iris no longer thought about her imperfections when she was with Dane. She thought only of him. "There will be time for slow later," Iris replied. "I need you now."

He gave her a devilish grin and lifted off her long enough to peel her jeans and panties from her trembling body, baring her completely to his gaze, to his touch, to his mouth. Then he was stripping his remaining clothes from his body and joining her on the floor.

But before they made love, she had something to say. Something that needed to be said. She grasped both sides of his cheeks with her palms. "I have to say this, Dane, and get it out while I can."

"Whatever it is, sweetheart—" his eyes peered into hers "—you can tell me."

"I'm sorry," Iris responded. "I'm truly sorry. And I promise I won't hurt you again. I promise to always fight for you and for everything we have built together. I will be strong for you as you've been strong for me and Jayden, and I won't let anyone or anything come between us again." She was his, body and soul, and she would love him to the day she died, with everything she had. "I love you, Dane."

"I love you more than anything in this world, other than Jayden," he responded.

"More than your career?"

"Yes," Dane stated emphatically. "Now let's quit talking and let's start loving." His lips slanted over hers, his tongue plundering inside her mouth while his hands moved lower to part her thighs. She granted him access, enjoying every sensation, especially when one of his skilled fingers slipped into her tight channel.

"Dane..."

"Yes, baby..." He swirled his fingers across her nub, again and again, sinking deeper and deeper inside her. It felt so incredible she began to shake.

"That's right, Iris. Let go." He slipped out and this time inserted two fingers. Her muscles clenched and began tightening around him; she could feel herself about to come.

But Dane didn't let her. Instead, he slid home inside her and she tilted her hips, welcoming his length while locking her legs around his back. Dane filled her so completely. With clarity Iris knew what she'd found with Dane was life changing. When he moved, she followed, matching him until the pressure began to build and he was surging inside her over and over and over again. Ecstasy came swiftly, suspending them momentarily in time as Dane pumped his release and gave a low groan. He collapsed on top of her before withdrawing to lie beside her, and tried to catch his breath.

Dane turned his head to look at her and whispered, "I love you, Iris."

"I feel the same," she said with a smile.

He sat up and leaned on his forearm, becoming serious. "Yeah, but this time I'm telling you I can't imagine my life without you, and I don't want to live like I did this last week in a half existence. I want to live fully and completely with you and Jayden for as long as we have."

"What are you saying, Dane?"

"I guess I'm going about this all wrong," Dane said. He rose from the floor and slipped on his boxers. "Let me do this the right way." He bent down on one knee. "Iris Turner, will you do me the supreme honor of being my wife?"

The words felt good on Dane's lips and he liked the way they tasted.

Iris bolted upright. Her eyes were wide and luminescent, searching his for an indication he was serious.

He was.

"And before you ask me if I'm sure, Iris, I am. I'm not doing this out of duty. I'm asking you because I want to be with you."

He could see her battling herself, as if she wanted to say something. All he wanted Iris to say was yes. "I wasn't about to say no," Iris responded. "I was just thinking I'd like to wait until Jayden's better."

Dane grinned from ear to ear. "Does that mean…"

Iris chuckled. "It means I'm saying yes. A thousand times, yes!" She threw her arms around him, closing the distance between them. "I can't wait to spend the rest of my life with you."

His lips dipped lower and his mouth found hers in a

heady kiss that bloomed with love he'd never known he could find. And Dane gave himself up to the feeling because Iris had shown him how good love could be. It didn't have to be distant like his parents'; it could be wondrous, crazy, joyous and everything in between.

"You seem deep in thought," Iris said, looking up at him.

"I was. For so long I wondered if I'd ever fit in or be a part of a family, but I've found my home with you and Jayden."

But there was one pressing piece of business he still had to attend to when he returned to Los Angeles and it couldn't wait.

"Dane, what are you doing here?" Jason asked when Dane stormed into his manager's office bright and early on Monday. "You should be filming."

After Iris had stunned him with her trip to North Carolina, they'd taken the weekend to get reacquainted in every sense of the word. But now it was time for business.

"Yeah, I should, Jason, but instead I'm here," Dane replied with a satisfied smile. "To fire you."

"Excuse me?" Jason huffed. "W-what the hell are you talking about, Dane?"

Dane narrowed his eyes. "You know exactly what I'm talking about, Jason. I guess you thought a dumb schmuck like me would never find out that you went behind my back to my woman and lied to her. Put doubts in her head about the relationship."

"I didn't say anything that wasn't true," Jason countered. "You were losing your edge after you worked so hard to get here. I was *helping* save your career. That's my job!"

"Well, I don't need your brand of help anymore. You're fired."

"You can't do that. We have a contract," Jason said.

"That I have the right to terminate on ethical grounds. If you recall, there's a morals clause in the contract."

"I was doing what was best for you and I stand behind that," Jason said. "How else do you think you got here, Dane? I've stood behind you, boosted you up, been your advocate when no one would look at you. And now, you're turning your back on me for a woman who couldn't even get laid to have a kid?"

The punch was quick.

Dane had tried to remain calm, but he wouldn't abide anyone talking ill about Iris. "*That woman* is my fiancée, soon to be my wife, and if you ever disrespect her again, you'll live to regret it."

"I'll blackball you," Jason responded.

Dane laughed. "I'd like to see you try. You must forget who the celebrity is here, who has the star power. Because if you come after me, I promise you I won't rest until I ruin you, Underwood."

"Just go, Dane. I hope you're happy with all that domesticity."

"Oh, you can believe it, I will be," Dane replied. After saying his piece, he strolled out, leaving a stunned Jason staring after him.

When he got outside, Iris was waiting for him in his convertible with the top down surrounded by cameras and reporters eager to get a quote and a glimpse of the enormous rock he'd put on her finger just that morning at the jewelry store.

"You ready?" Iris asked, glancing at him from the driver seat.

"I am." Dane slid inside the car and rode off into the sunset with the woman he loved.

Epilogue

Six months later...

Dane nervously waited under the simple arbor draped in white chiffon and laden with fresh white roses. He glanced around at the family and friends gathered on the sunny La Jolla beach for his simple yet elegant wedding to Iris Turner.

Fallon, Gage and Dylan were there in the first row. Seated beside them was his sister-in-law, Maya. She was holding her new baby girl, Elyse, who was sleeping peacefully. Then there were his parents Henry and Nora Stewart. They'd finally visited Jayden when he was in the hospital and now were attempting to get to know their oldest grandchild. Dane didn't expect much, but he appreciated the effort if nothing else for Jayden's benefit. Whitney was there, but Dane frowned when he didn't see Morgan. *Where is she?* She'd been instrumental in ensuring Iris found him six months ago in North Carolina. And she'd been excited to finally meet his parents.

Dane shook off the unease and glanced at his soon-to-be mother-in-law, who was beaming proudly at him. Charles Turner would be walking Iris down the aisle, while Shelly was her maid of honor. Ayden stood beside him as his best man. It was hard to believe Jason, someone he'd considered a friend, had sold him out and wouldn't be in Ayden's place.

But today wasn't a day for looking back.

He was looking ahead.

And as the waves gently lapped the shore, he saw Iris walk down the aisle in a stunning gown fit for a queen.

His queen.

The ceremony was sweet and heartfelt, with each of them saying vows they'd personally written. The words were easy for Dane because he'd never found a woman quite like Iris. He was proud to stand before God and everyone he knew and pledge his undying love and devotion to her. It was all the more special because Jayden, their ring bearer, was standing by. After all the chemo treatments, the transplant had been a success. Dane had recovered easily once his stem cells were harvested, but had worried incessantly over Jayden. Luckily his son accepted the transplant and after spending months in the hospital under quarantine to prevent any infections, Jayden bounced back. He wasn't 100 percent yet, but his health had improved by leaps and bounds, which was why Dane and Iris felt it was finally time to get hitched.

"I now pronounce you husband and wife," the reverend said. "You may kiss your bride." Dane lifted Iris's veil, pulled her into his arms and planted a big one on her mouth. The kiss wasn't meant to elicit passion, but that was what he felt. Because Iris did it for him. She always had and she always would.

And now she was his forever.

They walked down the aisle with Jayden at their side to their happily ever after.

* * * * *

COMING SOON!

We really hope you enjoyed reading this book. If you're looking for more romance, be sure to head to the shops when new books are available on

Thursday 12th December

To see which titles are coming soon, please visit

millsandboon.co.uk/nextmonth

JOIN US ON SOCIAL MEDIA!

Stay up to date with our latest releases, author news and gossip, special offers and discounts, and all the behind-the-scenes action from Mills & Boon...

 millsandboon

 millsandboonuk

 millsandboon

It might just be true love...

LET'S TALK
Romance

For exclusive extracts, competitions
and special offers, find us online:

facebook.com/millsandboon

@MillsandBoon

@MillsandBoonUK

Get in touch on 01413 063232

For all the latest titles coming soon, visit
millsandboon.co.uk/nextmonth

MILLS & BOON

HEROES

At Your Service

Experience all the excitement of a
gripping thriller, with an intense romance
at its heart. Resourceful, true-to-life
women and strong, fearless men face
danger and desire - a killer combination!